continued . . .

"The most powerful and emotionally gripping entry into the series . . . Jacka has visibly grown as an author over this series, and I am thrumming with anticipation for what comes next."
—*Fantasy Book Review*

TAKEN

"The action is fast and smart, playing with thriller conventions so that while readers get excitement, they also are encouraged to think about what magic might mean in human terms. A superb book in an outstanding, provocative series."
—*Publishers Weekly* (starred review)

"Tons of fun and lots of excitement in this fast-paced thriller . . . [Benedict Jacka] writes well, often with the ability to bring places to life as much as his characters, especially the city of London."
—*SF Site*

"This series rocks . . . The characters are well crafted, the story well written, and each book filled to the brim with nonstop action. [A] must-read."
—*Whatchamacallit Reviews*

CURSED

"An even more impressive tale of gunplay and spellcraft in present-day London . . . Readers will savor this tasty blend of magic, explosions, and moral complexity."
—*Publishers Weekly* (starred review)

"A wonderfully fun, action-packed story with witty dialogue, making it another great installment for the Alex Verus series."
—*All Things Urban Fantasy*

"Benedict Jacka is a master storyteller . . . A brilliant urban fantasy that is so professionally polished and paced that you barely remember to come up for air . . . Fun and action-packed but now bigger, angrier, and absolutely nuts. I loved it."
—*Fantasy Faction*

"An action-packed, magic-fueled story . . . Captivated me from start till finish and had a complex mystery that you could really get into." —*Under the Covers Book Blog*

FATED

"Harry Dresden would like Alex Verus tremendously—and be a little nervous around him. I just added Benedict Jacka to my must-read list . . . An excellent novel, a gorgeously realized world with a uniquely powerful, vulnerable protagonist. Books this good remind me why I got into the storytelling business in the first place."
—Jim Butcher, #1 *New York Times* bestselling author

"Benedict Jacka writes a deft thrill ride of an urban fantasy— a stay-up-all-night read."
—Patricia Briggs, #1 *New York Times* bestselling author

"[An] extremely promising urban fantasy series starter . . . Jacka deftly invents the rules of magic as he goes along, creating an emotionally satisfying story arc and a protagonist who will keep readers coming back."
—*Publishers Weekly* (starred review)

"Benedict Jacka will become a favorite for fans of Jim Butcher, Simon Green, and/or John Levitt. His recipe for success combines believable and well-developed characters, lots of action, enough suspense to keep one up all night, and a new twist on magic . . . *Fated* is one of the strongest first books in a series I've read in a long time." —*SF Site*

"An excellent example of not just great urban fantasy but also of brilliant storytelling. There is a near-perfect mix of everything, and it has been masterfully crafted with a meticulous eye for those pieces of humanity that make a great protagonist and a fantastic story." —*Fantasy Faction*

Ace Books by Benedict Jacka

FATED
CURSED
TAKEN
CHOSEN
HIDDEN
VEILED

veiled

BENEDICT JACKA

ACE BOOKS, NEW YORK

ACE

An imprint of Penguin Random House LLC
375 Hudson Street, New York, New York 10014

VEILED

An Ace Book / published by arrangement with the author

ISBN: 978-0-425-27575-7

PUBLISHING HISTORY
Ace mass-market edition / August 2015

PRINTED IN THE UNITED STATES OF AMERICA

10 9 8 7 6 5 4 3 2 1

Cover photographs: St. Paul's Cathedral © Tim Gartside / Trevillion Images;
fractal pattern © Quka/Shutterstock.
Cover design by Judith Lagerman.
Interior text design by Laura K. Corless.

Penguin
Random
House

veiled

chapter 1

I t was midwinter.

A cold wind blew down the street outside, beating at the houses and rattling the windows. The night was overcast, the air a few degrees above freezing. It was the early hours of the morning, and the noise of the clubs and bars had faded to a distant murmur until the loudest sound from the city around us was the whine of the wind.

Inside, the warmth of the living room held back the cold. Variam was sitting on the sofa with Anne tending to him. Luna was pacing back and forth beside the table, while I was leaning against the wall next to the mantelpiece, my arms folded and my head down. There was a tension in the air.

"You should have got out earlier," Luna said, still pacing. Invisible to normal sight, the silver-grey mist of her curse swirled and snapped around her. Luna's curse is tied to her emotions; being around her when she was angry used to be dangerous. She's better now, but the movements of her curse still broadcast her emotional state to anyone with the skill to see it.

"Didn't have time," Variam said.

"We said to evac when the alarm was raised."

"We needed a couple more minutes."

"You do this every time. I told you the militia were coming in—"

"Well, they weren't the problem, were they?" Variam twisted around to face Luna. "If we'd—"

"Vari," Anne said.

"Fine, okay." Variam turned back to where he'd been before. Anne placed one hand on Variam's left shoulder and the other on his wrist, and went back to studying the limb, eyes slightly narrowed.

My eyes rested on Variam's arm. The sleeve of his coat was brittle and shredded from where the ice blast had hit, and the skin beneath was swollen and tinged an unnatural bluish-white. I wanted badly to ask Anne whether he'd be okay but knew it'd only distract her. I'd never yet seen Anne run up against an injury she couldn't heal, but there's always a first time . . .

"What the hell was Talisid thinking?" Luna asked.

"I don't know," I said.

"There wasn't supposed to be any magical security. He said—"

"I know," I interrupted. "We'll get into it when he picks up."

Luna is my apprentice, half-English and half-Italian with wavy light brown hair. Although she's an adept and only twenty-four, she's got more battle experience than most mages ten years her senior. She'd been on backup duty for the mission this evening, and she'd done her job well, but from the look in her eyes I knew she wanted to take her frustrations out on someone. Still, she kept quiet.

Anne straightened slightly from where she was sitting. It was only a small movement, but both Luna and I turned towards her. "So?" Luna asked before I could open my mouth.

"He'll be fine," Anne said in her soft voice.

I felt some of the tension go out of Luna, and to my eyes, the tendrils of mist around her slowed. "How bad is it?" I asked Anne.

Anne and Variam make an odd pair. Anne is tall and

slender while Variam is small; where Anne is soft-spoken and shy, Variam is confident and quick. When the two of them are together, it's Variam who usually stands out in the conversation, while Anne's content to stay in the background. Despite that, it's Anne who might be the more powerful of the two. She's a life mage, and due to various events that she doesn't like to talk about, she was forced from a young age to become very good with her magic. It's given her more than her share of issues, but it's also made her the best healer I know.

"The skin, nerves, and blood vessels are frozen along the left side," Anne said. "But there's no serious tendon damage and the muscles are okay. It'll take me ten minutes or so."

"You're getting slow," Variam said.

"Regrowing nerves *is* slow. Unless you don't want to be able to feel anything along your forearm—"

"He's just being a dick," Luna said. "Vari, shut up and let her work."

Variam rolled his eyes. Green light began to glow around Anne's hands, spreading into Variam's arm as Anne's healing magic took hold. It wasn't the first time I'd seen Anne heal Variam, or the fifth for that matter, and the two of them made it look very everyday and ordinary. All the same, I couldn't help but think of how close it had been. I'd shouted a warning, but if Variam had been just a little slower to get that shield up . . .

There was a chime from the mantelpiece. Luna's head snapped up instantly, but I was already reaching for the item that had made the sound: a small blue-purple disc with serrated edges. I picked it up and channelled a thread of magic through its centre.

The edges of the disc lit up and a small figure materialised at the centre, twelve inches tall and sculpted from blue light. The shape was that of a man, middle-aged and straight-backed, with thinning hair. "Verus," the figure said. His voice was as clear as if he'd been standing in front of me. "How did it go?"

My name's Alexander Verus. The "Verus" part is my

mage name, the "Alex" part comes from my parents, and I go by either or both depending on which society I'm interacting with and how much I like the person I'm talking to. I'm a diviner, which means that I can perceive the sensory data of my short- to medium-term potential futures in the form of if-then conditionals.

I've also got some serious long-term problems, most of which stem from my history. Mages are split into two factions, and I was originally trained by a particularly notorious Dark mage named Richard Drakh. The mage I was talking to through the communication focus, Talisid, was from the other faction—the Light Council, the dominant power in magical society—and I'd been working for him on and off for several years. It had been a low-key, freelance relationship . . . at least until last April, when Anne was kidnapped and taken away into the shadow realm of her old master, Sagash.

I went after Anne and found her, and together we fought our way out. But despite all the battles and dangers we went through, it wouldn't have been even a footnote in the records as far as any other mages were concerned, except for one thing. While I'd been in Sagash's shadow realm, we'd run into my old master, Richard.

There had already been rumours of Richard's return. When I told my story, it was treated with the same scepticism as the rumours. I'd only seen someone who *looked* like Richard—it could have been an illusion, or a construct, or some other trick. Richard had been gone for eleven years, and as far as many of the Light mages were concerned, this was probably just someone trying to trade on his old reputation. But I knew that it hadn't been a trick. It had been Richard, returned after all this time . . . and worst of all, he hadn't forgotten about me. He'd asked us to join him.

It didn't matter that we'd said no. I never came to really know Richard back when I was his apprentice—I don't think anyone did—but there were some things about him of which I was certain. One was that he was very, very patient. And another was that when he wanted something, he took it. In my mind, ever since that April, a clock had been ticking. I didn't know how much time was left on it, but I knew that sooner or later it would run out.

One mage who hadn't been sceptical was Talisid. He'd believed the rumours of Richard's return even before I had, and in the months since then, he'd begun approaching me more often, asking for my help with operations. Surveillance, reconnaissance, even some covert insertions, all with the same ultimate goal: finding out what Richard was doing, and how to stop him.

Things were easy at first. We discovered that Richard had returned to his old base of operations, the mansion in Wales. Once he'd set up again, he started to receive visitors in increasing numbers. All were Dark mages. We couldn't get close enough to risk actually eavesdropping on one of the meetings, but we were able to discover that Richard was trying to build a coalition, uniting as many Dark mages as he could. At the same time, another Dark mage named Morden was making a push to get Dark mages admitted to the Light Council. From several pieces of information that we'd uncovered, we were sure that the two of them were working together. Morden was the public face, dealing with the mages on the Light side of the fence, while Richard kept the Dark mages in line. A few Dark mages had spoken out against Morden's proposal; all had disappeared without a trace shortly afterwards.

But since October, our investigations had become harder. We'd taken all the low-hanging fruit, and the closer we drew to Richard's real secrets, the more we risked revealing ourselves. Talisid started sending us further afield, chasing rumours with no guarantee of safety or success. Some of the leads we pursued turned out to have nothing to do with Richard at all, while others turned out to be dangerous.

The mission we'd just returned from had been the second kind. Talisid had sent us to Idlib, a contested city within Syria. He'd told us that there was a lightly guarded warehouse in the eastern district containing a shipment of goods intended for Richard's mansion. Talisid had been right about where the goods were headed. He hadn't been right about much else.

"How did it go?" I repeated. "Badly."

"Is everyone—?"

"Alive, yes," I said. "Healthy, no. We need to have a talk about your definition of 'lightly guarded.'"

"The militia—"

"The militia weren't the problem," I said. "Although there were a lot more of them than you said there would be. The *problem* was the ice elemental."

"What kind?"

"The kind that's seven feet tall, made of solid ice, and can freeze things from thirty feet away. I didn't stick around to classify it."

"You said there wasn't going to be any magical security," Luna cut in.

"Did you get a look at the shipment?" Talisid asked.

"Is that all you care about?" Luna demanded. "What, it's okay if we get killed, just as long as—"

"That's not what I meant."

"Well, that's the way it sounded!"

I held up a hand. Luna's gaze flicked to me, and she shut up. She still looked pissed off, though, and I didn't blame her. "Talisid," I said. "This is the second time in a row."

"I know. I'm sorry. All of the information we have indicated that this militia group was entirely mundane."

"And it didn't occur to you to wonder how a mundane group would be selling—?" I checked myself, took a breath. "Forget it."

There was a moment's pause. Over on the sofa, Variam was listening in. Anne was still working on Variam's arm, the green light of her magic casting a soft glow. "You weren't able to get close enough, then," Talisid said.

"Oh, we got close enough," I said. "To some empty crates. Whatever that shipment was, it's gone. Your intel was wrong about that too."

"Empty?"

"Yes."

"You're sure they—?"

"Yes, I'm sure they were empty, and no, they weren't

anywhere else in the warehouse. We checked. For as long as we could, anyway, until that elemental pulled its Mr. Freeze act. Whoever gave you those timings, they screwed up."

"I see. Would it be feasible for your team to go back and do another sweep?"

I stared at Talisid, then took a breath and counted to five in my head. "No," I said, once I was sure I could keep my voice calm. "It would not."

"All right," Talisid said. "I'm going to need to make some calls. I'll get in touch with you when I know more."

"Fine."

"Until then." Talisid paused. "I know there were setbacks, but well done on returning safely. We'll talk tomorrow." Talisid's image winked out and the lights around the edge of the communicator went dark.

"Arsehole," Variam muttered.

"There," Anne said. The green light around her hands faded and she let go of Variam's arm. She hadn't even glanced at Talisid throughout the whole conversation. "Try moving."

Variam worked his arm, flexing his fingers, then nodded. "Feels good."

"Do we need to keep him warm?" Luna asked.

Anne shook her head. "No, you could get it frozen again and it wouldn't make any difference. Though I'd rather you didn't." She glanced at me. "You didn't tell him about the papers."

"No," I said. I walked to the armchair, then picked up some of the papers lying scattered over the table. There were a dozen or so sheets, grubby with dirt and damp and cracked at the edges from where the ice blast had grazed them. Variam had managed to keep hold of them during the fight.

"Next time, leave the papers and just get out," Luna said.

"Will you stop whining?" Variam said. "We're alive, aren't we?"

Luna scowled. "Can you read them?" Anne asked.

"In Arabic?" I said dryly. "No." The papers had notes scribbled across them in a right-to-left scrawl. It could be battle plans, shipping manifestos, a history of Richard's dealings with the group . . . or someone's laundry list, for all we knew. But there was a reason we'd picked the things up: three of the pages were rubbings, not writings. They were crude and it was hard to figure out where they'd been taken from, but if I'd had to guess, I'd have said that the pictures and text they showed looked old. More like carvings.

"Are they from what was in those crates?" Luna asked.

"Or from something else," I said. "We're going to need a translator." Who not only spoke whichever dialect of Arabic this was written in, but also knew enough about Middle Eastern magical history to be able to identify the content. This wasn't going to be quick.

"Are you going to go back if Talisid asks?" Anne asked. Despite her spell, she didn't look tired. Life magic healing tends to drain the caster, but Anne's very good at what she does.

"No," I said.

"What's up with Talisid, anyway?" Luna asked. "When we did jobs for him before, this kind of thing didn't . . ."

"Well, it's because of what Morden's doing, isn't it?" Variam said. "Talisid wants us to dig up some dirt."

Luna frowned. "I thought the Council didn't buy that Morden's working for Richard."

"They don't," Variam said. "They've got him down as 'potential associate' and that's it. If Talisid could prove that Richard's behind him, though . . ."

"I think you're right," I said. "Talisid still won't tell me exactly who he works for, but I'm pretty sure he's with the Guardian faction. And Richard's reputation still carries. If they could link Richard with Morden it'd scare a lot of people off."

"Yeah, well, he hasn't done much of a job of it so far, has he?" Variam said. "And doesn't sound like his faction's winning."

"Mm," I said. I wasn't sure how to feel about that.

Politics in the Light Council are complicated. There are seven primary factions: Guardians, Crusaders, Isolationists, Directors, Centrists, Weissians, and the Unity Bloc. They're closer to social cliques than to the political parties of Westminster or Congress, but the stakes are just as high and the consequences for mistakes are a lot more deadly.

Most of the issues the Council argue over are transient, changing from month to month. But there are some questions that don't go away, and one of the biggest is the issue of how to treat Dark mages. At one extreme are the Crusaders: they're the most militant of all the factions and think the Light Council should be actively fighting against Dark mages, going to war if necessary. They hate Dark mages and anyone who's associated with them, including me. Which is ironic, given that my feelings towards Dark mages aren't any more positive than theirs, but the Crusaders don't care. As far as they're concerned, if you were trained by a Dark mage, you don't get any second chances.

Less extreme than the Crusaders are the Guardians. Like the Crusaders, they're opposed to Dark mages, but their philosophy is basically defensive rather than aggressive. While the Crusaders want to go out and take the fight to the Dark mages, the Guardians just want to hold things together. They'd rather do the minimum to prevent Dark mages from hurting other people, then leave them to fight among themselves (something Dark mages tend to do quite enthusiastically). And opposing both the Guardians and the Crusaders is the Unity Bloc. The Unitarians want the Light and Dark factions to unite, bringing Dark mages into the Council and involving them in the political process. It's not a new idea, more of a cyclical one, and it's been attempted and abandoned many times before.

If it had been just the Unity Bloc versus the Guardians and Crusaders, the Unity Bloc wouldn't have a chance. But increasingly the Unity Bloc was coming into favour with the Centrists, and the Centrists had more members than the Guardians and the Crusaders put together. And now Morden was making a push not only to get Dark mages recognised, but to get a Dark seat on the Light Council itself. It hadn't yet come to an open contest, but if things kept going the way they had been, that was where it was headed.

Morden's actions had given Talisid a second reason to be interested in Richard. As far as most Light mages knew, Talisid was just a mid-level Council functionary, but for several years now I'd been pretty sure that he was one of the Guardian faction's black-ops guys. The Guardians did *not* want Morden on the Council, and if Talisid could prove that Richard was up to something and link him to Morden, that would kill Morden's proposal stone dead. Unfortunately for Talisid, he hadn't found anything. Unfortunately for *us*, that had caused him to take increasing risks with our missions in the hope that we'd find him something he could use. But while we'd found out plenty about Richard's activities, we hadn't found anything much that we could *do* about it, to the point where it had become almost like checking the weather forecast. Yes, that tornado's moving in your direction, and yes, it's going to be a bad one, and isn't it going to suck if it decides to hit your house?

"Okay," Luna said. She'd had long enough to calm down, now. "If no one else is going to say it, I will. Should we still be working for Talisid?"

"He can still get us in with the Council," Variam said.

"Not really," Luna said. "Hardly anyone knows about what we're doing. It's all under-the-table stuff."

"Yeah, and it's going to stay that way," I said. "Talisid still hasn't given up on getting me to go spy on Richard as a double agent."

"Which is frigging insane, by the way," Variam said.

"No kidding," I said. Talisid hadn't tried to sell it to me again, but I knew he hadn't forgotten about it. "But as long as he thinks he can use us as plants, he's not going to want us to get any recognition. He wants to stop Richard. Keeping us alive is an optional extra."

"But that's going to screw us over, isn't it?" Luna said. "People are talking about Morden's new proposal. I see it in my classes. All the Light mages who've got an axe to grind with the Dark ones, they're all coming out of the woodwork. They're going to be looking for someone to take it out on, and we're right in the crosshairs. Well, I guess Vari isn't, but . . ."

"Yeah, it's not that easy, you know," Variam said. "Just because I'm a Keeper apprentice doesn't mean they don't give me shit over Sagash and Jagadev."

"They're still not going to go after you. But they might go after Alex."

"The Council's never liked me," I said. "That's nothing new."

"We know Richard's going to make a move sooner or later, right?" Luna said. "If that happens and the Council are after us as *well*, we're going to be totally and utterly screwed."

"Thanks, Luna, I figured that out already." I still had no idea how we were ever going to stand up to Richard. He was one of the most feared mages in the country. And the Council was the most powerful *faction* in the country. The thought of trying to fight either of them was insane. Fighting both at once . . .

"Is there anything we could do to stop that?" Anne said. Anne tends to be the quietest one in our discussions—quiet enough that it's easy to forget she's there—but she pays attention.

"Okay, what if we just go public with the whole thing?" Variam said. "We take everything we've figured out about Richard and shout it as loud as we can. People'll listen."

"We'll also be painting a giant target on our backs," I said. "You seriously think Richard and Morden are going to take that lying down?"

"Um," Anne said. "I don't really like that plan."

"Nobody likes that plan," Luna said.

"I don't mind a fight," Variam said.

"That's because you're an idiot."

"Oh, stop being—"

"Guys," I said. "Not helping."

"Fine," Variam said. "You just want to hurt Morden and Richard? We take what we've found and leak it anonymously."

"No," I said. "First, we haven't found out anything important enough to make any real impact. Unless we have solid proof that Morden's working with Richard, it'll just be another rumour. Second, it won't stay anonymous for long. They'll figure out where it came from. And third, it doesn't actually do anything to make it less likely that we'll end up fighting both Richard and the Council."

"It's not as though Richard can afford to focus on us, either," Variam said. "His big problems are going to be other Dark mages. They're not going to be happy taking orders from him."

I nodded. "But he's going to get around to us eventually."

"Okay," Luna said, "so if we can't do anything about Richard, what about the Council?"

"What do you mean?"

"Well, the reason they won't go after Vari is that he joined the Keepers, right?" Luna said. "Talisid can get us work, but he won't get us what Vari has. So why don't you join the Keepers too?"

Anne, Variam, and I are all quite different people from who we were three years ago, but out of the four of us, it's probably Luna who's changed the most. When I first met Luna she was lonely and depressed, smiling rarely and laughing not at all. Nowadays when you look at her the first thing you notice is her confidence. Being an adept in mage society isn't easy, but Luna's managed to take that and turn it into a strength; it gives her a different perspective and she's often the one to come up with ideas that don't occur to the rest of us.

Anne, Variam, and I all turned to stare at Luna. "What?" Luna said.

"The Council are—" Anne began, and stopped. She'd been about to say *our enemies*. The Council haven't given me many reasons to like them; the treatment Anne's received from them has been worse. "They're not our friends."

"Yeah, no shit," Luna said. "I don't like them either, but we might as well use them."

"It doesn't matter," I said. "Keepers recruit from apprentices or from Light mages. No way in hell they'd take me."

"Well . . ." Variam said. "Kind of."

Luna looked at him.

"You couldn't actually be a Keeper," Variam said. "Not without spending years and years. But you could be sanctioned."

"What does that mean?"

"Means you count as an auxiliary and they can recruit you for jobs. Some of those guys spend as much time in the station as the Keepers do . . . well, it's halfway there, I guess. It doesn't make you a member of the club, but it's next best."

"Which order, though?"

"Probably Order of the Star. Order of the Shield only takes battle-mages and the Order of the Cloak spend all their time dealing with normals."

"I dunno, that could work if—"

"Hey," I interrupted. "Can you two stop talking as though I've agreed to this?"

"You've basically told us that sooner or later, we're going to be fighting Richard," Luna said. "If you're tied in with the Council, that'll make it harder for him, right?"

"That doesn't matter. The Council don't like me either. Have you forgotten about Levistus?"

"If Levistus wants to get us, then if we're split off from the Council without any friends in the Keepers, that'll make it easier," Luna said. "Not harder."

I didn't like the idea. It was true that what Luna and Variam were suggesting wasn't actually all that big a step. I'd helped the Council out with investigations and police work before—if I was being honest, becoming a sanctioned auxiliary would just be a way of recognising what I'd effectively been doing anyway. But it *did* mean making the relationship official, and while it might not have been a big step in reality, it felt like one to me.

What it really came down to was the simple fact that I don't like the Council. Maybe not all of them are bad—and I'll admit, I know a lot more of the better ones than I used to—but I've got too many old grudges to forget easily. Every single time in my life that I've really needed help, the Council have left me in the lurch, and more than once they've been the *reason* I needed help in the first place.

"Look," Luna said when I didn't answer. "We've been at this for how long now? Six months? Maybe a bit more. And all we've really been doing is just reacting to what Richard's done. Okay, we've been finding out what we can, but basically he does stuff, and we spy on it. We're not going to win anything this way."

"I know that," I said. "But we're the underdogs here. You know the kind of resources Richard can draw on. We *can't* move against him directly."

"So doesn't that mean we need some more friends, then?" Variam said with a frown. "Otherwise, what happens when he gets around to us?"

"I still don't want to deal with the Keepers."

"That was what I said," Variam pointed out. "You told me to join them anyway. Remember?"

That brought me up short. When I'd first met Variam a couple of years back, he'd been just as hostile towards the Keepers as I was. More, actually. But I'd managed to persuade him otherwise with . . .

. . . with pretty much the same arguments Luna and Variam were using now.

Luna and Variam were looking at me. I looked at Anne. So did Luna and Vari.

"Um," Anne said. She looked a little troubled. "It's not really my decision."

"What do you think though?" Luna said.

"I . . ." Anne looked at me, hesitated. I didn't say anything. Somehow I was hoping Anne would give me a reason to say no.

"I don't trust the Keepers," Anne said at last. I felt my heart lift slightly, but Anne kept going. "Especially the Order of the Star. So I wouldn't blame you if you said no. But . . . it's worked for Vari. And they don't hate you as badly as they do me. If it could keep you and Luna alive . . . maybe it's worth it."

"We still don't know that they'd say yes," I said.

"So you'll try it?" Luna said.

"I didn't say that."

"You didn't say you wouldn't, either."

I rolled my eyes, then paused. All three of them were looking at me. "What?"

"So?" Luna said.

"Slow down," I said. "Even if I did agree—which I haven't—we've got no place to start. It's not like I can show up and ask for an application form."

"That's easy," Luna said. "Just go to Caldera. You've worked with her enough times already, right?"

"We're not exactly best friends."

"Yeah, but she doesn't hate you or anything," Variam said. "Actually she kind of likes you."

"And all you have to do is ask," Luna said. "I mean, what do you lose if she says no?"

I tried to think of a good answer to that and didn't have one. All of them were still watching me and I felt weirdly trapped.

"So are you—?" Luna began.

"All right! I'll ask."

⁘⁘⁘⁘⁘

Which was how, one week later, I found myself standing outside Keeper headquarters in Westminster.

The main Keeper HQ for all of Britain is just south of Victoria Street, in one of the little off-roads. That particular area of London has always felt to me as though it's so full of history that it becomes commonplace—you can't cross the street without passing something historical or architec- turally significant. The actual headquarters is one of those big grand Victorian buildings, with pillars and carvings on the front, as well as statues of some goddess or other and a few of the more photogenic predatory animals.

Like a lot of old London buildings, the inside of Keeper HQ is a lot less impressive than the outside. The walls are covered in flaking paint that's a similar colour to coffee mould, and the stairs and floors use that particularly horrible type of linoleum that got popular in the mid-twentieth cen- tury and for some reason has never quite gone away. I checked in at reception and got told to wait. There were half a dozen other people sitting on the chairs against the wall, and none of them seemed especially happy to be there. I sat down and crossed my legs.

Now that I thought about it, this was probably the first time I'd been to a Keeper facility voluntarily. All the other times that I'd been here or to one of their other stations, it had been because I'd been forced to. I've never been *officially* arrested, but in practice there isn't very much difference between "you're under arrest" and "you're going to come here and answer our questions or we'll make you." It tends to colour one's memories of a place. I didn't have good associations with this building, and I wasn't really looking forward to talking with Caldera. A small but definite part of me was hoping she'd say no and give me a reason to leave. After fifteen minutes an apprentice came and escorted me upstairs.

Once you get past reception, Keeper HQ gets a lot busier, filled with noise and people. The stairs and corridors are narrow and there are always people squeezing past, and there's a clamour of typing and talking in the background. If you were dropped in the middle of it and didn't know what to look for, you'd probably think it was a civil service building of some kind. Keepers don't wear uniforms or carry weapons (they don't need to), and to most people they just look like ordinary men and women. But if you *do* know what to look for, it's not too hard to spot them. Keepers move differently from ordinary people; there's a sort of unconscious power and arrogance in how they carry themselves. They have a different way of looking at you too—a quick once-over, sizing you up as a suspect. I didn't let myself get visibly tense, but I'd be lying if I said I was comfortable. I might not be a suspect, but I didn't belong here.

Caldera's office was on the second floor. It was medium-sized, with two desks, two computers, some paperwork, Caldera, and another Keeper I didn't know. Caldera gave me a glance, held up a hand, then turned back to the other guy. "I know what it says," she was saying. "This isn't a Section Three."

"So you want to do what?" the other Keeper said. He was tall and athletic-looking, with blond hair. "Just let the guy go?"

"There's sod-all we can charge him with."

"Karla's not going to be happy."

"Fuck Karla," Caldera said. "She wants this guy so badly, she can do it herself."

"Or she'll just take it out on us," the man said, then held up his hands to forestall Caldera's answer. "All right, all right. I'll try and sell her." He walked out, giving me a curious glance as he passed by.

"Hey, Verus." Caldera typed something into her computer and blanked the screen, then waved me over. "Grab a seat."

Caldera is a member of the Order of the Star, the division of the Keepers that enforces the Concord and national laws amongst adepts and mages. She's an Englishwoman of thirty or so, shorter than me and a fair bit heavier, broad and stocky.

I first met Caldera about a year and a half ago. I was being chased around London by a bunch of adepts who wanted to kill me for something I'd done while still an apprentice, and Caldera had become involved because of the Richard connection. The whole thing ended badly for pretty much everyone concerned, but if there'd been one silver lining from my point of view, it had been the working relationship I'd developed with Caldera. I'd seen her a few more times since then, usually under similar (if slightly less dangerous) circumstances—I'd want some favour or a bit of information, she'd want something I could find out with my divination magic, and we'd figure out some sort of deal that gave us both what we wanted. We'd even had a couple of drinks together, from time to time. But we'd never quite made the jump from acquaintances to friends, and to be honest that was probably because of me—I could never quite forget the organisation she worked for.

If I was going to do this, that was probably something I'd have to get over.

"Right," Caldera said after we'd exchanged the how-are-you-how-have-you-beens. "So you want to be a sanctioned auxiliary."

"That's the idea."

"Why?"

"What do you mean?"

"It's not a difficult question," Caldera said. "Why do you want to join?"

"Excitement and glamour?"

Caldera gave me a look.

"Well, we've worked together a few times before and it's more or less worked out, right? I just thought it was worth giving it a try."

"Uh, yeah," Caldera said. "The times we've worked together, you only did it because you needed the help."

"Hey," I said. "What about last April? Anne was the one in trouble, not me."

"And you disobeyed every single order I gave you."

"There were extenuating circumstances?"

Caldera gave me a flat look.

"Okay, okay," I said. "I know there's been some friction, but I was hoping to mend fences with the Council, and this seemed like a place to start. Besides, I'm a good diviner and I know you guys are shorthanded."

"It's not about whether you're a good diviner," Caldera said. "Working as a sanctioned auxiliary is different from being a freelancer. You need to pass a security screening."

"Okay, how do I do that?"

"You don't. They investigate you."

"How long does it take?"

"Yours is finished."

"That was fast."

"I don't think you quite understand," Caldera said. "Council security screenings are current for two years. They didn't do a security screening because you called me. They'd *already* screened you because they'd investigated you *anyway*."

"What for?"

"Do you really need me to answer that?"

"I'm just curious about what I was being charged with."

"Well, first on the list, you're one of three people listed

as being responsible for the destruction of the Nightstalker group the summer before last."

That wiped the smile off my face. "All right," I said. "As far as I know, it was the Nightstalkers who broke the law that time, not me."

"And you and your associates were involved in the apprentice disappearances around the White Stone."

"Oh, come on. I was working *for* the Council that time. It's on file. And I was the one who found out what *happened* to those apprentices."

"Then there was the break-in at—"

"Okay, look, I already explained how that one wasn't my fault. And I offered to help, it wasn't as though you were—"

"And," Caldera continued, "the deaths of the mages Griff and Belthas three years ago."

I shut up.

"Not going to justify yourself?" Caldera said.

"I didn't kill either of them," I said. I kept my voice level.

Caldera was watching me, apparently casually, and I noticed that her eyes stayed on me as I spoke. Cops tend to be very good at picking up on when people are lying to them, and I had the feeling Caldera had been paying close attention to how I answered that question. I hadn't quite been lying. *Technically* I hadn't killed either of them, in the same way that if someone comes after you and you lead them into a tiger pit, then from a certain point of view the ones who actually killed them were the tigers.

Unfortunately for me, both Griff and Belthas had been Light mages in good standing with the Council. The Council may turn a blind eye to infighting among Dark mages, and they really don't care very much about what happens to adepts or Orphans, but that definitely does not apply when the victims are Council mages themselves. To make matters worse, Griff and Belthas had also been working for a Junior Council member named Levistus. Offing them (and messing up his plans in the process) had placed me firmly on his shit list. Levistus didn't come after me personally—that's not his style—but since then he'd taken the opportunity to bureaucratically screw me over in several ways, some of them quite lethal.

My past history with Levistus was one of the other reasons I wasn't comfortable here. Logically, I knew that staying away from the Keepers wouldn't actually make it any harder for Levistus to mess with me—if he really wanted to nail me, he could do it no matter where I was—but I still didn't like the idea of being any closer to him than I had to.

But at the same time, I knew that Luna was right. For too long now we'd been just reacting to Richard, gathering up scraps of information and waiting for him to make a move. I didn't know how we were going to beat him, but I knew we had to do *something*. Trying to make more friends amongst the Keepers was at least a place to start.

"Okay," I said. "Cards on the table. Are you saying you don't want me?"

"No," Caldera said.

I paused. "No, you don't want me, or no, you don't not want me?"

"Do you know who makes the final decision on security screenings?" Caldera asked.

I shook my head.

"After that call last week, I wrote up your submission for auxiliary status and sent it off to personnel," Caldera said. "They sent it to the Keepers in charge of your cases. Those Keepers have a dozen active cases already and didn't have the time to go reopening yours, so they passed it to Rain. And Rain passed it down to me."

I tried to follow all that. "So . . . ?"

Caldera looked at me. "So right now, there is exactly one person who's been given the job of deciding whether to take you on or not. Me."

"Oh. So is that a yes or a no?"

⁙⁙⁙⁙⁙

"So was that a yes or a no?" Luna asked.

We were in the Islington gym that we use for training. Luna was in her exercise clothes, white T-shirt and tracksuit bottoms, with a book balanced on her head. My clothes were similar to Luna's, but instead of a book, I was holding a weapon: a simple but functional-looking katana.

"She didn't say no," I said. I stepped forward and aimed a two-handed blow at Luna's head. The swing was at seventy percent speed, and my grip was angled so that the impact would be with the flat of the blade, not the edge. It wouldn't break the skin, but it would hurt. Luna stepped back, spine straight and movements smooth to keep the book from falling, and I followed up, continuing to threaten her.

"So she said yes?" Luna asked. She adjusted her position on the mats slightly, keeping just enough distance that I had to move to come within strike range.

I made a couple more head-level strikes; Luna stayed out of range. "She didn't actually say that either."

"So what *did* she say?"

I began another step, then changed it into a low glide, striking at waist level. Luna was caught within the sweep and had to block cross-hand, the flat of the blade meeting her palm with a slap. The movement left me within striking distance and she had to block twice more before she could open the range again. "Making it onto the sanctioned list is out," I said, glancing at the blade. The colour hadn't changed. "At least right now."

"That sounds like a no."

"Kind of." I closed into range again and began a series of attacks, measured and steady, switching targets from waist to shoulder to thigh, each strike flowing into the next one. Luna had to keep blocking, catching the blade against her hand each time. She couldn't move too abruptly without making the book fall. "The deal she offered was a probationary membership. It means I'm not an auxiliary, but I'm allowed to be treated as one for a trial period, so long as she's the one supervising."

"So it's what, a trial?"

"Pretty much. I'm still doing exactly what a Keeper auxiliary would be doing, it's just not official."

"So how—?"

I broke my pattern, sending the sword flashing up at Luna's face. Luna had to jump back, both hands coming up instinctively to block the blade with a *smack*. The book wobbled and she had to catch it with one hand as she backpedalled. I paused to examine the blade. Where Luna had touched it, there was a pale patch on the metal. "You let a bit through."

"Oh, come *on*," Luna said. "That wouldn't even give you a nosebleed."

The mist that swirls around Luna is the manifestation of her curse, a spell of chance magic, and the fact that Luna's spells are applications of her curse rather than effects she produces herself is the reason that she gets classified as an adept rather than a mage. Luna's curse is very hard to spot, invisible to normal vision and difficult to see even with magesight, and it brings good luck to her and bad luck to everything that mist touches. "Bad luck" at low concentrations of that mist means stuff like tripping or breaking a nail, but at high concentrations it can do anything from making a building fall on your head to directing a serial killer into your neighbourhood to say hi. It's also *cumulative*, and the more of it you get, the worse it'll be.

The exercise was a simple one; Luna had to avoid the sword without letting her curse touch it. The sword is a simple focus, designed to react visibly to magic. Once upon a time just having Luna touch it would have turned the whole blade white in seconds, but Luna's put a lot of time and effort into learning to control her curse, and nowadays she can touch something for a second or so without letting any of that deadly mist stick—which is long enough to push that something away. We'd been playing this particular game for six months or so and Luna's become very good at it, which was the reason for the conversation and for the book on her head—I'd had to keep upping the difficulty.

In this case I'd managed to shake her concentration, although not by much. "Keep talking," I said, moving in to threaten her again. "And take your hand off the book."

Luna rolled her eyes and obeyed, retreating to a safe distance. "So how long does the probationary thing last?"

"Caldera didn't say." I aimed at Luna's eyes again, but this time she was ready for it. The blade slapped into her palm less than twelve inches from her face. "But I'm guessing it's going to be until she makes her mind up."

"So what, you have to not piss her off for however many weeks it takes until she decides she can trust you?"

"Let's not expect miracles."

We kept going for another five minutes but I didn't manage to break Luna's concentration again. "All right," I said at last, lowering the sword. "Free sparring."

Luna perked up instantly, letting the book slide off into one hand as she headed for her bag. When she came back she was holding a short sword in one hand and an ivory-coloured wand in the other. "Ready?" I asked.

Luna took a stance. "Ready."

I attacked, slashing down at an angle, and I wasn't using the flat of the blade this time. Luna stepped back and I followed.

This particular part of our training sessions is the reason we use an empty gym. Last year someone saw one of my bouts with Luna and thought I was trying to murder her, which led to an extremely awkward conversation with a pair of police officers. Luna found the whole thing absolutely hilarious, but it's the reason that these days I take the trouble to schedule our training sessions in a Council-owned gym.

Right now we were alone, which was just as well. My arms are longer than Luna's, and coupled with the longer reach of my weapon I was able to pressure her, driving her back. Luna's face was set in concentration as she defended against my attacks, stepping away from most, occasionally parrying offhand with a clash of metal. To anyone watching, it probably looked as though Luna's life were at stake . . . but when it comes to magic, appearances are deceptive. Luna wasn't in any serious danger. Her curse makes her hard to hurt at the best of times, and while I was trying to get through her defences, I wasn't trying to cut her. With my divination, it's easy to see if an attack has a chance of landing, and the half second's warning is more than enough to pull a blow.

The one who was *really* in danger was me. Luna's curse is tied heavily to her feelings and instincts. She's learnt to bring it under conscious control most of the time, but if she ever feels genuinely threatened, all bets are off. But by that same token, if I *didn't* threaten her, force her to struggle, then she wouldn't gain the practice she needed to keep her curse under control when she really needed it. It was a game of brinkmanship, trying to push Luna just far enough to make her work for it, but not so far as to trigger a backlash.

The only sounds in the empty gym were the clash of metal on metal and the thud of our bare feet on the mats. Usually Luna has trouble holding me off in these matches, but this time to my surprise I realised she was holding her own. She couldn't really strike back, but as long as she kept giving ground she was managing to hold off my attacks. All the duelling she'd done had made a difference.

Of course, I wasn't really trying to hit her. There's a big gap between a sparring match and combat, and I didn't want to push it too far.

But then, if I *didn't* push her in training, I wasn't really doing her any favours.

Here goes.

I went up to full speed, and for the first time I moved with real killing intent. Instead of picking out futures where I nearly got through Luna's defences, I searched for ones where the blade landed. Luna's eyes went wide as the first stroke hissed by, and she jumped back. The second stroke she parried, the third she dodged—and stumbled. In the instant she was off balance I reversed the swing, striking down at her neck.

In my mage's sight, the wand at Luna's hand flared to life. A whip of silver mist leapt out, and for just an instant, all the visions I had of the future were of that silver mist surging into my body as the sword cut through Luna's skin.

I dropped the sword, turning the attack into a dive and roll. As I hit the mat I heard a gasp and a thud—then silence.

I came up, suddenly sick with the conviction that I'd just made a really horrible mistake. Luna had dropped her own sword and her hand was pressed to the side of her neck, and for a moment my stomach lurched . . . and then she took her hand away. The skin was reddened but unbroken.

I closed my eyes for a second, taking a breath. *Too close.*

"Wow," Luna said. Her eyes were a little wide. "That was intense."

I didn't answer. Checking, I couldn't see any of that lethal grey aura clinging to me; we'd both pulled our attacks at the very last instant. "We're done for today. Meet me up on the roof."

⁞ ⁞ ⁞ ⁞ ⁞ ⁞ ⁞ ⁞ ⁞ ⁞

"This isn't working," I told Luna twenty minutes later.

The roof of the gym was cold but not freezing, the air carrying just enough of a chill to numb the tips of your ears and nose. The gym was set a little back from the street, meaning that while we couldn't see any cars or roads, we did get an interesting view of the buildings around us. TV aerials and chimneys rose from the gravelled roofs like some weird kind of urban forest, and a couple of roof gardens sprouted up to our left, greenery against brick and concrete. A hundred feet away, a couple of young men in suits were talking animatedly on a balcony, and off to the other side a cat was washing itself on a balustrade. The breeze ruffled my hair, carrying with it the scent of car exhaust; over the buildings to the south the afternoon sun glanced off the skyscrapers of the inner city, and high above, wispy clouds hung in a clear blue sky. Just another London winter day.

"Wait a sec," Luna said. "We're not going to have the 'this is why it's dangerous for you to learn martial arts' conversation again, are we? Because you agreed—"

"It's not that. I don't think these lessons I'm giving you are doing enough."

That made Luna pause. The breeze blew her hair across her face and she brushed it back absently. "But I like them."

"You like the parts that are dangerous," I said dryly. "That was about a tenth of a second away from being a really nasty accident."

"I can control it better—"

I shook my head. "Your control's good. Not perfect, but good. The problem's me, not you. For a while now all of the exercises I've been giving you have been hands-off. I'm not teaching you how to use your magic, I'm just sticking you with some sort of problem and making you figure out a solution."

"I thought that was the only way we could do it?" Luna said. "It's not like you can learn to use chance magic."

"And that's the issue. You've gotten good at *directing* your curse, but it's been a long time now since we've made any real breakthroughs. If chance magic were an academic subject, I'd be qualified to teach it up to high school. You need a professor."

Luna hesitated. "So am I still your apprentice?"

I looked at her in surprise. "Of course."

"Oh." Luna relaxed a little. "Okay."

"Wait, was that what you thought this was about?"

"Well, I was wondering . . ."

"I'm not kicking you out or anything. We just have to find you a part-time teacher, is all. You're still my apprentice, and you'll stay that way until you decide to leave or until you pass your journeyman tests. Okay?"

"Okay," Luna said with a smile. "So are you going to find a chance mage?"

"Try to, anyway. But we can ask."

We started walking back towards the stairs. "This isn't going to be like when you were trying to find Anne and Vari a master, is it?" Luna asked.

"Let's hope things go a little more smoothly this time."

"So you're getting a new job, and I'm getting a new teacher."

"Pretty much." I pulled the door open for Luna, then followed her through. "Should be an interesting few weeks."

chapter 2

Ever since I broke away from Richard, my life's tended to go in cycles. There are short bursts of chaos and danger, then there are longer periods where things are relatively calm. The month that followed that conversation with Caldera was one of the calmer ones.

Just because things were calm didn't mean they were safe. Richard was still out there, along with all my other enemies. But there were no more missions, and beyond a couple of brief check-ins, Talisid didn't contact us again. I took advantage of the breather to search for someone who could read those notes that Variam had brought back. None of the people I asked could do it themselves, but one acquaintance claimed to have a friend due to return to the country soon who'd be able to help. While I waited for that I kept sniffing around, but as January turned into February with no further movement on Richard's end, it began to look as though my old master had put his operations on temporary hold.

Richard's sudden inactivity probably had something to do with events in the political world. Morden's proposal was edging closer to a Council vote, and as it gained attention, old arguments were raised. The anti-Dark side dug up every crime and atrocity the Dark mages of Britain had committed over the past hundred years, while the pro-alliance side accused them of witch-hunting and pointed to everything the Council had done wrong over the same period. Neither side had any shortage of material to draw upon, and as the date drew closer, the arguments became increasingly nasty. For most members of magical society the events in the Council were way over their heads, but you didn't have to know much about mage politics to see that battle lines were being drawn.

In the meantime, I kept looking for a teacher for Luna. I didn't make any instant progress, which was more or less what I'd expected. Chance mages are underrepresented on the Council, and the one or two I found who seemed as though they might be a good fit weren't taking new students. I put out some feelers, let my contacts know that I was looking for a chance teacher, payment negotiable, and kept looking.

But mostly, the thing keeping me busy was my new job with Caldera.

            ı ı ı ı ı ı ı ı ı

"This is so utterly stupid," I told Caldera.

Caldera didn't look up from her screen. We were in her office, and she'd been typing for the past ten minutes.

I leant back in my chair in disgust. "We could have caught this guy two days ago. We knew where he was and where he was going to be. Now he's God knows where and we've got zero chance of finding him."

"We didn't have authorisation for an arrest."

"You mean 'don't.' We still don't have authorisation, despite the fact that we asked the day before yesterday, and again yesterday, and *again* today, which your higher-ups *still* haven't gotten around to answering, which would have taken them all of *ten seconds*—"

"Would you stop whining?"

"How can you be so calm about this?"

The subject of our conversation was a Dark mage who went by the name of Torvald. He'd drawn Council attention by shooting up an adept bar—according to the reports, Torvald had been given the brush-off by some girl he'd had his eye on, and while he was still smarting from that, an adept had made the mistake of hitting on the same girl and succeeding where Torvald had failed. Torvald, who clearly did not handle rejection well, had expressed his unhappiness with this turn of events by applying lightning bolts to the adept, the girl, the bar, and several other people in the vicinity. The casualty count at the end of the evening had been six injured (two seriously) and most of the bar—luckily Torvald left before the police and fire brigade showed up, or there probably would have been fatalities. Caldera had been out in Shepherd's Bush on another call, so she'd sent me to handle things instead.

Given that Torvald had displayed all the discretion and subtlety of a stampeding elephant, tracing him hadn't been hard. It had taken me an hour to learn his name, a day to track him down. I'd called it in to Caldera, she'd reported it to her captain, we'd been told to wait for authorisation before taking further action . . . and we'd sat around for forty-eight hours without hearing anything.

During which time Torvald had figured out that he was being traced, and promptly vanished.

"We know what the guy did," I said. "We know where he lives. Or where he *lived*, anyway, God knows where he is now. What was the point of following this up if we weren't going to do anything about it?"

"He didn't break the Concord."

"Oh, bullshit. Maybe he didn't hurt any mages, but this was a *blatant* breach of the secrecy-of-magic clause. Besides, even if he didn't break the Concord he must have broken half a dozen national laws."

"Probably."

"Did you tell them that?"

"No, I turned in a blank report. What do you think?"

"Then why haven't they authorised us to do anything about it?"

Caldera sighed and finally looked up at me. "How am I supposed to know?"

"Well, give me your best guess."

"The fight got reported as a bar brawl that started an electrical fire," Caldera said. "The police threw out the supernatural stuff, and the only witnesses who believed what they were seeing were adepts and sensitives. Fourth clause of the Concord is only *gross* violations of secrecy; this doesn't qualify. Without that there isn't enough to justify a raid, especially when we don't know anything about his master or potential allies."

"This is such bullshit. So what—the guy lies low for a while, then goes right back to doing the same thing?"

Caldera didn't answer. "Okay, this?" I said. "This is why people don't trust the Keepers. Those adepts at the bar, how do you think they're going to see this? They just saw one of their friends get fried right in front of them. When Torvald shows up again two or three months later and no one's doing anything about it, what do you think their takeaway message is going to be?"

"And what do you think we should be doing?" Caldera said. "Kick Torvald's door down, and go in shooting? Start a fight with whoever's there, maybe end up with a few dead bodies? Is that your plan?"

"I didn't say—"

"Really? 'Cause that's what it sounded like. What did you think was going to happen if we got the go order? You thought Torvald would come along quietly?"

". . . No."

"So what? You want to see dead bodies that much?"

"I'm not looking for a fight. It's just . . . I don't like being able to do something about it and doing nothing."

"No." Caldera pointed at me. "You don't get it. You're not the one who makes that decision."

I was silent. Caldera gave an irritated shake of her head and went back to her typing. "You know, if you want to be an auxiliary, you're going to have to shift that attitude."

"I thought the reason I was probationary was because I was a murder suspect."

"No, that's the reason the *other* Keepers have a problem with you."

I paused at that. "Wait. Does that mean you actually trust me?"

"Didn't say that."

"You didn't *not* say it either."

"Let's just say I'm not worried about you going psycho on us," Caldera said. "But it takes a bit more than that."

"Like?"

"You have to be part of a team," Caldera said, looking up at me. "You're still thinking of this as a solo act. That's not how it works. When you're on call, you're part of something bigger than you, and that means you're not in charge anymore. If head office says no, you listen to them and you drop it. You don't pretend you didn't hear them, and you *definitely* don't go and do what they specifically told you *not* to do and then pretend it was all just a misunderstanding."

"You're still pissed about that thing at the Tiger's Palace last year, aren't you?"

"I know you can handle the practical side of the job," Caldera said. "That's not the issue. You're on probation because I want to see if you can follow orders."

"I haven't broken any of your rules," I said. "Which you should already know, given that you've been checking up on me."

"That just means you haven't done it where I can see."

"Are you always this paranoid?"

"It's called taking precautions. Look, just keep doing what you've been doing this last month and you'll be fine. You done with your report?"

I shrugged. "Can't exactly finish it, but it's up to date."

"Let's knock off, then. You coming to Red's?"

"Yeah. Let me pick up my stuff and I'll meet you there."

◦◦◦◦◦◦◦◦◦

There were some perks to working with the Keepers.

I wasn't a Keeper auxiliary, so I didn't get the full package. I didn't get a Keeper signet, or even the limited version that auxiliaries carry, and I didn't get one of the access keys that would have let me gate in and out through the wards around the Westminster station. But I got paid, and I had a temporary access card that got me past the front desk, and it did give me a bit more status in dealing with Council personnel.

More interestingly from my point of view, it opened up a few doors I hadn't known about beforehand. It turned out that when they weren't on the job, Keepers were still human beings, and they had hobbies like everyone else. Shouldn't have come as a surprise, I guess, but it's always easy to forget that members of an institution do actually have personal lives. And one of the centres for those hobbies was Red's.

The best way I can think of to describe Red's is that it's kind of like the magical version of a mixed martial arts gym. When I say "mixed," I'm not talking about the bare-handed fights you see on TV, I mean *really* mixed. It's also got a highly restricted guest list, and that list doesn't extend to ex–Dark diviners with dubious reputations. It does extend to Keepers, though, and the more martially inclined ones hold practice sessions there on Tuesday and Thursday evenings. This was the third time Caldera had brought me along.

By the time we'd arrived and changed, things were in full swing. There wasn't a guest teacher this time, meaning that everyone was broken up into small groups, and even though I'd seen it before, I still paused to watch. The group on the left side of the gym was practising elemental magic, shields and lances of fire and wind slamming into each other in controlled explosions. They were keeping a check on their power level, but I could still feel the heat in the air from the flame bursts. Another group was practising with rubber knives and staffs, while a third group was standing facing each other in pairs; it didn't look as though they were doing anything, but I could feel traces of mind magic. Caldera headed off to join the weapons group, and I was left on my own.

I took a few minutes to check what sort of reception I'd get if I just walked up and introduced myself. Divining how a conversation will go is difficult; predicting the first line or two of the exchange is hard enough, and reliably calling it any further than that is virtually impossible unless the guy you're talking to already has made up his mind about what he's going to say. Human interactions are close to the absolute worst things to try to predict with divination—they're too unpredictable, dependent on sudden decisions and random chance. But there are ways around it, and one of the more effective ones is not to try to predict exactly what someone will say, but to look at the general shape of the possible replies—they might vary, but from where they're clustered, you can get a sense of what kind of reception you're going to get. It's a good way to figure out if somebody likes you or not.

From looking at the futures in which I approached the mages here, I was pretty sure the general answer was "not." It's not really a surprise. Keepers tend to lean towards the Guardian side of the political spectrum, and they aren't the most trusting of people. As far as they're concerned, once a Dark mage, always a Dark mage. I suppose they've got reasons to see it that way, but it's hard not to get frustrated about it sometimes.

In this case, as far as receptions went, about half the Keepers in the room were going to be guarded, and most of the rest would be anywhere from unfriendly to downright hostile. They'd also noticed me—they weren't being obvious about it, but I knew I was being watched. Following Caldera was an option, but if I kept doing that it would seem as though I were hiding behind her. Instead I approached one of the few other Keepers I knew, a mage called Haken. "Oh, hey, Verus," Haken said. "Ready for me to kick your arse again?"

"You wish," I said with a grin. "Give me a sec to warm up and I'll join you."

Haken was the same guy who'd been in Caldera's office that first day—tall and fit, with blond hair, blue eyes, and an easygoing manner. He was also one of the few Keepers who didn't seem to have a problem with me, and I'd liked him immediately. I picked up a focus weapon and squared off against him.

Despite our banter, the fight wasn't very serious. Haken's a fire mage, and while fire magic is very good at hurting things, it's hard to use nonlethally. Fire magic has a natural tendency towards aggression and destruction, which means that fire mages tend to go one of two ways: either they learn a lot of self-control, or they're the kind of people you really don't want to spend time with. Haken was the self-controlled type. Although the sword of carved flame in his hands *looked* dangerous, the fire was tightly focused and didn't expel much heat, and none of his strikes came close to touching my skin. I returned the favour by being careful to pull my blows. When you're dealing with someone who's considerate enough to restrain themselves from hurting you, it's a good idea not to provoke them.

I was absorbed enough in the fight that I didn't notice anything else was happening until a burst of laughter broke my concentration. I stepped back, lowering my sword, and looked left to see that the other groups had merged, congregating into a loose circle. At some point while I'd been busy with Haken they'd switched to one-on-one sparring while the others watched. Right now most of the group were calling out comments; whatever had just happened, it had obviously been good entertainment.

Caldera was in the middle of the circle in her white gi. Opposite her was a stocky Keeper with close-cropped hair that I knew vaguely. His name was Slate, and right now he was hunched over and scowling. "Sorry," Caldera said. She was trying not to grin, and not doing a very good job of it. "Slipped."

"Bullshit," Slate said.

"Hey," one of the men sitting around the edges called out. "Not like you were using those anyway!"

There was another burst of laughter, and Slate's scowl got uglier. "Come on," Caldera said. "Let's go again."

"Fuck that."

"Wussing out already?"

"You know what?" Slate jerked his head in my direction. "You want to do shit like that, why don't you try it on your *friend*?"

The laughter died away at that. Heads turned in my direction. Caldera gave me a glance, then shrugged. "Fine with me."

All of a sudden everyone was looking at me. There were still a few Keepers grinning, but most of them looked expectant.

I hesitated. I really wasn't sure I wanted to take on Caldera—doing it alone might have been fun, but having her mop the floor with me in front of an audience didn't appeal. Unfortunately, that same audience was waiting for my answer, and from the looks in their eyes I knew I was on trial. They wouldn't pressure me into it if I said no, but the Keepers already thought I was morally suspect. Backing down now would *also* make them think I was a wimp. Not a good combination.

"You know, we could—" Haken began.

"It's fine," I said. I was going to have to make an impression sooner or later. "Here." I handed Haken my focus sword and walked forward.

The Keepers sitting on the ground scooted aside to let me in, and the laughter and conversation died away. All of a sudden everyone was looking *very* interested. I came to a stop about fifteen feet from Caldera. "Don't want a weapon?" Caldera asked.

I shrugged. "You haven't got one."

Caldera raised an eyebrow. She didn't say the obvious, namely that she didn't need any.

We faced each other in the middle of the circle. Caldera was wearing a worn and dirty white gi with a red belt: she wasn't carrying any tools or weapons, but given her magic type, that really didn't make much difference. There was a mirror on the wall behind her, and in the reflection I could see myself, tall and long-limbed and wearing a black gi of my own. Thinking about it, it hadn't been the smartest of clothing choices—having Caldera in white and me in black looked altogether too symbolic. Oh well.

Caldera bowed, and I did the same. Then she stepped back into a fighting stance and I put everything else out of my mind.

It's hard for a nondiviner to understand what it's like to use divination in a fight. I've tried to explain it a few times, but usually I can tell the other guy doesn't get it—the abilities divination gives you are just so weird, so alien. Standing on the floor of the gym, I could see Caldera standing opposite, one foot back and hands ready. Her stance was a generic one, rather than one that identified with any particular martial art. From her posture, I could tell that she was taking this moderately seriously.

Layered on top of that was the additional sense of my magesight. I could see the spells of Caldera's earth magic hanging around her limbs and body, solid and heavy, reinforcing her movements and keeping her braced against the floor. Other spells showed in my peripheral vision: the protective and sensory spells of all the other Keepers, the wards around the gym. All of this was what any mage would see, and it was a lot, enough that you could spend minutes analysing it all.

But on top of all that, I had another sense—my diviner's sight—and it multiplied what I could see a million times over. Instead of just seeing the picture before me in three dimensions, I saw it in *four*, all the possible futures of every single person in front of me. To me, Caldera's actions seemed to branch a dozen different ways, ghostly movements taking her back or forward or sideways, aggressive or defensive, depending on chance and whim and her responses to my own actions. And every one of those futures branched into a dozen more, and every one of *those* into a dozen *more*, hundreds and thousands of futures shifting and changing, winking out to be replaced by new ones as paths were closed off, never to become real.

For a normal person, the problem in a fight is lack of information. Diviners have the opposite problem: they have too *much* information. Even interacting with another person in a stable, predictable environment gives you more possibilities than you could explore in a lifetime. In something as chaotic as a fight, it's a thousand times worse. Novice diviners usually go catatonic the first few times they're thrown into a stressful situation: they get overloaded by trying to process the sensory input from all the possible futures at once. If you stick with it though, a diviner can actually be quite an effective fighter, in an unconventional sort of way. We aren't any stronger or faster than regular folk, but all that information gives us an awful lot of leverage.

The futures ahead of me shifted. Now the next few seconds were all going to play out the same way; Caldera was going to close in and attack. By the time she moved I'd seen the punch and made up my mind about how to block, and I barely noticed as her fist glanced off my forearm. Caldera specialises in reinforcement magic, and the spells sheathing her arms and hands were strengthening effects, boosting her power and durability. She can punch through concrete with her bare hands, and a full-power blow would shatter my skull. But for now she was just probing, and it was easy for me to deflect the strikes, keeping a safe distance.

A minute passed, two. Neither of us was going at anywhere near full strength, so we weren't getting tired. I made a few casual counterstrikes which Caldera brushed aside, but I wasn't seriously trying to hit her. As seconds ticked by with neither of us landing a blow, Caldera grew more aggressive. She closed the range, aiming for a body strike. I didn't really want to escalate things, but I wasn't going to stand there and be a punching bag. Caldera's attack left her head open, so as she moved in for her attack I hit her open-palm in the forehead. The impact rocked her back and pushed the two of us apart again.

I heard a murmur but didn't look around. Surprise flashed across Caldera's face, followed by annoyance. I hadn't hurt her but she hadn't been expecting to be hit like that. She came in again, and this time when she attacked, she put a bit of force behind it. I blocked and countered, striking back when I could. Caldera's fighting style was solid and workmanlike, straight punches with the odd elbow or knee. She wasn't fast, but there was little wasted motion and she didn't give any easy openings.

But when you can see the future, it changes things a lot. Caldera might be skilled, but she had a human body like everyone else, and she couldn't make an attack without leaving herself open at the same time. In a normal fight against an equally skilled opponent it's very difficult to execute a proper counterblow, since you need to start it the instant they begin the attack, but I could see the moves coming a second or two in advance. Doesn't sound like much, but in a fight that's a long time. I hit Caldera in the shoulder, head, breast, and head again. Caldera kept going, shrugging off another punch, and I put a snap kick into her stomach, using the impact to push myself off and keep the range open.

Caldera recovered and stared at me, eyes narrowed. From around, I could hear the murmurs from the crowd—I'd hit her maybe a dozen times, while she'd yet to land a punch. It probably looked as though I were winning, but appearances are deceptive. Just as with most of my fights with elemental mages, I could hit Caldera, but I couldn't hurt her. My hands were already stinging from the impacts on her skin, while I knew she wasn't so much as bruised. I was a wasp fighting a bear—I could sting and dodge, but one solid blow and I'd be crushed.

Caldera kept coming, speeding up. Now she was going all-out, and with each move I was getting a second or less to react. I kept hitting her back, but she'd obviously figured out that I couldn't hurt her and had decided to just ignore it. Sweat dripped down my forehead, and my arms and legs were starting to burn with fatigue. A spark of fear was starting to grow in my gut, the feeling you get when you're up against an enemy you can't defeat. Intellectually I knew this was just a sparring match and Caldera wasn't actually trying to kill me, but my instincts weren't listening.

A block and a grab sent me backpedalling into the circle of watchers; Keepers jumped to their feet and scrambled away as Caldera and I went through them. Caldera kept pressing me, then abruptly switched tactics and just charged. I hit her once on the way in, but I didn't manage to open the range in time and she tackled me.

It felt like being kicked by a horse. I hit the floor with her on top of me, driving the breath from my lungs. I couldn't get up or away in time, and for an instant panic took over. There were weapons where we'd fallen; without looking I caught one up and brought it under Caldera's chin with one quick slash.

Caldera scrambled back, coming up to her feet. Her eyes were wide, and she brought one hand up to touch her throat. I lay on the floor, breathing hard.

The Keepers came around, slowing to a leisurely pace as they saw the fight was over. "She took him down," one of them said.

"Yeah, and he cut her throat," someone else replied.

A few others were talking but I didn't listen. I looked down at the weapon in my hand. It was a training knife with a rubber blade; Caldera's group had been working with them earlier and when she'd tackled me we'd fallen into the middle of them. My fingers were still wrapped around the plastic handle and with an effort I made myself get up. The Keepers were still talking, but a good half of them were watching me. On a few faces I could see considering looks.

"Thanks for the match," I said to Caldera. I set the knife down and walked out without waiting for an answer.

⁙⁙⁙⁙⁙

I changed quickly, avoiding the rest of the Keepers, and headed outside. By the time I was out in the street and in the cold air I'd calmed down a little. Now that I could think clearly again I knew that what I'd just done had not been a smart move. The Keepers already suspected me of murder— going for a killing attack like that would not have made a good impression.

Why had I gone for that knife? The rubber blade had been harmless, but the move I'd used it for had *not* been, and I'd never even made the conscious decision to do it. I'd acted on instinct, and by the time I'd had the chance to think, it had all been over. Would I have acted like that a year ago? I was pretty sure I wouldn't, and I had a nasty feeling that I knew what had changed. Even though it had been ten months since I'd seen Richard, just knowing that he was out there was enough to put me on edge, quicker to feel threatened, quicker to strike back.

I'd been nervous about how Caldera was going to react, but when she finally appeared, gym bag slung over one shoulder, she didn't seem particularly bothered. She was on her phone and held up a hand to me as she approached. "Uh-huh," she was saying into the phone. "Yeah, but I'm off duty."

I leant against the wall, waiting for her to finish. "Okay," Caldera was saying. "No . . . Well, too bad, 'cause unless it's an emergency . . . Yeah . . . You okay with that? . . . Fine, you can check in with him later. Okay." She rang off and looked at me. "Got a job."

"Torvald?"

Caldera shook her head. "Some kind of magical fight on the DLR. It got called in through the Met and the liaisons flagged it."

"So they want us to do what, find out what it was?"

"Apart from the 'us' part."

"Come again?"

"I'm off duty as of three hours ago," Caldera said. "You can have this one."

"Seriously?"

"You want to be an auxiliary, you're going to have start doing solo jobs. Can't always be there looking over your shoulder." Caldera glanced at me. "You can handle it?"

"I guess."

"Central'll forward you the report." Caldera yawned. "I'm off. Have fun."

"Uh . . ."

"What?"

"About what happened in the gym?"

"What about it?"

I hesitated. Caldera looked surprised. "That bothering you? Don't worry about it."

"Oh. Okay."

"Best match I've had in weeks." Caldera grinned. "You won't get me with the same trick next time, though. I won't go easy on you."

"Then I guess I won't either."

"Promises, promises." Caldera gave me a wave as she walked off. "Have a good one!"

I watched Caldera walk away, then shook my head and turned away with a smile. At least there was one person who wasn't bothered.

ı ı ı ı ı ı ı ı ı

The message that arrived a few minutes later directed me to Pudding Mill Lane station, on the Docklands Light Railway. It wasn't a quick journey, and I had plenty of time to read through the incident report on my phone. Apparently a woman had made a 999 call claiming to have seen some kind of firefight on the station platform. The British Transport Police had shown up, found nothing, concluded that it had been a wind-up, and buggered off. Which was the end of the story as far as the authorities went, but the Keepers have listening posts in the police, and the report had raised enough flags to warrant sending someone over . . . though apparently not quite enough flags to send anyone important. I wasn't sure what I was going to do when I got there, but I supposed I'd just have to find out.

The Docklands Light Railway (aka the DLR) is one of the more unique ways to get around London, a raised railway crowded with small driverless red-and-blue trains that link up all the places in East London where absolutely no other lines go. It has four branches, winding and intertwining, and it can take you anywhere from Lewisham in the south to Stratford in the north or all the way eastwards towards Woolwich. I was on the northern branch, heading towards Stratford. Pudding Mill Lane was the last station before the Stratford terminus, and when the train arrived no one got off apart from me.

DLR stations are very lonely compared to the Underground. The DLR was designed with automation in mind, and just as the trains don't have drivers, the stations have the absolute bare minimum of staff. This one had none at all, and there were no passengers either. The station was a single-platform design with rails on either side, and all around was blackness. Pudding Mill Lane was right in the middle of what had once been the Olympic Park, the great centre for the London Olympics. For a few weeks the square mile in which I was standing had been the busiest place in London, but now it was a giant construction site, a jungle of concrete and fencing and metal scaffolds, abandoned and empty. Beyond the railway to both east and west, the land dropped away into half-constructed buildings, lying silent and unused. The old running track had been torn up and now was a giant heap of dark earth, filling the air with the scent of mud and water. According to the plans, this place was going to be turned into housing eventually, but there wasn't anyone living there now. Scattered towers rose up all around, and to one side I could see the skyscrapers of the Stratford skyline, an oval-shaped tower looming over us with a ring of rainbow neon glowing at the top, colours shifting from blue to purple to green. To the northeast, the Olympic stadium was a squat shadow in the darkness. Cars rushed along a main road to the east, but they were half a mile away and nothing else was moving. Despite being in the middle of the largest city in the British Isles, I was completely alone.

I looked around in the darkness, already starting to shiver. It had rained while I'd been on the train, and puddles were scattered around the platform; not enough to flood the place, but enough that the wind blowing off the stone was freezing cold. I looked around and tried to figure out what to do. Okay, so I was a Keeper—sort of—and I was investigating a crime scene. What was I supposed to do?

I'd come here with vague plans of finding witnesses, but as I looked around it became clear that that wasn't going to work. In the few minutes I'd been standing at the station I hadn't seen another living soul, and if there were any construction workers still on site I couldn't see them. Instead I focused on my magesight, trying to sense magic. Stone beneath me, cold and immobile, chill air whistling around, the silent menace of the electrical rails and wires. Nothing powerful enough to tell me anything. Spells can leave residue, but it takes repetition and time—one-off magical events have to be extraordinarily powerful to stick around. Nothing like that here.

I walked up and down the platform, trying different angles, hoping to get lucky. I didn't. Another passenger arrived and waited on the platform as I walked up and down it. A train arrived. She got on; one other person got off. I kept searching. The wind got colder, and so did I.

My nose and ears were starting to go numb. Times like this make me wish I were a fire or an ice mage. I took out my phone and called Caldera; it rang for what felt like much too long before Caldera picked up. "Hey."

"Hi," I said. "Look, seeing as this is my first solo job and all, mind giving me some pointers?"

"Just a sec," Caldera said. There was a lot of noise in the background, voices and glasses clinking. Wherever Caldera was, it sounded warm, comfortable, and a much nicer place to be than here. "Didn't catch that, say again?"

I took a breath, restraining the urge to hate her. "What the hell am I supposed to be doing here?"

"You're at the station?"

"It's cold, wet, and empty, and there's sod-all to find."

"Magesight?"

"Comes up blank. Look, you know about this stuff. What do you do when you're sent out somewhere where there's nothing to see?"

"You got the report, didn't you?"

A train pulled up at the platform in a swell of light and noise. The doors opened with a hiss and I edged closer, hoping the air from inside would be a little warmer. It didn't help much. "It just says 'investigate.'"

"Hey, you're a diviner. You're supposed to be good at this."

"Oh, sure." The doors shut and the train pulled away, accelerating into the darkness. I walked after it, heading up the platform. "I'll use my divination and look into the future. Hey, you know what, I'm seeing the future right now. If I stand here and wait, then in three minutes a train's going to come. And after that, *another* train's going to come. Here,

I'll let you guess what's going to happen afterwards. I'll give you a hint—there's a train."

"Hey, can you hear that?"

"What?"

"It's the sound of me playing the world's tiniest violin."

"Yeah, laugh it up, you're not the one freezing your balls off. Why didn't they send a time mage?"

"You know how many incidents we get called out to per day?" Caldera asked. "Have a guess. Then have a guess how many time mages we've got on retainer."

I was silent. "Here's another question," Caldera said. "You think you're the first guy who's noticed that some of the jobs we get sent on probably aren't going to accomplish much?"

"No."

"You have to search an empty station," Caldera said. "Given what usually happens when you're around, you ought to be happy."

"It's still a shit job."

"This is not even *close* to what our really shit jobs look like. Now, are you going to do the work or are you going to keep being a whiny little bitch?"

I sighed. "Fine."

"Because I'm not running out there to hold your hand."

"I get it."

"Besides, I've got a pint waiting for me and it's nice and warm in here."

"I hate you so much."

"Sucks to be you. Later." Caldera hung up. I glared at my phone and shoved it into my pocket. Another gust of freezing wind swept across the platform; the air was damp and even without my magic, my London upbringing was telling me it was going to rain again soon.

I had another try at finding a witness, but after fifteen minutes of searching I was forced to give up. The closest guy I could find was one lonely security guard still on duty at the construction site, bundled up in a booth with a space heater. He was several minutes away, had no line of sight to the platform, and from his body language didn't seem to be interested in anything except trying not to freeze. It was theoretically possible that some other construction workers had been on site when whatever-it-was had happened, but if they had they hadn't called 999, and I had absolutely no idea how I would find the right individuals out of an indeterminate-but-almost-certainly-large number of construction workers who (a) had gone home for the night, (b) would probably be disinclined to talk to me, and (c) were unlikely to have seen anything useful in the first place.

In the end I was forced to fall back on my divination, which was ironic given that I'd just been complaining at Caldera about how useless it was. But while divination isn't really designed for CSI work, there are a few tricks you can pull which kind of do the same thing. In particular, it's good for searching. If you've already decided to search an area, you skim through the possible futures of yourself doing the search and look for ones in which you find something. It's not all that reliable, mainly because it's hard to tell the difference at a casual glance between "future in which you find something useful" and "future in which you find something that looks useful but turns out on closer inspection to be irrelevant or worthless." But it beats turning over rocks with your bare hands.

I was right on the edge of calling it off when something caught my attention. The wind had grown even colder, my ears had gone numb, and the first spots of a new rain shower had started to fall. I was towards the north end of the platform, and most of the futures I could see led to nothing but damp and frustration—but beyond the platform was a future that was different. The end of the platform was fenced off with a big sign on the gate reading *Danger: High Voltage— No Admittance Beyond This Point*. I pushed the gate open and walked down the ramp between the sets of railway lines, tufts of scrubby grass growing between piled gravel.

The thing (whatever it was) was lying in the midst of the damp stones. It was small and spherical, about the size and shape of a marble. But it had a trace of magic—just a tiny, tiny trace—and now that I was closer I could sense something from it. A weak one-shot, or a *very* weak focus. If my mage-sight hadn't been better than most mages', I'd never have noticed it.

I picked the thing up—it felt like a marble too—then straightened and looked around. Spitting rain was falling onto the railway lines around me, the drops briefly visible in the orange glow of the station lights. If there was anything else here, I couldn't find it.

To my right the rails were vibrating: another train was coming. I walked back up onto the platform. This time, when the train pulled up, I got on.

Back home, I took a hot shower, then once I was warm again I sat down at my desk and studied my new find. It seemed to be a glass marble, a little bigger than my thumbnail, pale green and translucent. Under the desk lamp I could see little white flecks floating inside. Now that I had the chance to study it, it was definitely a focus. It didn't have any energy stored—what I'd sensed was the residue of its previous uses. The magic felt universal rather than living or elemental, but it was pretty generic. It didn't seem closely tied to any of the magic types.

I ran it through a few basic tests but came up blank. It didn't respond to any standard command words, which given that it didn't have any energy storage was exactly what you'd expect. It was tougher than glass, but not indestructible. My best guess was that it was designed to respond to some sort of magical input, but channelling into it didn't do anything. Maybe it needed a type of magic I didn't have.

I thought about calling it in but decided against it. I'd show the thing to Caldera when she got back on Monday. With that settled, I left the focus on my desk and went to bed.

chapter 3

"   and unfortunately I don't think it's going to open up
. . . any time soon."

"That's a pity," I said. "No chance of that changing?"

"Right at the moment my schedule's fairly fixed, I'm
afraid. I'm committed all the way through the spring."

"Sorry to hear that. If anything does change and you have
an opening . . . ?"

"Of course. I'll give you a call."

"Thanks for your time."

"Have a good day."

The man on the other side of the video feed reached
forward to his keyboard and the window closed. I leant back
in my chair with a sigh. "Well, that was a waste of time."

"I didn't like him anyway," Luna said.

It was the next day and we were up in my living room. I was
at my desk, Luna was sitting on the sofa, and we'd just finished
a call with another prospective teacher. I'd had Luna around
just on the off chance that the conversation might have gone
well, but as it turned out she could have saved herself the trip.

"Is it me," Luna said, "or are there not many chance mages

with the Council? Because every time I get a class on chance magic, it always seems to be some *other* mage telling us *about* chance magic. I'm starting to think I know more than the teachers."

"You know magic types have a bias towards factions," I said. "Death mages are more likely to be Dark, mind mages are more likely to be Light . . . well, chance mages tend to be independent or Dark. They might go through the apprentice program, but they don't stay there."

"Yeah, can't imagine why. So have we run out yet?"

"Of the Council-approved ones, yeah."

We'd been at the teacher-hunting game for a month, with no luck so far. Trying to find a magic teacher who matches your magic type *and* has the time and inclination to teach *and* is trustworthy is not easy. When I'd tried it with Anne and Variam, it had taken longer than this and I'd only managed a fifty percent success rate. "Guess it's time to go farther afield," I said. "We could try looking abroad, start in America or Europe and work our way out. Only problem with that is that I don't really have any contacts over there."

"Or . . . ?"

"Or we broaden our search by person instead of by country. So far I've been keeping it to Light mages and the reputable independents." I tapped my fingers on the desk. "I know there are a whole lot more chance mages out there, but they don't advertise. And you don't know what you're getting . . ."

"Soooo . . ." Luna said. "Funny you should mention that."

I looked at Luna. "What have you done this time?"

"What do you mean, 'this time'?"

"Just give me the bad news."

"For your information, I got an offer for a teacher already," Luna said.

"Who?"

"Her name's Chalice."

"She's a finder?"

"No, she said she's a chance mage. And she said she wanted to meet you."

I frowned. "That's . . . strange." Magical teachers who are thinking about taking on a new student usually want to interview the student. The only explanation I could think was that she wanted some sort of payment. Still, there was only one way to find out. "All right. How?"

"She gave me an e-mail address, asked me to give it to you. I'll forward it."

"Okay. When was this?"

"Just this morning." Luna paused. "By the way, there's one other thing . . ."

I'd been waiting for the other shoe to drop. "What other thing?"

"She's . . . not an independent."

And if she were a Light mage, Luna would have told me already. "She's Dark."

"Yeah," Luna said. She was watching me carefully.

"How do you know?"

"She told me. She didn't keep it a secret or anything."

"How did she get your contact details?"

"She said it was through the apprentice program," Luna said, shrugging. "It was only my public mailbox."

I was silent. "Is that a problem?" Luna asked.

"Yes."

"You did just say we'd have to widen the search."

"I said we *might* have to widen the search, and when I said 'widen,' I didn't mean take anyone we could get. Let's try some independents before we get crazy."

"I thought you *had* been trying most of the independents."

"Then we'll find some others."

"Okay," Luna said. "But while we're doing that, it won't do any harm if we see how it goes, right?"

I looked at Luna. "Are you actually serious about this?"

Luna paused, then nodded.

"Luna, this isn't a good idea. She's a Dark mage."

"Most of the people I hang out with are ex-Dark anyway."

"Okay," I said. "Bit of a difference here I don't think you're seeing. I was *originally* trained by a Dark mage, a really long time ago, and in case you've forgotten, it didn't work out so well. And Anne and Vari's experience was worse."

"It's not like the Council are so much better."

"Maybe not, but they're safer."

"They didn't feel much safer to me," Luna said quietly.

That brought me up short. Luna officially became my apprentice two and a half years ago, but she got her feet wet in magical society the year before. And when I say "feet wet," it was more like "someone trying to drown you." Back then Luna had been a novice, inexperienced and vulnerable, and on two separate occasions she'd fallen into the hands of Light mages who had done a very good job of demonstrating to her that being a Light mage did not make you a nice person. Those sorts of experiences leave an impression.

But just because Light mages can be bastards, that doesn't make Dark ones any less dangerous. "I don't think you're thinking this all the way through," I said. "You're twenty-four. In another year or two you're going to want to take your journeyman tests, and that means going to the Council. You already know how much grief you get for being my apprentice, and I'm only ex-Dark. If you've been studying under a Dark mage directly, it's going to be worse."

"So the Council are going to be upset," Luna said. "The Council are *always* upset. They're never happy and they're never going to like me, and you know what? I'm pretty much okay with that. I know doing this might be dangerous but . . . ever since I've been in the magical world, ever since I walked into your shop, I've been taking risks. And I kind of like it. I don't *want* to be a hundred percent safe. Besides . . . the last few years, it feels like it works. Okay, yeah, sometimes it goes wrong, but everything *good* that's happened to me, it's because I took the chance and did something that could have turned out badly, isn't it? I mean, that was the only reason I met you. If I hadn't decided to go for it, I'd be back at home alone, sleeping most of the day and trying to find a reason to get up every morning. And that's if I was lucky. So I don't know what'll happen, but . . . maybe it's worth it."

I looked at Luna. She was sitting up straight, meeting my

gaze, and I felt a pang. *She's growing past the apprentice stage, isn't she?* How much longer before she'd be ready to strike out on her own? Two years? Less? I didn't know, but all of a sudden as I looked at her, I felt sure that Luna was past the halfway mark. The time ahead of her as my apprentice would be shorter than the time she'd spent already. It was a strange feeling, proud and melancholy at the same time.

And if she was going to be a journeyman soon . . . then maybe it was time to start treating her like one.

"I'll talk to her," I said. "But I'm not promising anything."

"Thanks."

। । । । । । । ।

Once Luna was gone I opened up and spent the rest of the day running the shop. My shop's called the Arcana Emporium, and it's in the back streets of Camden. As far as I know it's the only magic shop in Britain that sells actual magic (there are rumours of one in Ireland, but I've never gotten around to checking them out). The weather outside was cold, but I didn't have any shortage of customers.

I get two general categories of customers in my shop: the ones who have a clue (the minority), and the ones who don't (much more common). Generally speaking, the clueless ones aren't a big problem—all they want to do is browse around and poke things. They're just here for entertainment, and as long as they don't break anything, I don't really mind.

The ones who *are* a problem tend to be the ones at the far ends of the scepticism-to-credulity scale. First you get the sceptics, who are absolutely certain that magic isn't real and will explain this to you at length. This is generally irritating rather than dangerous, but still gets old fast, particularly since a large fraction of said group seem to believe that if you don't agree with them, then all that means is that you must not understand what they're saying. So they'll go back to the beginning and explain all over again about how all of this magic stuff is superstition and why no one in their right mind could *really* believe in it, while I try to explain in turn that yes, that's very interesting, but there are three other customers waiting behind you and would you mind getting out of the way so I can talk to them instead?

At the other end of the scale you get the excessively credulous types, who believe in magic just fine, as well as everything else. Today's representatives of the latter group included a guy who'd come into possession of a vase that he wanted identified because he thought it was magical (it wasn't), another guy whose girlfriend had left him and who was convinced that it was for supernatural reasons (it wasn't), a woman who thought she was the reincarnation of Cleopatra and wanted to talk to me about her destiny (that one went downhill fast), and some bunch of lunatics calling themselves the Circle of the Serpent who wanted my help with initiation rites (don't ask).

In other words, a normal day. Hey, at least it isn't boring.

But mixed in with the ones who have no idea what they're talking about are the ones who do. And mixed in with *those* are the ones who might not know how the magical world works but have enough common sense to figure out that if they're going to be involved in it, then learning as much as they can is a really good idea.

"For the last time, I'm not checking up to see if your wife is cheating on you," I said. "I'm not a private detective."

The man left in a huff and I turned back to the person I'd been talking to before he'd butted in. The adept was shorter than average, with scruffy clothes and overly thick glasses, but the eyes behind the lenses were perceptive.

"Kind of," I told him. "I mean, the way the law is right now, it doesn't actually draw any distinction between Dark mages and Light mages anyway."

"So what *is* the proposal going to do?"

"The big issue is Council membership," I said. "Some mages want the Junior and Senior Council opened up to Dark mages, some don't. This proposal of Morden's is going further than that. If it goes through, there'll be one seat on the Junior Council that's *only* open to Dark mages."

"But why?"

"Affirmative action, I suppose. If it's any consolation, it's not going to affect you and your friends directly. It only applies to mages."

"But it'll make a difference, won't it?" the adept said. "If there are Dark mages on the Council, then it's like saying that they're approving what they do."

"Yeah."

"So isn't that going to filter down? Like that thing that happened with that Dark mage, Torvald. The next time that happens they'll be even less likely to do anything, won't they? It'll just keep getting worse."

I sighed. "You might be right."

"So what are we supposed to do? It's not like the Council's going to listen to us."

"I don't know. I wish I had some better answers for you, but I don't. And it's not as though the Council's going to listen to me, either."

"But you're still a mage."

"There is that. Look, how many are there in your circle?"

The adept (his name was Lucian) hesitated for a second before deciding to tell the truth. "Five."

"So at least you're not on your own. Okay, I'm guessing there's something specific you're worried about, so why don't you give me a rundown on which of your friends you think are in danger and why. I can't promise anything, but I can probably give you some advice that'll make it more likely that if something goes wrong, it won't happen to you guys."

We talked it over. It took a while because the conversation kept on being interrupted by other customers: a girl who wanted to sell a dagger focus, three people buying various mundane items, two different guys wanting to buy magic tricks, and a latent mage just starting to come into her power who'd gotten in touch with me via e-mail. I bought the dagger off the first, sold the next three the things they wanted, gave the two would-be magicians business cards from the box on the counter, and booked a time with the last girl for a longer chat.

"Anyway, that's the best advice I've got," I said at last. "Look, you can give me a call if anything happens. Doubt

I'll be able to do anything directly, but I can give you some suggestions."

"All right." Lucian started to leave, then hesitated. "Thanks."

"You're welcome."

"No, I mean . . . Kath said I shouldn't come. She thought you were supposed to hate adepts."

"I've heard that too."

"But you don't, right?" Lucian said. "I mean, that thing with the Nightstalkers. You didn't go after them because you wanted to, did you?"

"I wish everyone else would believe that. Look, you want to do me a favour back? Tell the other adepts you know that I'm trying to be one of the good guys."

"Oh." Lucian paused. "Okay." He left, and I went back to dealing with the rest of the customers.

When you're forced to see things from someone else's point of view, it helps you put things in perspective. I often feel vulnerable in mage society—in both power and influence, compared to someone like Caldera, I'm a lightweight. But just as other mages are above me, there are others that I'm above in turn. I might be weak by mage standards, but I'm still a *mage*, and that gives me a certain automatic level of status and bargaining power. For adepts like Lucian, and for novices like that girl, magical society is a very scary place. Things can go wrong very fast and very badly, and when they do there isn't much of a safety net. It was a reminder that my life could be a lot worse.

It was also a reminder that this wasn't just about me. Whatever Richard and Morden were planning, it was going to have trickle-down effects to everyone. More lives than our own were going to be affected by this.

⁛⁛⁛⁛⁛

The sun was setting when I finished with the last customer and locked up. I used to spend most of my days like this, but over the last couple of years the amount of time I've spent running my shop has been going steadily down.

Officially the Arcana Emporium's supposed to be open six days a week, and okay, I don't think I've ever *consistently* kept to that, but I used to average about four and a half. Nowadays it's more like three. Either there's a job, or a problem, or I'm training Luna, or researching . . . and when push comes to shove, running my shop is one of my few responsibilities where if I skip out, then nothing immediately bad is going to happen. Over the last few months I'd actually got into the habit of having Luna run the place every Tuesday, just so there'd be one day the place would consistently be open.

If things kept going the way they had been, though, then before long the average number of days I was putting in at the shop per week was going to hit zero, and that bothered me a little. Weird as it sounds, my shop's one of the only public faces for magic in this country; for people like Lucian who have some sort of magic-related problem but aren't plugged into mage society, this is one of the few places they can go. Maybe I needed to start taking steps so that the shop could survive without me . . . I shook it off and checked my e-mail. There was a message from Carol, one of the Keeper admins; they'd received the report I'd sent about yesterday and had sent a form-letter acknowledgement back, which for some reason left me vaguely disappointed. I'd been half-expecting to get chewed out, but it didn't sound as though they'd even particularly noticed.

Luna had sent me Chalice's address. I sent her an e-mail agreeing to meet, then spent a couple of hours trying to dig up information. She was a Dark chance mage, but beyond that her affiliation was unknown. No apprentices or dependents that anyone knew about. Trained (and presumably born) outside the U.K., so there wasn't as much information as there would have been if she'd grown up here. No obvious red flags, and no connection to Morden or Richard that I could find, but I was still uneasy. Dark mages always have an agenda. What was hers?

I was so lost in thought that I didn't even see it coming when the phone rang. I picked up absently. "Lensman."

"Hello, Verus." Lensman is a mage with a voice that sounds like he should be on the BBC. He's in the same business as me, more or less—while I sell items to adepts and apprentices, Lensman sells to mages. It's higher profit but a lot more dangerous. I get some of my items from him, and over the years we've become friends of a sort, though we rarely meet in person. "Just to let you know, that focus you delivered looks excellent. I've already got a buyer lined up."

"That's good." Honestly, I didn't really care. The item in question had been a concentration-based shielding focus. Completely useless in a combat situation, but for some reason Light duellists love the things. My mind was still on Chalice.

"Well, in the meantime, I've sure you'll be glad to hear that I've finally heard back about that archaeological project of yours."

"Archaeological . . . ?"

"The rubbings?"

"Oh, right." All of a sudden I was paying attention. I'd forgotten about those notes of Vari's. "How did it go?"

"Well, it took some time." Lensman sounded entertained. "You certainly picked a puzzler. Where did you dig them up, anyway?"

"Can't really discuss it, sorry." I knew that Lensman would assume that meant it was Council-related. "If you wanted somewhere more secure . . ."

"No, no, nothing sensitive about the information." I heard the rustling of papers in the background. Lensman doesn't like using computers—like a lot of mages, he's the old-fashioned type. "So, the long and the short of it is that the inscriptions are almost certainly Heraclian."

"As in the philosopher?"

"Not Heraclitus, Heraclian."

"Okay, I have no idea what that means."

"Yes, obscure, isn't it? They were a mage tradition dating back to the Byzantines. Heavy associations with magical creatures. It looks as though those rubbings were taken from a storage device of some kind. Probably their version of a Minkowski box."

"Any idea what was inside it?"

"No, it seems that whoever took those rubbings left the box sealed."

"You said they 'were' a mage tradition," I said. "Don't suppose there's any chance they're still around?"

"Unfortunately not. Apparently they got a bit too close to magical creatures for their own good. Came under vampiric control and the Council had to wipe them out in the vampire wars."

"Anything else in the notes? Where it came from, what it could be used for?"

"Sorry. We were lucky to get this much really."

Damn it. "Well, thanks."

I hung up and put the phone on the desk, staring down at it. I tried to puzzle out what all that meant and came up with nothing. Magical creatures in our world have been declining for centuries. Most of the types the Heraclians had been in contact with would probably be extinct by now. What would Richard want with relics of extinct magical creatures? It could mean anything, or nothing . . . and without more information, there was no way to know which. Another dead end.

I leant back, closing my eyes with a sigh. Ever since I saw Richard last year, I'd had a sense of doom. As though I were stumbling around in the dark, blind and clumsy, while Richard was looking down on me from some place of power. He hadn't contacted me since last year, yet wherever I went and whatever I did, I could feel his presence like a silent shadow. Worst of all, no matter what we did to move against him, I couldn't shake the creeping feeling that Richard knew *exactly* what we were doing and wasn't responding in kind for the simple reason that nothing that I or Anne or Vari or Luna could do was the slightest threat.

I leant back and stared out of the window, wondering what to do. From above the rooftops, stars shone down from a clear sky, and I knew that it would be a bitterly cold night. It was hard not to feel hopeless. I was struggling and clawing to become a Keeper auxiliary, working for weeks and months at a time to gain a tiny bit more favour with the Council.

Meanwhile, Richard and Morden between them had more power than I could gain in a hundred years. They could have us all eliminated at any time and place of their choosing, probably with no more than a phone call. Was I really accomplishing anything? Or were all my efforts with the Keepers and with finding a teacher for Luna just a way of passing time?

Then I shook my head. *This isn't getting me anywhere.* Maybe working with the Keepers would help and maybe not, but I'd chosen my course of action and all there was to do was stick with it. In the meantime, if I couldn't do anything about Richard or Luna, I might as well concentrate on something more productive.

All day long, in the back of my mind, I'd been puzzling over that focus I'd found last night and the question of how it had got there. Without it, I could have written off the 999 call as a waste of time. With it . . . well, focuses don't get left lying around for no reason. Why had one been sitting by the train tracks of an all-but-empty DLR station?

The bottom line was that I'd been told to find out what had happened, and I hadn't. Yes, I'd followed orders, but I didn't really want to leave it at that. Part of it was a sense of professionalism, but part of it was just simple curiosity. When you're a diviner, you have this constant urge to stick your head in for a closer look, and when you don't, it bugs you. If I wanted to find out what had happened at that station, how would I do it?

The easy answer was time magic. Time mages can look back into the past of their current location, playing out the events before their eyes like a video recording. It's a very useful ability, which naturally means that the supply of helpful time mages never meets the demand. I do know one time mage, a guy called Sonder, but we aren't exactly friends anymore and I didn't even think he was in London at the moment. That just left the mundane way. What would I do if I wanted to find out what had happened at a particular place and time and I *wasn't* a mage?

The obvious answer was CCTV. London has the dubious distinction of being the most spied-upon city in the world, with more security cameras per person than anywhere else on the planet. I couldn't remember if the station had had any cameras, but logic suggested that the answer was yes. I glanced at the clock to see that it was ten P.M. Trains would still be running.

Well, why not?

＊＊＊＊＊＊＊＊＊

One of the drawbacks of being a diviner is not having access to the gate spell. Gate magic is one of the more useful tricks that mages have up their sleeves; it creates a portal between two points in space, allowing you to step from place to place instantly. You have to know the two places you're gating between, but it's still a really useful ability to have—it would have allowed me to get to Pudding Mill Lane station in about sixty seconds, using my mental image of the place from the night before. Unfortunately, gate magic is restricted to elementalists. There are a handful of non-elemental magic types that can use the spell (death and space being the most well known), but divination isn't one of them.

If you can't use gate spells, the next best thing is gate stones. They're small, cheap items that can be used to produce a gate effect at will, and like most focuses they can be used by any mage. Only problem is, they'll take you to the same place every time, namely the spot the focus was keyed to. Great for going home, not so good for outbound trips.

Which is why when I'm travelling around London, I usually just take the train like everybody else.

＊＊＊＊＊＊＊＊＊

I stepped out onto the platform at Pudding Mill Lane, shivering in the cold air. Behind me, the doors of the train hissed shut and the carriages began to pull away from the station.

Now that I knew what I was looking for, it didn't take me long to find it. There were two CCTV cameras on the platform, pointing in both directions, and . . . *there. Perfect.* A third camera just a little way past the platform, pointing at the gate with the *No Admittance* sign and looking right down on the spot where I'd found the focus last night.

I wanted to go through the gate and poke around, but despite the late hour there were a couple of other people on the platform: a man fiddling with his mobile phone and a woman carrying a bunch of Sainsbury's bags. I didn't want to do anything to draw attention while they were so close. Although now that I'd found the right camera, it occurred to me that I didn't really know what to do next. How *did* you pull recordings off cameras? The Keepers would definitely have contacts at Transport for London, but I didn't know whether they'd do something like that on my request.

From the departure boards I could see that trains were coming every ten minutes. As I watched, a southbound train pulled up at the platform in a rumble of light and noise, newly arrived from the terminus at Stratford. The woman with the Sainsbury's bags got on. The man with the mobile phone didn't. The doors shut with a hiss and the train pulled away, heading south towards the towers of Canary Wharf, leaving the two of us alone on the platform.

I tried to figure out how I'd go about getting the recordings. The camera had to be sending the data somewhere—maybe a local node? I walked down the stairwell in the centre of the platform, looking for some sort of office. No good. There was hardly any station beyond the platform, just a few locked doors. One was a lift, another a supply closet. The third was some sort of switch room. They were locked, but it was only a simple padlock. I could probably pick it . . . I looked up to see that the man was still up there on the platform, and annoyingly, he'd chosen to stand right near the top of the stairs. He was talking into his mobile in French, and ignoring me completely, but he'd have a perfect view of anything I did. *Will you just get on your train and go away?*

Maybe there was some other way I could get the recordings. If I . . .

Wait a second.

That man had been here when I'd arrived. He hadn't boarded the northbound train that I'd taken to get here. And he hadn't boarded the southbound train that had just left.

If he wasn't waiting for a northbound train *or* a south-bound train, what was he doing here?

Without looking directly at the guy I studied him through the futures. He was a little taller than average, dressed warmly in a woollen cap and a long coat. Most of his face was hidden behind a beard and dark glasses. As I watched, he started strolling down the stairs towards me, still talking into his phone. *"Allons, ma chérie, ne sois pas comme ça. Tu sais que ce n'est pas elle. Je viens de . . ."*

He still wasn't looking in my direction. From his body language it didn't even look as though he'd noticed I was there, but my instincts were starting to sound a warning. *"Allez,"* he said. *"Allez, allez, allez. Ce n'est pas ce que j'ai dit. Non, tu sais . . . Je n'ai pas dit ca. Allez . . ."*

The two of us were alone in the station entrance. Fluorescent lights buzzed overhead, reflecting off the white tiles of the walls. The man was halfway down the stairs; his course would take him behind me and out onto the long path heading through the construction site to the main road. Something in my precognition was trying to catch my attention, and I looked into the short-term futures of what would happen when he—

Oh shit.

All of a sudden I realised just how isolated we were. There were no staff in the station, no passengers on the platform, and the next train was still four minutes away. The construction site around us was deserted. There were still security cameras . . .

. . . and how much help were they yesterday? I was on my own. Casually I shifted position, my right hand drifting to my belt. I didn't turn around and the man disappeared out of my field of vision. He was still talking. *"Tu sais que je n'ai pas . . . je n'étais—"*

I held very still, counting off the seconds. Four. Three. Now he was right behind me. *"Je n'étais même pas là . . ."* Two. One . . .

"Pourquoi de vrais—" Magic flared behind me and I heard a whisper of movement, soft and quick.

I was already twisting. Something slid past me and hit the door with a *thunk*. At the same time my hand came up in a flash of metal, stabbing upwards.

He was quick, very quick. The knife hit home but he was already jumping back and a shield flickered into existence as the blow landed. He came down in a fighting stance, a translucent blade that hadn't been there a second ago held in his right hand and pointing straight at me. He started to cast another spell, and before he could finish I lunged.

The man dropped the spell and struck, meeting my attack with his own. I hooked his blade and kept going, slamming him into the wall and forcing his knife hand out of position while I stabbed at his gut, one-two-three. The third blow sank home but as it did another spell blew me back, solid air striking like a hammer. I was thrown back to the steps, tripped, looked up to see him moving in a blur of motion, disappearing around the corner before I could react.

I scrambled to my feet. I could feel the signature of his spells moving out of the station towards the construction site. Air magic, soft and grey and whisper-quick. That spell he'd used to throw me away had been a wind blast, and that blade had been hardened air. I looked right to see that the door I'd been standing in front of had a narrow diamond-shaped hole, almost too thin to see. If I hadn't moved that would have been my back.

I looked at my knife to see a trace of blood, but only a trace. He'd been using an air shield. I didn't think he was seriously hurt, but—

My divination warned me first, my magesight second. Energy twined around the corridor where I was standing and I bolted up the stairs, putting distance between me and the centre of the spell. As I cleared the stairs and came down on the platform I felt a sudden tug of wind pulling me back and my ears popped as I heard a hollow *whump* from behind. I darted behind a pillar and held still.

Silence. I strained my ears, trying to make out some sound. Wind swirling around the platform, traffic on the main road to the east. I couldn't hear the guy's footsteps.

What had that spell been? Whatever it was, it wasn't friendly to human bodies. My best guess was some kind of implosion effect. *Air mage, has to be.* Too many spells to be an adept.

Movement in the futures. There was no sound, but looking into what would happen if I stepped out, I could sense the air mage coming back. He was floating, not walking, hovering a few inches above the ground at the foot of the steps. The air blade was still in his right hand, and as I watched he began to glide up the stairs, eyes searching left and right.

Not good. The platform had cover, but not enough. *Maybe I can hide . . .* The pillar I had ducked behind was more of a girder, really, holding up the roof over the platform. I held very still.

The air mage reached the top of the stairs, looking left and right. He was maybe twenty feet from where I was standing. I held my breath.

Silence.

The other man was standing quite still. The futures flickered, uncertain. In some of them he found me, in others he didn't. I couldn't see what I needed to do to shake him. He began walking down the platform.

I edged very carefully to the left, keeping the pillar between us. The wind had dropped and the air was still. I made it around and the air mage was walking away down the platform. *Hasn't seen me yet . . .* I drew in a soft breath and let it out.

The air mage's head snapped around.

Shit.

He cleared the benches in one jump, seeming to hang in the air, eyes locking onto me. I leapt back behind the pillar as a spray of something almost invisible and very lethal flashed down the platform towards me. I needed time. I grabbed a forcewall from my pocket, flicked the gold discs out to the platform edges, and said the command word just as another spell came flying at me.

The discs ignited, throwing up an invisible barrier, and the spell bounced off; it had been some sort of whirlwind. I backed out into the open, looking at the mage through the forcewall. "Can we talk about this?"

He threw another spell. Fragments of hardened air slammed into the forcewall, dissolving back into gas as soon as they struck. The forcewall didn't budge. "Okay, so you're not the chatty type," I said. "That's fine, we can work something out. So why exactly are you trying to kill me? I'm guessing it's got something to do with what happened last night?"

No answer. I couldn't see the guy's eyes behind the dark glasses, but the rest of his face was expressionless. Usually when someone attacks you, they want to talk, either to justify themselves or to convince you to give up. When they're silent and blank-faced, it's a bad sign. It means they've already written you off and they're not going to waste time talking to a dead man.

The air mage fired off another useless spell at the forcewall, then stopped. His head tilted up as he looked at where the forcewall met the platform roof and I knew he was studying the spell with his magesight. Forcewalls transfer energy into whatever they're anchored to when they're attacked, which makes them very hard to blast through. Air magic isn't much good at blasting through stuff. It's much better at moving things around.

Unfortunately the forcewall only went as far as the platform edge.

Magic curved around the mage as he floated into the air. He flew out over the train tracks and right around the wall.

Shit! I was already moving, jumping off the other edge down onto the tracks, putting the concrete bulk of the platform between us. I'd been hoping that the guy would chase after me, fly low over the platform where he'd have trouble manoeuvring, but instead he flew straight up, coming all the way over the platform roof to arc down on top of where I was hiding. I had to scramble back onto the platform to look for cover.

The mage did an attack run, sweeping past. Bullets of hardened air threw up chips of concrete as I darted behind the advertising boards at the platform centre. The shots tracked me as I moved, tearing through the flimsy plastic of the boards, punching holes in the posters from Transport for London announcing that *Being Careful Won't Hurt You* and urging everyone to *Report Anything Suspicious to Our Staff or the Police*. The boards went dark as the lights behind them fizzled and died, and the air mage soared up into the sky again, disappearing from my sight.

This was bad. As long as this guy stayed airborne I couldn't touch him. Running was useless; it was too far to the main road. I glanced up at the indicator. Three minutes until the next northbound train. Could I hold out that long?

The air mage did another flyby. The first attack was a hail of daggers made of hardened air, the second a whirlwind that would have picked me up and thrown me out onto the tracks. Next was a wind blast like a solid punch, and after that was another implosion spell, shattering more of the poster boards and sending a hollow boom echoing out over the construction site. I ducked and dodged, jumping behind the platform, using the forcewall as a barrier, pulling every trick I could think of to shake him. I was holding him off, but I wasn't stopping him. Magic doesn't run off some sort of limited resource, and while casting spells takes energy, it's no more tiring than any other demanding skill—apprentices might exhaust themselves after a dozen or so spells, but a journeyman or master mage won't. Which means that you can't make a mage run out of magic. As long as they want you dead badly enough, they can just sit there and keep casting the same spell at you over and over again until you roll over and die.

And just as I was thinking that, my luck ran out.

The air mage had fallen into a pattern, aiming spells at the same points on the platform. He started to cast another dagger burst, and I began to jump down behind the platform edge . . . and in midcast he changed target, placing the centre of the burst right above where I'd been about to take cover.

You don't have much margin for error when you're dodging spells. I tried to get to the stairwell before the detonation.

I didn't make it.

There was a *bang* that hurt my ears, and something hit me in the side and back, sending me flying. I hit the stairs and rolled down, scraping to a halt on the landing, pain stabbing from a dozen places. I couldn't see my attacker but

I knew he was coming and I fumbled for an item in my pocket. On the second try my hand closed over a small sphere—one of my condensers—and I threw it at the top of the stairs. My head was still spinning and the throw went long, hitting the pillar behind and shattering. Mist rushed out, cloaking the platform and the top of the steps in fog.

I struggled to my feet. Pain lanced from my side; I put my hand to it and felt wetness. Another spell in the futures, but no danger; it was going to miss. A moment later I heard the *boom* of another implosion spell and felt the whack of wind as air rushed by. The mist swirled slightly.

I could feel a faint rumble through the concrete: the train was coming. I crouched on one knee, waiting. Above, I saw the glow of lights through the mist. No more attacks, not yet, but if— He was waiting for me to move. I held my breath, keeping very still.

The rumbling grew louder and with a whine of metal the train pulled up by the platform. I still couldn't see it, or him, but I knew where he was: up and to the left, waiting for me to show myself. The train doors opened with a hiss. I looked to see when they would close, counted down. *Nine . . . eight . . . seven . . .*

Now.

I ran up the stairs. The air mage detected me, waited for me to clear the top of the stairwell, fired. I checked just as he cast his spell, fire stabbing my side, heard the hiss of projectiles slashing through the mist ahead of me. *Three seconds.* I ran right, the mist parting to reveal a blue-and-red carriage, curious faces peering out; the doors were just beginning to close and I jumped through. They met behind me with a *thud*, and with a jolt of acceleration the train started to move.

All of a sudden I found myself in the middle of a scattered crowd of people, all staring. "Excuse me," I said to the nearest guy, a black man in a peaked cap. He got out of my way, and I began moving forward to the front of the carriage. As I did, I glanced back over my shoulder through the train windows. The mist cloud was a grey patch, fading away on the platform behind. I couldn't see my attacker.

"Are you all right?" a woman said. She was on one of

the seats at the front, twisted around to look. I wondered briefly how I looked to everyone else, and that made me remember my wound. I touched it with my left hand again and drew in my breath. Looking down, I saw blood smeared over my fingers and palm.

"Oh, shit," the woman said. "You want me to call an ambulance?"

"Might not be the best idea." Now that I was out of combat, my side was really hurting. I didn't think it was going to kill me, but it was deep. *Not good.*

"I'm calling 999," the woman announced. She pulled out a phone and started tapping.

There was a *thump* from above, echoing through the carriage. It was hollow, and heavy. It was, in fact, exactly the kind of noise a grown man would make when landing on the roof of a train.

Shit.

The passengers in the train looked upwards. They looked confused rather than worried; I had the feeling that wasn't going to last. "Hello?" the woman was saying. "Ambulance."

I held still, scanning futures. The people around were making it harder, their actions tangling with my own. What was this guy going to do, smash his way through the windows?

"Hello? Yeah. There's a man here, I think he's hurt . . . I mean, yeah, he's definitely hurt . . . what? Marie Gilman . . . Yeah, my number's, wait a sec . . ."

I couldn't see any futures in which the air mage broke in, but it was looking like he wouldn't have to. Up ahead, the lights of the shopping centres were getting brighter and I could see what looked like a platform. The next station was barely a minute away. And it was the terminus, which would mean everyone would be getting out . . .

"No, the DLR," the woman was saying. "What? Hang on, I'll check. How old are you?"

It took me a second to realise the woman was talking to me. "What?"

"I think about thirty?" she said into the phone. "Oh. Okay . . . Do you have any existing medical conditions?"

I stared at her.

"They want to know if you've got any existing medical conditions," the woman said. "Oh, she was asking if you've got any chest pain?"

"No, I have a pain in my side, because someone just stabbed me through it. And you might want to forget that call and get out of here, because the man who did the stabbing is probably on the roof of this train."

"What?"

The train was pulling into Stratford and the doors would be opening in twenty seconds. Stratford's not Pudding Mill Lane: the station was well lit, skyscrapers rose up around us, and another train was waiting to go on the other side of the platform. We were still at the edge of the station, but there would be staff farther in—the closer I could get to the main floor of the station, the more pressure there'd be for this guy to back off. Why was he even after me? The only explanation I could think of was that he wanted that focus I'd picked up last night. *Maybe he's planning to take it off my corpse.*

The train stopped with a hiss. The passengers got off, filing out through the doors, heading for the stairs down. I followed them, hands in my pockets, head down. My side was hurting badly, but I didn't let it show and I didn't look up. It's hard to pick one person out of a crowd, especially from the back. All I needed was for this guy to hesitate for a few seconds and I'd make it out. I scanned through the futures—he wouldn't be aggressive enough to attack me right in the middle of a bunch of commuters, right?

Right?

Oh, *fuck!*

I jumped out of the way as a blade hissed past. The air mage was right on top of me. I'd lost my knife somewhere back in the last fight; I fumbled for another weapon but he was already aiming another spell and I dived for cover behind the struts at the centre of the platform. There was another *boom*, deafeningly loud and very close; the shock wave made me stagger as something seemed to punch my back.

Shouts and curses echoed from all around. We'd been right at the only exit and suddenly people were scattering, some running away, others standing and staring and trying to figure out what was going on. It would have been the perfect cover, except that the air mage was already there, stalking around to block my way out, another air blade low and by his side. He could see me and I backed up, keeping the platform struts between us. "What the hell is wrong with you?" I shouted at him. "Just go away!"

He didn't answer, and I felt a trace of fear. Usually I deal with battle-mages by outmanoeuvring them, using my divination to avoid their attacks and putting distance between us. But air mages are the skirmishers of the elementalists, fast and light and agile. They aren't as strong in a stand-up fight as a fire or earth mage, but they have more than enough power to crush someone like me.

The air mage tried to circle around and I dodged again, keeping cover between us. If I couldn't outrun this guy, I'd have to outthink him. Was he after that focus? I glanced through futures in which I tested it. With the chaos going on around it was hard to be sure, but I thought it was getting his attention. Maybe he'd seen the auras of the items I was carrying—

"Oi!" a new voice shouted. "You!"

The air mage stopped and turned. It was the woman from the train. She was standing behind the air mage in the mouth of the exit tunnel, but instead of running she'd stopped and was pointing at the air mage and glaring. She still had her mobile phone to her ear. "You back off!"

We both stared at her. I think we'd both forgotten that the bystanders were even around. "You're the one who stabbed him, aren't you?" the woman said. "Well, I've called the police, so you better back off!"

I looked at the woman in disbelief. "Are you crazy?" I shouted. "Get out of here!"

"Yeah, you're welcome," the woman said. She actually sounded offended. "Not like I'm helping you or anything. Now *you*"—she turned back to the air mage—"you going to beat it, or do I have to get serious?"

The air mage studied her for a second. Other people had turned to watch too, and for an instant everything was still. Then the mage flicked one hand and air struck out in a hammer blow. It smashed into the woman with the distinctive *crack* of breaking bones and threw her twenty feet down the tunnel, sending her rolling over and over to lie still.

Someone screamed and suddenly the platform was chaos, people running, dodging, getting out of the way. The air mage started advancing towards me again, glass crunching under his boots. "That," I said tightly, "was not necessary."

The mage didn't answer. He was still studying me from behind his glasses, and the air blade was by his side again. He'd obviously figured out that I was hurt, and he was intending to get in close to finish the job.

There. To my right, people were running onto the train at the platform. Behind me I could sense a man in an orange TFL vest staring down at the activity, and he was next to the train's control panel. DLR trains don't have drivers, but they do have a manual override. All of a sudden I had a plan. "You know what, screw it," I said. "This isn't worth dying for." I pulled a pouch from my pocket.

The air mage paused, studying me. The pouch was the one I use for my condensers, padded to stop them from breaking. There was one left, still inside, a marble-shaped item about the same size and shape as the focus I'd found last night. I let him get a brief look at it, and then from behind me I sensed the TFL man hit the button and I moved.

The air mage's hand came up and another spell flashed down the platform. He'd been expecting me to run for the train, but I hadn't; I'd thrown the *pouch* into the train, and the shards of hardened air crossed paths with it midflight. It landed on the train floor and skidded, just as the doors closed behind it with a thump. With a whine of electrics the train started to move.

The air mage looked between me and the train. "Now what?" I said. I had to speak loudly over the rumble of wheels. "You can get me, or you can go after that focus. But you stay to finish me and that focus'll be gone by the time you catch up." I stepped back. "Which is it going to be?"

The air mage hesitated and I held my breath, feeling the futures swirl ahead of us. So many things could go wrong. He should have had just enough time to sense the magic from the condenser, but if he'd gotten a good enough look at that pouch before the doors cut his magesight off, he would have seen that it wasn't the right one. Or I might have guessed wrong and it was me he was after. Or maybe—

Then the air mage gave one quick shake of his head and started running down the platform. I scrambled for cover, but he sprinted right past, matching the train's speed and then leaping off the platform. The jump was impossibly high and graceful, arcing through the air to land with a *thump* on the train's roof. I had a last glimpse of him straightening, holding his balance easily on the rocking carriage, before starting to walk towards where I'd thrown the pouch. He didn't look back.

I watched the train pull away into the distance, running lights fading into the sea of neon. Only when I was sure that he wasn't coming back did I sigh and relax. I was hurting in a dozen places, and now that the adrenaline was fading away, I was realising just how bad the wound in my side was. Blood had soaked through my shirt and coat, and I was starting to feel light-headed.

I looked at where the woman was lying. She wasn't moving, and that was enough to kill any satisfaction I felt at having escaped. From a quick check I could tell that she was alive but badly hurt. I didn't have anything that could help her, and I could hear sirens in the distance; the paramedics were on their way and the police would be too. *Time to go.* I turned and limped away, looking for somewhere out of sight where I could gate home.

chapter 4

"Hold still."

"Ow."

"I said, hold *still*."

I was back in my flat, lying on my side on the sofa. My shirt was off, and Anne was leaning over, studying me.

"You're sure it was just hardened air?" Anne asked. "He wasn't using something else as a missile?"

"I didn't exactly get the chance to—"

"Don't lift your head."

I obeyed, putting my head back down on the sofa and talking to the floor. "Pretty sure. There isn't . . . ?"

"There's nothing in the wound. I just wanted to be sure." I heard Anne sigh slightly. "You were lucky."

"Doesn't feel like it."

It was about fifteen minutes later. I'd gated home, called Anne, and had been lucky enough to get her on the phone. She'd used a gate stone to make the journey to my flat immediately.

Other members of the magical community have mixed feelings towards life mages, viewing them rather as they would nuclear reactors. They're good at what they do, but

you don't want to get close to one unless you're *really* sure
it's safe. Given Anne's history, very few mages would will-
ingly allow her within arm's reach. I never used to really get
that attitude, but after last year, I think I understand it a little.
I still don't share it though. I've always instinctively trusted
Anne, and as soon as she'd arrived, I'd felt myself relax.

"I'm serious," Anne said. Her sleeves were rolled up but
she hadn't touched me. Anne can look at a living body and
read its condition and injuries and state of health as easily
as you or I can read a clock. "You were *really* lucky. The
shard must have been almost flat—it went deep but it didn't
have much volume. That's the only reason it didn't hit anything vital. An inch or two up or sideways and it would have
penetrated the kidney or the bowel."

"Is that bad?"

"What do you *think*?" Anne said in exasperation.
"There's muscle damage, internal bleeding, and you've got
some bacterial contamination."

"Oh." I paused. "Uh, can you . . . ?"

"Can I?"

"Fix it?"

"Of course." Anne sounded surprised. "Did you think I
couldn't?"

"Okay."

"When you were stabbed in the casino it was with a sword,
and it was a stomach rupture," Anne said. I felt her hand on my
side; she was touching the skin around the wound, but it didn't
hurt. Soft green light glowed at the edge of my vision as Anne
started to weave her spell. "*That* was hard. The thicker the blade
and the more tearing it causes, the worse it is to treat—the really
bad ones are the ones where the blade's serrated or where it was
twisted and pulled out. Air blades are easy. They're nearly flat,
and they're so sharp they're like surgical knives. Plus they just
dissolve in the wound . . . Move your arm up."

I did. "Would you have trouble with injuries like that?"

"Like what?"

"Where the blade's serrated or twisted."

"Well, no. But it takes longer."

I couldn't feel anything on my side. Anne was still using her magic, but I couldn't tell what she was doing. "Is there anything you *can't* heal?"

"Not really." Anne's voice was absentminded. "I always think of it like a flame. As long as there's a spark left, you can build it up . . . There. Done."

I looked down in surprise. The ugly gash in my side was gone. Blood was still crusted over it, but underneath the skin was clean and unbroken; I couldn't even see where I'd been hurt. "Wow," I said. "I didn't feel anything."

"I had the signals from your local nerves turned off."

"Don't you have to worry about a patient suddenly getting up when you do that?"

"Actually, I was controlling your movements as well."

"Oh."

"You just didn't notice because you weren't fighting it. Could you get up and move around?"

I did. I felt a little light-headed, but no more. "Looks good," Anne said. She didn't wait for me to tell her how it felt; she probably knew better than I did. "Oh, and you had some bruises and sprains, so I fixed those too. Some were from today and a couple looked like you did them yesterday evening. You didn't get attacked twice, did you?"

"No, the first time was a sparring match." I worked my arm; it felt good as new. "Are all life mages this good at healing, or is it just you?"

Anne smiled. "I've had a lot of practice. Is there any food in the house?"

⁙ ⁙ ⁙ ⁙ ⁙

I showered and changed my clothes. I felt *really* good; I must have been carrying a bunch of minor injuries that I hadn't noticed until Anne fixed them. By the time I stepped out of the shower I could smell something very appetising coming from the kitchen and my stomach growled. "Wow," I said as I walked in. "Smells good."

"It's a stir-fry with tuna." Anne was over the stove; she'd

washed the blood from her hands. "Sorry, there were only so many things in the fridge so it'll be a bit makeshift."

"Knowing you, it'll still be better than anything I could come up with."

"That's not saying much."

I laughed. Anne never used to say things like that out loud, but she's a lot more relaxed around me these days. "There's a catch, you know," Anne said.

"With tuna?"

"What you were asking. About whether I can heal any-thing." Anne had turned to look at me and her face was serious again. "I have to be there. If I'm next to someone, I can bring them back, no matter how close they are. But if you bleed out, or if that shard had hit you in the brain or the heart . . ."

"I know."

"This was why I wanted you to have a gate stone for my flat."

"You've got one for here. It works out about the same."

"What if I hadn't answered my phone?"

"I'd have had to think of something else," I admitted. "But you're pretty good about that kind of thing."

"That's because you never ask for help unless it's some-thing incredibly serious." Anne had been opening a can; now she drained off the water and poured the contents into a frying pan with a hiss. "Um, by the way, don't you have a set of armour?"

I sighed.

⁞⁞⁞⁞⁞⁞⁞⁞⁞

Luna and Variam arrived just as Anne was finishing up; she'd called them and given them the news, which come to think of it was something I should have done myself. They took a little time catching up on the story, then once they were sure I was okay, promptly started critiquing my performance.

"So let me get this straight," Luna said. "You have a set of imbued armour designed specifically to stop attacks like this one, and you left it at home."

"Yes."

"Because you forgot to wear it."

"I didn't forget, I just didn't realise I was going to get attacked."

"Even though you're a diviner."

". . . Yes."

Variam and Luna shared a look. "You know," Luna said, "I think that has got to be one of the stupidest possible ways to get killed."

"Yeah, seriously," Variam said. "What's the point of having armour if you're not going to use it?"

"It's *armour*," I said. "I can't walk around London every minute of the day looking like I'm going to a SWAT raid. Anyway, I didn't think it was going to be dangerous."

Variam stared. "You didn't think a police investigation could be dangerous?"

"Well, none of the others have been."

Variam and Luna looked at me.

"All right! It was stupid, I get it. Look, you don't have to worry about this stuff. You can just throw up a shield whenever you feel like it."

"Honestly, doesn't work as well as you'd think," Variam said. "I can dispel anything that's magic, but not if they just shoot through."

"And I can't shield either," Luna said. "So none of us can really. Though I guess Anne can do the 'healer's shield.'"

"Healer's shield?"

"You let them shoot you, then you heal yourself."

"I'd rather not," Anne said mildly. "It still hurts."

Anne had made enough for about six normal people, which was just as well since I was starving—one of the side effects of life magic healing. I wasn't the only one, either. "I wish I could eat that much and stay that thin," Luna told Anne.

"I don't really have a choice, you know."

"Yeah, but you still get to pick how much goes into body fat. That would be *so*—"

"Okay," Variam said. "I'm preemptively cutting you both

off before you start talking about your diets. What are we going to do about this assassin guy?"

Luna and Anne turned to me. "Right now, not much," I said. "He's long gone and we don't have any way to trace him. I'm going to call Caldera in the morning."

"What if *he* traces *you*?" Luna asked.

"Then we'll just have to see who finds who first."

"Do you still have it?" Anne said.

I went to my desk and took out the focus, returning to the dinner table to put it down in the centre. "So that's the thing you nearly got killed for?" Luna asked, studying the green marble with interest.

"Looks that way. You guys seen one of these before?"

"If I had, it would have been on your shelves," Luna said.

Anne had picked the focus up and was studying it curiously. She shook her head. "I don't recognise it."

"I do," Variam said.

Luna and I looked at Variam in surprise. "Really?" Luna said.

"You don't need to sound so bloody shocked."

"You've seen one?" I asked.

"It was a different colour, but yeah, I think so. My master was doing something with it."

"Doing what?"

"Dunno," Variam admitted. "Wasn't paying attention."

"You and Luna have a lot in common, don't you?"

"Hey," Luna said to me, then looked at Variam. "Could you show it to him?"

Variam shrugged. "Got a lesson tomorrow. I can ask him then."

Anne glanced at me. "Is that okay?"

I thought about it for a second. Variam can look after himself pretty well, and having the focus up in Scotland with his master would probably be safer than keeping it here. It did mean trusting Variam's master with the information, but it wasn't like the thing was doing any good sitting in my desk. "All right. Call us when you know anything?"

"No problem."

. . . .

We talked a little longer, but it was past midnight and it wasn't long before everyone was yawning. Anne decided to stay over (she said she wanted to keep an eye on me). Luna wanted to go home but didn't want to cycle back this late, so Variam gave her a lift. By the time I went to bed, the aftereffects of the healing had sunk in, and I was asleep as soon as my head hit the pillow.

I woke up to a tickling feeling. Something thin and light was brushing the side of my face; I twisted away and buried my head in the pillow and duvet. There was a moment's pause, and I had just enough time to vaguely register a presence on the bed before something round and cold was shoved into my ear.

I woke with a yelp and opened my eyes to see a long face with red-brown fur and a pointed muzzle ending in a black nose. The eyes were yellow and less than six inches away, and they were staring right at me.

I glared. "Will you stop doing that?"

The fox pulled its head back and sat on the bed, blinking twice at me. "Alex?" Anne called from the kitchen. "Everything okay?"

"Fine," I called back. "Just Hermes." Apparently satisfied that I wasn't going back to sleep, the fox jumped off the bed, trotted to the door, then looked back at me expectantly.

Hermes is a blink fox, a magic-bred creature with human-level intelligence and the ability to perform short-range teleports. I met him last year at about the same time that I ran into Richard, and after making it out of the shadow realm he followed me home. Ever since then he's dropped by at irregular intervals, expecting a meal. I probably shouldn't have fed him the first time.

Finding out the fox's name had been less straightforward than you'd think, since while blink foxes can understand human speech, they can't talk. Luna had wanted to name him Vulpix, but I'd put my foot down and gone to Arachne instead. After a private conversation with the fox, Arachne had told me to call him Hermes, though she'd been evasive about how she'd found out. "Seriously?" I said. "You want me to feed you *now*?"

Hermes blinked.

Grumbling, I got up and dressed. Anne was already in the kitchen when I got there, cooking something on the stove. "Morning," she said. "Hi, Hermes."

"'Scuse a sec," I said. Anne moved out of the way and I opened a cupboard, rooting through the cans. "You didn't see how he got in, did you?"

"No. Sorry."

"Goddamn it." I pulled out a can of cat food. "I have gate wards specifically to *stop* stuff like this."

"Um, I don't think he wants the cat food," Anne said. "He'd rather have some of the bacon."

"How do you know?"

There was a soft *thump*. I turned around to see Hermes sitting up on the kitchen counter, tail curled around his feet. He was ignoring me and looking at Anne. "Just a guess," Anne said.

"We don't have any bacon."

"I bought some this morning."

I glared at the fox. "Why exactly did you wake me up again?"

"Maybe he just thinks you sleep in too much."

"I got stabbed!"

"Actually, you're completely recovered."

"You know, that lifesight of yours really takes the fun out of acting injured."

"You seem to get injured often enough anyway."

"I didn't use to!"

Anne fed Hermes while I (reluctantly) got in touch with Caldera. I wasn't looking forward to the conversation, so I put the story in an e-mail in the slim hope that that way I wouldn't have to tell her face to face. With that done, we settled down to breakfast.

I suppose if you're not used to how my life works, the way I was acting probably seems pretty weird. I'd just had someone try to kill me and my response had been to call my friends over for dinner. If this had been some episode of a TV series, we'd have spent the night racing around interrogating people, having dramatic adventures, and trying to find the suspect in forty-five minutes plus commercial breaks.

There were two reasons I wasn't doing that. First, on a strategic level, that's not how conflicts between mages work. If you're trying to catch a mage, the rule of thumb is that once he breaks contact, you've got one to five minutes to find him. After that, he's gone. He'll have gated away, and you're not going to track him down without serious effort. Realistically, there wasn't anything I, Anne, Luna, or Vari could have done to find my would-be assassin, and given what had happened last time, finding him probably wasn't even that smart an idea in the first place. Caldera was the one with the resources to track him, and since that wasn't going to happen quickly, it made more sense to get a good night's sleep before calling her in.

The second reason was much simpler: I'd needed to recover. Having someone come that close to killing you is traumatic, especially when you hadn't had time to prepare. I'd been in a state of mild shock last night, and all of the others had known it. That was why Luna and Vari had dropped everything to come over, and why Anne had stayed the night. I've been in this kind of situation enough times to know that when something like this happens to you, the best thing to do is hole up somewhere safe, try to relax, and spend your time doing safe, everyday things, like arguing about what to feed a blink fox. Soon Caldera would arrive and everything would start moving, and before long I'd probably be in danger again. But for now, we could rest.

"How's the healing business going?" I asked Anne.

"It still feels weird thinking of it like that," Anne said. "It's okay, I think. I'm making enough money. Actually more than enough. But it still feels awkward charging people."

"I thought you were only charging the ones who could afford it."

"I am . . . well, I guess I'm not really the entrepreneur type. Though they do seem to treat me better than when I did it for free."

"I noticed that too," I said. "Back when I first took over the shop, I tried giving stuff away. Never seemed to turn out that well. I think people value something more if they pay for it." I paused. "Are you still seeing Dr. Shirland?"

Anne nodded. Dr. Shirland's an independent mind mage. She'd offered to treat Anne a year and a half back but had been turned down. After last spring, Anne had reconsidered.

"Going okay?"

"It's not easy, but it helps. I'm glad you and Luna pushed me into it."

"Have you been talking about . . . ?"

"About her?"

I didn't need to ask who the "her" was, and Anne didn't need to say it. Anne has her own problems, and there's a side of her she doesn't get on well with. "She calls her my shadow," Anne said. "Other things too, but . . . She thinks I can work something out, but it'll take a long time."

"I guess now's as good a time as any to start."

Anne smiled slightly. "Let's hope so."

My phone rang, and I put it to my ear with an inward sigh. *So much for quiet.* "Hi, Caldera."

"Are you at home?" Caldera said.

"Yeah."

"I'm on my way. Don't go anywhere." She hung up.

I lowered the phone. "Well, it was nice while it lasted."

Anne rose to her feet. "I guess that's my cue to go."

I looked at her in surprise. "You don't have to."

"I think it might be easier."

I started to answer, then stopped and looked down. The bell was about to ring. *Already?*

I went downstairs and opened the door to see Caldera, dressed in her work clothes. "Hey."

Caldera gave me an up-and-down look. "You all right?"

"I got better."

Caldera pushed past me. "Then how about you explain,"

she said over her shoulder, "how the *hell* you managed to nearly get yourself killed on the bloody DLR?"

I closed the door and followed Caldera upstairs. "Nice to see you too."

"One job. You had *one job*. All you had do was investigate."

"You were the one who sent me there. Shouldn't I be the one blaming you?"

"I should have known it was a bad idea to send you on your own. I could—"

Caldera walked into the living room and stopped. I followed her in to see that Caldera had come face to face with Anne. Anne was in the middle of packing up her bag with her medical gear. She looked up at Caldera. There was a pause.

"You could what?" I asked when Caldera didn't go on.

"In a sec," Caldera said. She didn't take her eyes off Anne.

"It's okay," Anne said. "I was just going." She did up the straps on her bag and slung it over her shoulder. "Give me a call if you need anything."

"You don't have to," I said with a frown.

"I should probably be getting back." Anne walked to the door. Caldera let her pass, moving noticeably farther out of Anne's way than she really needed to, and I saw her eyes track Anne as she went by. Anne disappeared down the stairs, and a moment later I heard the sound of the front door opening and closing.

I turned to Caldera. "Was that really necessary?"

"She's not a Keeper or an auxiliary," Caldera said. "She's not cleared for this information."

"She just patched a giant bloody hole in my side. You don't think that earns at least a thank-you?"

"A thank-you, yeah," Caldera said. "Just leave it at that next time. You know there are Keeper-sanctioned healers."

"Anne's saved my life at least twice."

"She's also—" Caldera checked what she'd been about to say, shook her head. "Never mind. All right, I want you to go through *exactly* what happened last night. Don't leave anything out."

I still felt annoyed, but suppressed it. I sat down at the table with Caldera and started the debriefing. It took the best part of an hour, and by the time we were done I felt strung out.

"You were lucky," Caldera said once I'd finished.

"*Lucky* would be not getting attacked by an assassin-mage in the first place," I said. "Seriously, can you stop acting like this was my fault?"

"You still shouldn't have gone back. If you suspected something—"

"Suspected *what*? There was no evidence that it was going to—"

"All right, all right," Caldera said with a wave of her hand. "I'll admit, you didn't totally screw up."

"Is that supposed to be a compliment?"

"Anyway, we're officially assigned to the case. So you can consider yourself on the clock as of yesterday."

"Do we get anyone else?"

"Rest of the Order are stretched thin right now," Caldera said. "The ones who aren't tied up with security ops are off looking for some missing Council guy. You get me."

"One case, one Keeper?"

"It's usually enough." Caldera closed her notepad. "Okay, here's how things stand. Liaisons are pulling the CCTV from Pudding Mill Lane and Stratford stations for the past seventy-two hours, so we should have that by the end of today. Next priority is this air mage. I've checked the watch list and there's no one recently active who meets your description."

"He was speaking in French," I said. "At least, before he was trying to kill me."

Caldera nodded. "We can try the French Council, but that'll take time. Anyway, we'll need a better description before we go to them. Once the CCTV footage gets in, we should have a photo."

"Timesight?"

"The waiting list for time mages is a mile long," Caldera said. "I've put in a request flagged as urgent, but don't hold your breath."

"Maybe we can get this air mage to try to kill you, too. That ought to bump it up the priority list."

"Next up, this focus. You got it here?"

"It's with Variam's master," I said. "Landis. You know the guy, right?"

"Yeah," Caldera said, and sighed. "Fine, let's see if he's got anything."

⁙⁙⁙⁙⁙

Gate magic makes travel so much easier. If I'd been on my own, getting up to Edinburgh would have meant either an overpriced rail ticket and hours on the train, or a path-finding exercise involving gate stones. With Caldera, we were there inside five minutes.

Edinburgh's a weird city; castles and ancient buildings and modern shops all piled together down the length of sloped streets, with that giant grass-and-stone hill looking down over the rooftops. In the summer it's crammed with tourists, but this was February, generally accepted to be the most miserable month in the British year, and not too many visitors were braving the cold winds and drizzle.

In magical society, Edinburgh's famous for a different reason: it's the location of the second and smaller of the Council's two apprentice programs. Sometime back in the sixteenth or seventeenth century, there was a treaty signed giving the Edinburgh mages the right to run their own teaching establishment separate from the ones in the south. Over the centuries most of the mage schools were assimilated into the association that would eventually become the London apprentice program, but the Edinburgh faction resisted it for long enough that having a second apprentice program became a tradition. There's still the odd attempt to merge the two, but the proposals have always fallen through, partly due to Scottish nationalism but mostly because a number of British mages find it useful to have a secondary power centre in the British Isles that's not quite so closely connected to the Council.

We wound our way through the streets, away from the tourist centres and to a stone house down a side alley. We rang the bell and the door opened to reveal Variam. "Hey, Vari," I said.

"Hey," Variam said. He looked more subdued than usual.

"Landis in?" Caldera asked.

"He's up there," Variam said, pointing his thumb at the rickety staircase behind him. "Good luck, you'll need it."

Up until a year and a half ago, Anne and Variam were living with me. Anne moved out in the summer to a flat in Honor Oak, but Variam came here to Edinburgh, taking up the role of apprentice to a mage named Landis, a Council Keeper from the Order of the Shield.

The Keepers of the Flame have three orders. The largest and most well known is Caldera's order, the Order of the Star. The Order of the Star police magical society; if a crime is committed that breaks the peace of the Concord or the national laws of the Council, they're the ones who are supposed to deal with it. Next is the Order of the Cloak, the ones responsible for preserving the secrecy of the magical world. They work with (and on) the mundane authorities, dealing with normals and sensitives, and they're much less high-profile. They rarely deal with other mages, to the point that a lot of mages forget that the Order of the Cloak even exists.

And then there's the Order of the Shield. Once the biggest of the orders, their name's a hint at their original function: they were battle-mages, meant to protect the population from magical predators. But as magical creatures declined, so did they, and nowadays they're the Council's military reserve, called in when a situation is violent or expected to get that way. Ninety-nine percent of their time is spent sitting around doing nothing or guarding against threats that never show up. The last one percent involves getting sent into the most horrendously dangerous situations imaginable. Let's put it this way—the Order of the Shield are the ones who get sent in when the Council thinks that mages like *Caldera* aren't enough.

It shouldn't be a surprise that Keepers of the Order of the Shield have a reputation for being weird. The Council gives them more leeway than the other orders, probably because people who were entirely sane wouldn't be volunteering for the job in the first place. Mostly, they just point them at a problem, then get out of the way. I'd met Landis two or three times, but this was the first time I'd visited his house.

The top floor of the building was a wide room with a beautiful view out over the Edinburgh skyline. The room was a workshop, with desks and benches covered in half-built or disassembled clutter, and papers and books were stacked in piles or scattered in the corners, and bent over the desk at the centre was Landis. He's tall and rangy, with sandy-brown hair and an angular face, and he always seems to be moving. As we walked in he thrust a finger towards us without looking. "Caldera! Lady of the hour! Excellent timing, I'm quite sure you did it on purpose, and don't think it's not appreciated. Or was it you, Vari?"

"It's not that." Variam had followed us into the room and was looking at Landis in a long-suffering sort of way. "They just wanted to know—"

"Wanting to know, the source and saviour of our problems, but there's no escaping it, is there? Oh, hello, Verus, of course I don't need to tell you that. Right then, let's be about it!" Landis bounded up and covered the distance to Caldera in three long strides, holding something out to her. "There! No goodly state in the realms of gold, but a thing of beauty in its way."

I peered at the thing warily. It looked like a wide-bodied dart, about the size of my hand, with a body of beaten copper that gleamed in the daylight through the window. I could also feel fire magic radiating from the thing, and a *lot* of it, which made me more than a little nervous. Fire magic's good at what it does, but "what it does" mostly involves burning things.

"It's very nice," Caldera said. "But what we came for—"

"But time and tide wait for no man, eh? Or woman, or child, or elemental spirit, so no sense admiring the weather." He tossed the dart to Caldera, who caught it; I felt Variam flinch. "Now just take a twiddle at the top and we'll be on our way."

Caldera sighed. "I have no idea what you're talking about."

"Disassembly, my dear girl—give that gadget you're

holding in your delightful hands a closer inspection by way of its inner parts, field-strip and cleaning, don't you know?"

"Oh, I give up," Caldera said. "Fine—like this?"

Caldera fiddled with the dart, trying to find a way to open it as Landis watched eagerly. After a moment, she found the right angle and unscrewed the top until it came off in her hand. Beneath was a complex arrangement of crystal rods, each glowing with a small but powerful orange light. Together they looked like a weird miniaturised furnace, and very dangerous. Out of reflex I started searching through possibilities, figuring out whether this thing was safe.

"Excellent!" Landis clapped his hands happily. "There you go, Variam! Doubting Johns, eh?"

"Are we done here?" Caldera said. "It's not as though—" She started to move her hand towards the glowing crystals.

A future suddenly jumped into my sight in horrible clarity. "Don't touch that!" My voice came out as a yelp.

Caldera paused. "Don't touch what?"

"That thing's a bomb!" I couldn't take my eyes away from Caldera's fingers, only a few inches away from the central rod. I'd just had a vivid image of what would happen if she touched it. "The crystal in the centre's a pressure sensor. You hit it and it's going to blow up the whole room!"

Caldera stayed still for a second, then, very carefully, moved her hand away from the trigger. "Landis?" There was a dangerous note to her voice. "Would you mind explaining?"

Landis had disappeared to a bench in the corner and was digging through spare parts. "Yes, yes, the tragedy of our violent natures, but what can one do, hmm? Certainly can't deny the artistry in the affair . . . Ah! There you are, you little rascal!" He strode back with a slim-handled tool in one hand.

"Mind telling me *why* you wanted me to open it?"

"Fluctuations, my dear girl! No use in setting the circuit if it'll lose containment as soon as it brushes up against some unfriendly spell, eh?" Landis paused, stroking his chin. "Though earth's not quite the *ideal* test, should really have brought a water mage—no chance you're planning to spontaneously change to that type, is there?"

"I don't know why I expected anything else," Caldera muttered. She thrust the bomb and its cap at Landis. "Take your little do-it-yourself suicide kit back, all right? I'm not your lab assistant."

Landis took the parts from Caldera and spent a moment juggling the things in a way that made me cringe. He ended up with the bomb in one hand, the tool (which I recognised as a conductor probe) in the other, and the cap in his mouth. "Look," Caldera said, following him back to the bench. "You said you knew what that focus was, right?"

"Mf crth uh dr," Landis said around the cap, his attention on the bomb as he fiddled at it with the probe. "Brth urf yrr crld yrf way uh mrmuh . . ."

"How often does he do this?" I said under my breath to Variam.

"All the bloody time," Variam said gloomily. He'd withdrawn to behind a bench, and I could sense he had a fire resistance spell up.

"Hah!" Landis dropped the tool on the bench, spat out the cap, and looked at the bomb in delight. "A thing of beauty is a joy for ever, eh? Well, until it goes off, but only in life's transience do we truly see, et cetera et cetera."

"Landis?" Caldera said.

"Hm?"

"The focus?" Caldera was obviously trying very hard to be patient.

"Secrets hidden in the craftsman's hands! Of course!" Landis flung himself into a chair and put his feet up on one of the desks, crossing his legs. "Variam, make us some tea, there's a good chap. They must be parched."

Variam disappeared quickly, probably glad to be out of the blast radius. "Right then!" Landis said. He was still holding the bomb in his left hand, and the safety cap was still off. The pressure sensor glowed menacingly; I knew it would only take a strong tap to detonate it, and I had to restrain myself from flinching as Landis waved it in my direction. "Good old Vari told me the story. Fascinating account, wish I'd seen the fellow who went after you, Verus, must have been quite the spot of exercise, hmm?"

"You could say that."

"Wish I'd been there, but we're still on standby. Tedious business, but ours not to reason why." He sighed for a moment, then visibly brightened, set the bomb down on one arm of the chair, and rooted around in his pocket to produce the same focus I'd given Variam last night. "Not much to look at, is it?" he said with interest, studying the green marble. "Hidden depths, though, the data array is mightier than the sword, hmm? At least when we're talking Council politics."

I kept a wary eye on the bomb. Landis had balanced it on end on its fins. It would only take one jerk of the chair to knock it to the floor, in which case it had roughly a fifty-fifty chance of landing on its tip and blowing apart the chair, the benches, the floor, and probably us. "Data array?" Caldera said.

"Indeed! Good old-fashioned storage device. Lovely craftsmanship, don't see many of them these days." Landis studied the focus admiringly, then glanced up as Variam came back. "Ah, man of the hour! Just in the nick of time."

Variam distributed teacups. Landis leant forward to take his, making the chair sway, and I winced. "Okay, so you're saying . . . um . . . is there any chance you could put the cap back on that bomb?"

"Eh? Goodness, you're right! Memory like a sieve." Landis caught up the bomb, twirled the cap back onto it, and then threw it without looking in the direction of the sofa. Even though I knew it wasn't going to blow up I couldn't help but close my eyes briefly. The bomb thumped into the cushions, bounced once, and lay still. I let out a sigh of relief and shared a glance with Caldera. She looked relieved too. Variam hadn't moved—maybe he was desensitised to it.

Landis, meanwhile, was in full cry. ". . . marvellous design! Completely stable once they've been set to the user, and no energy requirements at all. You see that distinctive little fractal pattern at the centre, little universal-tinged beggars? That's the Halicarnassus influence. Tricksy things, bugger to forge but worth the effort." He beamed at the two of us.

"So let me get this straight," Caldera said. "It's a data storage?"

"Right on the bull's-eye!"

"Can you read it?"

"My dear girl, weren't you listening? What'd be the point of a signature lock if any Tom, Dick, or Jehosaphat could come along and take a gander?"

That rang a bell. "Wait," I said. "It's a signature lock?"

"The very same!"

"Okay," Caldera said to me. "You know what he's talking about, right? Any chance you could say it in English?"

Landis watched with interest, steepling his fingers, and gave me an approving sort of nod. "It's a type of security system," I said. "I've read about them, but . . . oh." Suddenly it all made sense. "*That's* why the thing didn't respond. I mean, I was looking for a password, but if it's signature-based—"

"Then no more use than common pebbles!" Landis looked very happy. "So nice not to have to explain everything, you wouldn't believe how slow these young fellows can get."

"Yeah, well, I *don't* get it," Caldera said, "so if you don't mind slowing down for the benefit of those of us who *don't* spend their free time messing around with magic items, maybe you could spell it out?"

"It's a data focus," I said. Now I understood how the thing worked. "Mind magic core, you channel a bit of energy in and access the information telepathically—you guys use them, right?"

Caldera frowned. "*Those* things? We stopped using them years ago. Capacity's great but you can't transfer the data, and finding anything is a pain in the arse."

"But those were the regular kind, right?" I said. "Anyone could use them?"

"Yeah, why?"

"Because these are signature locked," I said. "That's their selling point. They're made in a morphic state, can't hold anything to begin with. Once a mage uses them, they shape to that specific magical signature and they won't react to anyone else. Kind of the magical equivalent of a DNA lock." I glanced at Landis. "Right?"

"Seven out of ten!" Landis said. "This particular design is set to two signatures, not one."

"Does that mean we can read it?" Caldera asked.

"'Fraid not, dear girl. Set, locked in, and unchanging for ever."

"Any way to break the encryption?"

"None whatsoever. Otherwise they'd hardly keep using the things, given that searching for any one particular piece of data inside them is, as you so succinctly observed, a pain in the arse."

"So it's useless," Caldera muttered, and rose to her feet. "Damn it."

"Just a second," I said. "What was that you said about Council politics?"

"Well, Council are the only ones that use 'em, aren't they? The old-fashioned isolationist types. Dull buggers, the lot of them, but if you're going fishing for the owner, that's where I'd try. Here you go!"

Landis tossed the focus to Caldera, who caught it and shook her head. "Yeah, that's not really an option. Thanks for the help."

Caldera and Landis said their good-byes, and Caldera disappeared downstairs with Variam following. I was about to go after them when I heard Landis say, "Oh, Verus?"

I stopped in the door and turned.

"You might be getting into deep waters." All of a sudden, Landis's voice was serious. "I'd be careful who you trust the next few days if I were you."

I frowned, but as I was about to say something Caldera called up from downstairs. "Hey, Verus! You coming or what?"

"Well, you'd best be off!" Landis said, and just that quickly his old manner was back again. "Tally ho and all that, eh? Good luck out there!"

chapter 5

I came downstairs to find Caldera and Variam talking on the ground floor. Neither seemed to have noticed my delay. "Wait," Variam was saying. "So you guys were apprentices together?"

"Trainees."

"Was he always . . . ?"

"Oh, yeah," Caldera said. "You're lucky you didn't know him back in his tech phase. There was this time in our second year when we were living in the same house. Kitchen table kept wobbling so Landis shoved this metal saucer under one of the legs. Wasn't until two weeks later we found out it was a land mine." Caldera shook her head. "Crazy bastard. Good guy to have at your back in a fight, but . . ."

"Caldera?" I said. "Does Landis know much about politics?"

"God no," Caldera said in surprise. "Knows his stuff when it comes to items, but don't take anything he says too seriously."

I frowned. "Hey, listen," Variam said. "Can I help you guys out?"

"Haven't you got work to do?" Caldera said.

"He's on standby for that missing apprentice case," Variam said, pointing up. "So all he does is mess around with his projects. He doesn't need me here, I can gate back if anything comes up."

"Sorry, Vari," Caldera said. "If he's on standby, you're supposed to be with him."

"Oh, come on . . ."

"Don't give me that. You know the rules. We're not running a daycare."

Variam made a face and disappeared upstairs. "Well, that was a bust," Caldera said. "Let's head back to the station."

"What do you mean?" I said. "We know a lot more."

"Yeah, except none of it's useful."

"Yes, it is," I said with a frown. "We know the focus has some kind of information on it, and it's keyed to two different magic-users, probably mages. If we can find out who they are—"

"How? Get every mage in the country to try the thing and see if it works? This isn't bloody Cinderella."

"So what's your take?"

"Your air assassin tried to commit a murder and broke the Concord in the process. *That's* why we're here. The focus only matters if it can lead us to him."

"The focus is the *reason* that guy was after me," I pointed out. "Otherwise he wouldn't have broken off to chase a decoy. Whatever's on there, it's important."

"Important to him doesn't mean important to us. And yes, I know you've got that famous diviner curiosity, but given that the crime was *your attempted murder*, I would have thought you'd be a bit more focused. He might be getting ready to try to kill you again right now."

"I thought about that," I said. "I don't think it's likely. He only went after me to get to the focus, and he'd know that I'd have figured that out afterwards, which means *he'd* know the first thing I'd do once I got back would have been to take the focus to someone else or put it in a safe place. There's no reason for me to be carrying the focus around on my person, so there's no reason for him to take the risk of coming after me again."

Caldera sighed. "You know, normal people, when someone tries to assassinate them? They care a little less about finding out what happened and a little more about staying alive."

"I've got you around to protect me, haven't I? Come on, let's get back to London. I think I know someone who can tell us a bit more about this thing."

॥ ॥ ॥ ॥ ॥

We gated back to London and started working our way through the streets around Brick Lane. "Her name's Xiaofan," I said. "I met her last year."

"Mage?"

"Time adept."

Caldera looked interested. "Timesight? We always need more of those . . ."

"Not exactly. She does objects."

We'd reached the place: a dimly lit shop with a faded red sign above the top saying *Libra Antiquities*. Clothing stores were on either side of it, carrying the smell of leather. "Before we go in," I said. "Xiaofan . . . hasn't had the best experiences with mages. Try to be nice, okay?"

Caldera shrugged. "Sure."

The inside of the shop was gloomy, weak yellow lights doing their best to push back the darkness. Furniture and household ornaments were piled all around: chairs, coffee tables, mirrors, vases, figurines, silverware, plates, lamps, and everything else, taking up so much of the space that it was hard to move. They created a muffling effect, and when the door swung behind us, shutting out the noise of the street, the shop was suddenly very quiet. "Hello?" I called. "Anyone there?"

There was the sound of movement, and a young woman appeared from behind a carved wardrobe. I'd known she was there, but I've learnt over the years that sometimes it's better not to advertise. Xiaofan was Chinese, conservatively dressed and pretty, with glasses and long dark hair. Her manner was cautious, but as she saw me she relaxed a little. "Alex. I didn't know you were coming."

"Yeah, sorry. I tried to text but it didn't go through."

"I changed my number," Xiaofan said. Her English was good, though not perfect; understandable but slightly stilted. She glanced at Caldera. "Hello . . . ?"

"This is Caldera," I said. "A friend of mine. We were hoping you could help us finding out about an item."

Caldera nodded. "Hey."

"Pleased to meet you," Xiaofan said. "Just let me change the sign."

Xiaofan locked the door and flipped the sign on it to *CLOSED*, then went back and cleared papers and bric-a-brac off a small cluttered desk while Caldera and I took a seat. I looked at Caldera. Caldera gave Xiaofan a dubious glance but took out the green marble and handed it to her. Xiaofan took it in her small hands, then closed her eyes.

A minute passed, two minutes, five. Caldera shifted and opened her mouth to speak, but I put up a hand. She raised her eyebrows but stayed quiet. Divination magic and time magic are different in many ways, but they have a few things in common, and the informational uses of time magic work a lot like my path-walking. It doesn't look like the spellcaster is doing anything, but they are.

When Xiaofan opened her eyes, she looked troubled. "This is dangerous." She put the marble down on the table and pulled her hands away.

The marble rolled across the desk, and I caught it as it dropped off the edge. "And you know this how?" Caldera said.

"It is for secrets," Xiaofan said. "To hold power over others, as a threat."

"How many owners did it have?" I said.

"Many. One of them was you. You want the ones before?"

"Please."

"Then, three." Xiaofan tapped three places on the desk. "Maybe others, but those are too long ago." Xiaofan moved her hand up, tapped the first place. "The first owner was a woman. Not young. She was . . . I don't know the word. She held power over others, and others held power over her."

"Politician?" I said.

"That too." Xiaofan looked worried. "She was . . . cruel. Very cruel. She worked in secrets, and used this for secrets, too. You should fear her, I think."

That didn't sound good. "The second is a boy," Xiaofan said. "Young, afraid. He held it, but only for a little while. A few hours, maybe. He gave it up quickly, to the third." Xiaofan tapped the last spot on the desk. "A man. Young, but proud. He only held it a few minutes, and he lost it in violence." Xiaofan looked at me, and her eyes were troubled. "I think he died. I saw it falling from his hand, then nothing. What is this thing?"

"You already figured that out," I said. "It holds information. Secrets."

Xiaofan shook her head. "I don't want them."

"Can you identify any of the previous owners?" Caldera said.

"I'm sorry?"

"The people who held this thing," Caldera said. "We need to know their names."

"No names."

"Faces, then? If you saw them, would you recognise them?"

"I . . . don't know."

"All right, how about if you come down to the station and we show you some pictures? You think you could identify the person?"

"Wait," Xiaofan said. "You're with the Council?"

"Yes, I'm with the Council."

Xiaofan shook her head quickly. "No. I'm sorry."

"It won't take long," Caldera said. "Just an hour or two."

"I'm sorry. No."

"This is an important investigation. You just told us there was some sort of violence with this thing, and we need to find out what it was. You don't need to worry, we'll keep you safe."

"I don't want to go with the Council."

"You might not have a choice if you keep refusing to help."

Xiaofan looked alarmed. She looked at me, appealing.

"Okay," I said, and got up. "I think we've got all we need. Thanks for the help, we really appreciate it."

Caldera looked up at me in annoyance. "We're not done."

"Yes, we are." I met her gaze and held it. "I think we should go."

Anger flashed up in Caldera's eyes, but I didn't look away. We stared at each other for a second, tense, then Caldera rose with an abrupt motion and walked out. I shot Xiaofan an apologetic glance. "Sorry."

Xiaofan nodded but didn't speak. She was still looking warily after Caldera.

I followed Caldera out. Xiaofan shut the door behind me, and I heard the sound of the lock.

। । । । । । । ।

"Okay, what the hell was that?" Caldera said as soon as we were together out on the street.

"You were pushing her too hard."

"That's not your call to make." We were a few shops down, out in the bustle of the street; Caldera stopped by a postbox and pointed a finger at me. "You are not in charge. You do not get to cut me off like that."

"She's *my* friend, not yours. The only reason we were there was because I know her."

"I don't care! You don't act like that, ever. Clear?"

"Okay," I said. "You remember when I said that you should be nice to her because she's had issues with mages? Do you want me to explain *why* I told you to stop and *why* the way you were acting was a bad idea, or do you want me to stand here while you shout at me?"

Caldera glared at me for a few seconds longer, then turned and started walking down the street. "This better be good."

I caught Caldera up and matched her pace. "I met

Xiaofan last February," I said. "She'd come over from China only a little while before. Her English was bad and the most marketable skill she had was her object reading, so she tried to make a living with that. That brought her into contact with mages, and somewhere along the line she met a Dark mage called Pyre. Know the guy?"

"Vaguely. Dark mage based in London."

"Yeah, well, in Dark society he's got a reputation for other things. Remember Torvald, Mr. I-Don't-Take-Rejection-Well? Pyre's kind of the less-nice version of Torvald. I did some investigating and it turns out he's had quite a few girlfriends who were adepts and sensitives. A handful of them seem to have disappeared. Funny coincidence—the disappearances always came right after they turned Pyre down or broke up with him."

Caldera was silent, and I knew she'd figured out where the conversation was going. "So Xiaofan tried to break things off with Pyre," I said. "He didn't like it. Xiaofan saw the way things were going and tried to get help. Went to a bunch of Keepers, they all turned her down. Pyre wasn't breaking the Concord, nothing they could do. You know the story."

"Yeah," Caldera said. Her anger had blown over. "I remember the guy now. He's had a bunch of warnings, but . . ."

"Yeah, well. Xiaofan's got a regular job nowadays, so she doesn't have to work with mages anymore. And given what happened last time she got too close to them, I don't think it's that surprising that she wants to keep her distance."

We walked a little way in silence. "And?" Caldera said.

"And what?"

"You just said she doesn't like working with mages," Caldera said. "Looked like she got on fine with you."

"Not really."

"So what did you do?"

"I just gave her some advice."

"Advice?"

"Back when she was having that trouble with Pyre."

"And Pyre just suddenly decided to leave her alone?"

"More or less."

"Was there a reason for that?"

"Pyre might have picked up the impression that Xiaofan had a curse on her causing anyone who got too close to her to suffer horrible accidents."

Caldera eyed me. "How exactly did he get that impression?"

"It's hard to tell how these things get started."

Caldera gave me a look. "Anyway," I said. "Xiaofan's object reading is metaphorical, not precise. You heard what she told us. She can get a sense of the personality of an object's owner, what they used it for, how it got passed on, that sort of thing, but she can't give you the kind of stuff you'd search a database for. She's not going to read off height, weight, and eye colour."

"But she might be able to recognise them if she saw them in a picture."

"It's not really the way she works."

"But it's *possible*."

"Maybe," I said reluctantly.

"Then why didn't you get her to come in?" Caldera asked. "You just said she trusts you."

"Because she *does* trust me, and I don't want to take advantage of that. If everything hinged on what she could tell us, then maybe, but I'm not going to force her to do it on a tiny off chance of getting something that might help."

"Verus, if you never want to make people upset with you, you're in the wrong job. We're the *police*. We're not here to be nice."

It was still a line I wasn't comfortable with crossing, but I knew I'd taken the argument as far as I could. "Have you checked your phone?"

Caldera gave me a suspicious look but pulled the phone from her pocket. As soon as she read what was on the screen, her brow cleared and the futures in which she kept asking me about Xiaofan vanished. "They've got the CCTV. Come on, we're going back to the station."

"After you."

I couldn't help but relax slightly as I stepped through the gate back into Keeper headquarters. I still didn't feel one hundred percent comfortable in the place, but you can get used to anything, and the sound of Keepers, auxiliaries, and admin staff talking and typing and walking through the narrow halls was familiar now. Besides, when you've got an assassin to worry about, hanging out with a bunch of cops suddenly doesn't seem like such a bad deal.

Once we were back in her office, Caldera tapped at her keyboard for a second, then beckoned to me. "Take a look."

I walked around the desk. Filling most of the computer screen was a headshot of a man in his thirties. The face was long and angled, eyes expressionless and grey. The beard was thinner, and there were no sunglasses this time, but I recognised him all the same. "Look familiar?" Caldera asked.

I reached to the keyboard, scrolled right. A series of photos went past, different angles, different places. Alone, none of them was a perfect match, but putting them together . . . "It's him."

"You sure?"

"Ninety percent."

Caldera nodded. "Jean-Jacques Duval, thirty-four years old, mage name Chamois. Born in Lyons, travels all around Europe as a freelance battle-mage—he works for Dark or Light, anyone who'll pay the bills. Suspected assassin but he's never quite made it onto the wanted list. He uses France as a base and does all his dirty work out of the country, then stays on just good enough terms with the French Council to get away with it. Pretty tough reputation. The people who want to talk him up call him Silence, or The Silent."

"Yeah," I said. I'd found the video of the battle in Stratford station. It was grainy and low quality, but it wasn't hard for me to recognise myself. "I think I know where that came from."

We watched the fight play out. I saw myself jump away

from Chamois's implosion spell. "You run fast when you want to, don't you?" Caldera said.

"Practice." On the video, Chamois leapt onto the train and disappeared from view. "How long's he been in the country?"

"His passport's not registered as having entered," Caldera said. "Not that that means anything."

"Any other sightings?"

Caldera shook her head. "He probably gated out as soon as that attack failed."

"Huh." The video ended and I searched quickly through the folders. "Where's the video from Pudding Mill Lane?"

"Yeah, well, that's the bad news," Caldera said. "You know those cameras you saw at Pudding Mill Lane, the ones you went back to take a closer look at? All dead. Early Thursday evening, they lost the feeds from platform and approach CCTV."

I looked up at her sharply. "That's the same time that report was called in."

"Mm-hm."

"What killed the cameras?"

"'Electrical failure,' whatever that means. Not like a bunch of TFL engineers are going to know what to look for in a magic attack."

"Yeah, I'm guessing we can rule out coincidence." I thought for a second. "When did the feeds go?"

"Between six twenty-three and six twenty-six. The call-in was seven-oh-four."

"Not collateral damage, then."

"Safe bet," Caldera said. "So someone decides to do some business around the station, and they don't want anyone watching."

"Why would they pick a station?" I said. "Why not some-where private?"

"Maybe they didn't *want* somewhere completely private. Picked a place that was away from the public eye, but public enough that it'd discourage a fight."

I tried to picture it in my head. Two people, maybe more,

coming to that station to do . . . what? A meeting, an exchange? I remembered what Xiaofan had told us. A younger boy and a man, and the man had held the focus only a little while. Maybe the data focus had passed between the two of them, given or taken. Then the man had lost it, for it to fall into the gravel beyond the platform . . . but how?

"So something goes wrong," Caldera continued when I stayed quiet. "There's a fight, we get the call. Somewhere along the way, that focus gets lost. You pick it up, and sometime after that our Mr. Chamois figures out the thing's missing. He gets the idea that if he hangs around, he might find out who took it. You show up, he spots you, and everything plays out from there."

"Why was he trying to kill me then?"

"Probably wasn't. Just wanted to cripple you badly enough that he could take you somewhere for a proper interrogation before he finished you off."

"You're a real ray of sunshine about this stuff, aren't you?"

"Well, that's enough guesswork for now," Caldera said. "Check the folder. I've got every CCTV recording I can find from the Stratford area over that time period, plus all the recordings from Pudding Mill Lane from earlier. I've shared access with your computer, so go through them and see what you can turn up."

I clicked on the folder and started scrolling down. When I saw just how much footage there was, my eyebrows went up.

⸱ ⸱ ⸱ ⸱ ⸱ ⸱ ⸱ ⸱ ⸱

I t was a few hours later.

The sun had set, and the sky through the small office window was dark. Around us, Keeper headquarters was quieter, though still nowhere near empty. Every now and then footsteps would go past in the corridor outside, but Caldera and I were alone in the office.

I leant back from the computer with a groan. My eyes were aching and it was getting hard to focus on the screen. "I'm not getting anything."

"Nothing from the stations?" Caldera said.

"He jumped on that train at Stratford, but he didn't get off at Bow Church or any of the stations after that. No sign of him on the station cameras before or after. I don't think he was even there." I shook my head. "And once he stops casting spells and walks into the crowd, he looks just like all the other five thousand people on these tapes. This is like looking for a needle in a haystack, except you don't know if the needle's *in* the haystack. I don't think he's on any of these tapes at all."

"Probably."

I stared gloomily at the computer screen. "I wish we had Sonder for this."

"Yeah, well, you're not the only one who's figured out that timesight's useful," Caldera said. "Sonder's on the upward track now. He's on the exchange program in Washington."

"What are we doing here?" I asked Caldera. "I mean, we're looking at footage from one to two days ago. Even if we see anything, is it going to help us catch this guy?"

"If he's smart, he's out of the country by now."

"So . . . ?"

Caldera shook her head. "You're like all the other mages. You think Keeper work's all about mage duels and chasing people down. We only have those kinds of fights when stuff goes *wrong*."

"So what's the plan?"

Caldera laughed. "We know what happened, we know what crime was committed, and we've got a positive ID on the suspect. We basically solved the case already. This is just the wrap-up."

"But we have no idea how to find the guy."

"Don't need to," Caldera said. "IDing the suspect and proving what they did is the hard part. Once we're done with this, you can write up a report and we'll get a warrant issued for Chamois's arrest. He attacked you and a civilian on camera: it's pretty open-shut. Then we pass it on and wait for the next case."

"And wait for some other Keeper to pick him up?"

"What, you wanted to take the guy down yourself? We're an organisation. Quit with the lone-wolf stuff."

I shrugged. "Seriously, though," Caldera said, "you did a good job on this one. As soon as you managed to get away from the guy at Stratford, you won. The rest is just cleanup."

"Doesn't feel like we've won."

"You get used to it. Come take a look at this."

I got up and crossed the room to look over Caldera's shoulder. On the screen was a nighttime video of a London A-road, two lanes each way. The time stamp read 7:03, two days ago. "What am I looking at?" I said.

"CCTV from Stratford High Street," Caldera said. "Same time that the 999 call was made." She pointed at the bottom-right of the picture. "See the corner there? That's the side street that leads over the canal to the Pudding Mill Lane construction site. Watch."

Caldera hit the Play button. Vehicles began to travel back and forth on the main road, cars mixed with the occasional lorry or bus. A few pedestrians were scattered along the pavement. As we watched, a figure appeared at the bottom right corner, running from the direction Caldera had pointed out. He darted out across the road, forcing cars to brake to avoid hitting him. The figure didn't stop but kept going to the far pavement, then headed southwest towards the big overpass. A few pedestrians had turned their heads to watch.

"In a hurry, isn't he?" I said.

"Yep," Caldera said. "999 call was at seven-oh-four, and that spot's about two minutes' run from the station. Could have come from somewhere else, but that street's mostly a dead end."

"You think he was the one who made the call?"

"Nah." Caldera pointed to the screen; the figure was disappearing down the road, and the time stamp had clicked over to 7:04. "Call would have been made by now. Besides, the one who called in was a woman. That's a boy."

"It is?"

"Early teens, maybe younger."

The figure just looked like a grey outline to me, but then I don't spend long periods of time studying CCTV footage.

Caldera rewound the video and again we watched the figure dash across the road. "He's running pretty blind," I said.

"He's running from something," Caldera said. "Look. After the car brakes, see how he turns his head and looks back? He's more worried about what's behind him." Caldera looked thoughtful. "Wonder what got him so scared?"

"He could have been a bystander?"

"Timing's a little off for that. Besides, remember what your friend Xiaofan said? Second-to-last owner was a boy."

I raised an eyebrow. "Thought you didn't believe her?"

"Didn't say that, did I?" Caldera said. "Have another look at the Thursday footage and see if you can find any trace of this kid. Oh, and while you're up, get us a coffee."

"I'm not your secretary, you know."

"Uh-huh."

I rolled my eyes and went out into the corridor. Even though it was a Saturday night, I could hear movement from elsewhere in the building. An office after working hours has a different feel from one during the daytime: there's a kind of energy you don't get when everyone is just doing their nine-to-five. It's not the sort of environment where you can really relax, but there's a weird sense of camaraderie.

Haken was at the coffee machine. The last time I'd seen him had been at Red's, on Thursday night: he hadn't looked so tired back then. "You're working late," I said.

"Oh, hey, Verus," Haken said. "Yeah. This bloody missing-persons case."

"I keep hearing about that." I opened the fridge and glanced through for milk. "Who are you guys looking for?"

"You know that Council mage, Nirvathis?"

"Vaguely. Is he one who's got his eyes on that Junior Council seat that'll go to the Dark mages if . . . ?"

"Yeah, him. Well, his ex-apprentice did a vanishing act. So now he's accusing the Dark mages, and the Crusaders have jumped on it from one side and the Unitarians from the other and it's a giant bloody mess." Haken sighed and pinched the bridge of his nose. "We've got four different factions riding us and they all want us to solve the case, except they all want us to solve it different ways, so they're calling for reports every hour. Everyone's had their leave cancelled and we're spending more time answering calls than we are actually working. Total balls-up."

"Guess that explains why we're not getting any help."

"Yeah, sorry about that. You two are going to be on your own for a few days." Haken yawned. "How's it going anyway?"

I shrugged. "We IDed the guy. No idea if we'll catch him."

"You figured out why he was after you?"

We know that already. I opened my mouth to say that the assassin had been after the focus I'd picked up, then something made me change my mind. That last thing Landis had said to me . . . "Not really."

"Well, keep at it." Haken walked out.

The coffeepot was empty, so I had to make a fresh batch. When I was done I took the mug and headed back to Caldera's office. The corridor was deserted but I could hear the sound of voices coming from the open door: Caldera and Haken. As I approached the doorway I saw Haken walk out.

I went back into the office. Caldera was still in her chair, and I set the mug down on her desk. "Nice one," she said without looking up.

"What did Haken want?"

"Oh, just being nosy," Caldera said. "His guy went missing around the time we got that call-in, so he was checking to see if the cases might be connected."

"You think they are?"

Caldera shrugged. "Suppose they could be."

"You told him about the focus?"

"Uh-huh."

Something was nagging at the back of my mind: a little seed of unease. It might be nothing, but . . . "Do you mind if I knock off? I'm still not a hundred percent."

"Sure. Go get some rest."

I headed for the door. "Oh," Caldera said after me, "put that focus in storage before you go home, okay?"

"Okay."

।।।।।।।।।

I took a train to Hampstead Heath and met up with an old friend. We talked a while, and I left the focus there before gating back to my shop. The focus was being stored somewhere safe, and I'd put it there before going home, so I'd done what Caldera had told me to do . . . technically.

I knew that I was playing with fire, doing this. Obeying the letter of Caldera's orders but not the spirit was something I'd done a few too many times already, and I'd discovered from experience that it really pissed her off. But I had the feeling that it might be a good idea to be prepared. If things went well, what I'd just done would be irrelevant and no one would really care. But if things went *badly* . . . then I'd be glad I'd taken the precaution.

The gate closed behind me, leaving me in the darkness of my shop storeroom, and I sagged in sudden exhaustion, catching myself on a set of shelves. Operating a gate stone is difficult for me—my magic is very bad at affecting the physical world—and it had been a long day.

The doorbell rang.

I held still. The echoes died away, fading into silence, and the shop was dark and quiet again. It was nine o'clock on a Saturday night. Who was calling at this hour?

I looked ahead. The caller was a woman, and she was outside the door, waiting. I filtered the futures, searching for danger. Nothing that I could see. I changed my focus, looking to see how she would introduce herself . . .

. . . oh.

I forgot all about her, didn't I?

I checked my one-shots, touched the hilt of the knife under my coat. I didn't really want to answer the door. But I'd invited her—had it only been last night?—and it was too late for second thoughts. I walked out into my shop. Neon light glowed from the street outside, slits of it passing through the security shutters to cast strips of orange across the counters and shelves. Out in the road, a car rumbled by, making the shadows flicker. I opened the front door.

The woman outside was a little below average height, with light brown skin and dark eyes. Her hair was black and shoulder length, blending into her black coat so that only her face stood out in the darkness. "Mage Verus?"

"And you would be . . . ?"

"Chalice." She held out a hand. "Pleased to meet you."

I checked with my magesight: no active spells that I could see. I shook her hand. "That's right. Good to meet you."

"You aren't too busy? I know it's late."

I looked back at Chalice. A Dark mage . . . and Luna's prospective teacher. "No, it's fine." I smiled. "Why don't you come in?"

chapter 6

I handed Chalice a cup of tea. "Here."

"Thanks."

We were up in my living room. Chalice was sitting on the sofa, knees together. I sat in the chair opposite her and put my own cup of tea on the table with a click. The sounds of the Camden night came filtering faintly through the window—shouts and laughter, running footsteps, the thumping of music from over the rooftops—but inside, the room was quiet.

I studied Chalice. Her coat was slung over the sofa along with her scarf, and she was leaning back, apparently relaxed. She wasn't obviously pretty but she dressed well and held herself with a sort of pleasant confidence. She didn't look like a Dark mage, or any sort of mage for that matter. She looked like a professional London woman in her late twenties or early thirties.

But she *was* a Dark mage, and the fact that she didn't look dangerous just meant that I hadn't yet figured out *how* she was dangerous. Being Luna's master has given me a good basic understanding of chance magic. Chalice would be able to lay curses, protect herself with good luck, arrange for coincidences to happen when they most benefited her . . . and unlike Luna, she'd be in full control of it. "Thanks for coming on such short notice."

"Oh, don't worry." Chalice spoke with a faint Indian accent, but her English was perfect. According to what I'd been able to learn, she'd grown up and trained in India before coming here in her midtwenties. "I had a free weekend, so I thought I'd drop by."

"Hope you didn't have to wait long."

"I didn't wait at all."

"Actually, I was out of the shop all day. You rang just as I was getting home."

Chalice smiled at me. "Just good luck, then."

"Very."

Silence fell. From outside, men's voices echoed down the street, laughing and drunken. Inside, Chalice and I watched each other across the coffee table. If we'd been cats, our tails would have been twitching.

"I like your house," Chalice said.

"It's pretty small by mage standards."

"I know, but the places most mages live are so cut off." Chalice glanced back at the window; the sound of the boys had faded away to be replaced by the rumbling of a car engine as someone tried to park. "This feels more like the middle of the city. More alive."

"That's why I do it. I grew up here in London; I don't like to be too apart from it."

Chalice nodded, and I felt the tone shift. Pleasantries were complete. "So I understand you're looking for a teacher."

"That's the idea." I leant forward, picking up the teacup. "Do you mind if I ask you something?"

"Of course."

"Usually, when a mage is thinking of taking on a new student, the first thing they want to do is talk to the student," I said. "You wanted to talk to me."

"Oh, I'd like to talk to your apprentice, too," Chalice said. "But I thought it would clear the air if I spoke to you first."

I raised my eyebrows.

"You're deciding whether you trust me enough to teach her. Yes?"

"That's pretty accurate," I said. "If you don't mind, I'm a little curious as to why you approached Luna in the first place."

"Actually, I've been aware of Luna for a while," Chalice said. "Word got around when you started looking for a teacher. She's an unusual girl."

"And how much *do* you know about her?"

"Her name's Luna Mancuso and she's twenty-four years old. She has an Italian father and an English mother, no brothers or sisters, and she was born and went to school in southwest London. She left school at age sixteen and started living away from home shortly afterwards. She became your apprentice at age twenty-two, two and a half years ago, and joined the apprentice program at the same time. She's at the bottom of her class in magical history and metaphysics, and at the top of her class in duelling. She won the Novice Open in early spring last year, placed third at Greengrove, practices at the Islington gym in her spare time, likes Japanese food, and she's a Leo."

I looked at Chalice. "Also," Chalice continued, "she's the carrier of a family curse that protects her and harms everyone else. Which makes her an adept, rather than a mage. Which technically means it's illegal for her to be in the apprentice program."

"*Technically*, adepts are defined by being only able to use one spell," I said. "You just said that her curse protects her and harms others. That's two effects, not one. Which makes her a mage."

Chalice smiled. "You sound like a lawyer."

"I've become very familiar with the adept laws in my spare time."

"Don't worry," Chalice said. "That wasn't a threat. I'm sure that if you had to, you could prove to the Council that Luna's a mage. Or at least muddle things enough." Chalice paused. "But you're still wrong. She isn't using different spells; she's using one spell. She's simply channelling it in different ways."

"Why are you interested in her, then? If you don't think she's a mage—"

"I didn't say that."

"So what do you think she is?"

"I think where you get your power from is less important than what you do with it. Have you tried teaching her any other spells? Luck control, blessings, slay machine . . . ?"

"We've done some practice."

"Did you get anywhere?"

I hesitated an instant, deciding how much to give away. "No. Directing the curse, focusing it, yes. But we haven't managed to change that into anything affecting probability more generally."

"That's because you're doing it the wrong way."

"How do you know?"

"Because of what you just said," Chalice said. "Probability. Diviners always see it like that."

"Isn't that's exactly what chance magic does?"

"Probability is mathematicians' language, something separate from you. For a chance mage, it's not separate. Chance is the air you breathe and the ground under your feet. You can't set yourself apart."

I thought about it for a second. I didn't really follow what she was saying . . . but then, I didn't need to. "Can you teach Luna?"

Chalice nodded. "I think so."

I looked at her. "So."

"So?"

"What's in it for you?"

"There are a few minor things. I'm curious to see how that apprentice of yours develops. Then there's the chance to study—"

"How about you just skip to the big one?"

"I want an alliance," Chalice said. She wasn't smiling anymore. "Which means your help. If I need information, or a favour of some kind, you give it."

I looked back at her for a second. "That sounds dangerous."

"Magic is dangerous. Your apprentice is dangerous. *You're* dangerous. From what I understand, you've dealt with much worse."

"That doesn't mean I do it by choice. Isn't there anything else you want? Money?"

"You couldn't offer me enough."

"Items?"

"More tempting, but I'm afraid I'm not bargaining. I told you my price and I meant it."

I checked to see what Chalice would do if I said no. Sure enough, every future in which I turned her down led to her walking out. She wasn't bluffing. "Your price isn't cheap."

"Don't act as though you were expecting to get this for free. Did you think the Light chance mages were going to give lessons away?"

"No, but I wouldn't jump on that kind of offer from a Light mage either." I thought for a second. "What kind of help?"

"Right now, there's nothing I need," Chalice said. "I expect that'll change, sooner or later. Most likely, I'll need your help against other Dark mages."

"Because *that* doesn't sound like a bad idea."

"You're qualified to deal with it, aren't you?"

I was silent. "Besides," Chalice said. "I did say an *alliance*. You can call on me for help too."

"Except that you'd expect that to happen less often, since you're also teaching Luna."

Chalice shrugged. "It's only fair."

"I'm not going to sign any blank cheques," I said. "There are things—a *lot* of things—that I won't do. If you're expecting me to . . ."

"No blank cheques," Chalice said. "No oaths of obedience. You can always turn me down. But I want good faith. If I ask you to do something, and it's something you would be willing to do for an ally, then you should be willing to do it for me. If you say no, and you don't have a *very* good reason, then no more lessons."

We sat in silence for a minute.

"What are you thinking?" Chalice asked.

"I'm thinking . . . it sounds like a fair offer." I met Chalice's eyes. "If I trust you."

"That's the question, isn't it?" Chalice tilted her head. "How about I give you a little good-faith gesture? I'll help you out with your current problem. Then if it checks out, maybe you'll be a little better disposed for the next time."

"How are you going to help me?"

Chalice smiled. "You've never worked with a real chance mage before, have you?"

"Why do you ask?"

"If you had, you wouldn't have that tone of voice." Chalice extended her hand. "For this trick, I'll need a pen and paper."

I looked back at her for a second, then walked over to the desk to get them. "Want a top hat too?" I said as I put them on the coffee table.

"Is this one of your British humour things?" Chalice pushed the pen and notepad over to me. "Now, are there any things you're looking for at the moment? People, places, items?"

"You could say that."

"Think about them and draw something."

I raised my eyebrows. "What kind of something?"

"Whatever you like."

I shrugged and decided to play along, taking the biro and beginning to draw. I've never been much of a sketch artist, but I'm good with patterns. I let the pen move across the paper as I thought about what I was looking for right now. Straightaway my mind went to the case with Caldera. Xiaofan's three owners, and where they were now. The boy Caldera had seen on the camera footage. The assassin who'd wounded me, and who was still out there . . .

"Done?" Chalice asked.

"More or less." I studied what I'd drawn for a moment—it looked like a sea, the shapes of creatures beneath the surface, with a sky above. Geometric shapes formed a border over the water.

"Now give it to me."

I handed Chalice the notepad. She glanced at the picture, took up the pen and scribbled something on it, then stood up and reached for her coat. "There you go."

"Wait, what?"

Chalice put her coat on, flipped her hair out, and began winding her scarf around her neck. "You were looking for something, weren't you? That's where you need to go."

I looked at the pad. A two-digit number was written on top of the picture, followed by what looked like a street name and postcode. "An address?"

"Looks that way."

"What's there?"

Chalice finished with her scarf, then gave me a smile. "How should I know? You're the one who picked it." She walked to the door. "Send me a message once you've made up your mind. I'll let myself out." She disappeared down the stairs.

I stared after Chalice, listening to her go. When her footsteps faded away, I switched to the future in which I followed her, tracking her movements. She crossed the shop floor and let herself out into the street, shutting the door behind her, before walking away down the street.

So that was Luna's potential teacher. I tried to figure out how I felt about her, and didn't come up with any definite answers. She wasn't telling me everything . . . on the other hand, I hadn't been telling *her* everything, and it's not like I'd expected more at a first meeting. I still didn't completely trust her, but I didn't know whether that was just natural suspicion.

I *did* know that I wasn't a hundred percent comfortable with leaving Luna in her hands.

But Luna wasn't a child anymore. I had a responsibility to protect her, but not to overprotect her. This was a decision I should be making with her.

I looked down at the pad Chalice had written on. She'd taken two of the lines I'd sketched, and turned them into the numbers of the street address, 34. If I squinted a bit and looked sideways, those lines I'd drawn *did* kind of look like a 3 and a 4.

That didn't make any sense. I'd just been sketching. How could she turn that into an address that I didn't even know?

But hadn't that been exactly what Chalice had been getting at? That chance magic didn't work by the same logic as divination? Maybe that was why I'd never managed to make any real breakthroughs with Luna . . .

I shook my head and stood up. No point thinking in circles. I walked to my computer, typed in the postcode, and hit Search.

A map result came up of a district in west London. The postcode was UB8, out in Uxbridge. I switched from map to satellite view and saw nothing but a street full of houses. I wanted to path-walk and see what I'd find, but I didn't have an unobstructed route. If I could gate to that location it would have been easy, but I didn't have a gate stone that went anywhere near. That just left car or train, and the cumulative uncertainty of that kind of transport would cut off any path-walking before I'd covered a fraction of the distance.

But I had time to spare, and my divination magic to warn me of danger, and Chalice's visit had left me wide awake. The sounds of the Camden night were all around me, life and noise and activity, and I felt full of energy. Nothing makes me more curious than a mystery. I wanted to go and see what was there.

I grabbed my coat off the hanger . . .

. . . and . . .

. . . wait a minute. This was *exactly* what I'd done last night. I'd gone rushing off on my own to investigate, without my armour and without backup. It hadn't turned out well.

Maybe I ought to do this the smart way. I laid my armour out on the bed, then started making phone calls.

⁚⁚⁚⁚⁚⁚⁚⁚⁚

I took the tube out west to Hillingdon, then caught a bus for the last leg. I think I'm possibly the only mage in London who uses public transport on a regular basis. Most use gate magic or get a bound creature to ferry them around, and the ones who don't either get chauffeured or drive a car. Part of it's paranoia—I've had a couple of bad experiences with taking cabs, and while the tube can be crowded and slow, being several hundred feet beneath the surface of the earth makes it much harder for someone to pull an assassination attempt in the middle of your commute. But if I'm being honest, the real reason's something else. When you're a mage, you live in a different world from normal people. Your lifestyle is different, your problems are different, you have a new set of hopes and fears and worries. And the longer you spend in magical society, the further away you get. If you put a sixty-year-old master mage in the same room as a twenty-year-old college student, they can't hold a conversation with each other. Their lives are so far removed that they don't have enough points of similarity to be able to meaningfully communicate.

Something about that bothers me. I'd have trouble putting my finger on exactly what it is, but I don't like the idea of ending up like that. So I take public transport and go shopping in Sainsbury's and skim the news on the internet. It's part of the reason I run my shop too. I don't know if it really accomplishes anything, but I do it all the same.

The address Chalice had given me was just off Uxbridge Road. I walked down the side streets, hearing the rush and noise of the main road fade away behind me. The sky had cleared a little, and a half moon shone down brightly through patches in the clouds. Stars twinkled above and to the east; we were far enough away from the centre of London that the constellations were a little easier to see. I came to a halt one street away and scanned ahead.

The address was a house, small and cheaply built, with a concrete drive for parking at the front. Red-brown peaked roof, two floors with no basement, square windows looking out onto a curving street. It was the kind of house you find all around the suburbs of London, duplicated a hundred times in this street and ten thousand times in this borough. More streets like this one wound away to the east and west, with a small park to the north. There were no real landmarks; a couple of small tower blocks rose up a mile away, but for the most part the area was flat and unremarkable.

In a way, places like this are the real London. When most people think of my city, they think of Big Ben and the Houses of Parliament, the London Eye, the skyscrapers of Canary Wharf and Liverpool Street, the parks around Buckingham Palace, and all the other tourist spots that show up on TV and in the movies. But if you marked all those places on a map, you'd find you'd dotted only a tiny little patch in the middle of a vast sprawl. London is *huge*, and most of it isn't tall historic buildings; it's streets like the one I was standing in now, row after row of suburban houses that all look pretty much the same. For most Londoners, these are the places that matter—the school around the corner where they spent their childhood, the council estate where their friends live, the high street where they go to work. The landmarks at the centre of London are where people go to visit, but streets like this are where they *live*.

I sensed Caldera coming a long time before I saw her; like me, she'd made the last part of the journey on foot, though she'd probably used a gate to shortcut the journey. I waited on the pavement for her to approach.

Caldera turned the corner onto my road, walked up, and looked at what I was wearing. "Expecting trouble?"

"Let's just say I wanted to be prepared this time." My armour is a full-body suit of coal-black mesh, moulded plates covering vital areas. It doesn't exactly look like most people's idea of what armour's supposed to look like, but it sure as hell doesn't look normal either.

"So," Caldera said. "If you're out in the open, I'm guessing we're not in danger."

"Not yet," I said, and pointed around the corner. "Though if we go in there that might change a bit."

"What's inside?"

"First off, the house is warded," I said. "Subtle, but it's there. No attack spells or barriers to entry, but scrying spells won't work and you can't gate in or out. Standard privacy wards. Also, there's someone inside." I'd had plenty of time to explore the futures in which I broke in, and while they'd been chaotic, it hadn't been hard to notice a pattern. "A kid, and he's aggressive. If we just smash the door down and go charging in, he's going to attack us."

"With what?"

"A knife."

Caldera shrugged.

"Yeah, I know, not exactly a threat to you. I think it's a panic attack, not something calculated. He's scared, and if he's cornered, he's going to fight."

"Can we talk him down?"

"Not sure. But I don't think he can hurt you, so it's not like we lose anything for trying."

Caldera nodded. "Okay, let's do it. Stay behind me."

We turned the corner and walked down the street, passing a scattering of parked cars. Out of habit, my eyes went left and right, checking the terrain. Electrical substation on the corner, leading to a small park and a council estate. Not much cover apart from that—nothing but rows of houses. Number 34 was a detached house with no car in the driveway and no lights in the windows. Streetlights cast it in a dim orange glow. Caldera walked up to the door and knocked.

Silence.

Caldera knocked again.

"He's not going to answer," I said.

Caldera looked at the route around to the back of the building. "He going to do a runner?"

I shook my head.

"All right." Caldera took out a focus and channelled her magic into it. I watched with interest. After a second, the door rattled open and I followed Caldera in.

The inside of the house was dark and silent. I tapped Caldera on the shoulder and pointed upstairs. She nodded and we climbed to the top floor. The stairwell was cramped, a little too low for me and a little too narrow for Caldera.

There were three rooms on the top floor, and the house's other occupant was hidden behind the middle one. I started to signal to Caldera but she was already moving in that direction; she'd probably sensed him through vibration. "Hello?" Caldera said, stopping in the doorway. "Anybody there?"

Silence.

"I'm Keeper Caldera of the Order of the Star. I'm with the Council. I'm not going to hurt you or arrest you. I just want to talk."

More silence.

"Look, I know you're in there. You don't have to come out if you don't want to. How about you tell me your name?"

The futures shifted, started building. "He's going to make a break," I murmured.

"Okay, how about you tell me what you'd like to do?" Caldera said. I saw her shift position slightly. Through the open doorway I could see a desk and the window. The boy was just on the other side of the door, only a few feet away. "We can just stay here if you want. You can—"

A shape bolted for the window, trying to pull it open. Caldera was on him in two strides. The shape turned on her, there was the flash of light off a blade, then they were struggling. I held back: if I went in, I'd only be in Caldera's way. I heard a thud, fast breathing, then a clank and a pause. More struggling. Silence.

Caldera spoke. "Get the light."

I flipped the switch. Yellow light flooded the room and I shielded my eyes.

As my eyes adjusted, I saw that Caldera was holding on to a boy dressed in ragged jeans and a sweater. He was young, no more than ten or eleven, and small and thin to the point of looking actively malnourished. His chest rose and fell with rapid breathing, and his eyes flicked back and forth, trapped. A knife lay on the carpet in front of him; I stepped forward and picked it up.

"Like I said, I'm not going to hurt you," Caldera said. She was holding the boy by his wrists, and compared to him she looked like a giant. Even without her magic, she could probably have picked him up one-handed. "If I let you go, you going to stop trying to stab me?"

A pause, then the boy nodded.

"I didn't hear you."

"Yeah," the boy said in a high voice.

"You going to tell me your name?"

". . . Leo."

Caldera let the boy go. He stepped back, watching us silently, rubbing his wrists. Futures in which he made another dash for it flickered and disappeared. Caldera pointed to the bed. "Sit down."

It was an order, not a request, and the boy sat instantly. "There anyone else around?" Caldera asked.

The boy shook his head.

"You hurt? Hungry?"

Another head shake. He was watching the two of us very closely.

"Go check out the house," Caldera told me.

I nodded and left the room. Behind me, I heard Caldera start questioning the kid.

The house was small: an open-plan living room and kitchen on the ground floor, a bedroom, spare room, and bathroom upstairs. There were basic furnishings, but no posters or paintings on the walls and no books or DVDs on the shelves. I hadn't seen any personal items in the bedroom either. It was the sort of look a house has if it's just been rented or sold.

I took a closer look at the knife I'd taken from the boy. Kitchen knife, black-handled. No blood on the blade. I opened one of the kitchen drawers and . . . yep, this was where it had come from. The kid had taken the knife upstairs. What had he been scared of?

Checking the cupboards, I found canned and long-life food. Judging by the date stamps, all had been here for some time. I used my magesight to study the wards and found a similar story. This place hadn't been used in a while.

I went back upstairs to find Caldera and the boy talking quietly. To my surprise, Caldera wasn't pressuring the kid— she was firm, but her voice was gentler than usual and she wasn't pushing him too hard. I guess after seeing how

Caldera had dealt with Anne and Xiaofan, I'd been expecting her to play the threatening cop, but she wasn't, and the kid seemed to be responding. "No," he said. "No one."

"No family you could go to?" Caldera asked.

Leo shook his head.

"You were at Pudding Mill Lane station two nights ago, weren't you?" Caldera asked.

Leo hesitated, then nodded.

"Did you go there alone?"

Another nod.

"What happened when you got there?"

Leo's eyes flickered from me to Caldera. He hunched his shoulders. *He's scared,* I thought. *Scared of what?*

"It's all right," Caldera said, and her voice was reassuring. "I'm not going to get angry."

Leo didn't answer. Caldera kept trying to talk to him, and I searched through the futures, trying different lines of questioning. Most petered out in silence, others led to nothing. One approach caught my attention. "Leo?" I said. "Where did you stay before?"

Caldera shot me a warning look. "At Phil's," Leo said.

"But that was connected to a group, wasn't it?" I said. "An organisation. What's their name?"

Leo was silent. "It's okay," Caldera said. "You can tell him."

Leo looked down at the floor. "White Rose."

I felt Caldera go still. Leo didn't meet our eyes. "You mean the ones here in London?" Caldera asked. "Around Leicester Square?"

Leo nodded.

Caldera got to her feet. "I'll be back in a second, okay?"

"How did—?" I started to ask Leo.

Caldera walked past me, grabbed my arm, and towed me out the door. "Come with me a sec."

Once we were out in the hall, Caldera let go. "You could have asked," I said. She hadn't been trying to crush me, but my arm still hurt. Earth and force mages tend to forget their own strength.

"We might be in over our head," Caldera said quietly.

I blinked at that. "Wait. Who are these White Rose people?"

"Independent group based out of London," Caldera said. "Did you check this place out?"

"I think it's a safe house. Supplies, gate wards, shroud wards. No one lives here."

Caldera frowned. "That woman, the one you said divined this address. She tell anyone else?"

"She didn't divine it—" I saw Caldera's expression and decided this wasn't the time to get into technicalities. "I don't know. Maybe."

Caldera shook her head. "I'm calling for backup."

"Wait." I caught Caldera's shoulder as she started to move past. "Why? Who *are* these guys?"

"They're a brothel."

"You're scared of a brothel?"

"I'm not scared of them, and if you knew more you wouldn't be arguing. These people are bad news."

I looked towards the room where we'd left Leo. He hadn't moved. "So he's . . ."

"The kid's a sex slave."

I stared at Caldera. "How did—?"

"If he's with White Rose, that's what they use him for," Caldera said. "Look at the way he sits and the way he answers. He's used to adults telling him to do a lot worse than that."

I looked towards the room again. Now that Caldera had said it, it fit in an unpleasant way. "I didn't spot that," I admitted.

"You run a shop," Caldera said. "If you were an expert on sexually abused ten-year-olds I'd be a bit worried." She shook her head. "But I'm not an expert either. I'll try and get someone from the psych unit."

"I don't like this."

"You're not supposed to."

"Not just that." I gestured around to the house. "This.

The kid's been here for two days. Okay, what you said, if he's a slave . . . why hasn't someone from White Rose come to get their property back?"

"It's warded. They can't find him."

I was silent. "What's getting to you?" Caldera said.

"Something about this feels wrong."

"Wrong how?"

"I don't know. Just . . . out of place. Do you ever get the feeling you're being set up?"

"You looked for danger?"

"As far as I could. Nothing I could see."

Caldera didn't answer. "You think I'm being paranoid?" I asked.

"No, I was getting the same feeling."

I looked at her in surprise. "If you got this address, other people might have got it, too," Caldera said. "Besides . . . it's White Rose. There is a *lot* of shit going on with that group. I'll feel a lot better when we have some support."

I nodded. "I'll watch him. You make the call."

Caldera disappeared downstairs and I heard her start talking into her communicator. I hesitated, glancing through the futures again, but with Caldera talking they were too unpredictable to search far ahead. That's the problem with divination—it doesn't handle free will well. If I'm on my own somewhere deserted, I can look ahead hours, maybe even a day or more. But when you have people talking to each other, making decisions, then the futures keep changing and fuzzing, like clouds in a strong wind. You can see the shape, but they change so quickly.

I went back into the bedroom. Leo was still sitting there, tense. He hadn't relaxed, and now that I knew what to look for, I could see the signs. His expression was blank, but his eyes didn't move away from me, always watching. He was looking for any signs of a change in my mood. I wanted him to trust me, but I knew that would be almost impossible. The best I could hope would be that he would answer my questions.

"You remember two nights ago?" I said, sitting down. "When you went to the station at Pudding Mill Lane?"

Nod.

"You had something with you, didn't you?" I said. I was careful to make my voice normal, unthreatening. "A little green marble."

Leo hesitated, but I already knew the answer was yes. It's one of the tricks of divination: by looking ahead to catch glimpses of replies, you can see all the possible answers that someone might give. Very revealing when someone's deciding whether to lie. More experienced mages know to guard their reactions, making it harder, but Leo was too young. "Yeah."

I looked to see what would be the best path to take. I wanted to find out who'd given him the focus, but that line of questioning would make him freeze up. I'd have to go the other way. "Were you supposed to take it to someone? Give it to someone?"

Another nod.

"Who were you supposed to give it to?"

"Dunno."

"But you know what he looks like," I said. I was trying to sound reassuring, though I wasn't sure how good a job I was doing at it. I wished Anne were here—she's good with kids. "Don't you?"

Another nod, this one reluctant.

"Could you describe him to me?"

"I dunno."

Footsteps sounded on the stairs and Caldera walked back in. "They're on their way," she said. "Should only be a few minutes."

I nodded and turned back to Leo. "But it was a man?"

Leo nodded.

"Tall? Short?"

I kept asking, drawing information out piece by piece. Leo answered reluctantly, but he still answered—he was probably afraid of what we'd do if he said no. I didn't much like that, but it didn't seem the time to push it. The person Leo had met at Pudding Mill Lane had been a mage. Male, brown hair, tallish but not too tall, suit, light skin . . . "How old was he?" I asked.

"Old."

"Forty? Fifty?"

"Twenty-five or something."

Caldera didn't smile. She pulled out her phone, tapped at the screen, then held it out to him. "Was this the guy?"

I looked at Caldera curiously. There was an edge to her voice that hadn't been there before, and Leo seemed to sense it. He shrank back. "I dunno."

"Leo," Caldera said. "I need you to look at this picture. Was this the man you saw on Thursday night?"

Unwillingly, Leo looked at the phone, stared at it for a few seconds, then nodded.

Caldera didn't take her eyes off Leo. "Are you sure?"

"I guess."

Caldera swore under her breath and got to her feet. "Find out what happened at the station. Fast. I need to call this in." She disappeared downstairs again.

I frowned after her. *What was that about?* "So you took the green marble to Pudding Mill Lane," I said to Leo. "And you met that man there."

Nod.

"Were you supposed to give it to him?"

"I guess."

"You were supposed to give it to him, if . . . ?"

"If he said the right thing."

Code phrase, I thought. Leo was getting uncomfortable again. The subject he didn't want to talk about seemed to be the person who'd sent him to the station. I was getting the strong feeling that was who he was scared of. "What happened at the station?"

"It wasn't my fault."

"We know it's not your fault."

"They'll say it was." I realised suddenly that Leo was trembling. He wasn't scared—he was *terrified.* "I was supposed to give it to the man in the suit."

I tried different lines of questioning. *Not that one, not that one . . . ah.* "But someone else came," I said. "A man with a beard, wearing sunglasses."

Leo nodded.

"And there was a fight, so you ran away."

"It wasn't my fault."

"I know." So Leo had been there to meet the mage at the station when Chamois had attacked. "Did you see anyone get hurt?"

Leo shook his head. *He's leaving something out . . .* "There was something you were supposed to do," I said. "Wasn't there?"

Leo nodded.

Say something? No. Take something? "Was the man in the suit supposed to give you something, too?"

"I was supposed to take it back," Leo said. He'd started trembling again.

"It's not your fault," I said again. "You did what you could."

"He was supposed to give me another one back," Leo said. He hunched up defensively. "She's going to be . . ."

"She's going to be what?" I kept my voice calm. I was right on the edge of getting him to talk. I tried out different routes through the futures, probing delicately. I just needed to find the right thing to say.

There was a clumping from the stairs and Caldera appeared again. "We might have to move him."

I didn't take my eyes off Leo. "Can this wait a sec?"

"Leo," Caldera said. "Who sent you to Pudding Mill Lane? Can you tell us?"

Leo looked back at Caldera with wide eyes and hunched over on the bed. All the futures in which he spoke to us vanished.

I sighed and got up. "Let's talk outside."

We went back into the hall. "Wrong question to ask," I said once we were out of earshot.

"Priorities just changed," Caldera said. "That guy in the picture? That was Rayfield."

"Who?"

"You remember the guy Haken and the others were looking for? Nirvathis's apprentice? That guy." Caldera shook her head. "This is getting too big too fast. I'm trying to get the station but I can't raise them. If the guys don't show up we might have to take him there ourselves."

"If they're coming here we— Wait. You can't raise them?"

"Com disc's dead."

I frowned. "Just now?"

"What did you manage to get out of him?"

"Leo? Uh . . . yeah, he saw Chamois. That was why he ran . . ." Something was bugging me. "Wait. Your communicator focus isn't working?"

"Yeah, let me try it again." Caldera pulled out a serrated blue-purple disc and focused on it. The design was similar to mine, though slightly more streamlined.

I waited. Thirty seconds went by, a minute. "Anything?"

"Worthless piece of crap," Caldera muttered. "'Work every time,' my arse. We could just use radios but no, they're not *secure* enough . . ."

Something was nagging at me. "Those things have a locator beacon, right?"

"Yeah."

"You activated it?"

"Yes," Caldera said shortly.

"Should they be here by now?"

"Yes." Caldera shot me an annoyed glance. "I'm going to try out back. Wards must be screwing with the signal." She started down the steps.

I frowned, watching her go down. I'm not an expert on defensive wards, but I'd had a close look at the ones on this house, and as far as I could tell they were low-power and basic. They shouldn't block communication—definitely not something as advanced as a synchronous focus. Anyway, hadn't Caldera used that same focus to call for backup just a little while ago? Why should the wards suddenly start blocking it *now*?

Something was wrong. Caldera was heading for the back door. I looked ahead, searching for danger.

And froze. Something was about to . . .

. . . *oh, shit.*

"Caldera!" I shouted down the stairs. "Get up here NOW!" Then I ran for the bedroom.

Leo looked up as I burst in, then as I reached for him he flinched and shielded his head. I grabbed his wrist and hauled him off the bed before pulling the wardrobe door open and shoving Leo inside. Coat hangers bounced off his forehead but he was small enough to duck under the clothes rail and I slammed the door, shutting him inside.

The window burst inward in a spray of glass and something sleek and deadly hit the bed right where Leo had been sitting. Its momentum sent it to the floor, and as it landed it turned its head towards me.

chapter 7

The thing in the room with me was dark grey, four-legged, and fast. I had a fleeting impression of a low-slung body and glowing blue eyes, then it lunged. I dodged, kicked; the thing lurched away but seemed to twist in midair and was on me again in a blink. For a few crazy moments everything was a blur of motion, claws and teeth and icy cold. A paw raked for my face, I blocked and hit the thing in the belly, then it was slamming into me, sending me staggering against the wall. It snapped at me, wispy blue light trailing from its fangs; I scrabbled for its neck, got a grip, tried to force it back. It strained against me, trying to reach my skin with its teeth, and it was hellishly strong. Empty glowing eyes stared into mine as it bit at me again and again. Cold was sinking down my fingers and into my joints, numbing my hands, and I tried frantically to push it away—

A big hand shot down across my field of vision and pulled the thing off me. I looked up to see Caldera holding the thing up one-handed. It struggled and Caldera smashed it into the door frame, once, twice, three times, the door frame splintering and breaking, then she slammed it to the floor, drew back her other hand, and hit it with a downward blow. There was a *crack* and the thing went still.

All of a sudden the house was silent again. The whole fight had been over in seconds. "You all right?" Caldera asked.

"I think I need new pants." I scrambled to my feet. "Thanks. What was it?"

"Icecat. There any more?"

I took a breath, heart pounding, and looked ahead. The creature was lying on the floor, still and dead. It was cat-shaped, the size of a leopard or jaguar, but now that I could see it more closely, I could tell it was a construct. The eyes were lifeless now, the spell that had powered it broken. "At least one out the back. Maybe more."

Caldera opened the wardrobe door to reveal Leo huddled in the corner. "We're leaving," she told him. "Stay close." She pulled him out.

Leo's eyes lit on the body of the icecat and his face went pale. "Oh God."

"Just stay with me." Caldera dragged Leo downstairs.

The fight with the icecat had been so fast that I hadn't had the chance to draw a weapon. I pulled out my phone and started typing, trying to search through the futures at the same time. Danger flickered through the possibilities, getting closer. I hit Send, shoved the phone back into my pocket, and followed Caldera.

Caldera was down in the living room behind the dividing wall, crouched low and holding on to Leo tightly. Leo was huddled into a ball, breathing fast. "Where are they?" Caldera said quietly.

"Don't go out the front," I said, keeping my voice down. From our position we could barely see the front door, and couldn't see the back at all, but I knew what would happen if we went there. "There's someone covering the front door. We step through it, we're going to eat a spell to the face. Something else too . . ."

"The back?"

"More icecats." I scanned future after future in which

we left the house. In most of them we got shot the instant we came into view. "A mage as well."

"So we're surrounded."

All around us, the house was dark and silent. After the brief flurry of the battle, there had been no sound from outside; only my divination let me know that anything was there. I could hear Leo's rapid breathing, and the whites of his eyes showed in the gloom. "Don't let her take me back," he said, his voice high and scared. "I'll do whatever you what. Just don't let her, please—"

"No one's taking you anywhere," Caldera said, then looked at me. "Can you tell when our backup's going to be here?"

I'd been scanning the futures for exactly that. "No."

"*Shit.* Where are they?"

"I don't know, but if you're expecting the cavalry to come riding to the rescue, you're going to have to wait."

"If we break out the back?"

"We'll go right into a fight," I said. "Two icecats, the guy controlling them—ice mage, I think—and something else. Something bigger."

Caldera was silent, and I knew what she was thinking. Caldera might be able to beat that many, but she couldn't protect Leo at the same time. "All right," she said at last. "We hold here and wait for backup. I'll try the com disc—"

"Forget that bloody focus. It's not helping."

"You have a better plan?"

"I called for backup too. We just need to hope these guys wait long enough—" The futures shifted and I trailed off. All of a sudden the ones with violence in them were much closer. "Shit."

"What?"

"We've got incoming." Movement from the back. Had they left the front exposed? No—if we made a break for it that way, we'd still run straight into fire and—

"*Verus.* Talk to me."

"Icecats." I kept my voice low. "They're going to force

an entry at the back. They'll come through the kitchen and the picture window, then sweep towards us."

"Can we get them as they come in?"

"No, it's a trap. They're going to pause at the entrances—get you to show yourself so they can get a clear line of sight. That ice mage is somewhere in the back garden—"

There was a scraping sound from the kitchen, very loud in the darkness. Leo whimpered and tried to huddle into the corner. Caldera glanced back at the front door. "They going to come from the front as well?"

"Don't think so."

Another scraping sound, and I heard the sound of splintering wood. "I'll take the cats," Caldera said, and I knew she'd made her decision. She came up to one knee, staring into the dividing wall as though she could see through it. "You stay with the kid."

"Wait. There's something else." I could see confused futures of another path through the combat, something hulking and big. "Another construct, I think . . . but it's not there yet . . ."

The door broke with a crunch and I fell silent. I could hear the distant sounds of the city drifting in through the now-open back door: traffic, an aircraft overhead, a TV from somewhere. No voices or shouts. There were people in the houses all around us, but no one had raised the alarm. It seemed crazy that we were fighting for our lives and the neighbours hadn't even noticed, but they couldn't see the futures that I could. All they'd have seen was the window breaking and the scuffle with the icecat, and that had been over in seconds. They probably hadn't even heard it over the TV, and by the time they'd gotten to the window to look, it would have been all over.

Footsteps padded through the kitchen on the other side of the divider. I could hear the icecat's movement, smooth and heavy. No breathing. To my sight the construct's futures were solid lines in the darkness, easy to predict. Another was about to break in, and I signalled for Caldera to stay where she was.

There was the crash of breaking glass, shockingly loud. Leo jumped, and I covered his mouth before he could yelp; his eyes were wide and I could feel his quick breath against my palm. The dividing wall blocked our view of the icecats, but I knew where they were—one was to the left in the kitchen, the other in the broken remnants of the picture window, a little more than five feet from where Caldera was crouching.

Silence. The icecats were waiting. There was no variation in the lines of their future; they were following a program, not under direct control. They would wait another ten seconds, then close in. I tapped Caldera, then took my hand away from Leo's mouth and held up ten fingers where Caldera could see. Then I held up nine fingers, then eight.

Caldera nodded, came quietly up to one knee. *Seven, six, five.* Broken glass crunched from the other side of the dividing wall as the icecats moved. *Four, three.* Caldera braced herself, ready to lunge. *Two.* A shadow appeared on the wall, the long shape of the icecat outlined by the ambient light from the garden behind it. *One.* I took hold of Leo, making sure he wouldn't run.

Zero.

The icecat came around the corner and Caldera met it in a rush. The blow threw the icecat into the wall with a *thud* and Caldera moved in, but it was already turning on her, eyes glowing blue in the darkness. Leo made as if to bolt, but I tightened my grip on his arm and he went still. The second icecat lunged for Caldera but she stepped back, using the dividing wall as cover, forcing them to come around the corner one at a time.

Shapes flashed in the darkness, fist meeting claw. The icecats were constructs, immune to pain and unnaturally strong, but Caldera was their match and more. Most battle-mages focus on ranged spells, learning to use their magic to kill safely from a distance, but Caldera is one of the ones who specialise in getting up close and personal. To my eyes her body was outlined in solid brown energy, flowing down her arms and legs and rooting her to the ground, one spell giving her strength and stability, another making her skin as hard as stone. The icecats' claws trailed cold mist in the shadows, but where they met Caldera's skin they scraped off harmlessly. Caldera's blows didn't scrape off. When she connected, the icecats went flying. Here in these tight quarters she was in her element, and even two on one, the icecats were losing.

I held back as Caldera fought. In one hand I had a silver dart, tapered to a point—a dispelling focus. It could disrupt the spells that powered the icecats, maybe even destroy one with a lucky hit, but it needed to be recharged between attacks and I'd only get one shot. I wasn't planning to use it unless I had to—this was a heavyweight fight and I was out of my league. Instead I kept searching the futures, trying to look past the chaos of combat to see what was coming. There were flickers of ice magic, but it looked as though our plan was working—the ice mage at the back couldn't get a straight shot. But there was something else, a construct or gate magic or a combination of the two. Whatever it was, it was bad news, and—

Caldera kicked at one of the icecats and it dodged, sliding away with an odd grace. The movement brought it farther into the living room, and for the first time, it had a clear line of sight to Leo.

Instantly the futures changed. The possibilities in which the icecat attacked Caldera or me vanished—it was locked onto Leo and no one else. Without hesitating it sprang.

"Caldera!" I shouted, but Caldera was already reacting. Her punch caught the icecat in midair, sent it flying into the wall. But she'd had to step back to do it, and the second icecat came around the corner . . . and as soon as it saw Leo *it* locked onto him, too.

They're not after us. They're after him—

The icecat lunged, and this time Caldera couldn't block it. Constructs are strong, but they're predictable. I plotted its course and managed to get my leg up in time; my heel met its head and the force of the construct's leap crushed its head into my shoe. Pain shot up my leg and I thumped back against the wall, but the impact twisted the construct's body around; it would have broken any normal animal's neck, and it was actually enough to stagger it for a second.

Caldera grabbed it before it could recover. As it struggled she lifted it in both hands, then broke it over her knee. It twisted and went still.

I felt a flare of space magic from the back garden.

A gate formed just outside the gate wards of the house, and *something* came through, massive and heavy. I felt the floor shift, trembling, first once and then again. I switched perspective, viewing the future in which I moved right to peer around the corner—

A giant hulking shape was right outside the picture window, nearly eight feet tall, ambient light gleaming off a polished body. It was shaped like an insect but moved with the precision of well-oiled machinery. Light caught on its eyes and on the blades and weapons in its arms, and as a triple-jointed leg came down through the broken window, the floor shook, first in the future and a second later in the present. The window frame shattered as it came through without slowing, its head taking out a chunk of plaster where the frame met the wall.

Mantis golem.

Oh, fuck.

Caldera was already facing the thing, and I felt her eyes go wide as it came around the corner. It swivelled towards her, the two of them facing each other in the darkened living room. Caldera is big, muscle and earth magic giving her the strength of stone, but compared to the construct towering over her she looked like a child. Mage and golem looked at each other, less than five feet apart.

Caldera hesitated, just briefly.

"Run!" I shouted.

The kind of magic you can use isn't something separate from you; it's a part of who you are. It affects your thoughts, your desires . . . your instincts. Air mages, when they're hurt or in danger, their first reaction is to break away, create space. Ice mages try to control the threat, lock it down. Fire mages attack. Earth mages . . . they defend and stand their ground.

Caldera stood her ground.

The golem struck, swords flashing out. Caldera ducked under the first swing and was about to punch when the golem's second hand came up, holding some kind of cylindrical device; Caldera twisted aside as a beam of golden light shot down, burning a glowing line along the floor, then had to dodge again as a sword blow nearly took her head off.

Mantis golems have four arms, and this one was holding two one-handed swords, the laser projector, and some other weapon I didn't recognise. No human can use that many weapons, but mantis golems aren't human and they have the strength and the parallel processing to use all four arms at once. The golem wasn't especially fast, and its strikes didn't have its full body weight behind them, but every one of its arms was attacking Caldera simultaneously and independently, like some kind of lethal golden windmill. No sooner had Caldera blocked one attack than she had to dodge the next.

I hesitated, caught between Leo and Caldera. I didn't want to fight this thing, but if I left Caldera alone—

A grey shape darted behind the golem, turned its blue eyes onto Leo, and lunged. I'd forgotten about the other icecat. Leo screamed; I tried to get my focus up in time but the angle was wrong and I was thrown onto Leo with the icecat on top of me.

For a few seconds everything was chaos. The icecat was raking with its claws, trying to shred through me to get to Leo; Leo was screaming; I was swearing and striking with elbows and knees, the floor shaking as Caldera fought the golem. A future of my arm being burnt off flashed before my eyes; I twisted right and the golden beam of the laser seared a glowing line along the floor. Leo broke away, dashing for the door; the icecat bounded after him and I grabbed it, hanging on grimly. The icecat dragged me a couple more steps, then the futures flipped as it switched targets and turned on me, jaws opening wide to bite at my head.

I'd been ready for it. My dispel focus was in my free hand, and as the head came round I rammed the spike right through the construct's eye. The focus discharged and the icecat spasmed, throwing me back. The spell animating the cat construct flickered and died. Icy claws raked the floor, then went still.

I looked up to see Leo fumbling with the front door. "Leo," I shouted at him. "Stay here!"

Leo shot me a terrified glance, then pulled the door open and ran out into the street.

I swore and went after him. To my left, Caldera somehow got through the whirlwind of steel and landed a solid blow on the golem's armour; plates cracked but a sword came around before she could pull back and I heard her grunt. I made it to the front door—

—and ducked back as a force blast nearly took my head off. Leo was out there but someone else was too, and the force mage was in the cover of a station wagon across the street. There was something going on, but as I looked back I saw that Caldera was struggling. The golem was pressing down on her, a golden swirl of death. I could go after Leo or help Caldera, but I couldn't do both.

I hesitated a second . . . then turned back to Caldera, bending as I did to yank my focus out of the icecat. The mantis golem brought all its weapons to bear, striking at Caldera with three limbs at once. Caldera blocked a downward slash, ducked under the laser, and *almost* dodged the stab. It didn't impale her, but blood sprayed and Caldera staggered and went down. The golem moved in to finish her off.

I charged with a shout. Futures shifted as the golem retargeted on me, and I felt a spike of terror as the golden eyes turned to look down at me. I feinted at the golem; for a second I had it on the defensive, then it moved into its attack routine.

All of a sudden the futures were a whirl of violent deaths, all of them mine. Move that way and I'd be impaled; move the other way and I'd have a severed arm; stand still and the laser would burn a hole through my chest. I ducked and dodged, staying half a step ahead of the gleaming blades. I caught flickers of futures in which I hit the golem, and none of them did anything. My dispel focus wasn't recharged, and even if it had been, it wouldn't even scratch a monster like this. I'd forgotten all thoughts of Leo, or the force mage who'd been shooting at me, or the ice mage who was still lurking around. My world had narrowed to the next two seconds, and nothing more.

The left sword came at my head and I half-parried with my forearm. Even using the angle to limit the blow, I felt the shock go up my arm, sending me lurching back. There's this terrifying sense of *power* to golems, a kind of smooth, unstoppable force. So many of the machines we meet on a daily basis have checks, safeguards; it's easy to forget how lethal they are until one's turned against you. The laser fired and I ducked, letting the beam pass an inch or two over my shoulder, feeling the air heat and seeing the armour of the golem's body backlit in the glow. Caldera was somewhere behind but I couldn't take the half second to check. The golem still hadn't used the device on its fourth arm: it looked like a torch with a gaping barrel. No time to study more closely. Swing, sword thrust, laser. Dodge and block and twist. There was a rhythm to the attacks, and I fell into it, matching the golem's movements like a dance, and for a moment I was holding my own.

But only for a moment. *I'm losing.* Had to change tactics. Couldn't break its armour. What to do?

Evade. Run.

I stepped into the next swing, catching the golem's sword arm. The blow was too powerful to stop and I let it lift me, pushing off the ground to let the golem swing me around like a roundabout. The golem stepped back, twisting, trying to bring its weapons to bear, and with the moment's breather I pulled a condenser from my pocket and smashed it against the wall.

Mist rushed out, filling the room, and suddenly all I could see was the shadow of the wall and the construct's golden body. It swung again and I ducked past; two steps brought me out of its visual range and I felt the futures in which it killed me fray and scatter. The futures opened up again and I could see where I was going.

Caldera was against the other wall, struggling to rise. I caught a glimpse of her side through her torn clothes; blood, a dark gash, something peeking through. I threw her arm over my shoulder, heaving her up. "This way," I whispered. "Quiet."

Caldera resisted for a second, then let me guide her. "Where is it?" she muttered. She was still half dazed and her voice was loud in the mist.

There was the sound of creaking metal and the floor shook as the golem zeroed in on the noise. I switched direction, pulled a stumbling Caldera to one side; a massive golden shadow loomed up, appearing out of the fog and disappearing again. The lines of its future didn't turn to intersect ours; it hadn't detected us. I held my finger to my lips and this time Caldera stayed quiet.

We'd reached the stairs. The golem was no more than ten feet away but it couldn't see us. Constructs aren't sapient, and they're very bad at dealing with unexpected situations. The golem had been sent into the house with a simple directive: kill us both. Now it couldn't detect either of its primary targets, and following the voices hadn't worked. It paused, waiting for input.

I led Caldera up the stairs. A future flashed up of a stair creaking under Caldera's weight, and the golem hearing and lasering us through the wall; I caught Caldera's shoulder, signalled for her to place her foot to one side. Blessedly, she didn't argue. The mist thinned and vanished as we made it up into the hallway.

The light was still on in the room where the icecat had attacked, and I led Caldera into the other one. She was silent and favouring one side. "How bad are you?" I whispered.

"Managing," Caldera muttered.

I looked sceptically at Caldera. She wasn't trying to order me around. Bad sign. "I don't think that golem can get up the stairs, so if you don't mind, I'd kind of prefer to stay up here. You might be able to fight that thing, but I'd just as soon not go another round with it."

Caldera didn't answer for a second and I wondered if she'd spotted what I was doing, but she didn't push it. "Leo?"

"Panicked and ran out the front door." I hesitated. "The force mage was right there. No way he could have missed him."

Caldera glared. "I told you to stay with him."

I looked away, stung. I wanted to make excuses—I'd been tied up fighting the icecat, I'd gone back to help her—but on the facts, she was right. Guarding Leo had been my job.

"Where are they?" Caldera said.

"Ice mage is in the back garden." I kept my voice very low. The golem was really damn close, and that laser could easily pierce the floor. "Lost the force mage. Golem's still waiting."

"What if we make a break for—?"

"Bad idea," I said. I'd been looking at the futures in which we did exactly that. "The street doesn't have enough cover—with you hurt, they'd chase us down and pick us off. Only reason they haven't done it already is they aren't sure where we are."

Caldera paused for a second, and I could sense her flicking through plans. "All right," she said. "We're going to have to stall them. I'll—"

The futures shifted. I took one glance at them and my heart sank. I caught Caldera's arm and pulled her towards the bedroom.

One of the few silver linings to these sorts of situations is that you learn pretty quick whether someone trusts you. Even wounded, there was no way I could have moved Caldera if she didn't want to be moved, but after one startled glance she let me drag her inside.

There was a weird low-pitched noise, like a deep cough.

I twisted around. Through the doorway and out in the hall, where there had been carpet, now there was a big circular hole in the floor. Through it, I could see the mist-filled living room. As I watched, there was another cough and most of what was left of the hallway disintegrated into dust.

From below, I felt the vibrations as the golem moved and

turned. The cough came a third time, then a fourth. There was nothing left of the hallway: if we stepped out of the bedroom we'd fall straight into the room below.

"Well," I said quietly. "I guess now we know what that fourth weapon does."

"What the *fuck* is that?" Caldera whispered.

There was another cough, followed by another. It wasn't going directly towards us . . . yet. "Disintegration cannon. Wonder why it didn't use it earlier. Maybe it's got too slow a charge-up time. Or it could be one of those spells that needs the target to be stationary to—"

"Did you hit your head?" Caldera hissed. "Focus!"

"We all have our ways of dealing with stressful situations," I said absently. Most of my attention was on plotting out futures. "It's going to shoot the floor out from underneath us. Probably collapse the house."

More coughs sounded. The golem was destroying the small guest room in which we'd found Leo, one section of floor at a time. We'd gotten lucky that it had decided to start there. Not too lucky, though. Our room was next.

Caldera hesitated one second, then lowered her head. "Fuck it." Her voice was harsh. "We fight."

"No."

"We don't have—"

I didn't raise my voice. I often get calmer in really dangerous situations. "If you go down there, you'll die."

"You don't—"

"I *do* know that, and that's without the ice mage interfering. He wouldn't have ordered the golem to force a confrontation like this unless he knew he'd win."

"Then—"

"Our best chance is to wait for backup. And no, I haven't seen it coming, I'm still looking. Please let me concentrate."

"When are—?" Caldera started to ask, then stopped.

Another series of coughs. The light in the next room blinked out and the house went dark. One of the shots must have cut the power cable. There was a groaning sound and a rumbling crash that I could feel through the floorboards. The floor shifted under my feet.

Caldera snatched a look out into the hall. "Mist's clearing," she said in a low voice.

"I know."

"Got another?"

"No." I don't stockpile condensers—they work best when they're fresh. I'd lost two in the battle with Chamois, and the one I'd just used had been my last. I kept scanning through the futures. There was some sort of disturbance up ahead, something like . . .

. . . fire?

Now I just needed to figure out how to keep us alive until they got here.

The coughing sound came again and the wall ahead of us shuddered. "I think I'm going to have to go keep that thing busy," I told Caldera. "Wait up here, okay?"

Caldera glared at me. "Screw that!"

The wall shuddered again. A few more shots and it would collapse. "Stay in the corner," I told Caldera. "When that wall goes it'll take down most of the floor, except for the far corner. As long as you stay there, you won't fall."

"If you—"

"You're hurt, I'm not." I kept my voice calm. "I've fought these things before; I can stall it for a little while. We just need to survive another forty seconds."

Caldera hesitated. I don't know much about medicine, and I hadn't had a close look at Caldera's wound, but I'd seen the futures in which she tried to fight the golem, and they'd been brief and messy. We didn't have time to talk it through. "Stay back," I said, and walked to the edge.

There was a final cough. The wall groaned and collapsed, taking the section of floor I was on with it. I'd been ready for it and rode it down, jumping off at the last second to land in the living room, rolling to soften the fall.

I came up to see the golem turning to face me. Plaster dust was in the air, and broken drywall littered the floor.

Taking down the wall hadn't collapsed the house, not quite, but it wouldn't take much more. Caldera was hidden by the remains of the ceiling. From the back garden I heard a yell, then the golem moved to attack.

The laser burned a line across the carpet as I dodged right. The golem approached, swords coming down, and I backed away. The living room flashed, lit in the glow of spells from outside: red, blue, red again. I couldn't take the time to look and see. All my attention was focused on the mantis golem.

The laser fired again and again, a glowing golden line of death. I stepped aside from each blast, calculating how to position myself to dodge the next. The golem was herding me, pushing me towards the corner. The spells from outside had stopped; the dust in the air was cutting the visibility but I could see the futures that were approaching and knew what I had to do. *Just need a little distraction . . .* I stepped forward to go under the next laser blast, letting myself be drawn into melee range. The golem's swords came down.

I jumped away, backpedalling, thumping into the wall. The golem adjusted its aim to focus on me, the laser emitter sighting on my chest.

Light bloomed from behind the golem. A blast of flame stabbed out, washing off the construct's back.

The golem halted, turned. A figure strode out of the dust, wreathed in flame. The fire around it hid its form; all I could make out was a vaguely humanoid shape with glowing eyes. A second blast hit the golem before it could finish turning around. This one was narrower, more focused, a near-white beam the width of two fingers that was too bright to look at. It burnt into the golem and I saw armour glowing and melting, molten gold spattering to the floor.

The golem fired, but as it did the figure raised a hand. The laser struck the fiery shape, hit a shield. The golden line fuzzed and faded. The white-hot beam didn't. It kept going, burning into the golem. The golem took one stride forward, then its back went white and the beam burst all the way through, streaming out the other side. The heat was so intense that I had to shield my face. Through my fingers I saw the golem jerk, shudder. The beam sawed, melting the golem from the inside out.

With a groan the golem fell, toppling with a crash that shook the house. Just for an instant I saw *something* expand from the metal body, stretching, sinking into the floor, then it was gone. The golem's remains lay still and some light seemed to have vanished from its golden eyes.

The fiery shape turned to me and I nearly flinched. It looked like a man sculpted from flame, invulnerable, god-like. Fires had broken out all around it, licking at its feet. For a moment I felt as though I were facing down some sort of fire spirit, not a human being.

Then all of a sudden the flame shield winked out and Landis was standing there. He was dressed in some sort of close-fitting body armour I didn't recognise, and he looked brisk and full of energy. "Verus! Glad to see you made it, good job on the distraction. What's your status?"

The floor around Landis's feet was on fire. He didn't seem to have noticed, and I dragged my eyes away. "Caldera's hurt," I said. Adrenaline was still pumping through me and I wanted to move, to fight. "The kid we were protecting, he ran that way. We need to find him."

"Leaving some of the fun for us, eh?" Landis said cheerfully. He turned just as another fiery shape came out of the smoke behind him. Again the fire hid the person's features, but I recognised the signature of the magic and I knew it was Variam. "He's running," Variam said. "Do we chase?"

"Not this time, we've got a civilian to find. Description, Verus?"

"His name's Leo. Boy, about ten, thin, blond hair. Wearing jeans and a black top. There was a force mage covering the door. He's gone, but—"

Landis was already heading for the door. Variam followed. "Shield off, Vari, there's a good lad. Standard cover. Verus, you stay with Caldera and take a breather. We'll take it from here." They disappeared out into the street.

I was left alone in the wreckage of the living room.

Flames were still licking around and I tried to find a way to climb back up to the first floor.

It took me a minute, and by the time I made it up, I found Caldera slumped on the bed. Blood had soaked through the side of her jacket and into the bedclothes. "Caldera." I kept my voice low. "Can you hear me?"

"Not like I could miss it, way you talk," Caldera muttered. "Was that Landis . . . ?"

"It was him." *Not good.* I hadn't realised how badly hurt Caldera was; she must have been forcing herself to keep going. "Vari's here too. We should be safe."

"Didn't call for Order of the Shield." Caldera's eyes opened; she stared at me suspiciously. "Should have been Star."

I sighed. "Seriously? You're going to give me a hard time about this *now*?"

"You were on your phone. When I took the kid down . . ." Caldera sighed and closed her eyes. "Never follow orders, do you . . ."

"Yeah, well, you can shout at me later." I was looking Caldera over. The gash on her shoulder didn't look bad—it was the side wound I was worried about. How deep was it? "We need to get you some help."

"Already called for—"

"On your com disc, I know. I think we can give up on that, all right? You guys must have backup ways of getting in touch. Phone number?"

"There's a number." Caldera didn't open her eyes. "For emergencies."

"You think this might qualify?"

"I'll read it. Type it in."

I made the call. It took longer than it should have to convince the woman on the other end that I was who I said I was. Finally I just passed the phone over to Caldera and let her give the authentication code. By the time it was done I could hear the strain in Caldera's voice.

At last it was done and Caldera hung up. "Hate those people," she muttered. "Bureaucrats . . ."

Caldera was still slumped on the bed; she'd stopped

moving except when she had to, and when she'd lifted the phone to her ear I'd seen that it had hurt her. "You doing okay?"

"You always ask such stupid questions?"

"Yeah, I've got the feeling it might be a good idea to keep you talking until the medics get here." I could still smell smoke; it wasn't getting any fainter. "Oh, and I don't want to worry you, but just so you know, the house is on fire."

"Lovely."

"On the plus side, I don't think it's going to collapse in the next ten minutes."

"You know," Caldera said, "even by my standards, this was a really shitty night out."

"Oh, come on," I said. "Quiet neighbourhood, door-to-door entertainment . . . there's even romantic candle-light."

"My ribs are sticking out of my side."

"You did say you wanted a match against someone who could challenge you."

"Does this happen every time you go out with someone?"

"Hey, at least I'm not a boring date."

Smoke rose from the floor below, ash drifting up into the night. We sat together in the ruined house as I searched through the futures, looking to see when help would arrive.

chapter 8

It was half an hour later.

Blue light flashed from the roofs of the police vehicles, reflected back from car windows and the fronts of the houses. The lights were out of sync, creating a weird strobing effect that made the shadows dance back and forth. Although the police were here, they weren't going into the house: the Keeper liaisons had done their job and the figures in the black uniforms and yellow hi-vis jackets were holding a perimeter and putting up crime-scene tape at either end of the road. People were leaning out of windows and watching from doors, peering at the house where we'd fought our battle, but there was nothing to see. Plastic screens had gone up at the door and windows and all the activity was taking place inside.

"What day is it?" the woman standing over me asked.

"Saturday," I said. I was sitting in the open boot of a car. A mobile command centre had arrived, Keepers and other Council personnel were bustling around, and it all looked very official.

"What's the nearest tube station?"

"Uxbridge."

"How old are you?"

"You don't know how old I am, so I could answer that question any way I liked, so long as I didn't lie too blatantly. I get it, you're checking to see if I have a concussion. How about if I tell you how old *you* are, will that prove I can think straight?"

She didn't take me up on the offer. "How are you feeling?"

"Beaten up, but I've had worse."

"Nausea, headaches, problems with your balance?"

"Not yet, but shining that light in my eyes isn't helping."

The woman clicked the light off. "Make sure you see a doctor before you go home."

The rush from the battle had worn off, and I was utterly exhausted. My arms and legs were heavy, and I could feel all the bruises and scrapes I'd taken fighting the icecats. All I wanted to do was sit there. "Sure."

The woman left. I looked down, examining the forearm of my armour. Both of the icecats had raked my arms and I could see light score marks on the mesh, but the claws hadn't penetrated to the skin. My armour had probably saved my life. The icecats might not have been able to kill me on their own, but if I'd been carrying those wounds when I went up against the golem, it would have slowed me down enough to make the difference.

I felt a presence to my left. "Looks like you got off easy."

I looked up. It was a man, medium height and heavyset. The flickering blue light showed brown hair and a sour expression. A Keeper, one I'd met before . . . What was his name? Oh yeah, Slate. The one who'd goaded Caldera into that fight with me at Red's a couple of nights ago. *Just what I need.*

"So the kid's gone," Slate said when I didn't respond. "Only witness, from *our* case, and you lost him. Fucked it up right and proper, didn't you?"

"Yeah, it's not as if Caldera called you guys for backup as soon as we found out who the kid really was." I was tired, bruised, still working through the aftereffects of an adrenaline rush, and not in the mood to be diplomatic. "Oh wait, she did. You know what? Maybe if you'd pulled your finger out of your fat arse and come to help, your witness'd still be here."

I'd expected Slate to lose his temper, but he just looked at me with a twist of his mouth, as though I were something a dog had produced from its rear end. "Don't see any blood."

"And?"

"Kid got taken," Slate said. "Caldera got hurt. You look like you got off pretty okay." He studied me. "So what were you doing while Caldera was dealing with the golem?"

"Busy."

"With what?"

"With one of the icecats."

"That's convenient."

I didn't answer. "How about you run through that fight for me," Slate said.

"How about I don't?"

"I wasn't asking."

"Well, that's great, because I'm not answering, so I guess we're all happy, aren't we?"

"You think you're pretty special, don't you?" Slate said. "Rules don't apply to you, right?"

I just stared him. "Don't think that card you've got makes you a Keeper," Slate said. "You're not even an auxiliary. I could arrest you and take you down to the station right now and no one'd look twice." He leant in close, eyes staring into mine. "What happened in that house?"

I looked up at Slate. I could have looked down on him if I stood up, but I didn't. "Let's get something straight," I said. "Taking crap from Caldera is one thing. But I'm not going to fold to every Council mage who strolls up. You want to be my supervisor, you can go ahead and fight Caldera over it. But you might want to bear in mind that the last time you tried duelling her she kicked your balls up your arsehole, so if I were you I'd think twice before going back for a rematch."

I saw Slate flush. That one had finally managed to piss

him off. "You can—" he began, then stopped as a hand fell on his shoulder.

Slate turned. Haken was standing there. "Captain wants you," Haken said. He was watching Slate steadily.

Slate narrowed his eyes. I saw futures of him choosing to stand and argue; they flickered and disappeared. He gave me an ugly look and left.

Haken watched Slate go. "I know he's an arsehole," Haken said once Slate was out of earshot, "but you don't need to pick a fight."

"He picked the fight. I just fought back."

"Slate's . . . he's got some history with Dark mages. I know how he acts, but he's got his reasons."

"And I just nearly got my head hacked off trying to keep Caldera and your witness alive." I felt bitter, and the fatigue was making it worse. "I can deal with taking shit from Keepers when I deserve it. But taking shit from you guys when I'm risking my life to *help* you is pretty hard."

Haken sighed. "World doesn't always work the way we want it to, Verus." Haken was maybe in his midthirties, but all of a sudden, in the flashing police lights, he looked much older and very tired. "Just have to live with it."

"Isn't that the truth."

"They've run the maker's marks on that golem," Haken said. "It's part of a set of three that were reported stolen a few years ago. We didn't know White Rose had got them till now."

"You think they were the ones behind it?"

Haken looked surprised. "Who else would it have been?"

I shrugged.

"That kid was from there, right? And he was meeting Rayfield?"

I remembered that last glimpse I'd had of Leo, shooting a terrified glance back at me before disappearing out into the street. I wondered if any of us were ever going to see him again.

Haken took my silence as agreement. "I know we don't have enough for a warrant yet, but we're going to be going for one tomorrow. Could use you, if you can make it. Caldera'll probably still be out."

"I'll check with her. Do you know what happened?"

"About . . . ?"

"Caldera called for backup," I said. "Before the fight started. More than long enough for other Keepers to gate."

"Yeah, I heard." Haken frowned. "That shouldn't have happened."

"Her communicator went dead during the fight." I turned my head to look up at Haken. "Thought those things were supposed to be fail-safe?"

"That's what they told me too. Best guess, it was a glitch. I know these things are supposed to be good, but they're still new tech. We've had trouble with them before."

"Pretty crappy reason to get killed."

"Yeah, I'm not arguing. Look, I'll see if I can track down whatever the problem was, okay? I'm guessing someone screwed up, but at least we can stop it happening again."

"Thanks."

Haken turned to leave. "Oh," I said. "Haken?"

"Yeah?"

"When Caldera made that call, did she talk to you?"

"What do you mean?"

"Caldera told me a couple of weeks ago that you were her primary contact for cross-case work." I kept my voice casual, but I didn't take my eyes off Haken. "Aren't messages like that supposed to go through you?"

"Usually, yeah, but I was out on the Rayfield case. Would have done if it hadn't been for everything else, but I didn't get the call."

I nodded. Haken walked away.

Chatter and voices washed around me from the police and the Council personnel. The people at the police tape and the windows were still there, taking photos and watching. From inside the house, I felt a gate spell. I couldn't see through the screens, but I knew they were transporting the remains of the golem away.

So much movement, so much activity. In a way it was all

because of me, and yet everyone was ignoring me. It was good, I supposed—safer that way—but it felt weirdly isolating. I pushed myself up, holding the side of the car until the wave of dizziness passed, and headed for the ambulance that Caldera had been moved into.

I heard the sound of laughter as I drew closer. Walking around the back, looking into the brightly lit interior, I saw Caldera lying on one of the stretchers. She hadn't been bandaged, but her hands were clasped over her stomach and she was smiling. Landis was sitting on a chair by the stretcher, long arms and legs sprawled out like an ungainly spider, and he was in the middle of a story. "So then the fellow gets indignant and tells me, 'I don't know what you mean, I haven't anything like that in my family tree.' Well, as I'm sure you know, I wasn't going to stand for that. I got up and told him—"

"Hey, Verus," Caldera said, glancing up at me. "Thank God you're here—maybe you can shut him up. Nothing I do seems to work."

"You wound me, dear lady." Landis clasped a hand to his chest. "Can I not ask for a token of your favour?"

"Oh, bugger off," Caldera said, but she was laughing. "I swear, you're lucky I'm not allowed to get out of this bed . . ."

I had to grin. There's a weird rush from making it through a combat. When you come out of one alone, then it doesn't last, but when you have friends around it turns into something happier. A celebration, I guess. You're alive, your friends are alive, and all of a sudden you're intensely aware of it. "Let me guess," I told Landis. "You're on duty to make sure she doesn't try to run off for another round?"

"A fearsome duty, 'tis true, but needs must, eh? You hear that, my girl? Bed rest, that's the ticket."

"Oh, you wish."

"Well, well, one can hope. Ah, Verus, Vari and I had no joy, I'm afraid. Gave the place a good old search and quarter, but the boy's vanished into the ether."

I nodded. It wasn't really a surprise. "Thanks for showing up so fast."

"A bit of a sticky situation, eh? No need to worry, happens to the best of us. I remember this time out in Guernsey when—"

"Okay," Caldera interrupted, "before you start another of your endless stories, how *did* you show up so fast?"

"Oh, just a friendly request from your new junior." Landis leant back against the wall, nodding at me. "He mentioned you two might have a spot of bother, so I had Vari toodle over and take a look at the place so he could open us a gate. Better safe than sorry, eh?"

Caldera gave Landis a sceptical look. "Weren't you on standby for the Rayfield case?"

"And wasn't it fortunate that it turned out to be related? Happy endings for all!"

"Lucky for some." Caldera glanced at me. "They have any idea who those people were?"

"Leo was connected to White Rose." I looked at Landis, keeping my expression carefully neutral. "They seem to be the obvious suspects."

"Yes," Landis said, drawing out the word. "They do, don't they?" He jumped to his feet. "Well, I'll leave you in Verus's safe hands. If you see Vari, let him know he can take off for the night, eh?"

"I'll tell him."

Landis hopped out of the ambulance, and I took his seat with a sigh. Caldera cocked an eye at me. "You all right?"

"I should be asking you that." I nodded at Caldera's side. "How bad was it?"

"Oh, you know life mages. Always make it sound worse than it is."

I raised my eyebrows. "Not quite sure that's true."

"Yeah, well, they're going to keep me out for at least a day. You okay to go to the War Rooms as my stand-in?"

I nodded. "I'll be there."

"Good." Caldera paused. "Sorry for giving you a hard time in there."

I looked at Caldera in surprise. "About the kid," Caldera said. "Wasn't your fault. Just pissed off at myself."

"For what?"

"Don't like not being strong enough to do the job," Caldera was silent for a second. "Don't like losing people, either."

"Neither do I."

Caldera glanced up at me. "Why'd you go back?"

"When?"

"Middle of that fight, after the second icecat went for you and the kid. After you were done with that, you went straight for the golem."

"Yeah."

"Wasn't Leo out the door by then?"

"I thought you were too busy with the golem to notice stuff like that."

"I've been in enough fights to know what's going on around me." Caldera looked at me, eyebrows raised. "Don't dodge the question. You could have gone after the kid. Why didn't you?"

"There was a force mage covering the door," I said. "At least one other guy too. If I'd gone after Leo, it would have meant going one-on-one with a force mage in an open street. I couldn't have won that. The best I could have managed would have been to get away in one piece, and they probably would have got Leo anyway. And I knew the golem was going to kill you if I left you. I figured that two on one, we had a chance to beat it. It was a choice between losing two people, and giving up one person to have a decent chance of saving the other. I picked the battle I thought we could win."

Caldera snorted and closed her eyes. "Always the pragmatist."

A man I didn't know stuck his head around the corner. "Hey," he said. "We're heading back. You riding along?"

I shook my head. "It's just her."

The man disappeared. I got up, started to leave, then paused. "Caldera?"

"Yeah."

"That was half the reason. The other half . . . I'd rather you stayed alive."

Caldera looked back at me for a long moment, then nodded. I climbed out of the ambulance and went to find Vari and go home.

· · · · · · · · · ·

As Vari and I walked out of my downstairs storeroom, there was a clatter of footsteps from upstairs. Luna poked her head out from around the banister, and she seemed to relax as she saw us both. "You're okay?"

"We're okay," I said, wearily starting up the stairs. "Looks like you're getting better at sensing gates."

Luna had an endless stream of questions, and I used the excuse of making tea to let Variam do most of the talking. When it came to the fight in the safe house though, I had to tell the story, sitting in the armchair with legs crossed, a tiny trail of steam rising up from the mug in front of me.

"You're so lucky," Luna said disconsolately when I finished.

"I just had an eight-foot golem try to redecorate the room with my internal organs," I said. "*Lucky* is not the word I would choose."

"Can I come with you tomorrow?"

"It's a police investigation. They don't run 'Bring Your Daughter to Work Day.'"

"Yeah, well, I spent the day on Theory of Magic makeup classes," Luna said. "At least you got to do something fun."

Even I have trouble believing Luna sometimes. "Luna, I swear, by the time you're thirty, either you're going to have more combat experience than any other girl in the British Isles, or you're going to be dead. And no, I don't know which."

"Okay," Variam said, "you're not going to like hearing this, but I'm going to say it. Your new magic teacher, this Chalice? Maybe this whole thing was a setup."

Luna frowned. "How?"

"She was the one who sent him to Uxbridge, right?"

"That doesn't prove anything."

"Yeah, well, she's a Dark mage, and the first place she

sends you, you nearly get your head chopped off. You don't think that's a funny coincidence?"

"Just because—"

I raised my hand and Luna subsided. "I did think about it," I said to Variam. "When Chalice was doing that spell, I didn't sense any magic. Could mean that I just didn't spot it, but it could mean she wasn't doing anything at all—she just knew the address already. That's what you were thinking of, right?"

Variam nodded, but I kept going before he could answer. "But there's a problem. Remember what I told you about the icecats? They went after Leo. Same for that force mage. Caldera and I weren't the primary target. Leo was."

Variam frowned. "Okay."

"So if Chalice was behind the attack, why send me to Uxbridge at all?" I said. "We'd never have found the place in time without her help. If she wanted Leo dead, all she had to do was go there herself. And if she *didn't* want Leo dead but she was behind the attack, why was Leo the target?"

"Maybe they didn't agree—"

I shook my head. "What Chalice did helped us get to Leo. Whoever was behind the attack, their objective was to get rid of Leo. Most logical conclusion: they're different people. Don't make things more complicated than they have to be."

Variam didn't look a hundred percent convinced, but he shut up. "So does that mean you trust her?" Luna asked.

"No," I said. "Just because she's not on *their* side doesn't mean she's on *our* side. But I think there's more going on than she's telling us."

"So if she wasn't behind the attack tonight, who was?" Variam asked.

"The Keepers think it's White Rose," I said.

"Who?"

"No clue," I said. I was starting to realise just how out of my depth I was on this case. I needed to talk to someone who was more up to speed on Council politics, and soon. "But whoever they are, I'm not buying that it's nothing to do with the Council. You know what mantis golems are used for."

"They're Council bodyguards," Luna said.

"They said these ones were reported stolen?" Variam said.

"Bullshit," I said. "That's like a Challenger tank getting stolen from the British Army. The army doesn't lose battle tanks, the RAF doesn't lose jet fighters, and the Council sure as hell doesn't lose mantis golems. Whoever went after us tonight, they're in close with the Council."

Luna started to say something, but I held up a hand. "There's something else. Leo was holed up in that house for two days or close to it. We find him, and he gets attacked less than half an hour afterwards. I don't think that's a co-incidence. I looked into the futures while I was waiting for Caldera. There wasn't any danger, not as long as we stayed outside. Maybe those guys were looking for Leo, but I don't think they would have found him on their own. I think something we did brought them there."

"Could have been tracking you," Variam suggested.

"There's a simpler explanation. Between going into that house and the attack starting, we did exactly one thing that could have given our position away. Caldera used her com disc to get in touch with her order. And she activated a locator beacon."

Variam frowned. "Wait," Luna said. "I thought you said those communicator things were supposed to be untraceable? And no one could intercept them?"

"He's not saying they were traced," Variam said. He was watching me, his voice flat. "You're saying you got set up."

"Wait," Luna said, her eyes going wide. "You're saying the *Keepers* want to kill you? You managed to piss them off that much *already*?"

"If the Order of the Star really wanted to kill us, we'd already be dead," I said. "I told you, the target was Leo."

"What happened to him, anyway?"

"We couldn't find him," Variam said. He didn't take his

eyes off me. "You think someone in the Order of the Star's a traitor."

"I hate to sound cynical, but it's probably more than one," I said. "You know how many factions there are on the Council—they've all got their agents and their areas of influence. Leo was connected to the Rayfield case, and Haken already told me that half a dozen factions are interested. One of those factions must have not wanted Leo brought in."

"Do you think they wanted to kill him first?" Luna said.

"More likely they kidnapped him."

"Who was it?" Variam said.

"That I don't know."

"You said there was an ice mage and a force mage," Luna said. "You could try that . . ."

"Doubt it'll help," I said. "Whoever's behind this probably isn't the kind to do their own dirty work. No, what we really need to figure out is what Leo knew that was enough of a threat for them to move like this."

"He was a witness," Variam said. "If he'd made it, first thing they'd have done would have been pull him in for an interview . . ."

". . . and find out what he saw," I finished. "But we do know what he saw, because of Caldera. He saw the guy the rest of the Order of the Star's been looking for. Rayfield."

Luna's eyebrows had been gradually climbing higher and higher, and at this point she put up her hands. "Ugh, God. This is *so* confusing. I have no idea what's going on anymore."

"Maybe if you actually went to your politics classes," Variam said, "instead of bunking off to go duelling."

"Oh, like you're some sort of—"

"Luna, Vari! Not now!"

Luna and Variam shut up. I pulled over the notepad that Chalice had used earlier in the evening, flipped to a new page, and began sketching. "It's not as complicated as you think. Here." I turned the pad around; I'd drawn an equilateral triangle with the three corners marked and labelled. "There are three factions that we need to worry about. First is White Rose." I tapped my pencil to the first of the three corners. "Whoever they are, they're the ones who sent Leo to that meeting with Rayfield two nights ago. As far as we know, they haven't done anything else, but if Caldera's that careful around them then they're not anyone we want to mess with."

Variam looked down at the diagram and then up at me. "You're explaining this by drawing it in a triangle."

"And . . . ?"

Variam shook his head. "You are *such* a geek sometimes."

I moved my pencil to the second corner. "Next faction is our mysterious group who were behind the attack tonight. We know they've got ties to the Council and some way of getting supposedly secure data from the Keepers. They also wanted Leo silenced, so I think it's a safe bet they've got some kind of investment in the Rayfield case. Either they don't want the truth getting out, or they want to learn it first."

"The Keepers think those people and White Rose are the same people," Luna said. "Right?"

"Right, which I'm not buying." I touched the tip of the pencil to the last corner, labelled with a name and a question mark. "And finally, we've got our dark horse. The ones who hired Chamois. That's where this whole thing started. Chamois crashed the meeting between Rayfield and Leo at Pudding Mill Lane, he either killed Rayfield or made him disappear thoroughly enough that no one's found him, and the focus got lost in the fight." I tapped my pencil on the question mark. "This is the key to the whole thing, I'm sure of it. If we can figure out who Chamois is working for, and why he attacked Rayfield, we'll understand what's really going on."

"Okay . . ." Luna said. "So how do we do that?"

"That's the problem," I said. "I have no idea. So we'll have to work on the two groups where we *do* have something to go on." I moved my pencil to the other two points. "I'll go talk to Caldera tomorrow, find out what she knows about White Rose. What I *can't* ask about is this Council group.

I've got my suspicions, but if I go poking around it could lead to really bad things. You guys are apprentices though. Especially you, Vari—I think Landis might know a bit he's not telling."

Vari nodded. "I want to try talking to Chalice," Luna said.

"In the middle of this?"

"Well, since *someone* won't let me come along on their important official Keeper stuff, there's not much else I can do, is there? Besides, none of the guys you're talking about would know anything about what's happening on the Dark side of the fence. And we already know she wants to talk to me."

I sighed. "All right, but I want you to take Anne along for backup. We don't have any good reason yet to believe that Chalice is a danger, but that doesn't mean she isn't."

"Oh well." Variam yawned and stretched. "I'm off home. Sounds like tomorrow'll be interesting."

ı ı ı ı ı ı ı ı ı

The next morning was overcast, white cloud filling the sky all the way to the horizon. It had rained during the night, and the weather forecast promised more to come. Luna had stayed over, and we had breakfast together and discussed plans before I went off to see Caldera.

Caldera lives in Hackney, in a seedy-looking area with a lot of council estates. It's not quite a dump, but it's not high-class, either, and I doubt you'd find many other mages living there. Caldera has a flat on the second floor of a converted house; I got inside, climbed the stairs, and knocked.

There was a pause. The door and walls around the flat were warded, and I could feel the latent energy waiting to be used. Then they shifted slightly, and all of a sudden the configuration was less threatening. Caldera opened the door and looked me up and down. "Oh, it's you."

Caldera was wearing a baggy T-shirt, tracksuit bottoms, and slippers. It was the first time I'd seen her dressed in something that you couldn't do heavy manual labour in. "Hi, invalid," I said, and held up a package. "I brought grapes."

"Okay, you can stay."

I handed her the bag and walked in. I've only been to Caldera's flat a couple of times, but I quite like it. It's messy and comfortable, filled with old bottles and coffee mugs, the kind of place where you feel as though you're allowed to put your feet up. "Going for the casual look?"

"I'm on sick leave," Caldera said in distaste. "Can you believe they wanted to keep me in the bloody hospital?"

"Yes. Yes, I can."

"Oh, and by the way, if you want to get inside, you're supposed to ring the bell and wait for me to buzz you into the building. Not knock on my door."

"Sorry." I dropped into one of the armchairs and grinned at her. "Every time I see a security setup that bad I just have to go through it. I'm doing you a favour, really."

"You're a pain in my arse is what you are."

"You feeling better?"

"Course I'm better. Only reason I'm here is because Rain made it an order."

I made a noncommittal sort of noise. I'd been watching Caldera since I came in and she didn't seem to be in pain. Still, as she went to get a bowl and a drink from the kitchen, her movements were more sluggish than usual, and it wasn't until she returned and dropped into the sofa that I saw her shoulders relax. Caldera's tough, but whatever healing she'd received had obviously taken a lot out of her. I had the feeling Anne could have done a better job but decided not to say that out loud.

"So the indictment's set for this afternoon," Caldera said. "I want you at the War Rooms at noon, okay?"

"What time?"

"Could be any time. Might want to bring something to read."

"Sounds great. Who's the indictment for, Chamois?"

"White Rose."

I blinked. "Seriously?"

"What do you mean?"

"Well," I said. "Remember Torvald? We put in a request

about him the beginning of last week and they still haven't got back to us. Chamois tries to kill me on CCTV two days ago and there's no movement on that either. This attack happens less than twelve *hours* ago, and there's a Council indictment already."

"Yeah," Caldera said dryly. "Kind of a difference there."

"Look, I haven't pushed you on who these White Rose people are," I said. "But if I'm going to an indictment in your place, you don't think maybe you ought to fill me in?"

Caldera sighed. "Get me a beer from the shelf."

I looked back at Caldera for a second, then got up, fetched the bottle that she was pointing to, and brought her a glass. Caldera twisted off the cap bare-handed, poured out half of the bottle, waited for the foam to subside, poured out the other half, and took a drink. I sat and waited.

"I guess you do need to know," Caldera said at last. "But get something clear. This does *not* get spread around. I know you like to chat with your friends and those magical creatures of yours, but you get caught discussing this, I'm not going to bat for you."

I nodded.

"All right," Caldera said. "Let's start at the beginning. The baseline law for mages is the Concord. Under that are the national laws."

"Okay," I said. The Concord is the international set of laws that all mages are required to follow. They're pretty useless if you're not a mage yourself, but breaking them is still a fairly big deal, as long as the victim is someone the Council cares about. Underneath that there are the national laws, passed as resolutions by the ruling Councils of each magical nation, and those vary from country to country. They aren't allowed to conflict with the Concord, and the penalties for breaking them are a lot less serious, but it's still a good idea to know what they are.

"Now, a bunch of those laws regulate how mages are allowed to deal with other humans," Caldera said. "There's the prohibition on slavery, and the laws against harming normals and sensitives and adepts."

"Uh, yeah, in theory. I'm not sure how much they actually get followed."

"Light mages and independents follow them most of the time."

"When it suits them."

"I said *most of the time*. Yes, those laws get broken. Yes, we don't always catch the ones who do it. But the fact that they follow those laws is the big difference between Light mages and Dark ones. How many Light slave traders do you know?"

"Maybe they don't do it publicly, but that doesn't mean it doesn't happen."

"And do you know for a fact any Light mages who do it? With evidence?"

"You aren't seriously telling me you don't believe it ever happens."

"I'm not a moron, all right?" Caldera said. "Of course it happens. But the laws are there, and they do have an effect. It's like the speed limit. Yes, everyone knows people break it, but if they get *caught* breaking it there are consequences. And so they don't push it too far. You get me?"

I wasn't particularly happy with having slavery and murder equated with breaking the speed limit, but I knew arguing about it wasn't going to accomplish much. "I get you."

"So, if you want to be a Light mage, especially if you want to work with the Council, you have to follow the national laws. You have to play nice. Okay?"

"Okay."

"A certain fraction of Light mages are not nice."

"You don't say."

"They want to be part of the Council and have all the perks. They also want to get to do all the same kinds of things that Dark mages get to do. They have a problem. White Rose is an organisation that specialises in solving that problem."

"So White Rose provides a nice discreet brothel service?"

"Okay," Caldera said. "When I told you they were a brothel, that's not the whole story. The kind of guys who go to White Rose . . . if they wanted sex they'd just hit up an escort agency. White Rose does the kind of stuff you can't ask for out in the open."

I was starting to see where this was going, and I didn't like it. "You mean kids like Leo."

"Kids, heavy-duty sadism, snuff scenes. The workers are slaves, obviously. Then you start bringing magic into it. Let's say you're a client of White Rose. There's some new pop singer you've got your eye on, you see her in her music videos. You decide you want a piece of that. White Rose is happy to help. They'll find one of their slaves with a good physical resemblance, maybe get themselves a new one if it's a special order. Then they'll get to work. Flesh-sculpting or glamours to make her look the part, mental control to make her act the part. They soften them up first, then do most of the heavy lifting with mind magic. By the time they're done, the girl thinks she *is* that person. They can put in other bits too. Make her in love with you, switch her programming so she has to do whatever you tell her, set it up so she goes for your fetish. Whatever you like."

"Jesus," I said in revulsion. "I knew Dark mages did stuff like that, but . . . They make a business out of this?"

"Yeah, and their business is booming. They don't just sell to mages either: they've got a whole regular client base. You wouldn't believe me if I told you how much they make off those custom orders."

"I don't think I want to. The Council knows about this?"

"Yeah."

"Then why—?"

"First, White Rose isn't staffed by Light mages. They're all Dark or independent. And they're careful never to break the Concord. Their slaves are all normals or sensitives, never mages. They even steer clear of adepts."

"Screw the Concord. That's not just violating the national laws, that's breaking them over your knee and stamping on the bits. Did you just say it was like—?"

"Second," Caldera said, cutting me off, "most of White Rose's clients are normals with a lot of money. But a few of them are Light mages who don't pay in money. Guess what they pay with instead."

"They'd . . . oh, *fuck*. White Rose wouldn't want money from them, would they? They could get that anywhere. From the Light mages they'd want influence."

"And they get it," Caldera said. "A whole ton of blackmail material." Her face was unreadable. "This is the fourth time I know about that we've tried to get an indictment against White Rose. The last three times the answer was no. They've got too much dirt on Council mages."

"And that's what I'm going into the middle of," I said, realising suddenly how this was going to affect me. "Do you think it's going to be different this time?"

"Maybe. For all the fucked-up stuff that they do, this is the first time White Rose has attacked a Keeper. They've crossed a line."

"Assuming it was them."

Caldera looked sharply at me. "Do you have evidence that it was someone else? Something you're not telling me?"

"No, I just saw the same things you did. You don't think it's a funny coincidence that that strike team showed up right after you called in our location on your communicator? Which stopped working as soon as we needed it?"

"What exactly are you suggesting?"

"You said it. White Rose has influence on the Council."

"Don't."

"And the Keepers work for the Council—"

Caldera made a short motion, cutting me off. "I said *don't*."

"Are you seriously going to stick your head in the sand about this?"

"Shut up," Caldera said. She was leaning forward on the sofa, staring at me, and her eyes were hard. "Get something clear—you are not a Keeper. You do not get to make accusations like that. Talk like that outside this room where other people can hear and you are going to get a fucking bridge dropped on you. You don't understand Keepers and you don't know how much shit you can get into doing this. I've gone to bat for you before, but I'm not jumping off a cliff just because you can't keep your mouth shut."

I drew back, slightly shocked. Caldera held my gaze for a few seconds more, then leant back again.

The silence stretched out. I knew it was supposed to be my place to say something, to keep things moving, but I felt jarred, out of place. "You know where the War Rooms are, right?" Caldera said once the pause had gotten long enough to become awkward.

"Yeah."

"You'll probably be with Haken."

"Okay."

"You got a number for him?"

"Not yet."

"I'll get you one."

Caldera took out her phone. I sat uncomfortably as she typed. From outside, I could hear the cars and the motorbikes on the main road, the sounds of their engines echoing through the brick and glass.

⁘⁘⁘⁘⁘

We talked a little longer, but it felt forced and our rapport was gone. When I said that I needed to go, Caldera didn't argue. I felt my shoulders relax slightly as I came out onto the Hackney street.

As I walked, I puzzled over what had just gone wrong. It wasn't the first fight I'd had with Caldera but it bothered me in a way the others hadn't. Mostly it was the unexpectedness. All the previous times that Caldera had been pissed off at me, it had been a direct consequence of something I'd done, and usually something I'd known full well she wouldn't be happy about. This was the first time we'd had a fight and I didn't know why.

It occurred to me that Caldera and I might have very different assumptions about loyalty. Amongst Dark mages, betrayal is an occupational hazard, something that comes with the lifestyle. It's like having one of your co-workers change jobs—you know it's going to happen sooner or later.

Apprentices talking to each other about their masters' plans, journeymen discussing whether the leader of their cabal is going to sell them out once the job is over . . . That kind of thing isn't a betrayal of trust, it's just good sense. It's not a big deal.

Maybe for Keepers, it *was* a big deal. They had an actual organisation, an ethos. Maybe there was a code, a way you were and weren't allowed to talk about it. Except . . . that hadn't been how Landis had reacted. I'd been pretty sure he'd understood what I'd been getting at last night, and he'd agreed with me, or at least hadn't told me to keep quiet.

So maybe it wasn't the Keepers. Maybe it was just Caldera. Now that I thought about it, I'd never really thought about her as a person. To me she'd always been a representative of her organisation, Keeper Number One. I wondered what her membership in the Order of the Star really meant to her, and what she thought of when she saw her other Keepers. Did she fit in? Or in her own way, was she an outsider too?

I shook my head. Whatever the reason, I needed to know more, and I wasn't going to get it from Caldera. I took out my gate stone and started looking for somewhere secluded.

Once I was back in my flat, I dug out my synchronous focus, programmed in a code, then channelled through it and waited. After only half a minute, it chimed and lit up. A figure appeared at the centre of the disc, carved from blue light.

"Hey, Talisid," I said.

"Verus," Talisid said. "I wondered when you'd call."

"Isn't acting all-knowing supposed to be the diviner's job?"

"You're not as unpredictable as you think." I heard Talisid sigh slightly. "Go on, then. Ask your question."

"Given your contacts, I'm pretty sure you already know what Caldera and I have been doing," I said. "I just asked her about how our case connects to White Rose. She didn't react well. Can you fill me in?"

"You don't ask much, do you?"

"It's just information," I said.

Most exchanges in magical society come down to trading favours. Cash is handy, and so are magic items, but all too often they just don't go far enough. Help from another mage, though . . . that's always useful. Over the past year, I'd done a lot of jobs for Talisid. They'd been for us as much as for him, but we'd still been helping him, and we hadn't asked for much in return. I didn't say *You owe me*, but Talisid understood exactly what I meant.

"All right," Talisid said. "How much did Caldera tell you about White Rose?"

"That they're an organisation that provides dark and highly illegal sexual services to mages, and they have a whole load of blackmail material on the Council."

"Strictly true, but a little misleading," Talisid said. "If White Rose directly blackmailed its clients, they'd have been destroyed long ago. They're more careful than that. They keep their client list absolutely confidential, and more importantly, that list is *known* to be confidential. However, they also make it known that should their organisation be seriously harmed, then that list would be released."

"So it's what—mutually assured destruction?"

"Yes. The number of Council mages who use White Rose's . . . services . . . is relatively small. But still large enough to cause a great deal of trouble. And the Council, as you may have noticed, dislikes trouble."

"So they just let them get away with it."

"Yes. In the same way that you, as an ex–Dark mage, support the torture, murder, and abuse that Dark mages perpetuate."

". . . What?"

"Don't make the mistake of thinking that the Council is monolithic." There was a slight edge to Talisid's voice. "The Guardians and the Keepers would love nothing more than to see White Rose eradicated. But Marannis, the Dark mage who runs White Rose, has no political ambitions. If he were using White Rose to expand his power base, he would be a strategic threat. But instead it seems he is quite content to preserve the status quo, which brings him into de facto alliance with the Centrists and Isolationists. As a result, White Rose has existed long enough for it to become . . . part of the landscape. A benign cancer. We have limited political capital, and making a concerted push to destroy White Rose would cause significant internal conflict in the Council. So for the past years our policy has been one of containment. Well, Vihaela's arrival on the scene could have changed that given time, but . . ."

I nodded, filing away the references to "our" and "we" to my mental dossier on Talisid and his position, and making a note to find out who Vihaela was. "Okay."

"So I hope you understand exactly how large a can of worms you opened when you and Caldera reported White Rose's name to the Keepers last night. You see, for all the crimes Marannis has committed in his time leading White Rose, the one thing he has been very careful to do is never break the Concord. Now all of a sudden, the Keepers have evidence linking White Rose not only with Rayfield's disappearance—or murder, as the case may be—but an attack on you and Caldera."

I still wasn't sure that it was actually White Rose that had been behind that attack, but I got the point. "How does the Rayfield case fit in?"

"Rayfield is—or was—apprentice to Nirvathis, who is attempting to secure a seat on the Junior Council. I assume you know this?"

"Yeah."

"What you may not know is that Nirvathis is an empty suit," Talisid said. "He was chosen by certain Light faction members to be a puppet. And the main controller of that puppet is your old acquaintance, Levistus."

"Shit."

"Yes. Levistus hopes to use this to secure himself a place on the Senior Council this coming year."

"Goddamn it," I said. "So that brings the whole thing with Morden in, too."

"Actually, at a conservative estimate, I would guess that by now around fifty percent of the active political population of the Light Council is involved in this affair of yours at one remove or another."

"And I'm in the middle of it."

"Yes." Talisid paused. "Verus . . . I haven't said anything about your choice to work more closely with the Keepers. I understand that in some ways it was a logical decision. However, given the direction things are taking, it might be advisable to reconsider."

"Right. Wouldn't want your prospective mole with Richard to associate himself too visibly with the other side, would we?"

"I understand that—"

"I'm not going back to Richard." My voice was flat. "Not as a double agent, not as a triple agent, not for you, and not for anyone else either. It's not going to happen. Ever. Understand *that*."

"Becoming involved in a conflict between Council factions will not help that goal in any way."

"I'll take that under advisement." I looked at the clock: it was past eleven. I needed to get moving. "I have to go."

Talisid paused again, and futures of him trying to persuade me further flickered briefly before vanishing. "All right. Good luck."

I cut the connection and prepared quickly for my trip, checking my phone as I did. There was a message from Luna: she'd arranged an appointment with Chalice for this afternoon. It was an e-mail rather than a voice mail, which I suspected she'd done so that it would be harder for me to tell her not to do it. I was still uneasy about sending her off to meet Chalice, but she had Anne, and I had too many other things on my plate already. I sent her a short message and put it out of my mind. Time to visit the War Rooms.

chapter 9

Beneath the Treasury in Westminster is an underground complex called the Churchill War Rooms. It's a museum, though not a well-known one; the tourists that crowd London in the holiday seasons usually want to see places like the British Museum and the National Gallery, and the Churchill War Rooms get less than a tenth of the visitors of either of those. It was built on the eve of the Second World War, a concrete labyrinth designed to withstand bombing raids, and during those long dark years it was the place from where Churchill and his cabinet directed the wartime efforts of Britain.

But the Churchill War Rooms isn't the only tunnel network beneath this city. People have been living in London for a very long time, and while there have been people, there have been mages. It was inevitable that the Council would set up their headquarters there. The original centre for the Council was a sprawling complex of spires and towers situated near the old St. Paul's Cathedral in the City. It was burnt to ash in the 1666 Great Fire of London, along with the old cathedral, the Royal Exchange, and pretty much everything else within the City limits. (Depending on who you believe, the destruction of Council headquarters might have been the *reason* for the Great Fire, and the "started in a bakery" explanation a cover-up, but that's another story.)

With their old base destroyed, the Council needed a new one, and an argument broke out as to where to go. The Isolationists wanted a place out in the countryside where they'd have as little interaction with normal humans as possible. The more moderate members wanted to pick a smaller city like Gloucester or Oxford. But the Directors wanted their power centre here, in the heart of the City, and as London was being rebuilt they took the opportunity to lay the foundations for what would become the new centre of magical government in Britain for the next three hundred and fifty years.

One of the reasons the Directors won the argument was that they'd noticed which way the wind was blowing. Traditionally mages had lived in towers, way up above the ground, to the point where it had become a status symbol. Unfortunately for the status-conscious mages of that time period, spells and technology had been evolving at a good clip, and the seventeenth century's brisk trade in Light-Dark warfare provided the more innovative mages on both sides with plenty of opportunity to give the new weapons a test-drive. Experimental data proved that that towers and artillery didn't mix. After several well-publicised incidents of traditionally defended towers being brought down by cannon fire, even the slower-witted members of the Light Council figured out that while towers might work for personal residences, they probably weren't the best choice for a military centre of government.

Building a centre of government *below* ground, on the other hand, was a different story. Compared to a traditional tower or castle, an underground complex would be harder to attack, easier to defend, and much more likely to go unnoticed by any normal people living on the surface. So in the aftermath of the Great Fire, the first tunnels were burrowed into the area beneath what's now modern Westminster. With earth and matter mages to do the bulk of the work, the tunnels expanded fast, and within a generation they'd become a sprawling warren. The Summer War did a good job of proving the security of the tunnel network, and the Council's stayed there ever since. Somewhere during one of the various Dark-Light skirmishes the tunnels started getting called the War Rooms, and the name stuck.

Or so the story goes . . . but I might have got it wrong. Light mages learn stories like this as they grow up, picking up the culture and the traditions, but I spent my childhood in the normal world and my apprenticeship surrounded by Dark mages, and a good part of my life since then has revolved around my shop. I've never really been inside the Light mage circles. For that matter, this was the first time I'd ever actually been to the War Rooms.

I suppose I should look on the bright side. I might be going to an indictment, but at least it wasn't mine. Yet.

Getting through security took longer than I expected. The security personnel hired by the Council are famous for their complete lack of any kind of a sense of humour, and I was kept answering questions until Haken finally showed up. "There you are," Haken said, then addressed the man who'd been interviewing me. "He's with me."

The security man checked Haken's signet, then handed my card back without a smile. "Took you long enough," Haken said as he led me into the tunnels.

"Sorry. First time."

"Fair enough. Just don't go wandering off, okay?"

We turned into a wider corridor, smaller passages branching off. To my surprise, the tunnels actually felt a lot more spacious than Keeper headquarters. The tunnel ceiling was high, a good twenty feet or so, and the walls were made out of some strange kind of stone, light grey with tiny white flecks that gleamed in the light. The tunnels were electric-lit, bright spherical lamps set at regular intervals along the walls, and the corridor was filled with people, men and women hurrying back and forth. There was a bustling, serious feel to the movement, brisk and impersonal.

The corridor opened up into a huge hallway with an arched roof. Craning my neck and looking upwards, I saw that the ceiling was divided by gold buttresses, each supporting chandeliers that glowed with white light. Massive cylindrical pillars ran from the buttresses down to the floor. The floor itself was grey-white stone, inlaid with patterns that looked like ancient coats of arms, and made of some hard material that echoed with our footsteps. And there were a lot of footsteps; I could see at least thirty people, some crossing the wide-open space at the centre and others talking in the shadows of the pillars. Circular alcoves were situated along the walls, and corridors led off deeper into the War Rooms. There were wooden desks at the far end, and beyond them I saw three sets of guarded doors.

"Come on, Verus," Haken said. I'd slowed down to stare. "You look like a tourist."

I caught Haken up. "Okay, I have to admit, this is impressive."

"This is the Belfry," Haken said. As we crossed the floor, he pointed out the doors beyond the desks. "Far doors lead to the Star Chamber and the Conclave. The ones on the right go to the Courts of Justice. If you're not Inner Circle, you aren't allowed in without a pass, so go to the clerk on the right."

We reached the far side and Haken spoke briefly with the woman behind one of the desks, then returned. "They've already started."

"What's started?" I asked as Haken headed towards one of the alcoves. "The indictment?"

"Yeah."

"So . . . how does this whole indictment thing work again?"

The alcoves were arched and lined in gold; a circular table sat in the middle of a curved bench. Haken dropped into the seat and leant back. "The indictment's a formal statement by the Council that someone's committed a crime. No indictment, no arrest."

I sat opposite. "I thought Keepers could make arrests on their own."

"Yeah, but it's not our authority—it's delegated. We can do small stuff on our own account, but anything important has to be authorised by a Council jury." Haken nodded towards the doors. "Rain—he's the Keeper in charge of the case—he's making an argument to a panel of judges. They say yes, we go out and arrest whoever's name's on the paper. They say no, we go back to the office and find something else to do."

I looked across at the closed doors. There was something vaguely disturbing about the idea that someone—maybe a lot of someones—was having their life decided by others right now. What would happen if an indictment like that was brought against me? "Are we supposed to be there?"

"We're on the witness list," Haken said. "They might call us up to give evidence, so we have to make ourselves available as long as the case is still going." He shrugged and pulled out a folder and a pen. "You might want to get comfortable."

I looked back at him, raised my eyebrows, then took a look around the Belfry. The place was still busy; it didn't seem as though nothing was happening. I settled down to wait.

          1 1 1 1 1 1 1 1 1

I t was three hours later.

"Okay, this is ridiculous," I said. "How long are they going to take?"

Haken shrugged. He had his folder open on the table and was reading through a thick report, making notes in the margins. "You're the diviner."

Watching the people walking back and forth over the floor of the Belfry had been interesting, for a while. After the first hour, I'd started checking everybody walking in our direction, looking to see if they were approaching us. I'd spent the second and part of the third hour writing e-mails on my phone. Now we were getting into the fourth hour and

I still hadn't spotted any future in which we'd be called for. "You know, I used to have all kinds of ideas about what working for the Council would be like. Never occurred to me that it mostly came down to sitting around waiting."

"Haven't worked with many bureaucracies, have you?"

"Not so much." I looked around. "Does this place have a sandwich shop or something?"

Haken looked at me. "You're asking whether the centre of government of the Light Council of Britain has a sandwich shop."

"Well, it'd be useful."

Haken shook his head.

"Does it usually take them this long?"

"No. Most indictments are open-and-shut. Five or ten minutes, once the formalities are done. Maybe an hour, if it's a breach of the Concord or they're authorising deadly force."

"So what does it mean if they've taken three hours?"

Haken leant back, resting his head against the padded bench, and tapped the table. His fingers rapped against the wood as he stared past my shoulder. "I heard there were going to be Council members at this one."

"I'm guessing that's not a good thing."

"Yeah. If they issue an indictment against all of White Rose, it's going to get ugly."

"Is that what they're arguing about? How seriously they're going to take this?"

"The ones who've really been on our case over Rayfield are the Guardians and the Unitarians," Haken said. "Probably the Guardians are going to be pushing for a full indictment and the Unitarians are going to want the whole thing dropped. Usually the Centrists are with the Unitarians on this one, but Rayfield was Nirvathis's apprentice, so . . ." He shrugged.

I tried to follow what Haken was getting at and couldn't. It was an uncomfortable feeling—usually I'm the one who understands what's going on. Now I was the clueless one and I didn't like it. Council politics are byzantine and I was out of my depth.

One part I did understand: the attack last night and what it meant. I studied Haken, searching through the futures to see how he'd react to what I was about to say. "Is that all there is?"

"What do you mean?"

"White Rose have their own areas of influence, don't they?"

"Maybe."

"From what I've heard, some of White Rose's clients work for the Council," I said. "Maybe they're *on* the Council."

Haken glanced out over the floor. It looked casual, but I noticed his eyes do a quick sweep of every area within earshot. "You might want to be careful where you talk about stuff like that."

"Yeah, well, if I'm getting called as a witness, you probably want me to have some idea what I should be saying. So am I right? It's not about which factions want to do something about White Rose, it's about which factions are in bed with them. Kind of literally, in this case."

Haken let out a breath and turned to me. "Look. You're coming into the middle of something that's been going for a long while. White Rose controls a lot of secrets, and if they get out, there are Light mages who are going to lose big. Now, you're not involved in the Rayfield case directly, but sooner or later someone's going to connect the dots and when they do, you need to keep your shit wired tight. If they can save their careers by disappearing you, they aren't going to think twice."

"Does this happen with every case the Order of the Star gets?" I asked. "One faction wanting one result, another faction wanting another, both of them willing to stab if you get the wrong answer?"

"Not every case. But the high-profile ones? Yeah."

I looked at Haken curiously. "How do you live with it? It's bad enough having to watch the people you're supposed to be policing without having to worry you'll get shot in the back by the ones who are supposed to be on your side."

Haken shrugged. "You survive. What else can you do?"

We sat in silence for a little while, listening to the murmurs and footsteps echoing around the Belfry. "Mind if I ask you something?" I said.

"Go for it."

"You've worked with Caldera a while, right?"

"Since last year."

"Does she have some kind of issues about this stuff that I should know about?" I said. "Because I was talking with her about this and it didn't go so well."

"What did you say?"

"I sort of implied that we might not be able to trust the people we were working for," I said. "Kind of like what you just told me."

"Ah."

"Ah?"

"You know what rank Caldera is?"

"In the Keepers? Journeyman, right?"

"That's right. Know how long she's been there?"

I shook my head.

"A while."

I looked at Haken. He looked back at me expectantly, as if he'd answered my question. "Maybe I'm being slow here," I said. "Could you lay it out for me?"

"Caldera's a bit of an idealist," Haken said. "You want a mentor at the investigation side of the job, she's great. Thing is, you want to get ahead, it takes a bit more than that. You have to play the game." Haken shrugged. "Caldera's good at what she does. But there's a reason she hasn't been promoted."

"Does that have anything to do with why she seems to get assigned the really dangerous jobs?"

"Not the really dangerous ones . . ." I kept looking at Haken and he raised a hand. "She volunteers, all right? I keep telling her to pass them up."

"You said she doesn't play the game," I said quietly. "Any chance she's made a few enemies in the Order of the Star? Some people who'd be happy to get rid of her?"

"No." Haken shook his head. "Caldera's a good Keeper. The brass know that. They send her out, they know she'll do a good job. But to get up the ranks, you need to do more

than be good at your job. You need friends in higher places."
Haken paused. "You want to make a go of it in our Order,
you might want to keep that in mind."

I raised my eyebrows. "I'm not a Keeper."

"Doesn't matter as much as you think," Haken said. "The
Council can always use people who know how to be discreet."

I gave Haken a sharp look. He held my eyes for a couple
of seconds, then shrugged and the moment was gone. "Just
something to remember."

". . . Sure."

Something moved in the futures. I looked to the right out
across the Belfry and saw a blond woman approaching us
over the polished floor, heels tapping on the stone. She was
dressed smartly, and as she came within earshot she
addressed us with an upper-class accent. "Keeper Haken?
You're required in court."

Haken nodded and put away his report. "See you when
I get out." Haken and the woman walked away towards the
opposite doors. They didn't look back.

As they disappeared behind the columns I went back to
scanning futures. With Haken gone I could look further—
it's always easier when you don't have someone nearby clut-
tering things up. After a moment, I spotted someone
relatively close. He was going to approach me this time, and
his name was . . . *Huh. Where have I heard that before?*

I sat for a few minutes, thinking. I didn't react as the
figure crossed the floor towards me and halted at the alcove.
"Mage Verus?" a voice said.

"Mm-hm." I looked up with a frown. I'd already seen the
man in my future sight: English features, nice suit, brown
hair, neutral expression. He looked like a Council functionary,
and I'd *definitely* seen him before. Where had it been . . . ?

"If you're not too busy, we'd like to speak to you concern-
ing your investigation," the man said. "My name is—"

"Barrayar."

Barrayar didn't react visibly. He obviously knew what I
was. "If you'd come with me?"

I rose and let Barrayar lead the way across the floor. He didn't speak, and I didn't either. Looking at Barrayar reminded me of . . . dancing? Music? Something involving the Council . . .

We reached the doors that Haken had disappeared through. The men guarding the position were Council security; they gave Barrayar a glance but didn't challenge him. We passed through into more corridors, branching left and right. There seemed to be fewer people around this time. Barrayar led me around a corner, towards a junction . . .

And suddenly I remembered where I'd met Barrayar before. I stopped dead. Barrayar paused, turned. "Is there a problem?"

I stared back at him for a second, then gave him a smile that didn't touch my eyes. "No," I said. "No problem." I kept walking.

We turned right at the T junction. I was searching through the futures in which I tried to open the doors we were passing, making myself a mental map of the place. The door on the right led into the back rooms of a courtroom, maybe the same one Haken was in. That could be useful. The one on the left led to an interview room. The one behind was some sort of cell. Next left was locked. Next right . . .

There you are. Next question: how was Barrayar going to react to what I was about to do? He didn't look physically imposing—he was shorter than average and on the slim side—but I'd already checked out the futures in which I attacked the guy, and I knew he was faster than he looked.

But then, so am I. Barrayar halted at the door on the right. "If you'd just . . ."

I walked past without slowing. "Excuse me," Barrayar said to my retreating back. "It's this way."

"I know."

Barrayar started to follow me. "Your meeting's in here."

I pointed forward. "Tell your boss I'll be in the . . . conservatory? Whatever you call the room with the water feature and the plants."

I kept walking. My back itched and I knew Barrayar was

staring at me. Watching the futures, I caught a few fleeting glimpses of action, there and gone too fast to see, then they cleared away and there was nothing. I reached the end of the corridor and turned the corner. Barrayar didn't follow.

You have to give the Council credit; they do build nice architecture. The conservatory was a large room with a high ceiling, structured as a kind of ceremonial garden. Small trees grew from carefully cultivated squares of earth, flowering bushes and shrubs grew up around raised sections of floor, and water bubbled up from a fountain into an indoor pool. There was enough greenery to provide concealment, and I had to scan through the futures to see whether I was alone in the room. I was, but I could tell that others were within earshot, close enough to hear a shout or scream. Good.

There was a stone bench by the pool and I took a seat. The only sound was the gentle splashing of the fountain. The air smelt sweet and flowery; there were rhododendrons and hydrangeas all around, blooming in red and violet. I breathed in and out slowly, forcing myself to relax. The things I said and did in the next few minutes were going to have very long-term consequences, and I needed to be calm.

Footsteps sounded from the direction of the hallway. I closed my eyes and kept them closed. The footsteps drew nearer, and I tracked their owner by sound and divination as he walked into the observatory, wound his way around the bushes, stepped up onto the rock garden, and came to a stop on the other side of the pool from me.

There was a silence. I didn't move.

The figure on the other side of the pool spoke. "Mage Verus."

I opened my eyes. Standing opposite me was a man in his fifties, with thin white hair. He was dressed in Council ceremonial robes, understated but expensive, and he had his hands clasped behind his back. His most distinctive feature was his eyes: they were pale, almost colourless, and they were watching me steadily.

"Councillor Levistus," I said. "I understand you wanted to see me."

It's strange how one encounter can change your life. Before today I had met Levistus exactly once. It had been in Canary Wharf, for a private conversation that lasted hardly any time at all. I'd been in and out of his office in under twenty minutes, and since then, we'd never communicated in any way—no phone, no e-mail, no messages. It was as though we'd never met.

And yet, as a result of that one brief meeting, Levistus had become my worst and most dangerous enemy out of all the Light mages in Britain. That fifteen-minute conversation had led to an escalating series of attempts on my life, ranging from subtle betrayals and reassignments that left me exposed, all the way up to outright assassination attempts employing everything from other mages to bound elementals to (on one particularly memorable occasion) a rocket launcher. Directly and indirectly, Levistus has tried to get me killed more times than any person alive, and given that he's a junior member of the Light Council, there's absolutely nothing I can do to him in return.

On the other hand, while I can't do anything to Levistus, the same doesn't apply to his agents. An awful lot of the people who'd gone after me on Levistus's orders were now dead, including a Keeper named Griff, a Light mage named Belthas, and an enslaved air elemental named Thirteen, as well as various lower-level employees whose names I'd never learnt. At some point Levistus must have gotten the message, because he'd stopped sending assassins. That didn't mean his feelings had changed. In fact, I was pretty sure it had made him like me less.

"I believe I asked you to come to the interview room," Levistus said. He had a measured, detached sort of voice. There was little variation in tone: his words were as expressionless as his face.

"Thanks, but I'm not walking into any more private interviews with you."

Levistus raised his eyebrows slightly. "And you believe that out here you are safe?"

"It makes it a little less convenient for you to get an air

elemental to asphyxiate me. Did you bring one along this time?"

"I would have expected you to know the answer to that already."

"I do. Just wondered whether you'd lie about it."

Levistus tilted his head slightly, studying me. "If I decided to devote my full resources to destroying you, how long do you think you would survive?"

"That's actually quite an interesting question," I said, raising a finger. "You *do* have a lot of resources, and I'm sure it's something you've done before. On the other hand, as I'm sure you've discovered, my particular type of magic is pretty good at dealing with this sort of problem. Personally, I'd put my chances of survival somewhere between thirty and forty percent. If you'd give me some more information about your plans, I'd be able to give you a more accurate estimate."

"Interesting," Levistus said. "So given that—by your own admission—your odds of survival would be less probable than the alternative, perhaps you could explain why you see fit to continue to antagonise me."

"I suppose you'd prefer if I came to you humbly and offered to apologise."

"It would be wise."

I sighed, then straightened my back and looked Levistus right in the eyes. "And if I don't, what are you going to do about it? If you had a way to kill me off efficiently, you'd have done it already. The only reason you stopped sending assassins was because it wasn't working. So no, I'm not going to bow and scrape. Maybe it'd make you a tiny bit less likely to *carry on* trying to kill me, but quite frankly, given the amount of shit you've caused me, it isn't worth the effort. Does that answer your question?"

I'd expected Levistus to get angry. Instead he only nodded. "Do you know why you are here?"

"Why I'm here in this room? Why I'm here on Earth? Why—?"

"Why the Council is currently deciding whether to issue

an indictment against the members of White Rose," Levistus said. "And why this situation has developed."

I shrugged. "Mostly because an assassin-mage by the name of Chamois decided to keep an appointment at Pudding Mill Lane."

"And do you know the name of his employer?"

I didn't answer.

"You know nothing of importance." Levistus's voice was unemotional; it was a statement, not an insult. "Once again, you have managed to involve yourself in a long-term conflict of which you have absolutely no understanding."

I spread my hands. "If you feel like educating me about the wider context, I'd be happy to benefit."

"Morden's goal for years has been to gain a seat upon the Council." Levistus watched me steadily. "As of this spring, a seat on the Junior Council will be open for reassignment. This is why Morden has timed his proposal as he has. Without Morden's involvement, the seat would be assigned to Nirvathis. At present, Morden lacks sufficient support to push his proposal through."

And Nirvathis is your puppet. Yeah, I could see why Levistus wouldn't want it to go to Morden. "Given our relationship, why exactly are you telling me this again?"

An expression of irritation flickered across Levistus's face. "This is common knowledge to anyone with an elementary understanding of Council politics. Please believe that I have an abundance of matters more pressing than providing you with remedial education."

That stung, especially since I knew it was true. "Go on."

"To push through his proposal, Morden needs to significantly change the political landscape of the Council," Levistus said. "He has chosen to do so by targeting White Rose. If he succeeds in destroying or suborning them, he will gain significant influence. Enough to win him his seat."

"Hold up," I said. "How exactly would destroying White Rose get Morden anything?"

Levistus had the expression of a teacher dealing with a particularly slow-witted pupil. "White Rose's influence is exercised through the information they possess. If Morden were to gain control of their records and databases, their influence would become his. He would become the most powerful Dark mage in the British Isles, in a position to begin taking over the Council from the inside."

"Somehow I doubt it'd be quite as simple as that, but I get your point. So if you get on so well with White Rose, why don't you use all of your abundant power to have the indictment squashed?"

Levistus's lips thinned. "Unfortunately, certain mages within the Council have taken this opportunity to pursue their existing feuds with White Rose as an organisation."

"Gosh," I said dryly. "I can't imagine why some of the Light Council would have a problem with an organisation based around sex slavery."

"This is not a laughing matter. If Morden achieves his goals, he will command more power than any Dark mage has had since the Gate Rune War."

"This is all very interesting," I said, "but I think there's something you've forgotten. You're right, I don't particularly like Morden. However, I also don't particularly like *you*. And since Mage Nirvathis is a friend of yours, it's a safe bet I'm not going to like him either. Why should I care whether the Council seat goes to a Light-aligned bastard or a Dark-aligned bastard?"

"I was under the impression that you claimed to oppose what Dark mages stood for."

"Yeah, you tried that one last time."

"And you claimed to be a mercenary. Perhaps it would prevent further miscommunications if you were more honest about your motivations."

"Okay then. I don't like you, I don't trust you, and I'm not helping you expand your political empire. Is that enough honesty?"

"And how does your old master factor into your calculations?"

My voice sharpened. "I don't see how that's anything to do with you."

"I assume you at least know that Morden and Drakh are working together?" I didn't answer, but after a moment Levistus went on as if I'd agreed. "Should White Rose fall, the greatest beneficiary will not be Morden. It will be your old master. Whatever his long-term plans, it appears they involve placing Morden on the Council." Levistus raised an eyebrow. "Perhaps you still serve him after all?"

"Go screw yourself."

Levistus watched me with an expression of polite inquiry. I drew a long breath and let it out, controlling myself. *Stupid. He's provoking me.* "I'm not responsible for what Richard does."

"You are Drakh's apprentice."

There was something in those words that was hard to describe. There was a kind of finality to it, as though Levistus were telling me something self-evident and timeless. Wind blows, fire consumes, I was Richard's apprentice, so it was and so it would always be. "I am who I choose to be."

"The steel does not choose to be made into a knife."

"I'm not your knife, or his."

"Then who are you, Alexander Verus?" Levistus asked. "What do you stand for? Whom do you serve?"

"You don't have the right to demand answers to those questions."

"Evasions. You have nothing upon which to stand. You do not understand yourself, and thus you are easily manipulated. Have you any conception of how far back your master has chosen your steps, shaped your path? You follow in his footsteps without the slightest understanding of how thoroughly you are controlled."

I felt a twinge of fear at that. I had no way of knowing how much Levistus knew, or whether he was simply guessing, but what he was saying was too close to the things I secretly feared. *If you can't defend, attack.* "Fine," I said. "Then what do *you* stand for, Levistus? You tried to have me killed, not once but over and over again. If I hadn't stopped you, you would have had Luna and Arachne killed too. You wouldn't have done it because you'd judged them as unworthy. You wouldn't even have done it because you particularly wanted them dead. They were just in your way. You ordered their deaths with no more concern than you'd have for checking your bank balance. You're talking as though you think I'm going to take your opinions seriously. What can you *possibly* say that can outweigh everything you've done? Why should I listen to you?"

"Because you are involved in matters beyond your control," Levistus said. "You no longer have the option of distancing yourself. Even should you abandon your position in the Keepers and go back to your isolation, it would only buy you a little time. You know that the confrontation will arrive. When it comes, on whose side will you stand?"

"I'm not on anyone's side."

Levistus made a disgusted noise. "Do not play the fool. If you hinder me, you help Drakh. If you fight against your old master, you assist me. This is elementary common sense."

"Is that how you justify what you do?" I asked. "Everything for the sake of victory?"

"The Council has maintained stability in this world for thousands of years," Levistus said. "Without us, the Dark mages and the monsters would have torn human civilisation apart millennia ago. Is that what you hope to accomplish?"

"And when Griff tortured Luna to get to the fateweaver? When Belthas tried to Harvest Arachne for her power? That was all for the greater good, was it? Don't give me that bullshit."

"Power will fall into someone's hands. Would you prefer that mages such as Drakh or Morden had it instead?"

"Don't dodge the question. How do you justify trying to kill me and my friends?"

"Agents are expendable," Levistus said. Those odd colourless eyes rested on me with no particular expression. "In the sufficiently long term, *everyone* is expendable."

"Including you?"

Levistus shrugged. It was an indifferent movement, and in an odd flash of insight I understood something about

Levistus that I hadn't realised before. Levistus *wasn't* doing this for himself, not really. He might act out of self-interest, but at some level he did genuinely believe that by keeping himself in power, he was making the world around him a better place.

It was a worrying thought. Someone who's amoral and selfish can be a threat to you, but they're also a threat to everyone *else*, and that tends to limit how much time they can spend on you personally. But someone who believes in what he's doing can convince other people that opposing you is the right thing to do. In the long run, that's a lot more dangerous. "Enough philosophy," I said. "What do you want?"

"The conflict between us has grown unproductive," Levistus said. "I am willing to consider a truce."

I studied Levistus. "In other words, you've got enough on your plate with Morden that you don't have the time to keep going after me as well."

"As I understand it, you have been making your own preparations for your old master's return," Levistus said. "I'm sure you have already calculated your chances of survival should you fight me and him at the same time. You would be wise to limit your enemies."

"I thought you said that Richard was controlling everything I did." I tilted my head, looking at Levistus curiously. "If I'm so much his servant, why would he be coming after me?"

"As I said—everyone is expendable."

"Including your allies." I tapped two fingers on my arm. "If all you wanted was a truce, all you needed to do was stop going after me. That means you want more."

"As a part of our agreement," Levistus said, "you will cease working against my interests. This means you will take no action against White Rose."

I'd carried on tapping my fingers; as Levistus spoke I stopped for a second, then continued. "You realise I'm working for the Keepers now," I said. I kept my voice casual. "I'm supposed to do what they tell me."

"The Keepers serve the Council. They do not all serve the same Council."

"Did it ever occur to you that this kind of corruption might be exactly why the Council has so much trouble effectively opposing Dark mages in the first place?"

"I am not here to engage you in a debate," Levistus said. "Well?"

"You know," I said, "I can't help noticing that this deal seems a little uneven. You started all this by telling me to work for you or else. When I took the 'or else,' you tried to have me killed. Now you're offering to *stop* trying to have me killed, and in exchange I'm supposed to commit treason yet again. Bit slanted in your favour, don't you think?"

"It is the offer you have."

"I'll make you a counteroffer," I said. "I'll go back to the Keepers and do my job. You go back to the Council and do your job. We both ignore each other."

"Please tell me you are not truly this stupid."

"You know something, Levistus?" I said. "I'm getting a little tired of your backhanded insults. You talk like you're the gatekeeper of civilisation and I'm the barbarian. It's irritating."

"Your irritation does not concern me," Levistus said. "And your counteroffer is noted and rejected. My terms stand. Do you accept them, or reject them?"

"Your 'terms' are a glorified threat. Either I do what you want, or you'll keep on being my enemy. You don't have anything to offer me."

"Correct. I will ask one final time. What is your answer?"

I looked at Levistus for a long moment. I could lie, obviously. Pretend to agree, then work against him. But I seriously doubted that Levistus was going to act any differently whether I told him yes or no. As far as he was concerned, I was just another Dark mage.

Just another mage . . .

"What happened to Leo?" I said.

Levistus blinked. It was a very small motion, there and gone in a second, but he didn't manage to conceal it. For the first time in the conversation, I'd surprised him. "Who?"

"The kid Caldera and I found last night." I kept my voice

calm. "The mages who sent the mantis golem took him. What happened to him?"

"I don't see how that's relevant."

I looked back at Levistus for a long moment. "No," I said at last. "I suppose you wouldn't."

"Well?"

"The answer's no," I said. "I'm not going to be your agent to protect White Rose. In fact, I'm not working for you in any capacity. I don't like you, Levistus. I've told you that twice already, and I don't think you've really listened, so I'll explain more thoroughly this time. I don't like how you act, I don't like what you do, and I don't like what you stand for. You represent everything I most hate about the Council. You have no respect for human life, you deal constantly in betrayals, and yet somehow you also manage at the same time to be completely convinced of your moral superiority over everyone who isn't a Light mage. Maybe you *are* Morden and Richard's enemy, and maybe helping one of you does mean hurting the other. But there's a certain point where trying to choose the lesser of two evils is just an exercise in futility. It doesn't matter which of you wins; you're both so bad that I honestly can't decide who'd be worse. Working for you would be just as corrupting as being Richard's apprentice, even if I trusted you enough to do it, which I don't." I looked up at Levistus. "Does that explain it well enough for you?"

Levistus looked back at me for a second. "You disappoint me."

"Not halfway close to how disappointed I am in you. When I was a kid, I read stories where the white wizards were all good and moral. Do you have any idea how depressing it was to find out what the Light Council was really like?"

"Enough."

Levistus didn't speak loudly, but there was something in his tone that made me fall silent. When I didn't speak for a few seconds, he went on. "You appear to be under the illusion that you have some level of choice. That this is an option that you are free to take or leave." He regarded me steadily.

"You claim that I have been your enemy. This is false. You are, at most, an inconvenience. Should you continue to work against me, that will change. For the first time, I will devote significant resources to your removal. I will not do so out of any personal grudge. I will do so because, as an active tool of Morden and of Drakh, you are a sufficient threat to warrant it." Levistus's voice was quite normal, and he looked at me steadily as he continued to speak. "You will be placed under siege. Your allies will be driven away or killed. Your bases of operation will be attacked. The process will not necessarily be swift. It is possible you will survive for months or even years. However, given enough time, the end is inevitable. You will be destroyed. And when you fall, there will be no one left to mourn your passing."

I looked back at Levistus, and as I saw the expression on his face I felt a chill. It wasn't so much the threat. I've been threatened plenty of times by mages, often in quite graphic and unpleasant ways. This was something different. I think what scared me the most was the matter-of-fact tone of voice. Levistus didn't think he was bluffing. He had absolutely no doubt that he could do what he promised, and it shook me more than I'd really expected. For the first time I had a real, almost tangible sense of just how dangerous the man standing in front of me was.

I didn't have an answer. Levistus turned and walked away. His footsteps echoed and faded into the background noise of the corridors, and I was left sitting alone by the pool. I looked down at the fish swimming in the water and wondered what I was going to do.

A few minutes later I heard footsteps and a woman in mage robes walked through the rock garden. As she saw me she paused. "Hello."

"Hi."

She gave me a doubtful look. "Should you be here?"

I took a moment to think about it. "I'm not really sure," I said at last. I rose to my feet and walked out the way I came.

chapter 10

It was a couple of hours later when Haken reappeared on the Belfry floor. He was frowning down at the stone and didn't look up as he made his way over. "How did it go?" I asked.

Haken glanced up. I was sitting in the alcove in exactly the same place I'd been in when he'd left. "What?"

"The indictment."

"Oh," Haken dropped onto the bench. "Could have been worse." He shrugged. "Rain got the worst of it, he's the one in charge. Going to screw up his chances for his next promotion."

"So what did they want to know?" I asked. "More about the case?"

"No one cares about the case anymore. This whole thing's become about White Rose. That's what the prosecutor was pushing for—they want an indictment against the whole organisation. Centrists aren't going to agree to that but . . ."

"Then what are they going to do?"

"Fuck knows," Haken said with a sigh. "All I know is

that we'll be the ones the shit lands on. Come on, let's get out of here."

We got up and started walking out of the Belfry the way we'd arrived. "They kept you in there a long time," I said.

"Lot of questions."

"When did they let you out?"

"Look, Verus, you know what 'closed proceedings' are, right? I'm not supposed to talk to you about this stuff."

I nodded. "Sure."

We headed down the tunnels, making the rest of the trip in silence. I didn't say what I was thinking. While I'd been free in the Belfry, I'd kept myself busy by searching through the futures of questioning the other mages there. Most hadn't been talkative but I'd found one clerk who'd been willing to help, and she'd told me (or rather, would have told me) that Haken had gotten out of the indictment proceedings forty-five minutes ago.

I was fairly sure it didn't take forty-five minutes to walk from the judicial chambers to the Belfry. I wondered what Haken had been doing before rejoining me.

। । । । । । । ।

Night was falling by the time we made it out onto the city streets. "You're not on the witness list anymore, but you're still on call," Haken said. "When they make their decision there's a good chance you're going to be called up. Make sure you're ready to move on short notice."

"Tonight?"

"Maybe. They might move fast on this one."

I nodded. "Oh, one more thing," Haken said. "You still have that focus you found at the station?"

"Sure."

Haken held a hand out. "You'd better hand it in."

I took a green spherical focus out of my pocket and passed it over. "You're going to drop it off at the station?"

"Yeah. You might as well go home and get some rest. Don't know when we'll get the order to move."

"See you tomorrow."

I walked away down the road. The entrance to the War Rooms that we'd used was on a side street, and there wasn't much traffic. Behind me, I could sense Haken taking out his phone to make a call. I turned the first corner, stopped, put my back up against the building, and waited.

Watching through my future selves, I saw Haken talk on his phone for a few minutes. Eventually he hung up, gave a glance in the direction in which I'd disappeared, then turned and went back into the building that led down into the War Rooms.

"That's not the way back to the station, Haken," I murmured. I waited for a few minutes more just in case he reappeared, then headed for Westminster.

ıııııııı

I caught the Jubilee line and then the London Overground, alighting at Hampstead Heath. By the time I stepped off the train and walked into the Heath itself, it was night. The sky was overcast, thick clouds blocking out both starlight and moonlight, leaving the Heath pitch-black. A cold wind blew as I walked deeper into the park, whipping at my clothes and filling the night with the sound of rustling leaves. There was no way to see and hardly any way to hear. Most people avoid the Heath on nights like this, and for good reason.

But I'm not most people, and a night like this suits me just fine. With my divination I can navigate in pitch-darkness as though it were broad daylight, and against the vast emptiness of the park, the few wandering people stood out like searchlights. As I strode through the night, the wind gusting through my hair, I felt my spirits rise. The War Rooms had been tense, claustrophobic. Out here, alone in the cold and the blackness, I felt at home.

I didn't hurry making my way to Arachne's cave. When I finally stepped down into the ravine, I took a moment out of the wind, then stepped to the overhanging tree, touched two fingers to a root that was quite invisible in the darkness, and spoke into thin air. "It's me."

Arachne answered instantly. "Alex! Come right in. Everyone's waiting."

With a soft rumble the earth parted, revealing a yawning cavern. I stepped through and the earth and roots wove themselves shut behind me.

ı ı ı ı ı ı ı ı ı

Arachne's cavern felt warm and peaceful compared to the park outside. Globe lights cast a soft glow over the rocky cave, picking out the rainbow colours of the clothes draped over the sofas. Arachne was crouched at the far end. She's a giant spider who looks almost exactly like a blue-and-black tarantula that's been scaled up to ten feet tall, and she's probably the nicest magical creature you'll ever meet, assuming she'd let you in her lair in the first place, which isn't all that likely. Nowadays my little group of friends are all on Arachne's guest list, but it took them a while. Arachne's got her own reasons to be cautious of mages, and it's lucky for me that she isn't the type to judge all by the actions of a few.

And speaking of my friends, they were all there: Luna, waving from a sofa; Variam, leaning back near to her with his arms spread out; Anne, cross-legged in a chair of her own. "Hey, sleepyhead," Luna said as I walked up to them. "What kept you?"

"Don't even start," I told her. "However bad you think your day was, mine was worse."

"Our day wasn't *that* bad," Anne said.

"Don't tell him that!"

I smiled, then dropped into one of the sofas and shut my eyes with a sigh. I spend so much of my time looking ahead, watching for danger. Arachne's cave is one of only a handful of places where I don't have to do that. Behind the webs and the wards, I'm protected, and for once I can turn off my precognition and just relax. It's good to have somewhere you feel safe, even if it's only for a little while.

"So who wants to go first?" Variam said.

"Oh, go on," Luna said. "I know you've been itching to tell us."

"Alex?" Variam said. "You awake?"

"Just a little tired." I opened my eyes. "I'm listening."

Variam didn't need any more encouragement. "Okay," he began. He looked as though he'd just arrived, although he was wearing his street clothes: some masters keep their apprentices to a formal dress code, but Landis isn't one of them. "We got a notice this morning that the Order of the Shield might be getting deployed, so we spent all day getting ready. First thing I did was look up the Order files on White Rose. Apparently the one from White Rose that the Council are thinking about going after is this woman called Vihaela."

I searched back and remembered what Talisid told me. "The leader of White Rose is a guy called Marannis. Vihaela's his second, right?"

"Kind of," Variam said. "From what I heard it's Vihaela who mostly runs everything. Some people are saying it looks like she's going to take over. Anyway, she's the one everyone's scared of."

"And she's a Dark mage, right?" I said. I thought for a second and shook my head. "Don't really know anything about her."

"I do," Anne said.

We all looked at her in surprise. "Not in a good way," Anne said. "When mages want to tell horror stories about life mages, she's one of the names they use."

"Records have her listed as a death mage," Variam said. "They're not as far apart as you'd think."

"What kind of horror stories?" Luna asked.

"She's a torturer," Variam said. "The one who breaks down the White Rose slaves before they get handed over to the mind mages. If the reports are true, that was how she got into White Rose in the first place. Apparently even though she pretty much runs the organisation, she still deals with the new slaves herself. It's hard to find out about her because there are hardly any witnesses. Most of the people she gets her hands on never get away, and the few the Council find are too afraid to talk. Even if they're miles away, they're so terrified of her coming after them that they don't even want to say her name. The only full account we've got is from some girl who used to be one of the brothel slaves. She said that Vihaela ran White Rose on a points system. If you did something to make a customer unhappy, you lost points. At the end of the month, whoever had the lowest points got transferred to her lab. They didn't come back."

"The stories are that Vihaela's supposed to use them for experiments." Anne shook her head. "I don't know if they're true. I want to believe that it's just other mages trying to justify being afraid of life mages, but . . ."

"How do you know this stuff?" I said curiously. "Is this common knowledge in the apprentice program, or . . . ?"

"First I've heard of it," Luna said.

"It's not," Anne said. She didn't meet our eyes. "I'd rather not talk about it."

"I'm afraid that Anne's stories aren't exaggerations," Arachne said. She'd been sitting quietly, working away on a complicated pattern of green and blue thread as she listened; now she spoke, her voice clicking gently. "From what I've heard, if anything, they understate the case."

"Have the Council tried to do anything about her?" I asked.

"No one'll agree to give evidence against her in court," Variam said. "Apparently she goes out of her way to hunt down anyone who tries to spread stories."

"Lovely," I said. "Well, she sounds absolutely horrific. I really hope I don't run into her."

"There's more," Variam said. "She's connected to some high-up people with the Council. Guess whose name comes up linked to her?"

"Please don't say Levistus."

"Nirvathis."

"Great," I muttered. *This just keeps getting better and better.*

"Wasn't he Rayfield's master?" Luna said. "The one who started all this . . . ?"

"Nirvathis does what Levistus tells him," I said. I frowned. "And Leo was meeting his apprentice at Pudding Mill Lane . . ." It sounded as though it must have been Vihaela who'd sent him there, or someone working for her. Leo had been carrying that little focus . . . What had been on it?

"This is really confusing," Luna said. "Who's on which side?"

"There aren't just two sides," I said. "More like four. How did things go with Chalice?"

Luna glanced at Anne, then turned back to me. "Good, I think."

"I'm guessing there wasn't any trouble."

Luna shook her head. "Nothing like that. Though . . . I got the feeling she might have known that we'd been preparing for it."

"Chalice isn't stupid," I said. Even from our brief meeting, that was something I was sure of. "She knows we've got reasons not to trust her. She'd have expected you to bring backup."

"I don't think she brought anyone," Anne said. "Not that I could see."

"Mm," I said. "She probably wouldn't need them."

"Well, we didn't talk long," Luna said. "It was mostly about chance magic. I was kind of expecting her to quiz me but she acted like she knew all she needed to already."

"Did she say anything about the case?"

"No. She did ask what I thought about Morden's proposal, though." Luna shrugged. "I told her that since I wasn't a mage, it didn't matter much to me. She told me not to be so sure."

"Huh." *I wonder what she meant by that?*

"So?" Luna said. "What about you?"

"Well," I said. "I spent half the day sitting around in a very nice waiting room, and about half an hour getting very thoroughly threatened by Levistus. He says if I don't play along with what he wants, he's going to destroy me. He also implied he'd do the same to you."

Luna, Anne, and Variam exchanged looks. "Um," Luna said. "Details?"

I told them the story.

Once I'd finished, there was a brief silence. "Okay then," Luna said.

"What do you mean, 'okay then'?" Variam said. "Fuck that guy."

"Vari, wait," Anne said in her soft voice. "We weren't there when you had to deal with this the first time." She looked between me and Luna. "Can he really do it? Everything he's threatening?"

I hesitated. "Put it this way—I wouldn't like to test it."

"We beat his assassins before," Luna said.

"I don't think it's his assassins that we should be worrying about," I said. "You remember the Nightstalkers? The reason they were left to go after me was because of him. It's that kind of thing I'm really scared of. If he sends an assassin, I can fight them. But if he just gets other Light mages to do the work instead . . . He could probably turn half the Council against me if he really tried."

"This is so *stupid*," Luna said. "He's got this fight with Morden. The whole Council is fighting amongst themselves about White Rose and this proposal with the Dark mages. And he decides to go after *you*?"

I didn't answer. What I was really thinking was something so childish that I was embarrassed to say it out loud: *It's not fair.* I already had Richard to worry about. Wasn't one overwhelmingly powerful enemy enough?

"So fuck him," Variam said. "He's not allowed to do this."

"Oh, yeah, that's really going to help," Luna said in exasperation. "We'll tell him he's not allowed."

"Yeah, well, what else are you going to do?" Variam asked me. "Do what he tells you?"

"It doesn't even sound as though he can," Anne said. "Levistus said that he wanted White Rose protected. If Alex stays here and they go through with their plan and arrest them, isn't Levistus going to blame Alex anyway?"

"Somehow I don't think he's going to give me the benefit of the doubt."

"So no point worrying, is there?" Variam said.

"I don't think it's that simple," Anne said.

"Well, we've got one thing going for us," I said. "We might be juggling multiple enemies, but Levistus is too. He's too busy with this political duel he's fighting."

"Until it ends," Anne said.

"And if he loses, he's not going to be happy." I sighed. "On the other hand, if he wins, then he'll have even *more* influence. And he wanted to go after me anyway. I'm not actually sure which would be worse."

"Alex?" Arachne said. "Would you like a suggestion?"

"Please."

"It seems to me that you have already established what your decision has to be," Arachne said. "Even if you could aid Levistus—which may or may not be possible—you could not trust him to uphold his end of the deal. You would be adding to the resources of one proven to be your enemy. As well as mine. That is without taking into account that aiding Levistus would by default bring you into conflict with other factions of the Council. Besides . . ." Arachne looked down at me. "You know what White Rose are. You know what they do. Do you really want to help them?"

"No," I admitted.

Arachne made a movement, something like a shrug. "Well then."

"I guess that does simplify things, doesn't it?" I got up and walked absentmindedly over to one of the tables, moving a pile of clothes aside to pull something out from underneath.

"Can't we do something about Levistus?" Luna said. "I mean, he's trying to subvert the Keepers. That's kind of like treason."

"It *is* treason," Variam said. "Problem is, all the rest of the Council do it too."

"But it's still illegal. Couldn't Alex go to the Council and tell them what he told us?"

"Levistus would just deny it."

"Well, what if Alex recorded him? Wear a wire, like they do on those police shows?"

"You ever heard of a Council case getting decided by audio recordings?" Variam said.

"What do you mean?"

"You know how sound mages can reproduce any voice they like?" Variam said. "That's why. No Council court's going to admit it."

"Well, what if—?"

"Um . . ." Anne said. "Alex? What's that?"

Variam and Luna turned to look at me. I'd returned to the sofa and I was tossing a pale green sphere back and forth from hand to hand. "Data focus," I said.

Anne looked puzzled. "It looks like the same one from before."

"That's because it is."

"Wait," Luna said. "Didn't you say you gave it to Haken?"

"I gave *a* data focus to Haken."

Variam stared for a second, then his eyebrows rose. "You seriously—?"

"Yep."

"Are you nuts?"

"Somehow I don't think they're going to take me to court over it," I said. "Besides, how are they going to know the difference?"

Luna was looking between me and Variam. "Wait. You gave Haken a duplicate?"

"Alex came to me yesterday and asked for my help," Arachne said in her clicking voice. She was still working away on the pattern of thread between her legs: it was beginning to take shape, looking like a dress of some kind. "Those old focuses are quite simple to duplicate when you know the trick. You can't copy the information inside, of course, but other than that there's no easy way to tell the difference."

"And what are you going to do when they *do* look inside?" Variam said.

"The only way they'd be able to look inside would be if they were the intended recipient," I said. "How exactly would a Council mage explain that they were receiving a private message from White Rose? And how would they explain how they'd got their hands on it when it was supposed to have been in a Keeper evidence locker? They can't go public either."

"But won't they know it was you?" Anne said.

"Maybe. Or they might just blame White Rose."

"Wait a second," Luna said. "Wasn't it Haken who asked for that focus?"

"Yup."

"You think . . . ?"

"I've been getting a bit suspicious of Haken over the last day or so," I said. "I don't know exactly who he's working for, but it's not just the Council. What I'd really have liked would have been to trace that focus he took and figure out where it ended up, but . . ."

"It would have been too easy to annul it," Arachne said. "Besides, it wouldn't have given you more than a direction."

Variam still looked sceptical, but he stayed quiet. "I've been thinking the same thing as you, about getting some sort of proof," I said to Luna. "I've got the feeling that's what this thing is—the information inside, I mean. White Rose might get money for what they do, but their real power's information. I think that's what's in here. Blackmail material. Probably meant for Levistus in exchange for some other information paid in kind." I sighed and held it up to the light. "Problem is, we can't read it."

"If you can't read it, why'd you take it?" Variam said.

"Bargaining chip."

"Wait a second," Luna asked. "It was Vihaela who sent this focus, right?"

"Can't prove it," I said. "But from what Xiaofan said, it sounds like it."

"Then if she was sending it to Levistus, why would she send it with someone like Leo?" Luna asked. "Wouldn't it make more sense to use someone who could fight? Or something that couldn't be intercepted?"

"That's the bit I can't figure out either," I said with a

frown. "Maybe Vihaela was so convinced it couldn't be read that she didn't care if it got lost?"

"There's really no way to read it if you're not the right person?"

"It's quite impossible," Arachne said. "Barring some extremely high-level methods that I seriously doubt anyone in this country could access."

"So it *is* possible?" Variam asked.

"Variam, the things I'm referring to are orders of magnitude more powerful than anything we've been discussing. If your enemies have access to *those*, then you have considerably bigger problems."

"Listen to Arachne," I told Vari. "If she says it can't be done, it can't be done."

"Isn't that a little strange though?" Anne said.

I looked at her. "What do you mean?"

"Well, you said that the air mage who attacked you wanted that focus," Anne said. "Now you're saying that Haken might have wanted it, too. If no one except the person it's meant for can read it, why would they care if it got lost?"

"Maybe they need to know what's on it," Luna said.

"But Alex said it had just been used."

"No, you're right," I said. "Everyone's been acting as though the information on this thing is something sensitive. They're not afraid of it being lost—they're afraid of it being read. But if no one can read it . . ."

"Well, maybe they don't know that," Luna said.

"But they'd have to . . ." I stopped.

"I still think there has to be some way," Variam said. "I mean, you can break codes in computers, right? So if there's some trick—"

"That's it," I said. "That's it, isn't it?"

Variam looked at me. "You mean—?"

"It doesn't matter if it's possible. It just matters whether they *think* it is." I jumped to my feet. "I need to go."

"Wait," Anne said. "What's going on?"

"And why are you running off?" Luna said. "Can't you explain why—?"

"I don't know if I'm right yet," I said. "But if I am . . . I think I know who's doing this. Meet me back at the shop. Arachne, thanks again." I turned and headed up the tunnel.

ı ı ı ı ı ı ı ı ı

Once I was outside Arachne's lair, I used a gate stone to go home. Then I started making calls.

Most of the mages I tried to get in touch with weren't much help. Mages tend not to make themselves easily available via phone, and the ones I did get through to didn't have a clue what I was talking about. But after an hour, I finally managed to find the mage I'd wanted to speak to.

"It's the middle of the night," Lensman said peevishly. He sounded a lot more irritable than he had been when I'd spoken to him on Friday. I'd probably caught him about to go to bed. "Can't it wait?"

"No, this is important. I need to know if you've heard anything about a new method of breaking the signature lock on a data focus."

"A what?"

"A data focus. You know, the old Keeper model."

"How did you hear about that?"

I snapped my fingers with my free hand. *Yes.* "Then it's real?"

"Well, I haven't confirmed it. But I just heard the same thing. Used almost those exact same words actually—"

"Where did you hear it from?"

"From Verde . . . he wasn't sure where it had come from. Is it true?"

"Not a clue."

"Because if it is, it'll have huge implications for data security. You know how many old Council records are on those things? The whole reason anyone used them was that they were supposed to be unbreakable, but if there's a way of getting round it—"

"Did you just hear about it today?"

"Yes, this morning. Look, Verus, what's this about?"

"I don't know yet," I said honestly. All right, half-honestly.

I didn't know for sure, but I had a *really* strong suspicion. "But I should know whether that rumour's true or not soon. I'll tell you when I do."

"All right." Lensman didn't sound entirely convinced, but I had the feeling he was keen to get off the line. "I'll talk to you then."

I hung up the phone, opened a notebook, and started writing. I kept going for a couple of minutes, then leant back and tapped the base of the pen against my teeth, looking down at what I'd written.

At least one group and probably more had tried to get this focus, in a manner that suggested that it contained important information involving White Rose. There were rumours going around that there was a new technique to break this focus's encryption. Arachne was convinced that that was impossible.

Put that together with what was happening right now—the indictment against White Rose. Talisid had explained that the reason White Rose had stayed safe for so long was through mutually assured destruction. As long as everyone believed that White Rose's data was secure, no one would move against them. But if you managed to convince enough people that it *wasn't* secure . . . and acted in such a way as to make them believe that the data being released was only a matter of time . . .

"Yes," I said out loud. It made sense. The only catch I could see was that for the plan to work, you'd need to be able to predict what Levistus would do. But given that all the signs indicated that they *had* successfully predicted that, that could just mean they had access to information I didn't know about.

If I was right, then I knew who was behind all this. It was the same person who'd hired Chamois. And the reason they were doing it was . . .

My excitement died as I realised the implications. Yes, I knew who was behind this. But they were on the opposite side to White Rose. I could stop their plan—maybe—but that would mean helping White Rose continue to do what they did.

Levistus had been right after all: if I hurt one side, I'd be helping the other. Whatever I did, someone I hated was going to profit from this. Was there a third option, some way I could make both of them lose? I couldn't think of one. It was too binary—if one side was weakened, the other would profit.

I stared down at the notebook, thinking. I didn't come up with any solutions, and at last I shook my head. Worrying about which side I wanted to win was a long-term concern—right now what I should be worrying about was staying alive. If I was right, then I didn't have much time. The indictment with White Rose was going to come to a head soon, and when it did, at least one of the factions involved in this was going to try to neutralise me somehow, probably by killing me.

The problem was, I couldn't do anything to preempt them. If I attacked them directly then I'd find myself up against the Keepers. I was going to have to figure out their plan and come up with a counter on the fly.

Still, that didn't mean I had to improvise *everything*. I could make some preparations of my own. And I had my own allies too. I just needed to figure out how to use them.

I got up and headed for my safe room. I was going to have to think very carefully about what to bring with me.

chapter 11

I never sleep well the night before a battle. In this case I hadn't even known for sure if it *was* going to be a battle, which actually made things worse, since I'd stayed awake for hours trying to plan for all the possible scenarios. I fell asleep late, got up early, and by midmorning I'd finished my preparations, meaning that I spent the hours around noon with nothing very productive to do. I ended up rechecking things I'd checked already, talking to Luna, and trying not to wear myself down. It was a relief when the call finally came.

"We need you down at the station," Haken said as soon as I picked up. "Briefing's in forty-five minutes."

"I'll be there," I told him, then put the phone down and looked at Luna. "We're on."

"It could be—"

"It's not."

"Yeah." Luna sighed. "Wish I could come."

"You know that's not an option. Besides—"

"I know, I know. I'll be ready."

"Well, you never know," I said as I got to my feet. "Maybe

when you pass your journeyman tests you'll end up joining the Keepers."

Luna raised her eyebrows. "Yeah, right."

"You're the one who gave me the push into joining them."

"I didn't think it was going to turn out like this."

"I think I would have been drawn into this one way or another." I glanced at Luna. "You going to be okay on your end?"

"It's not like we've got much to do, is it?" Luna said. "What if we don't get the call?"

"Then it means everything's been resolved in a nice peaceful compromise and all the participants have gone away happy."

Luna gave me a sceptical look. "Do you think that's going to happen?"

I slung my bag over my shoulder. "No."

"I don't like sitting around when you're going out like this."

"Don't worry," I said as I headed for the door. "I think you'll be getting your share of excitement."

"That's not what I'm worried about." Luna sighed again. "Good luck."

⁞⁞⁞⁞⁞⁞⁞⁞⁞

I arrived at Keeper HQ, went through security, and was directed upstairs. The building was busy, people bustling around and running errands. As I climbed the stairs I tried to feel if there was something different, some note of anxiety or tension in the air, but I couldn't sense it. The Keepers are a big organisation, and at office level it was business as usual.

I found the briefing room on the second floor, checked to see who was inside, and rolled my eyes. I was tempted to wait out in the corridor, but given the collection of magic types, it was a safe bet that someone was already tracking my movements. I took a breath and opened the door. The room was windowless and decorated in the same ugly cheap-looking fashion as the rest of Keeper HQ, with chairs, small tables, and a whiteboard, along with a battered-looking projection focus sitting on a stand. There were seven people in the room, and all of them turned to look at me as I walked in.

"You're fucking kidding me," one of the men said. It was Slate, my old friend from Red's. "What's *he* doing here?"

"Love you too, Slate." I walked in and dropped into a chair next to Haken.

"No," Slate said, addressing the room. "No way. We're not taking him."

"Slate," Haken said wearily. "Not now, all right?"

Slate shut up, but the look on his face made it clear that this wasn't over. "This is Mage Verus," Haken said to the others.

"We know who he is," one of the other men said.

"Good," Haken said. "Then you know why he's here."

A woman on the other side of the room was looking me up and down. "You're the one saying you fought a mantis golem?"

"Yes."

"How come you're still alive?"

"It wasn't just a mantis golem," I said. "And it wasn't just me."

"Aren't you a diviner?" the woman said, and laughed. "What was it really, a crawler?"

"Tell you what," I said. "How about you go find the cleanup team who spent Saturday night scraping mantis golem off the floor in Uxbridge? Tell them it was a crawler and see what they say."

"Hey!" Haken said. He looked between me, Slate, the woman, and everyone else, glaring at all of us. "You all finished?"

I shut up. Slate and the woman didn't exactly look submissive but they didn't open their mouths either. "You have a problem with each other, deal with it on your own time," Haken said. "We've got a job to do."

No one argued. Haken started doing introductions. I paid attention.

Haken I knew, obviously, and it became clear as he went from person to person that he was the highest-ranking mage in the room . . . although maybe not by much. Slate I also knew, unfortunately, and the man who'd spoken up earlier was one I'd seen in Red's but hadn't put a name to, big and tough-looking, mixed race with dark brown skin. From his body language and seating position I had the feeling he was on Slate's side. Haken introduced him as Trask.

The woman who'd been poking at me was called Lizbeth—I didn't know why she wasn't using a mage name, and I didn't ask. She was in her late twenties, with blond hair in a bob cut and a glint in her eye that suggested she wasn't done messing with me either. The other woman in the room was also the only other person besides me who wasn't a Keeper. She was tall with long brown hair, well-dressed and good-looking in an understated way. Her name was Abeyance, and she was apparently a Keeper auxiliary and timesight specialist. She greeted me with professional reserve.

The last two men were also Keepers, but ones I hadn't met before. One was fair-skinned and nondescript-looking, the other fat and Hispanic, and when Haken told me their names—Cerulean and Coatl—I was none the wiser. It wasn't really a surprise; there aren't all that many Keepers in Britain, but they keep to themselves and if you don't move in their circles you usually only see one when something's gone wrong. Slate had gone back to interrogating Abeyance about something or other, and Lizbeth was about to open her mouth again, when the door opened and the last man came in.

Keeper Rain was the captain of Caldera's section. He was tall and slender, with very dark skin and hair cut so short that his head was nearly bare. I'd never spoken to Rain, though Caldera seemed to respect him. He wasn't dressed in any way that particularly stood out—just a neat-looking business suit—but everyone turned to look as he stepped inside, and all conversation in the room cut off. "Good afternoon, people," Rain said as he walked to the front of the room. He had a deep voice and a measured, deliberate way of speaking. "We've got a lot to cover and not much time, so I'll get straight to it. The Council has authorised the interrogation of Mage Vihaela, the second-in-command of

White Rose. You"—his eyes swept the group—"are going to bring her in for questioning."

There was no audible reaction. I looked around to see that no one seemed particularly shocked. Obviously they'd seen it coming. "What's the charge?" Slate asked Rain. He seemed to have forgotten about me.

"Suspicion of involvement in the Rayfield case," Rain said. "Which as of today is being treated as a murder."

"So we're arresting her?"

"No," Rain said. "The Council has decided not to issue a formal indictment."

A murmur went up at that. "So what are we bringing her in for?" Lizbeth said. "Littering?"

"The Council believes that an indictment would risk escalating the conflict." Rain didn't show anything on his face, but somehow I got the impression he wasn't happy. "Vihaela will be brought in, but she will not be formally charged."

"Oh, this is bullshit," Slate said.

"What, we're supposed to say pretty please?" Lizbeth said. "What happens when she tells us to go fuck ourselves?"

"You may not have a formal indictment," Rain said, "but you are acting under direct Council orders. That means if you encounter any resistance, you'll be free to use necessary force."

Both Slate and Lizbeth perked up at that. Rain noticed. "I said *necessary* force." Rain didn't raise his voice, but his gaze rested on the two of them. "You are not pulling in some two-bit adept, and you are going to have eyes on you for this one. You pull some cowboy shit, I will hang you out to dry. Understand?"

Slate and Lizbeth had stopped smiling. "Yeah," Slate said.

"Lizbeth?"

"I got it," Lizbeth said.

"The six of you," Rain nodded to the Keepers, "will be the field team for this operation. You will have two auxiliaries attached to you for the duration, mages Abeyance and

Verus. Abeyance is a time mage and Verus is a diviner. They'll provide information support on the ground. Haken has field command. Slate, you're his second. The seven of you report to Haken, and Haken reports to me." He glanced around. "Any questions?"

"Uh, yeah." One of the other Keepers, Coatl, raised his hand. "So if I need to be excused to take a shit, should I be going to Slate, or do I ask Haken? You know, if it's an emergency."

"Hey," Lizbeth said. "If *you're* taking a shit, it's always an emergency."

"Love you too, Liz."

"Are you hearing this?" Slate demanded to Rain. "Why's this clown on the detail?"

"Kiss my arse," Coatl told Slate. "If the Council really gave a fuck, we'd have an indictment already."

"How about you—" Haken began, then stopped as Rain raised a hand. Rain looked at Coatl. "You have something to say?" Rain asked. "Say it."

"Council can't make up their mind what they want," Coatl said. "Everyone's got their own piece." He shrugged. "I'm just saying."

"Yeah, well, maybe they do," Rain said. "But we've got a missing apprentice and a missing witness, and that's not going away. So if we're going to do this thing, we're going to do it right." He looked around. "Does anyone have a problem with that? Because if you do, there's the door."

Coatl and Cerulean looked away. Lizbeth and Slate looked back at Rain with neutral expressions. Abeyance stayed quiet.

"All right," Rain said at last. "I take it from your silence you're ready to do some work." He fitted something into the projector, then glanced over at the light switch. It moved with a click and the room was plunged into darkness for a moment before the projection focus activated and a life-sized figure materialised in front of us, shedding a glow over the group.

Like most projection images, the figure outlined before us was brighter and clearer than an ordinary image would be, more real than real. The shape was that of a woman, outlined in blue light, perfectly detailed but frozen and still. She was tall and slim, with a long neck, a willowy build, skin so dark it was nearly black, and short wavy hair that curved outwards to frame her face. She wore a black-and-beige dress, cut long.

"Take a good look," Rain said. Standing behind the image, the reflected light cast him in deep blue. "This is your target, Mage Vihaela. Age thirty-five, apprenticed under Ylath. Became his apprentice at age sixteen, made Chosen one year later. After Ylath's death, she moved out on her own. Drifted between various cabals, picked up a few records but nothing serious. Even then she was building a reputation for herself. Joined White Rose four years ago, recruited personally by Marannis. Within a year she was in charge of their internal affairs, and after two she was the second-in-command of the entire organisation. Our sources say that she's now director in all but name."

"Type?" Trask said.

"Death-life hybrid, heavier on the death side. Specialises in incapacitation and inflicting pain. One bit of good news is that we've got no indication that she can bypass shields. Bad news is that she definitely has ranged capability. How she can handle herself in a fight is not well known. She's never been brought in and there are no reliable accounts from people who've gone up against her. For that reason and for *several* others, I do not want you to engage her in combat if there is any possible alternative."

"Anything on associates?" Haken said.

"No apprentices, no cabal mates. It's believed she does most of her work personally."

I studied Vihaela's image. The recorder had caught her with her arms folded, large dark eyes looking out into space. Her expression made it seem as though she were studying someone. She didn't look obviously intimidating, but there was something in her face that triggered warning bells. I had the feeling I didn't want to get into a fight with her.

"Everyone familiar with her face?" Rain said. "Good. Because I want her brought in by tonight."

I felt Haken start a little at that. "Tonight?" For the first time, Slate looked taken aback. "Seriously?"

"That's not enough time," Lizbeth said.

"That's the time you have."

"Captain," Haken said, "we need to set more groundwork in place before doing something like this. We should be putting in surveillance, figuring out associates . . ."

"That's why you've been assigned a time mage and a diviner. They should be able to give you all the information you need."

"You know how White Rose are going to take this. We march in there without preparation—"

"You're not arresting her."

"They're not going to care!"

"Believe me, I am aware," Rain said. "But these orders come straight from the top. The Council wants immediate action." Rain paused. "For what it's worth, I told the representative almost exactly what you just told me. It did not sway his opinions on the matter. As far as the Council is concerned, the subject is closed." Rain looked around. "Any other questions?"

"What if she just does a cut and run?" Slate said.

"Yeah," Lizbeth said. "There's no way we can get an interdictor up."

"If she runs, she runs," Rain said. "You search the premises and bring back what you can get. But White Rose is pretty entrenched. If I were you, I'd be ready for something else."

Lizbeth muttered something under her breath. "We at least have somewhere to look?" Slate said.

Rain touched the focus: the image of Vihaela disappeared, to be replaced by a map of London, projected on the whiteboard. Three red dots shone from points on the map: two in the inner city, one a little farther out to the west. "White Rose runs houses at these three locations," Rain said. "Best guess is that none of them are going to have anything too illegal on the premises. However, from what we've been able to gather, all three houses have a transport focus, probably a freestanding gate. The gates all link back to White Rose's primary base of operations."

"So where's that?" Slate said.

"They move it," Rain said. "Last known location was a warehouse in Manchester, but it's been abandoned. Rumour is they went out to some new location in the country. Wherever it is, that's where their holding and training facilities are. Vihaela will be there."

The Keepers started talking and the subject of the briefing switched to personnel and resources. Slate wanted more; Rain was telling him no. I listened with half an ear, studying the other mages in the room out of the corner of my eye. Slate, Trask, and Lizbeth seemed to have forgotten about me, at least for now. They were the most involved, and despite their complaints, the most committed. Abeyance was staying out of it, her stance indicating that this was Keeper business. Coatl was sprawled back on his chair, cleaning his ear with his little finger. Cerulean hadn't said a word. Haken was the one I was most curious about: he was silent, occasionally chipping in to the argument but mostly listening. He didn't look happy, and I had the feeling that it was because of the time limit.

"All right," Rain said at last. "You've got your tasks; let's get to it. Haken, I want to be kept in the loop on this. Hourly reports and you don't deviate from the brief without clearing it with me."

Haken nodded. Rain took the rod from the projector and walked outside.

"Can you believe this?" Lizbeth said as soon as the door shut. "This is such bullshit . . ."

Haken was staring at the door. "Everything okay?" I asked quietly.

Haken got to his feet. "I'm going to have to make some calls. I'll meet you downstairs." He headed out. Glancing over, I saw that the other Keepers were still arguing. I got up and made an unobtrusive exit.

I left the room to see Haken turning the corner. Scanning

the futures, I saw him slip through a door and . . . *damn*. It had locked behind him. I could have easily picked the lock, but not in a building full of Keepers. What was Haken up to?

I felt a familiar presence behind me and turned to see Caldera. She was at the door leading to the stairwell, and she was arguing with Rain. With an annoyed glance back to where Haken had vanished, I headed towards them.

". . . not an option," Rain was saying as I came into earshot.

"I'm fine," Caldera said. "The doctor said I was in good shape."

"I've got Dr. Cazriel's report on my desk," Rain said. "He prescribed a minimum of forty-eight hours before you'd be ready for light duty. Four days before any combat ops."

"That's bullshit. I can still—"

"The answer is no," Rain said. "I am not going on record as sending you on a combat mission against direct medical instruction."

"You need all the help you can get."

"There are six Keepers on this already. We've got enough hitting power."

"It's my case," Caldera argued. "I've got the background—"

"And your reports have been filed. You're already the Keeper of record for the Pudding Mill Lane investigation. You'll get the credit."

"Fuck the credit! I want to be there."

Rain gave her a steady look. "Go home, Caldera." He glanced at me, then turned and headed through the door.

Caldera glared after him, looked like she was about to start swearing, then looked at me and visibly ground her teeth. "Bad day?" I said.

"No shit." Caldera took a deep breath. "You're going?"

I nodded. "I don't know most of the team. Anything you can tell me?"

Caldera moved to one side, out of the way of a pair of men walking past. "Who've you got?"

"Haken, Slate, Trask, Lizbeth. Two others called

Cerulean and Coatl. And a time mage auxiliary called Abeyance."

"Yeah, I've worked with Abeyance," Caldera said. "She knows what she's doing. Slate you know. He's an arsehole, but at least he's not bent. Lizbeth's a bitch, don't turn your back on her."

"The others?"

"Trask is Slate's partner: he's smarter than Slate and he'll back him up. Coatl's a long-timer. Not as dumb as he looks. Cerulean I don't know, he's a transfer from Order of the Cloak. And Haken's Haken."

"Cool. Who are they working for?"

"What do you mean?"

"I'm guessing that at least half the team are in the pay of or onside with someone who's not the Keepers." I didn't lower my voice, but I'd already checked around us to make sure that no one else was within earshot. "Do you know who's with who?"

Caldera looked away.

"I'm just saying it'd help."

"They work for the Keepers." There was a definite warning note in Caldera's voice.

"Officially."

"*Verus.*" Caldera gave me a look. "This doesn't help. Okay?"

"I'm not sure if you quite understand the difference in our respective positions." I kept my voice calm and didn't look away. "You're a Keeper and a Light mage. I'm not. So given that I'm about to go off on a mission with a group of people whose collective objectives might include disposing of me, then yes, I'd say that knowing exactly who they're working for would *very much* help."

We stared at each other for a couple of seconds. Two more people passed by, skirting around us to head through the door and down the stairs. Caldera was the first one to look away, but she still didn't answer.

"Okay," I said. "How about a compromise? I'll head off to work and do my job. You stay on standby. If things don't go to plan and some of these guys turn out not to be so friendly, you can back me up."

"I'm not cleared for active duty."

"Thought you just said you were fine."

Caldera gave me a narrow look. "You're trying to get me to pull this too?"

Voices sounded from the corridor behind us. I looked back to see the Keepers coming out of the room: Haken and Lizbeth, Slate and Trask, Cerulean and Coatl, Abeyance on her own at the back. "Think it over," I said. "Talk to you later."

The other Keepers caught us up. I let them pass before falling in behind, leaving Caldera up on the landing as I followed the group down the stairs.

⁂

We geared up, moved out, and began gathering information. Hours passed, and afternoon became evening.

Sunset found me in Bank, right in the heart of the City. If you're not connected to the London finance industry, then Bank is one of those districts that you pass through without stopping in, a strange place of towering walls and narrow streets, where buildings a hundred years old house newly furnished offices. There's not much to see from the outside, just dingy stone frontings with faded nameplates. Tucked away around the corners are the sort of pubs where you pay for a drink and a burger with a twenty-pound note, filled with men in suits talking office politics and going outside to smoke. Around one of those corners was a plain black van.

I sat inside the van, eyes closed, and I path-walked. Every future began the same way, with me getting up, opening the rear doors, and heading left. From there they diverged. My future selves were meant to turn left, go right down the alley, and make their way into an unmarked door on an unmarked building about halfway down. It had been easier earlier in the afternoon, when everyone was still at work. Now the skies were going a dusky grey and the streets were filling up with bankers and stockbrokers and all the people who worked for them. The people on the streets kept disrupting my path-walking, breaking the delicate chain and forcing me to retrace my steps and start again.

I'd just made it into the building when the future thread splintered and broke for the umpteenth time. I went back, sent my future self out the doors again, saw him stop. Conversation; someone I knew. I looked to see who it was, then opened my eyes, coming out of my trance.

The van doors opened, letting in grey twilight and car exhaust. Abeyance ducked her head and stepped inside. I reached over to pull the door shut behind her.

"Hey, baby!" Coatl said with a grin. He and I were the only ones in the van's rear compartment: the security men were in the front cabin. "How's the view out there?"

"Dull," Abeyance said. She glanced around. "Where's Haken?"

"Vanished again," I said. I'd tried to shadow Haken with my divination, but he was being careful and I'd lost him in the crowds. "Did you see Vihaela?"

Abeyance frowned. "He should be here for this."

I didn't answer. "No sign of her," Abeyance said. "Any movement on your end?"

"Pretty sure they didn't spot you." In her dark blue business jacket and skirt, Abeyance fitted into the area perfectly. Like most passive senses, timesight doesn't show up to magical detection.

Coatl laughed. "You think she doesn't know we're coming?"

Abeyance turned to him. The two of them made a strange pair: Coatl, fat, bearded, and balding, sprawled out over two seats, and Abeyance, slim and straight-backed and slightly prim, looking at Coatl with her mouth turned down in disapproval. Briefly I wondered how they saw me. Maybe to them, I seemed even weirder.

"Is there something you're not telling us?" Abeyance said.

"You know what they say," Coatl said. "Two people can keep a secret if one's dead." He grinned. "The Council knows, the eight of us know, the ones who briefed Rain know. Just a matter of time."

"Presumably that's why Rain's ordered us to do it by tonight," Abeyance said.

"What makes you think it's not one of us?"

Abeyance sighed. "This is pointless." She glanced at me. "If I stay here and don't talk or move, can you find out when Haken's going to be back?"

I nodded. Abeyance was as good as her word and to my surprise, Coatl didn't do anything to disrupt the path-walk either. After a few seconds I looked up. "He should be here in five minutes."

Five minutes and twenty seconds later, the door swung open and Haken stuck his head in, looking at Abeyance. "What's the score?"

"No sign of Vihaela," Abeyance said. "At least, not from the front. Plenty of traffic in and out, but as far as I can tell they're all normals or sensitives."

"The front entrance is for their regular clients," I said. "The mages aren't going to walk in off the street."

"But it's definitely active?"

"The evidence would suggest that, but I can't confirm it without going inside."

Haken looked at me.

"It's locked down pretty tight," I said. "I haven't identified anyone yet."

"I've already scanned the easily accessible periods," Abeyance said. "The problem is the location. If you want more useful information, I'll need to be inside."

Haken nodded. "I'm calling in the other teams. Get suited up." He disappeared again.

⁝⁝⁝⁝⁝⁝

The van took us to a nearby building. Although mages can theoretically just gate around London wherever they choose, in practice familiarity and the need for secrecy act as limits. Partly for that reason, the Council has a network of properties around London and England that can be used as transport nodes. This one was an office block—scanning it, the rest of the occupants seemed to be regular business folk, but one of the floors was empty except for us. The Council would own or rent it, and would leave it unused when it wasn't needed, which was a reminder of just how enormous their resources were. London's one of the most expensive cities in the world, yet the Council can afford to leave a place sitting empty just on the off chance that it might be used. When you have that kind of money, it gives you a lot of options.

The floor was an open-plan office, scattered tables and benches, and it was busy. Men in black fatigues were standing around in knots, talking or unpacking things from long bags. Their clothes were dark and nondescript, with no insignias or logos, but there was no hiding the black body armour or the guns at their belts. These were Council security, the guards and foot soldiers of the Light mages. If mage battles are a chess game, these guys are the pawns. The jobs that Council security do put them up against everything from Dark mages to magical predators to unlicensed constructs. Sometimes those guns they carry do them some good. Other times, they're about as effective as thrown rocks. It's a hard job, and it breeds hard men.

The Keepers were standing around a flimsy table at the centre of the floor, talking quietly amongst themselves. Everyone else was there already; we were the last. "Hey, hey!" Coatl called out as we walked over. "Where's the bar?"

Haken ignored Coatl. "The Order of the Shield aren't an option," he was saying. "Council wants this low-key."

"Right," Lizbeth said sarcastically. "The one time those nuts would be useful and we're not allowed to call them in?"

"The idea is *not* to escalate things."

"Yeah, good luck with that," Slate said.

"Fine," Lizbeth said. "So we pick up someone from White Rose and squeeze them."

"They won't have the base location."

Slate shrugged. "Get one of the mages, then."

The argument went on. Abeyance stood with arms

folded, not getting involved. Coatl had wandered off. I checked my phone: it was six o'clock. Time was running out.

"No," Haken said at last. "We're going with the original plan. We go in and talk." He looked around. "Slate, Trask, Cerulean, you're on point with me. We'll go through the front door and find someone who can make the decision. Verus, you stay close. Watch for wards and tell us if there are going to be any surprises. Understand?"

I nodded.

"Lizbeth, you take a squad of four and stay with Abeyance. Cover the front and make sure no one does a runner. When it's clear, escort Abeyance inside and cover her while she uses her timesight."

"Babysitting?" Lizbeth rolled her eyes. "Fine."

"Coatl—" Haken looked around. "Where is he?"

"Think he went to the bathroom," I said.

Trask laughed. Haken looked as though he wanted to swear, but controlled himself. "He's taking another squad and covering the back." *Where he can't screw anything up* was the unspoken message. He looked around. "Any questions?"

There was a few seconds' silence. "If we're going to do it, let's do it," Slate said at last.

"Okay," Haken said. "Move out."

:::::::::

There was no conversation on the journey back. The van ride was silent but for the rumble of the engine and the sound of the city streets around us, and everyone seemed lost in their own thoughts. There's a particular kind of tension you get when you're in a group going on a dangerous mission. You're isolated, yet at the same time you're intensely conscious of the people around you. If you trust them, that's your reassurance. You know you're not going in alone, and that there'll be someone to back you up.

If you *don't* trust them . . . well, that's not very reassuring at all.

I studied the other mages in the van. Who would be the most likely to stick a knife in my back? Slate didn't like me.

Neither did Lizbeth. Haken seemed to be on my side, but he was playing some game of his own.

Maybe if I looked at it in terms of magic types. Haken was a fire mage. Slate and Trask were death and water. Abeyance was a time mage, Cerulean an illusionist, Coatl used mind magic, and Lizbeth was a water/air hybrid. Based on that, it was Cerulean and Coatl I should be worrying about. They were the ones who could screw me over without anyone else noticing . . .

I shook my head in frustration. This was impossible. I didn't know *any* of these people—until today I hadn't known that half of them even existed. There were people who spent their whole lives immersed in Council politics, tracking the shifting loyalties and affiliations of the Light mages. Divination or no divination, I couldn't figure it out in just a few hours. I'd have to play this by ear. I didn't know whom I should be watching, but my magic would give me a few seconds' warning if anyone made a move on me, and that would just have to be enough. I needed to focus on being ready for whatever came at me.

The van came to a halt. Haken was speaking into his sleeve, giving quiet instructions to the security men in the other two vans. I could picture what would be going on inside: guns being loaded, equipment double-checked.

I waited.

"Go," Haken said.

The van doors opened and we streamed out into artificial light. We were in a subterranean parking garage near the White Rose facility in Bank, the other two vans parked on either side of ours, lined up in military precision. The security detail were heading up the ramp. At the top, one of the men was talking to the tollbooth attendant, who was trying to reply and stare at us at the same time. We walked past, up onto the street, and around the corner.

We got a lot less attention than I'd expected. I think it was the lack of fuss. No one ran or shouted; we just moved at a brisk walk, and while the odd passerby turned to stare, the looks they gave us were puzzled ones, as if they weren't quite sure what was going on. As we moved down the street Haken made hand signals. Coatl split off with four men, Lizbeth and Abeyance with two more. The rest of us turned the corner and headed straight down the alleyway.

Old buildings loomed over us, orange and brown in the artificial light, and unmarked doors passed by to either side. We were in detection range now. I hadn't seen any cameras on the White Rose house, but it was just a matter of time before they figured out we were there. Haken signalled; Slate and Trask accelerated and I quickened my pace to keep up. Slate reached the door first and banged on it.

There was a moment's silence, then with a rattle a small slot opened at eye level and I saw the outlines of a face. "What?"

"Hey, mate," Slate said. "I'm Keeper Slate of the Order of the Star. You've got a count of ten to open this door before I break it."

The eyes in the face saw us and widened. The viewing window rattled shut and I heard a muffled shout. "Hey, Mr. Seer," Slate said over his shoulder. "Anyone going to get hurt when I smash this down?"

I checked. "No."

"Pity." Slate lifted a hand and black energy lashed out.

Death magic blends kinetic and negative energy, and it's well suited to combat. Slate's magic was heavier on the kinetic side; the first blast buckled the door, the second smashed it off its hinges. Two Council security men moved in, guns up and ready. Slate and Trask were third and fourth, and I went in behind. The inside looked liked a converted townhouse, with a central hall and doors leading off, and already the men inside were reacting to the attack, shouting and converging. Guards came bursting out into the hall and ran down the stairs from the floors above. The men from White Rose guarding this building were outnumbered, but they were armed and they had the advantage of the choke point.

It didn't make any difference.

It's easy to forget just how powerful mages are. Slate took the first two down before I could even react, black rays sending them stumbling to their knees. One on the upper landing, quicker or dumber than the others, managed to get a handgun up and start firing down into the crowded hall-way, *bang bang bang*. Trask already had a shield up, blue energy smooth and polished, the bullets making white flashes as they bounced away. The man got off four shots before Trask sent a hydroblast up the stairs; it caught the guy in the chest, smashing him up into the wall, sending him sprawling limp on the landing.

And just that fast, the battle was over. Four men were down, none of them ours. One of the Council security was advancing on a man at the end of the hall, his submachine gun up and levelled. "Down on the floor!" he was shouting. "Drop the gun, down on the floor!" The White Rose man looked pale and scared; he dropped his gun and backed away, hands up. The Council security man grabbed him and shoved him down.

The Council security started restraining the men on the ground, while more came through the front door. Haken stepped through behind them and looked down at the prone figures before glancing at Slate. "Minimum force?"

"They're alive, aren't they?" Slate said. He headed towards the kitchen at the end of the hall. Shouts and calls were echoing down from the floors above. "Hey," I said to the Council security about to start up the stairs. "There's a guy about to come down shooting."

The security man glanced at me, then stepped down, sighting on the top of the stairs. Someone stepped up next to me and I looked left to see the illusionist, Cerulean. His eyes were slightly narrowed, and he waved a hand towards the security man.

The security man lowered his gun and stepped aside. We waited a couple of seconds, then there was the sound of running footsteps and a round-faced guy with a gun appeared on the landing.

Cerulean looked at him. Round Face's eyes went wide and he screamed. He clapped his hands to his face, bashing himself with the side of the gun in the process, and staggered sideways, tripping over the body of the one Trask had stunned. He went down and kept screaming.

"Clear ground!" someone shouted from the back of the hall. Haken reappeared, skirting around the Council security and the men on the floor. "Verus—" he began, but the screaming from the landing above drowned out his voice. He frowned.

I shook my head and gestured upwards.

Haken looked up, then down at Cerulean, and spoke loudly enough to be heard over the screams. "Could you please shut that off?"

Cerulean shrugged. "It's not an exact science."

I stared at Cerulean. I couldn't see any active spell, but illusion magic specialises in invisibility and it's notoriously difficult to detect. Illusionists usually manipulate light, but against weaker-willed opponents they can plant phantasms directly inside their targets' heads. I used my magesight, searching through the frequencies: for a moment I thought I saw something, twisting blue-purple wires linking Cerulean to the man up on the landing, then Cerulean glanced at me and the wires vanished. From above, the screaming cut off abruptly, to be replaced with sobs.

"You two, you're with with Slate and Trask," Haken said into the sudden quiet. "Full search, bottom to top. Check every room."

Cerulean nodded. "Okay," I said.

Haken headed back towards the end of the hall. I knew Slate and Trask were coming. Cerulean looked at the stairs, then gestured slightly to me, as if to say *after you*.

I looked back at Cerulean's expression, polite and indifferent, then as Slate and Trask reappeared I headed upstairs. I could feel Cerulean right behind me.

ııııııııı

We cleared the rest of the building, and the remaining White Rose personnel surrendered without a fight. The clients in the process of using White Rose's facilities were slightly more troublesome, and I got shouted at and threatened by a few men in various states of undress, but once they saw the guns and warrant cards they shut up. Cerulean and Slate told each of them in turn not to use their mobile phones, but funnily enough none of them seemed all that keen to get in touch with their friends and family. The girls (and the one boy) didn't give any trouble—they'd obviously learnt when not to put up a fight. There were no traps, and more to the point, no mages.

The top floor attic hadn't been converted into individual bedrooms. It was a studio, with some desks over to one side, but the main point of interest was the arch mounted against the far wall. I'd been using my magesight, searching for wards, and I recognised the thing instantly. Gate magic focus, and . . . password locked? *Interesting.* The only other person with me was one of the Council security men, and he was helpfully staying just outside the door. I focused on the archway, eyes narrowed. Cracking the password took about a minute. After that, I started path-walking to see what would happen if I stepped through.

I'd been at it for ten minutes when I heard footsteps from behind. Lizbeth and Abeyance's futures intersected with mine, breaking the path-walk. I stirred and looked around just as the two of them came in. "Is that what I think it is?" Abeyance said as she saw the arch.

"Gate focus to White Rose's base," I said.

"Perfect." Abeyance stood against the wall and narrowed her eyes.

"Anything downstairs?" I asked.

"Several hundred scenes of illicit sex. Per day."

"That must have been fun to watch."

"I've seen it before."

"I always wondered how that worked," I said. "So when you go into some random bedroom and use your timesight . . . ?"

"Yes. That's exactly how it works." She shrugged. "You stop paying attention after a while."

"You two done perving?" Lizbeth said. "How about you get us something useful?"

Abeyance gave Lizbeth an unemotional look and turned

to the archway, concentrating. "Your raid worked, didn't it?" I said.

"Are you stupid?" Lizbeth said. "Did you look at those girls? They're not even underage. No flesh work, no kids—we haven't got shit. Probably can't even make a slavery charge stick."

"The mage clients aren't going to be somewhere like this," I said. "They'll have the incriminating stuff in their main base."

Lizbeth gave me a withering look. "Well, that's not much fucking help, is it?"

I shrugged. "You could go through the arch."

Lizbeth glared at me. Abeyance ignored us both. There was an uncomfortable silence.

It was broken by the sounds of the other Keepers climbing the stairs. ". . . not getting anything," Trask was saying in his deep voice. "Could sweat the others."

"No," Haken said. "They won't have anything useful." He appeared in the doorway, took one look at the archway, then turned to me. "What'll happen if we go through that?"

"It'll take us right into the middle of White Rose's base," I said. "That'll start a fight, no two ways about it."

"So we do it fast," Slate said.

"They know we're coming."

Slate eyed me. "You have something to do with that?"

"White Rose aren't stupid," I said. "There are silent alarms spread out through this building. The guys here aren't meant up to stand up to a Keeper raid; they're an ablative screen. Same way you guys use your security men."

"Any chance we can do it peacefully?" Haken asked.

"We step through that gate, they're going to shoot first and ask questions later. And if you try to talk them down, you might not live long enough to do it. They've got a barbican setup. Crossfire, wards, the works."

"So how about you go first?" Slate said. "They're your kind, right?"

I gave Slate a look. He grinned and looked at Haken. "So we doing it?"

Haken shook his head. "No." He threw me a phone; I caught it one-handed. "From one of the guys downstairs. Get me the password."

I nodded, thumbed the display to reveal the unlock screen, and started working through the numbers. Slate looked at me, then at Haken. "Seriously?" he said in disbelief. "You're still trying to talk to her?"

"We are trying," Haken said, "to do this peacefully."

"Hey, Haken," Slate said. "You might have missed it so here's a newsflash for you: Dark mages don't go peacefully. This is a fucking waste of time."

Haken looked levelly at Slate. "Go down and help Coatl."

Slate gave us a disgusted look and stalked off. "Well, this is the place," Abeyance said. "Vihaela's used this gate. At least once in the past week, maybe more."

"Good," Haken said. "Keep looking for anything else with her. Verus?"

I'd found the passcode and had been scanning the past calls and the messages. "Code is 1535," I said, tossing the phone back to Haken. "Look for the contact listed as B. It's not Vihaela, but he's got access."

"Uh," Lizbeth said. "Not to point out the obvious, but how's calling her going to help?"

Haken didn't look up from the phone. "Is there a problem?"

"Yeah, the fact that these guys haven't turned up shit and we've got nothing on Vihaela. You think she's going to just roll up?"

"If she doesn't," Haken said absently, "she'll be disobeying the Council."

"Oh yeah, that'll scare her."

Haken looked up at Lizbeth. "I want you and Trask up here. Set up a defence in case anyone comes through that gate. Verus, you're on early warning. I want to know at least two minutes before anyone steps through." He looked between the three of us. "If you make contact, you notify me immediately. You are *not* to attack first under *any* circumstances. Clear?"

Trask nodded. "Fine by me," I said.

Haken looked at Lizbeth. "Clear?"

"Your funeral," Lizbeth said.

Haken turned and left. "This is the most fucked-up operation I've ever seen," Lizbeth said. "Can you believe this?"

"Mm," I said. I was trying to see if I could eavesdrop on Haken's call, but he wasn't making it yet—he was just heading downstairs. Maybe if I followed farther . . . no, he was going to gate away first. *Is he on to me?* Worrying thought . . .

"Hey!" Lizbeth told me. "You awake?"

"I can watch for trouble, or I can talk to you," I said. "Which would you prefer?"

Lizbeth glowered at me, then crossed her arms and looked away. Trask still hadn't spoken, and Abeyance was still lost in the trance of her timesight. I looked between the three mages and inwardly sighed.

ı ı ı ı ı ı ı ı ı

Twenty minutes passed, then forty. The noise level from below diminished as the Council security cleared out the building. A team arrived and set up on the landing, weapons ready. I wanted to go down and find out more, but I was too concerned about the possibility of what Haken had said. It sounded as though he was inviting Vihaela here to talk. By now she'd have to know what had happened here. Would she really leave her fortified base to walk into the middle of a Keeper team like this?

If I were Vihaela and I wanted to talk, I'd do it remotely. If I wanted to fight, I'd just blow up the building. There was no scenario I could think of in which Vihaela's best option was to come walking through that gate, yet that was what Haken had set me to watch for. I checked future after future, looking for alternate lines of attack: a gate to a different part of the building, a triggered explosive, a toxin or gas. Nothing pinged. Maybe Haken was talking to Vihaela right now . . .

Something shifted in the futures, a ghostly possibility, there and gone again. I stopped, searched, lost the strand, found it again. Movement, lots of movement. A person . . .

My eyes went wide and I looked up. "Trask! Get Haken. Vihaela's coming."

Trask put a hand to his ear and started speaking, his voice low and urgent. Lizbeth snapped out orders to the security men on the landing and all of a sudden the room was full of movement. Footsteps came running up the landing. Cerulean was first in; he must have been very close. Haken and Slate followed. Within a minute the small attic was crowded with people. Slate and Trask were at the front, Lizbeth and Haken a step behind. Abeyance had made herself scarce. Half a dozen Council security took up positions covering the gate, kneeling with their submachine guns ready. They weren't about to fire . . . yet, but between them and the mages, there was enough firepower trained on that gate to kill anyone. Vihaela wasn't going to step through into that, was she?

"Verus?" Haken said.

"She's coming," I said. "Two men with her. They're not going to shoot first."

"Good," Haken said. "Everyone hold fire."

Seconds ticked by. The room was silent but for the sound of breathing. Council security shifted position, adjusting their guns. Ahead of me, I saw Lizbeth flex her fingers, eager. I took a step back. Cerulean was in the corner, arms folded. There was a lot of power in this room, and it was pointed away from me. So why was I suddenly so nervous?

The gate lit up in my magesight. I heard half a dozen men draw breaths as the surface of the arch darkened and went black, forming a lightless plane. An instant later, Vihaela stepped through.

chapter 12

There's a saying that military life is long periods of bore-
dom punctuated by brief moments of terror. As soon as
Vihaela stepped through that gate, things started happening
very fast.

Vihaela was dressed in brown and black, similar to her
image in the Keeper records—actually, *exactly* like her
image in the Keeper records. She stopped abruptly at the
sight of all the people facing her. Two figures in suits stepped
out behind her, brushing past on either side. They looked
like men, but their blank expressions and the solid lines of
their futures marked them as constructs.

The futures went crazy. All of a sudden dozens of new
possibilities started unfolding, combat and confrontation and
magic and violence all blending together, overwhelming me
with information. It was too much and for a second I froze.

"Mage Vihaela," Haken began. "Under the authority—"

Danger, pain, death. There was a threat, and it was directed
at me. Instinct broke my paralysis. "Haken!" I snapped.
"Trouble!"

"—of the—" Haken stopped.

Green-black light bloomed around Vihaela's hands, tendrils materialising out of the air. In an instant they'd formed into snakelike shapes with skull faces, rearing back like scorpion tails, ready to strike. The two constructs reached up under their coats, their movements perfectly synchronised, pulling out handguns.

"Gun!" someone shouted.

"Drop the—!"

Magical auras filled the room, overwhelming to my sight, air and fire and death and water. I couldn't see the spell behind Vihaela's green light; she took a step back, eyes going wide in fright, then the snakes lashed out with a piercing shriek, casting a hellish glow. Guns fired, deafening in the enclosed space. There was too much going on, and I could sense danger but it wasn't matching up with the spells Vihaela was using. One of Vihaela's snakes hit Slate; his shield was already up and the green light splintered into shards. A construct was in the middle of firing when an air blade severed its shoulder; I caught one fleeting glimpse of the arm pinwheeling, no blood from the wound, the fingers still tightening on the trigger to send a bullet into the floor. Then all of a sudden my precognition screamed, images of pain and death and blackness flashing in front of my eyes. Someone was about to kill me and I didn't know who or how, but I could see the futures in which I lived and that was all I needed to know. I dived left, twisting; something tugged at my shoulder and I heard a splintering *thud*. I hit the floor hard, pain jolting through my side, and rolled left. I came up to my feet . . .

. . . and the battle was over. Vihaela and one of the security men were down. One of the constructs had been cut to pieces, its body parts scattered across the floor; the other was thrashing, headless, its remaining arm thumping erratically against the wall.

"Cease fire!" Haken shouted. "Cease fire!"

I looked left and right. The attic room hummed with magic, a dozen shields and protective spells brushing against each other. No one seemed to be paying attention to me. But someone had just nearly killed me. It hadn't been Vihaela—I'd been watching her. The constructs had been in my field of vision.

That just left the people who were supposed to be on my side.

Whatever had caused the threat on my precognition, it wasn't around anymore. Trask moved up to the thrashing construct and aimed a hand downward; there was the blue flash of a water spell. The construct went still and silence fell.

"No movement," someone called.

"Rick, you okay?"

"Yeah," a muffled voice said. It was one of the security men. "Just tripped."

"Slate, Lizbeth," Haken said. "Check her."

Slate was staring at Vihaela's still form. The Dark mage was lying facedown, crumpled against the wall. From a glance through the futures, I knew she wasn't getting up.

"Slate!"

Slate started. "Yeah." He and Lizbeth moved forward. Even though Vihaela looked out of it, the two of them treated her with wary caution. Lizbeth raised her hand, and I saw the grey flicker of a protection spell, then she cautiously kicked Vihaela's ankle. Lizbeth frowned.

"Is she out?" Haken asked.

"Yeah, you could say that," Lizbeth said. She straightened and looked at Haken. "She's dead."

"What?"

"As in, not alive."

"Are you serious?" Haken demanded. "Check her pulse."

"I don't need to. Living people do this thing called breathing. You don't believe me?" Lizbeth nodded at Slate. "Ask him."

"Slate?" Haken said. There was a dangerous tone to his voice.

"Well, I didn't fucking do it," Slate said defensively.

"What are you getting in your deathsight?"

Slate hesitated.

"Jesus *fucking* Christ!" Haken spun around. "Which one of you did this?"

No one answered. The other mages in the room avoided meeting Haken's gaze. Behind him, the bodies of Vihaela and the two constructs lay still and silent on the floor.

⌁⌁⌁⌁⌁⌁⌁⌁⌁

"I didn't hit her that hard," Slate said again.

Lizbeth passed a weary hand across her face. She was leaning against the wall. "Will you stop saying that?"

"Well, I didn't."

"Trask?" Haken said. "Give me something I can use."

The security men had all been shooed away, and it was just the mages—me, Haken, Slate, Trask, Abeyance, Lizbeth, and Cerulean. Abeyance was using her timesight, Cerulean had faded into the background, Trask was kneeling over Vihaela's body and examining her, and everyone else was arguing.

I listened with half an ear. I was less interested in the argument than in what I'd found in one of the walls: a pair of bullet holes. There was nothing especially remarkable about them . . . except for the fact that they were in the side wall, and Vihaela and her two constructs had been against the *far* wall. By my estimation, from the angle the bullets had entered, the only place they could have come from was the group of Council security and Keepers.

Which was highly relevant, since I was pretty sure those two bullets had been fired at me. I've been shot (well, seen my future self get shot) enough times to recognise it. That just left the question of who'd done the shooting . . .

"Nothing," Trask said.

"What does that mean?" Haken said.

"Don't have a cause of death."

"Then what *do* you have?"

"Stomach bruising." Trask pointed down, then moved his finger up. "And a shot to the leg."

"She got shot?" Lizbeth looked hopeful. "It was their fault then . . ."

Trask was shaking his head. "Why not?" Haken asked.

"Muscle wound," Trask said. "Missed the arteries."

"What did you hit her with anyway?" Lizbeth said to Slate.

"It was just an enervation bolt."

"Well, those are dangerous."

"I know how to do my job, all right?" Slate said. "Was the same thing I hit those guys downstairs with, and they're fine, aren't they?"

"People have died from enervation spells . . ."

"She's a fucking *life mage*," Slate said. He gave Vihaela's body an angry gesture that seemed to imply that her death had been a personal insult. "You have any idea how tough they are to kill? They're like frigging cockroaches."

Lizbeth shrugged. "Didn't seem that tough to me."

Haken put a hand over his eyes. "Abeyance?"

"I'm not getting much," Abeyance said. She'd stayed out of the argument. "Best guess is the bullet was from a burst aimed at one of those constructs. What took her down was Slate and Lizbeth's spells, but I can't tell what killed her."

"What do you mean, you can't tell?" Haken said. "The more recent an event, the easier it is to timesight it, right? So why can't you see?"

Abeyance shot Haken an annoyed glance. "There's interference. A shroud maybe, or spell static. It's not as though I have lifesight—I'm not going to be able to tell you the exact moment she went from alive to dead."

I ran my fingers along the bullet holes, then turned around, crouching slightly and angling my head to look back along the line they'd come from. I tried to remember who'd been in that position. It hadn't been Vihaela or the constructs. Hadn't been Haken or Slate, either. Coatl had been downstairs. That left Trask, Abeyance, Cerulean, and the Council security.

More to the point, no one seemed to have noticed anything. No one had said anything about my dive sideways, or about any shots going in my direction. That meant that either they'd seen it and said nothing, or there hadn't been anything to see. The first was technically possible, but seemed like an unreasonable risk. I didn't believe that *everyone* on the Keeper team wanted to kill me, which leant me towards the second option. It was always possible that the shooter had just hung back and taken a shot while all eyes were turned on Vihaela, but even in the confusion, that seemed unnecessarily dangerous. With the number of magical senses around, there was too great a chance that someone would notice. The simplest explanation was that it had been done in such a way that no one had been able to see anything at all.

Assuming that logic was correct, it gave me one very obvious suspect. And if *they* were a traitor . . .

I looked at Vihaela's body. *Wait a second.* Could that be it?

The others were still arguing. I crossed the room and knelt; Trask gave me a glance, then rose and stepped away. Vihaela was lying on her front, head turned towards me, eyes closed in death. Her face was drawn and still. I blanked my mind, put all thoughts of who Vihaela was out of my head, and simply looked at her.

She looked young. I've seen a lot of Dark mages, male and female, and Vihaela didn't really fit. It's hard to say exactly what it is, but there's something about a Dark mage's looks that marks them. Maybe an apprentice . . . no, I wouldn't even have pegged her as an apprentice. Not enough force. She looked like someone who'd had things done *to* her, instead of the other way around.

I thought back, remembering what I'd seen of the fight. In the few seconds I'd seen Vihaela alive, how had she looked? She'd looked afraid. Startled and frightened.

But looked at another way . . .

Yes. I couldn't prove it, not yet, but I was sure I was right. I looked up. Slate was still arguing with Haken, something about giving the report to Rain. Cerulean and Lizbeth had been watching me; Cerulean glanced away, Lizbeth didn't. I was pretty sure I knew who was working for White Rose, and I knew how they'd staged this. What was I going to do about it?

Accusing them openly . . . bad idea. I didn't have enough status here, and I didn't have any hard evidence. I could report what I knew up the chain of command. That was the dutiful thing to do, and what I was getting paid for.

Problem with that: I didn't know who the people above me were working for either.

So let's find out.

"It wasn't Slate," I said.

Slate frowned. Haken turned to look at me. "Say that again?"

I rose to my feet. "I know who killed her," I said. "It wasn't Slate."

Slate gave me a suspicious look. This obviously hadn't been what he'd been expecting. "Okay," Haken said. "Then who?"

I glanced around the room, letting my eyes pass very briefly over everyone in turn. "You might want to hear this in private."

Haken wasn't stupid. His eyes narrowed as he realised what I was saying. "So who?" Lizbeth said.

I didn't answer. "Rest of you, clear the room," Haken said. "Wrap up downstairs."

"Seriously?" Lizbeth said.

Haken looked at her. Lizbeth gave us both a disgusted look, turned on her heel, and walked out. Cerulean, Slate, Trask, and Abeyance followed. Abeyance lingered, looking curious, but when Haken waited pointedly, she shut the door behind her.

I listened to the footsteps going downstairs. Haken put a hand into his pocket and red light glowed. A shroud focus, possibly more . . . so that was why I'd had so much trouble eavesdropping on him. "This had better be good," Haken said.

"It was Vihaela."

Haken stared at me for a second. "You think it was suicide?"

"No. I'm saying Vihaela killed *her*." I nodded down at the corpse.

"We don't have time for—"

"Think about it," I said. "What did we actually see? We saw someone who looked like Vihaela walk through the gate. Then the fight kicks off and there's no time for anything else. She's dead before she has the chance to talk."

"You're saying that wasn't her."

"You remember the briefing. Vihaela's supposed to be the freaking death queen of White Rose. She shouldn't have gone down this easily. White Rose uses fleshcrafters, remember? Perfect duplicates of whoever their clients want. If you were a Dark mage and you had those kinds of resources, wouldn't you make some body doubles while you were at it?"

"She used magic—"

"Did she?" I asked. "Did your magesight actually see her cast any spells? Because mine didn't. Yes, those green snake things *looked* scary, but they didn't register as battle-magic, did they? Everyone was just so keyed up to fight that they reacted as if they were."

Haken frowned at me for a second. "You're saying they were faked."

I didn't answer. I didn't need to. There had been exactly one person in the room who'd had the ability to create that convincing a show. I wasn't openly accusing him, but there was only one way it pointed . . .

"What killed her?" Haken said.

"Here's how I think this went down," I said. "Vihaela's on the other side of that gateway. She knows we're waiting, and she's got her body double ready. But she knows it won't hold up under any kind of stress. So she makes sure the girl won't be around to answer any questions. She uses some kind of spell before this girl steps through the gate. Time delay, maybe a triggered effect—but whatever it is, it was meant to make sure that this girl didn't survive the encounter. She was dead from the minute she stepped through."

Haken was silent for a few seconds. I knew he was going through what I'd just told him, checking it to see if it held up. "I'm going to make some calls," he said at last. "Don't tell anyone what you just told me. Understand?"

I nodded. Haken walked out.

I started to follow, then paused. I turned and looked back. The girl's body was lying on the floor, alone in the room, still and lifeless. She hadn't been involved in this at all, not really. She'd been a pawn, prepared and sacrificed. It was so utterly casual. They had treated her like one of my one-shot items, expended to produce a desired effect. Just like Leo.

Fuck these guys. The depth of my hatred surprised me. All of a sudden I didn't care about the long-term consequences. I just wanted to see White Rose go down. I took out my phone and started making some calls of my own.

⁙⁙⁙⁙⁙

Haken called half an hour later, giving me instructions to meet him at the office where we'd planned the attack. He didn't offer any explanations, and I didn't ask.

The house was mostly empty now. Some Council forensics teams had arrived and were starting to go through the rooms, but most of the mages and security men had been called back to headquarters. It made sense really. The mission had been to bring in Vihaela, and now that Vihaela was apparently dead, things had ground to a halt. Outside, some yellow tape had been used to block off the alley, and bystanders were craning their necks to see if anything interesting was going to happen. I got a few glances, but no one challenged me on the way out.

I took a taxi to the office block and went inside. Night had fallen, and the building was dark and empty. My footsteps echoed up the stairwell as I climbed. When I found the door, I stopped and unslung my bag. I hadn't worn my armour today, but I'd brought a light backpack. Reaching inside, my fingers brushed against soft cloth before closing on a stone attached to a chain. The item I took out wasn't much to look at: a smooth-cut rock on a thin chain, teardrop-shaped and dull grey. But it wasn't a rock, it was a fire-hunger stone, and I'd primed it before leaving the house. I checked to make sure it was still charged, then hung the chain over my neck, tucking the stone inside my shirt. I pushed the door open and walked in.

Haken was at the far side of the office, next to the windows. The lights were off and he was only a shadow in the gloom. Fire mages can see heat—it's not quite the same as seeing in the dark, but it's pretty close, and a fire mage can manage just fine with no light at all. Haken turned to me as I wound my way through the tables. The only light was the reflected glow from the street below the window: I could make out the lines of his face, but I couldn't see his eyes. "Thinking something over?" I asked.

"Yes."

I tilted my head. "Made up your mind?"

Haken looked at me for a second without answering. "Ready to go?"

"Where to?"

"White Rose's base," Haken said. "Maybe. I'm going to need you there to confirm it."

I shrugged. "Easy enough. How do you know where to go?"

"Can't answer that, I'm afraid."

"Then mind telling me *why* we're going there? Because it doesn't seem like the safest possible vacation spot."

"Our mission hasn't changed." Haken said. "If what you're saying is true and Vihaela's at their base . . ."

"Then we still have to bring her in?"

Haken nodded.

"If we're doing something like that, wouldn't it make sense to bring some backup?"

"This is recon," Haken said. "If you're right, then I can't trust the others on the team." He looked at me. "I hope you haven't discussed this with anyone else."

I kept a straight face. "No."

"Good." I felt Haken look me up and down. "Is that really what you're wearing?"

"You don't like my clothes?"

"Thought you had a set of armour?"

Funny thing about lying—the less often you do it, the more effective it is when you do. "Golem damaged it," I said. "Besides, we're not there to fight, right?"

"I guess not," Haken said. He took a breath and straightened. "All right." He turned to one side, and a minute later light bloomed as a fiery disc appeared in midair. The glow backlit his face, casting it in red and black. The disc shifted, becoming a ring. From the back, the gate was opaque; I walked around it to see that it led into an empty building. Haken stepped through and I followed.

We gated through three more staging points, each one another building. The air felt different in each, and I had the suspicion we'd just taken some very brief overseas holidays. Gating through staging points is a standard mage trick—it makes it much harder to track them—but usually they'll only use one or two. Four is getting to the point of paranoia. Haken *really* didn't want to be followed.

The last gateway took us outside, into what felt like the country. My feet came down onto grass, leafy bushes blocking my sightlines. Haken stepped through behind and cut off the gate instantly; he'd muted the glow this time, presumably to make us harder to spot. The air was cold, and looking up, I could see a black and overcast sky. There was no light reflected off the clouds: wherever we were, we were a long way from any settlements. "What can you see?" Haken asked, his voice low.

"Give me a sec." I had my eyes closed, path-walking, watching as my future selves spread out in every direction. No immediate danger. I searched further, creating a slowly spreading mental map. The darkness made it harder, but . . . *there*. Just to the left, over a small rise, was a giant building. Not just a house, a country estate. There were only a few scattered lights from the windows, but even from a glance I could tell it was busy. Spotting the estate let me orient myself. So if we went the other way . . . Ouch. Okay, I wasn't doing *that*.

"Anything?" Haken said.

"We're in the grounds of a big country estate. Can't confirm it's White Rose's base, but given that they have electric fences around the outside, I'm going to guess it's not anywhere friendly."

Haken didn't seem surprised. "Vihaela?"

"I'll check."

Haken nodded. Silence fell.

"So," I said after a minute. "You didn't tell me how you found this place."

"That's classified."

"I get that. It just seems a little odd."

Haken didn't reply.

"I mean, we kind of went to a lot of trouble to storm that place in Bank. And we already knew that Vihaela was going to be in their main base. Seems like it would have been more efficient to come straight here."

"Wasn't an option."

"Couldn't you have just done whatever you did to find this place, except first?"

"Verus," Haken said. "Not now, all right?"

Another brief silence. Off in the darkness, a nightbird called and went quiet. The wind blew, rustling the leaves of the trees.

"So," I said, "was there a reason you only brought me?"

Still no answer.

"I mean, yes, this is supposed to be subtle. But if we're trying to stay hidden, it would have made sense to bring along Cerulean."

"You know exactly why I haven't brought Cerulean."

"Sure," I agreed. "But it would have been useful, wouldn't it? I mean, illusionists are handy guys to have around. They can show you things that aren't really there, hide their spells so that no one else can see what you're really doing. Oh, and they can turn invisible. He could be right here, and we wouldn't have any way of knowing."

Haken looked at me silently. "So did you know he was working for White Rose?" I said. "Or did it come as a surprise?"

"That hasn't been confirmed."

I sighed. "You know the most annoying thing about you Keepers? It's that habit you have of shutting everyone out. This whole thing would have gone so much faster if you'd just been up front."

"You think I've been lying to you?"

"No, I just think you've been leaving out some really relevant information." I studied Haken. "But you didn't know about Cerulean, did you? Must have been a nasty surprise. You'd been trying to resolve the whole thing with Vihaela peacefully, then for a few minutes you thought you'd killed her."

"Yes," Haken said, an edge to his voice. "That *was* a surprise. Somewhere you're going with this?"

I shrugged. "Just making conversation."

Haken looked at me. I looked back.

"Vihaela's in there, by the way," I said.

". . . Good."

"So, we clear to go back?"

"Not yet."

"I think it's about time."

"First I want you to—"

"Maybe I didn't make myself clear," I said. "I'm about to take out a gate stone and use it to go home. Are you going to do anything to stop me?"

Haken hesitated. It was only a very tiny pause, but it was long enough. The futures in which he said something reassuring flickered and vanished. The silence stretched out.

"Well," I said at last. "This is awkward."

"Something you're implying?" Haken asked. His voice was flat.

"It's not easy to keep secrets from a diviner."

"Sometimes you don't get a choice."

"Oh, I don't know," I said. "I'm sort of inclined to the philosophy that there's always a choice. Just not necessarily one you like."

"If you know so much," Haken said, "what are you doing here?"

I shrugged. "Honestly? I wanted to see which way you'd jump."

Haken didn't answer. *Still on the fence?* Maybe I could find out a little more. "So, there's something I'd like to know," I said. "What happened to Leo?"

"I have no idea."

I sighed. "Can we quit the bullshit?"

"I didn't have anything to do with that."

"Fine," I said. "You weren't the one sending those golems out. But you sure as hell had something to do with why Caldera didn't get that backup until it was too late for it to matter. I'm guessing it was Levistus, or someone from his crew. He didn't want the Council moving against White Rose, so he tried to cut things off at the source. Only he didn't get there fast enough." I studied Haken. "I'm guessing they gave Leo the interrogation treatment. What happened to him afterwards?"

Haken sighed, rubbing his forehead. "You have no idea how this works, do you? You think this stuff gets decided with a boardroom meeting?"

"So you had no idea what was going on? That's your story?"

"Leo was in the way," Haken said. "He hadn't shown up, this whole confrontation between the Council and White Rose wouldn't have happened. We could have headed things off."

"Yeah, I imagine that would have suited Levistus just fine."

"This isn't about Levistus," Haken said. "No one wants to start a war with White Rose, not with Morden running around. You think Levistus would have taken this big a risk if most of the Council weren't on his side? Two-thirds of them just want this whole mess to go away. It's only the nuts who want to pick a fight."

"Interesting that you see it as picking a fight," I said. "Some people might think that picking a fight is kind of your job. You know, that whole enforcing-the-laws thing?"

"You don't try to enforce the laws against a group like White Rose," Haken said, his voice hard. "That's not how it works."

"So what did we just do?"

"Oh, for—" Haken made a frustrated gesture. "You think this operation was meant to be a *success*? Capture Vihaela with that bunch of fuckups? All we were doing was sending a message. We clear out one of their buildings, take a few of their low-ranking people. They get a slap on the wrist; we go back to the negotiating table. That's how the game works."

I tilted my head. "I doubt it's much of a game for the slaves."

"Yeah, well." Haken's voice was harsh. "Shit happens."

"Except this time it didn't," I said. "Looks to me like Vihaela's changing the rules."

"Well, if you've got any theories as to why, I'd love to hear them," Haken said. "Because right now I have no fucking idea what White Rose is doing."

"And that's a problem, isn't it? Because you're not here to do an arrest, you're here to negotiate with them."

"More or less." Haken looked at me. "I could still use your help."

"Yeah . . ." I said. "We might have a problem with that. You see, I don't really feel like helping White Rose *or* Levistus."

"You're working for the Council—"

"Oh, please."

"Fine," Haken said. "How much do you want? You help clean this up, a lot of people are going to be grateful."

"And that was why Levistus asked you to bring me along?" I said. "So that I could help out?"

The futures flickered. Again, it was fast, but I was watching for it. "Pretty much," Haken said.

"Ooh," I said sympathetically. "Sorry, Haken. You're not a good enough liar." Who had asked for me to be brought here—Levistus or Vihaela? I looked through the futures in which I accused Haken of both. If I'd done it cold, it would never have worked, but Haken was off balance, thinking on his feet. It takes more time to think up a lie than to tell the truth, and it showed.

"This doesn't—"

"Ah," I said. "Vihaela. So that was what was in those calls you were making, huh? She gives you the coordinates, and tells you to bring me as part of the deal." I raised my eyebrows. "I've got to say, as a negotiator, you don't seem to be doing all that well."

"She's not going to do anything stupid," Haken said.

"Uh-huh," I said. "Let's take stock, shall we? First, the White Rose plant amongst your Keepers tries to kill me during that fight with the double. When that doesn't work, Vihaela tells you to bring me here, out in the middle of nowhere, where no one knows where either of us is, to a mage who specialises in torturing people for information. This isn't setting off any flags to you?"

"That's not going to happen," Haken said sharply.

I shrugged. "Well, since we're on the same team, I guess you won't mind if I do a little solo recon." I turned to leave.

"Verus," Haken said.

I started walking. I didn't look back. All my attention was on the futures ahead. They were shifting, changing . . .

"Verus," Haken said. And I felt the futures settle.

I paused, turned. Haken was standing side-on with one arm raised. A dull red glow had gathered at his palm, casting him in an ominous crimson light. "Come on, Haken," I said. "If you love someone, set them free."

"Yeah, well the version I heard of that saying ends with 'if they don't come back, hunt them down and kill them.'" Haken gestured with his other hand. "Get back here."

I looked down at the spell in Haken's hand, then up at him. "I have to warn you, I think this is going to put a serious damper on our relationship."

"Here. Now."

I shrugged, took one step towards Haken, then burst into a sprint.

Haken snapped something, but I wasn't listening. I was focused on the presence behind me, the same person who'd tried to kill me back in Bank and who'd been eavesdropping on us ever since we arrived. He was silent and invisible, undetectable by sight or by sound, but no matter how well you hide yourself in the present, it doesn't hide the actions you're going to take in the future. I dodged left and a gun fired, the bullets whipping away into the night. Bushes loomed ahead and the futures of the next few seconds forked. Haken had two spells ready: one to block me in, the other to kill. He had only a second—

A wall of fire roared up in front of me, thirty feet long and ten feet wide, dazzlingly bright. It was just barely far enough away that I'd have enough time to stop. I took a breath, clamped down on the animal instinct to shy away, and ran straight into the flames.

The heat rose—and stopped rising. Flames licked hungrily at my skin, but the heat was drawn away, sinking into the stone at my neck. It lasted only a second, and then I was through and into the bushes. The fire-hunger stone was pulsing with heat and magic, but I was alive and unburned. My eyes were swimming with white-purple spots and my night vision was gone, but my divination still worked and I picked out a path over the broken ground, ducking and swaying out of the way of the branches. From behind me I heard a shout and felt the wall of fire vanish. I kept running, coming out of the bushes to swerve into a copse of trees. I knew that I was slightly faster than the two mages behind me. I also knew that if I kept going, they'd inevitably catch me. Mages have a lot of ways to track people.

And so instead of continuing to run, I ducked behind a tree, reached into my pack, and pulled out my hole card.

Most people don't really get how defences work. Every culture has a version of the Achilles myth, where someone's immune to every form of harm except getting shot in the heel, or hit with a dart of mistletoe, or having their hair cut off, or being stabbed in the left butt-cheek with a tuning fork while balancing one-legged on an aardvark, or something similarly stupid. In every single story, some dick goes out of their way to make sure all these ridiculous conditions are satisfied, and the supposedly invulnerable guy dies as a result. If you ask most people what the moral of the story is, they'll say, "No one's invincible," or "Everyone has a fatal flaw."

In my opinion, the *real* moral of those stories is: if you have some special ability that protects you, make damn sure people don't find out about it.

My reactive armour is really useful. Only problem: Haken had already gotten a look at it. He knew what it could do, and he'd already have figured out exactly how much extra power it would take to blast through it. Which was why, for this mission, I hadn't taken my armour at all. Instead I'd taken something that Haken *didn't* know about. The loose bundle I drew from my pack was soft cloth, coloured a neutral grey, long enough to fall to my ankles and with a hood to shield the head. I pulled the mist cloak around my shoulders, stepped back into the shadows, and held still.

My mist cloak was made for me by Arachne, and it's very good at what it does. When wrapped around a wearer, it functions as adaptive camouflage, changing its colour to blend with whatever's behind it—it's not invisibility, but if you keep still and stay in the shadows it's pretty close. More importantly, it blocks magical senses. Most magic types have some way of finding people who are trying to hide from them, and mist cloaks cause you to drop right off their radar. It's very, very useful, and it's saved my life more times than I can count.

It also nearly *ended* my life, or the next thing to it at any rate. The last time I used my mist cloak I made the mistake of wearing it too long, and bit by bit it started hiding me *so* well that no one would have been able to find me, ever. The thought of that still creeps me out, and I'm not sure what would have happened if Arachne hadn't pulled me out of it. I'd checked and rechecked obsessively with my divination, and I was as sure as I could be that as long as I only used it for a little while, the same thing wasn't going to happen again. *Probably.* I pressed up against the tree and held still.

Running footsteps sounded and Haken came into view, red light glowing about his hands. He came to a halt, looking left and right, frowning, and I knew he was looking through the trees, trying to pick out my heat signature. I kept my breathing slow and steady, not letting myself move. Haken stood, listening, and I could guess his thoughts. He couldn't hear me running, he couldn't sense my body heat, so where was I?

There was a soft rustle of movement. Haken turned

sharply, the light at his hands brightening. He stared across the grass for a second, then I saw his stance shift. A shield of fire sprang up around him, and he lifted a hand to point towards an empty patch of grass. "Show your face or I'll burn you out." His voice was sharp and dangerous.

For a moment the landscape was silent, then a man seemed to fade into view, standing on the grass only twenty feet from Haken. The gun he'd been using was nowhere to be seen, and the glow of Haken's fire magic reflected off his face. "No need for threats," Cerulean said.

"Why were you shooting at Verus?"

"Because I wanted to kill him," Cerulean said. He nodded over Haken's shoulder. "Haven't you got something to do?"

Cerulean looked far too relaxed for someone in his situation. Despite everything that had happened there was something bland about him—my eyes kept wanting to slide over him, and I had to keep dragging them back. "I'm getting really tired of your shit," Haken said. "Give me a good reason I shouldn't fry you right now."

Cerulean shrugged. "For one thing, you wouldn't make it off the estate alive. Where's Verus?"

"Gone, since you decided to fuck things up."

"I didn't shoot until he ran."

Haken swore. "That's how diviners work, you moron. It doesn't matter if you're invisible. All he has to do is look into the future to see what would happen if he runs, and if he sees you shooting, he knows you're there!"

Huh, I thought. *Haken's got a pretty good understanding of divination.* Would explain how I'd been having so much trouble spying on him. Though right now, I was a little bit *too* well placed for spying on them, at least for my own comfort. Maybe if I waited until they were busy with each other, then edged away . . .

"Maybe you should have used a fireball instead of trying to block him off with a wall," Cerulean said.

"You know what?" Haken said. "How about you explain to me why you want him dead."

Cerulean cocked his head, as though listening to something. "Vihaela."

"She didn't clear that with me."

"Guess you're not in the loop."

"Don't fuck with me." Haken's voice was dangerous. "This wasn't part of the deal."

"Why don't you tell her that?"

Haken started to answer, then stopped. He looked up, over Cerulean's shoulder, as though he'd noticed something. A second later, I heard it too: people coming closer, lots of people. The wavering white glows of flashlights were showing through the bushes. Shadows moved and Haken took a step back into a defensive posture. Then a woman stepped out into the light.

chapter 13

When I'd seen Vihaela's decoy a few hours ago, I hadn't realised at first that she was a fake. It's hard to identify someone from a picture—you can match the features, but what really sets a person apart is their actions, the way they move and stand and speak. I'd known that there was *something* off, but I hadn't known what it was. Often that's how it happens, when you see an imitation—it doesn't look totally convincing, but if you don't have anything to compare it against, you'll probably accept it.

Until you see the real thing. And then all of a sudden, you can't understand how you could ever have been taken in by the fake one.

Vihaela—and I *knew* this was the real Vihaela, knew it instantly and without needing to check—was tall and dark-skinned, though so perfectly proportioned that the only reason I even registered her height was that standing next to Cerulean, she was taller than him. She wore layered clothes of brown and black and red, with white gloves that stood out in the darkness, and moved with the graceful indifference of a bird of prey. Beautiful, but the kind of beauty that intimidates rather than attracts. Looking at her, I understood why Leo had been so afraid of her. She scared *me*, and I hadn't even seen her do anything.

This was way more than I'd bargained for. I'd been planning to lose Cerulean and Haken in the darkness, then either call for backup or gate out. All I could do now was hold very still.

"Hello, Haken," Vihaela said. Her voice was musical, quite pleasant to the ear. "Where's Verus?"

"Gone," Cerulean said.

Vihaela gave Haken an inquiring look. "He ran," Haken said reluctantly.

Vihaela turned to Cerulean. "Fetch the sniffers. Take the outer guard. Find him."

Cerulean nodded and slipped away into the darkness. Beyond the ring of Haken's light, I could hear him giving orders. The men outside the circle drew back; I saw Haken's eyes flick in their direction and he seemed to relax a tiny bit, though he was still on guard. "This would have gone a lot faster," Haken said, "if you'd just come to talk."

"Oh, did you like my little surprise?" Vihaela smiled. "Short notice, but I did my best."

"Hilarious," Haken said sourly. "You couldn't have just showed up?"

Vihaela raised an eyebrow. "You really thought I was going to surrender to your little task force? I would have thought you and Levistus would be grateful. You wanted a way to wrap this up quietly."

"Having your constructs come in shooting was not 'quietly.'"

Vihaela waved a hand. "Relatively quietly. I think you need more realistic standards."

Haken took a breath, obviously controlling his temper. "I don't have much time here. Can we get down to business?"

"Oh, business?" Vihaela clasped her hands and smiled. "That sounds good. So what does the great Levistus have to say?"

"I think you know. By now half the Light mages in

Britain have heard that those data focuses can be read. More importantly, they know that you *lost* one. Every mage who's used your 'services' is scrambling around trying to put a lid on things."

"Sounds very inconvenient for you."

"Look," Haken said. "I'm a Keeper. I don't know what you guys have got going on here. What I do know is that because of that focus getting out, a lot of Light mages have got a problem. And because Levistus depends on those mages for support, that means he's got a problem. And since he's got a problem, he makes it *my* problem, which means it becomes *your* problem. So I would appreciate it very fucking much if you could stop doing things like trying to assassinate a Keeper auxiliary in the middle of an operation."

"Hmm. You're right." Vihaela tapped a finger to her lips, studying Haken thoughtfully. "You really *don't* know much about what's going on here."

I heard Haken grit his teeth.

"Getting rid of Verus wasn't my idea, by the way," Vihaela said. "That came down from Marannis. He thought that with Verus gone, we could pick up his apprentice and find out what he did with that data focus. Or maybe it was his idea of mending fences with Levistus." She shrugged. "Oh well, who cares?"

"Killing a mage on Keeper business isn't going to mend fences with anyone. You're smart, you'll call off the hunt on Verus now."

Vihaela sighed. "No, that was what *Marannis* wanted. Try to keep up."

"I'm not here to—"

"No. You were here to deliver Verus. One simple thing." Vihaela paused. "Do you have any idea how much work it's been to get you Keepers moving? I'd thought you'd at least make your raid here. Instead you send your whole assault force after the smallest house we have. I suppose I should have expected it, really. Losing a mage seems to be the only thing that motivates you."

All of a sudden I knew what Vihaela was going to do.

Shit. Who's she really working for? I very briefly thought about doing something, then abandoned the idea and started looking for ways out.

Haken hadn't caught up yet. "Look, the way Levistus sees it, we can still keep a lid on this. The others think you're dead. Okay, we can work with that. That'll stall the investigation long enough to let us work out something—"

"Sorry, Haken," Vihaela said. "I'm afraid you and Levistus are a couple of steps behind."

Haken frowned. "What are you—?"

Light flashed from the small of Haken's back, magic surging at close range. Haken jerked, his spine arching, then collapsed to the ground.

"Fire mages." Vihaela shook her head, looking down at Haken. "So easy to misdirect."

Cerulean materialised out of thin air where Haken had been standing, slipping something back into his pocket. His invisibility was flawless: even with my magesight, I hadn't picked up any trace of his presence. Two figures came marching out of the darkness; they were the same humanoid constructs that had accompanied Vihaela's decoy in Bank. "Pick that up," Vihaela said, pointing down at Haken. The constructs moved to obey and she turned to Cerulean. "Where's Verus?"

"He couldn't have gated," Cerulean said. The constructs lifted Haken; focusing on him I could tell that he was unconscious but still alive. "Wards didn't trigger. Shroud?"

Vihaela frowned. "This isn't a good time for distractions."

"I've told the team that Haken's MIA and Verus is the suspect," Cerulean said. "Should keep them busy a while."

Well, shit. That was going to make my life a lot harder.

"Find him anyway," Vihaela said. She glanced around at the gardens. "You know, I might actually miss this place." Her voice was thoughtful, and she kept gazing around for a few seconds more before turning to walk away. The constructs followed, carrying Haken between them.

I watched the group disappear into the darkness. As soon as they were gone, I backed slowly away, then turned and started hurrying through the trees. I could still hear voices in the distance, and the flicker of lights. I wasn't worried about any of the men finding me the regular way, but I was pretty sure a slaver group would have more than just torches.

I ducked into another bush and crouched down in the darkness. I pulled out my phone and started to activate it, then frowned. No signal. I flicked through the futures, trying different numbers—all nothing. They must have a jammer of some kind. I looked into the futures in which I used a gate stone. A minute or two to get the spell working, and . . . oh, goddamn it. Cerulean hadn't been bluffing about the wards either.

I'd suspected that Haken was going to pull something like this—that was why I'd brought the fire-hunger stone and the mist cloak. My plan had been to wait for him to tip his hand, learn what I could, then bug out. Unfortunately, I'd been counting on either being able to gate away, or get a message to Luna and the others.

A sound rose up from the direction of the house, making my head snap around. It was a low-pitched, throaty *arrh-arrh-arrh*, something like what you'd get if you crossed a dog and a giant crow. I remembered what Vihaela had said about "sniffers" and a nasty feeling formed in my stomach. My mist cloak's great against magic, but it doesn't do anything against tracking by scent.

Plan C. I rummaged around in my bag for the serrated blue disc of my communication focus. I channelled into it, strained myself to give it a bit of extra energy, and waited.

A second later I heard Caldera's voice from the disc. "Who is this?"

Damn, that's loud. I wished this one had a volume control like the later models. "Keep your voice down."

"Verus?" Caldera sounded suspicious. "Is that you?"

I could hear voices behind me to my left. They were getting closer. "It's me."

"How do you have a synchronous focus?"

"Not the time. I could really use some help here."

"Yeah, no kidding. What's going on with Haken?"

"He's in deep shit and I'm not doing so well either. Any chance of some backup?"

"Orders are for you to come in—"

"I know. You got a call within the last half hour, telling you that Haken's MIA and that I'm to be arrested under suspicion of being involved. Right?"

"So are you going to do it?"

"Can't."

"If you don't—"

"I'm not saying I won't, I'm saying I *can't*. I'm at White Rose's base and they've got sink wards. Listen, I didn't do anything to Haken. He was dealing under the table with Vihaela and got burned. Cerulean's the mole, not me. White Rose has got Haken, and they're after me too. I need you to get the others and gate to the beacon from my communicator."

"That's not an option."

A sound went up into the night, the same throaty *arrh-arrh-arrh*. It was closer this time. I looked over in the direction, then huddled down, biting off my words. "Listen. This is me calling for help. I need you guys here."

There was a silence. It could only have been a few seconds, but it felt like more. "I can't," Caldera said. "Orders are to bring you in. I can't gate to your position on your say-so."

"Then call Vari or Landis or someone who *can*!"

"I can't do that either. You're asking me to disobey a direct order."

"Fuck the orders! If you wait for clearance, then Haken and I are going to be dead by the time you get it!"

I heard a shout from close by. I snatched a look around the tree and swore quietly. Two shapes were moving down the bank, torch beams searching in my direction. They'd heard me talking and I'd been too distracted by the conversation with Caldera to see them coming. "Verus?" Caldera said. "What's going on?"

Caldera hadn't kept her voice down. The torches zeroed in and I ducked back behind the tree before they could blind me. I heard a man's voice, and undergrowth cracked as heavy footsteps headed in my direction.

I took a deep breath and bent my head over the communicator. "Caldera. I know I've done things to piss you off and there have been times I haven't told you everything. But I've never actually lied to you and I'm telling you the truth now. I can't handle this on my own. Please. I don't know how much longer—"

Danger. I dropped the focus and turned just as the first man came around the side of the tree. His flashlight was up: he'd been expecting me to flee, and the ferocity of my attack caught him off guard. I hit him in the stomach twice, then as he doubled over, kneed him in the face hard enough to feel something break. I turned on the second man to see him backpedalling and I closed in on him, swift and wolflike. He struck out with what looked like a club; from the futures in which it hit me I knew it would discharge a stunning shock. I let it slide past and caught the arm. The torches were dazzling but narrow-beamed, and the other man couldn't see what I was doing. I closed my eyes as he shone the light into my face, ducked his attempt to club me over the head, then threw him. The fall knocked the torch and shock stick out of his hands, and while he scrabbled for them I had time to draw my stun focus; he'd just made it to his knees when I discharged the focus into his side. He went down and didn't get up.

Shouts and lights moved through the trees. My fight hadn't gone unnoticed, and others were closing in. I ran back to the tree where I'd been hiding, scooped up my pack, and scanned the futures: there were people coming from behind and to the left, and going right would bring me up against the perimeter fence. *Forward.* I wove through the woods, relying on my second sight to keep me from tripping and falling on my face. A couple of men were at risk of cutting me off: I reached down without breaking stride, scooped up a rock in the darkness, and threw it blind. A few seconds later there was a distant *tak* as it hit a tree. The futures of the men to my left shifted as they homed in on the noise, leaving me a clear path.

I came out of the trees and started up a grassy slope, wind

blowing in my hair, the overcast sky above. To my left, I could see the bright lights of the White Rose estate. These grounds felt like the size of a national park, but it meant that I had more space to hide, and that was to my advantage, not theirs. For a second I thought that I'd lost them.

Then I heard the *arrh-arrh-arrh* sound from behind me, followed by the sound of crashing vegetation. It was close—too close. I ducked behind a bush, blending into the shadows and looking back down the slope.

A shape moved in the darkness under the trees. It looked something like a huge dog, but the proportions were wrong, the shoulders too large. Its lines were solid light in the futures: a construct. There were men with it, though, catching up fast, and they *weren't* constructs. As I watched, the shape came out onto the slope and started trotting uphill, head low to the ground, heading straight towards my hiding place.

I calculated quickly. The thing was faster than me; if I kept going, it'd run me down. Maybe I could take it out and lose the men . . . but the light beams of more torches were appearing below . . .

No other choice. Silently, I drew out my dispel focus. I'd only have one shot at this.

The construct was still closing in. It had slowed down, and as it reached a distance of thirty feet from the bush it stopped. *Shit.* My dispel focus was a touch-range weapon. I held still.

The men were climbing the hillside, closing in on my position. The wolf construct was holding still. Three of them caught up, then five, then six. More were coming. ". . . in there?" I heard one say.

"Can't see shit . . ."

". . . a mage, right?"

They began to spread out, circling. They were wary, but that wouldn't last long. My only cover was the leafy bush, and as soon as they circled far enough around they'd have a clear line of sight to me. I looked into the future, and—

—*there*. I pulled off my cloak, stuffing it into my pack.

One of the men saw the movement and shouted something, the beam of his torch darting out towards me.

Pale brown light split the air, forming a vertical disc, lighting up the startled faces of the men. The light solidified, forming a gate, and Caldera stepped through, coming down onto the grass. She dismissed the gate behind her, called up an orb of light in her hand, and looked at the men surrounding her. "Hey there," she said. "Seen a diviner around?"

I grinned and took a step forward. Caldera turned instantly, shining the light on me. "Caldera, I have never been so happy to see you in all my life."

"I'll take that as a compliment." Caldera jerked her thumb at the ring of men surrounding us. "Who are the goons?"

"That's him!" one of the men shouted. "Get him!" He charged Caldera from behind, and as she began to turn he stabbed his shock stick into her side. Blue-white light crackled as the energy discharged into her body.

Caldera finished turning and stared at the man. He looked down at the stick, then up at Caldera. Caldera picked him up, lifted him over her head, and threw him. Not a martial arts throw, more the kind of thing a football player does with a throw-in. She got the same sort of distance too. The man went flying away into the darkness with a long trailing yell that was cut off a couple of seconds later by a *thud*.

The other men stared down at the flight path their companion had just described, then turned back to Caldera. "Anyone else?" Caldera asked.

There was a rustling, shuffling sound as all of them took a step back. The construct held its ground, staring at us, until one of the men called something and it retreated as well.

Caldera turned and walked to me. "You were supposed to be intel support," she said. "How do you keep getting into this shit?"

I sighed. "Would you believe I was just following orders?"

More people were gathering downslope. Another one of the wolf constructs had emerged from the trees, and I could hear shouts and see arms pointing in our direction. Caldera still had her light spell active, clearly illuminating us in the darkness. "I hate to be a downer," I said, "but I think they're coming back for another round."

"That's okay," Caldera said. "I brought some friends." She took out her communicator and spoke into it. "Beacon's lit. Gate when ready."

"Got it," a familiar voice said from the disc. "Sixty seconds."

The men started advancing again up the hill. They moved slowly at first, but we were illuminated by Caldera's light and they could see that they outnumbered us ten to one. There were three of the wolf constructs now, padding heavily through the grass, black eyes locked onto us. The men still didn't have guns out, only the shock sticks, but there were an awful lot of them. They closed to sixty feet, then forty. Someone shouted, "Go!" and the wolf constructs arrowed in, the men following behind. I took a step back, bracing myself . . .

And then a gate opened beside us, this one flame-red, lighting up the night. Figures came stepping through: Landis, wreathed in flame; Variam, his face bright and eager; Luna, her wand in her right hand, whip coiled and ready. The men hesitated, shouting. The constructs didn't. The first construct came face to face with Landis and was just starting its leap when a fireblast exploded it in midair, the wave of heat so intense that I felt it twenty feet away. Red-hot pieces of construct went rolling across the hillside, sending smoke rising up from the grass. "Verus!" Landis said cheerfully. Two more men had been behind the construct and were wavering; he gestured and a spell detonated with an explosive *whump*, sending them both sprawling. They scrambled to their feet and ran. "Saved a few more for us this time, excellent work. Any friendlies?"

Caldera was fighting to the left; to the right, Variam and Luna were taking on one of the constructs. Vari was holding it at bay with a wall of fire while Luna struck with her whip, the silver mist of her curse lashing eagerly into the construct's body. I was in a tiny oasis of calm at the centre of the circle, everything happening at once. "Just Haken, he's at the house—uh, there are two more mages at least, Vihaela and Cerulean. Cerulean is working for White Rose, he's somewhere around invisible—to your left!"

Landis gestured and one of the White Rose men who'd been in the middle of drawing a gun suddenly screamed and dropped it. The gun hit the grass with a hiss, glowing with heat. "Cerulean, eh?" Landis said. "Never did trust the bugger. Be a good chap and spot for me, will you?"

I looked through the futures, saw gunfire. "Group at the bottom of the hill, your one o'clock. They're aiming for Vari."

Landis lifted a hand and a glowing ball of dark red energy formed above one finger. He frowned down at the people below who were sighting on Variam. "Should have taken the hint, boys." The glowing spark flew downhill, disappearing into the night.

Fire bloomed, followed by a clap of thunder. For an instant everyone on the hillside was illuminated in fiery red, then a wave of hot air rolled over, making me stagger. The three men who'd been about to open fire were gone. In their place was a circle of scorched and glowing earth, shapeless masses burning at the centre.

The men still standing broke and ran. To the right, the construct Vari and Luna had been fighting tried to leap; Luna sent a pulse of some kind through her whip, flashing into the doglike body. The construct staggered and collapsed, its animating spell misfiring as Luna's curse set it against itself. Vari burned away its head with an incineration spell. "Boss!" he called at Landis. "They're running!"

"Let them go," Landis said. "This was just the small fry. Verus?"

"They're gone," I said, scanning the futures. "Can't sense any mages or adepts. They must be back at the estate."

"Yeah, and now they know we're here," Caldera said, walking up, glancing down at the last scattered men fleeing into the trees. Behind her, the third construct was broken on the grass. I hadn't even noticed her take it down. "Get behind me. The guys coming in aren't going to be so happy to see you."

"What do you—?" I saw what was going to happen. "Jesus. When you said you were bringing company, you weren't kidding, were you?"

"What, you thought I was going to come charging in on my own? That hero shit is for rookies." Caldera glanced sideways. "Landis . . . ?"

Landis made a reassuring gesture. "I'm here in a purely supporting role, my dear. You're the senior."

"Thanks." Caldera turned back towards the slope. "Here?"

"Here," I said. "Five seconds."

Caldera nodded.

Another gate opened up on the hillside, followed by another. Council security men came through, two by two, guns levelled. Torches shone on our faces, and I squinted against the glare. "I'm Keeper Caldera," Caldera said, arms folded. "These guys are with me. Point those things somewhere else."

The Council security glanced at each other, then lowered their guns. "Clear!" one of them called back through the gate.

The next one through was Slate. "You'd better have—" he started to say to Caldera, then he saw me and his face darkened. "You!"

"Okay, look," I said. "I can explain."

"You can do it in a cell. You, you." He gestured to the security men. "Arrest him."

"Belay that order," Caldera said.

"Do it!"

"If you touch him," Caldera told the two security men calmly, "then I will shove whichever body part you use to do it up your own arse."

The two security men looked at Caldera, looked at Slate, and clearly and visibly decided not to get involved. "Caldera," Slate snarled. "What the *fuck*?"

"Verus is my second," Caldera said. "Not yours."

People were still coming through the gate. There were a good fifteen security men with us now, but most had taken one glance at what was going on and hurried past to set up a perimeter. No Council auxiliary wants to get in the middle of a mage fight. "This is my case," Slate said.

"No, the raid in Bank was your case. You don't have seniority here."

Slate glanced at Landis, who made a very small gesture to indicate that he wasn't involved. "Look, maybe I can—" I began.

"Shut up," Caldera and Slate told me at exactly the same time.

I blinked, and did. "Cerulean fingered him for Haken being MIA," Slate said.

"Yeah, well, some new stuff's come to light," Caldera said. She jerked her head back towards the distant building. "Like the fact that Haken's in there. You want to argue jurisdiction, or you want to get him out before Vihaela gets to work on him?"

Slate gave Caldera a hard look. His eyes flicked to me and back to Caldera, and I felt the futures settle. "He doesn't leave my sight," Slate said. "And I've got tactical command, not you. Got it?"

Caldera nodded. "Fine."

Trask had appeared behind Slate, who turned to him. "Get on the com to Rain," Slate said. "Tell him we want more backup, as much as he can scare up." Slate raised his voice, addressing the crowd. "All right, ladies! Lock and load, we've got work to do!"

"Thanks," I told Caldera quietly.

"Don't thank me yet," Caldera said, her voice dry. "Slate would have had you safe at HQ. Now you're going to be leading the charge."

"You going to tell them about Cerulean?"

"You do not want to make it your word against a Keeper's." Caldera looked around then headed towards Slate, giving me a last comment over her shoulder. "Don't screw this up."

All around us, men were organising, sorting into teams. "That was fun," Luna said, walking over from where she'd been talking to Variam. Her eyes were bright and there was a spring in her step. "Thought you'd forgotten about us."

"Just keep your head down and stick with Vari and Landis," I said. "You're still not supposed to be here. And be—"

"Be careful, I know," Luna said, rolling her eyes. "Look who's talking."

"That pulse trick you used against that construct," I said curiously. I'd never seen Luna use that move before. "Where did that come from?"

"Oh." Luna shrugged. "Chalice showed me. Worked pretty well, right?"

I looked at Luna. "Yeah, it did."

"Hey!" Slate shouted. "Verus! I said where I can see you!"

I sighed and gave Luna a nod. "Stay safe." I walked to join Slate's group.

Slate was with Trask and Caldera, and he was giving orders to a group of Council security. ". . . through the gap," he was saying. "Once we've made the breach, I want two men on point. Stay in cover range for when things go wrong." He beckoned to me and started walking. "Let's go, fortune-teller. You're finding us a way in."

"It's Verus, not 'fortune-teller.' You're not waiting for backup?"

"*If* you and Caldera are right," Slate gave a sharp glance, "then we don't have time. And to make sure, you're going at the front."

I sighed. "Fine. Then stay quiet and let me work." I searched through the futures, picking out points of entry. White Rose's base loomed up in the futures and the present, growing closer each second.

⸻

Keepers can move fast when they want to. It took the whole assault force less than five minutes to make it across the grounds and to the White Rose estate. To no one's surprise, by the time we got there, the defending forces were alerted and ready for us.

When you're doing recon, five minutes isn't much time. With half an hour, I could probably have found a way to get in safely. With an hour, I might have slipped in a couple of other people too. Getting the whole assault force in subtly and cleanly was not going to happen, no matter how long I had.

Fortunately, "subtle" wasn't on Slate's priority list. The front doors of the White Rose estate were bound in metal, reinforced and warded. But the reinforcement didn't extend to the entire building, and my divination found the weak points in the walls. The elemental mages did the rest.

At which point things got busy.

। । । । । । । ।

"Pull back!" Slate shouted into his communicator. "Stay in cover!"

I was lying flat behind a low rise in the ground. I could just make out the edges of the right wing of the White Rose estate, but not the central block, which was just as well because that was where the fire was coming from. A low-pitched, hollow *duh-duh-duh* sound echoed from the roof, repeated and overlapping, mixing with the distant sounds of bullets sinking into earth. The man who'd been hit in the first volley had stopped screaming: treated or dead, I couldn't tell which. Slate shoved the disc away and glared at me. "Why didn't you tell us about this?"

"I told you those things on the roof looked like bunkers," I said absently. Most of my attention was on counting the sources of fire. There were only three that I could see, but that was enough to make it a bad idea to stick your head up.

"You didn't tell us they had machine guns!"

"You didn't give me a chance to check."

"Fuck it." Slate lifted himself up to squint out over the rise at the estate. "Let's just—"

"Get down," I said calmly.

Slate might have been obnoxious, but he wasn't stupid. He ducked instantly. A bullet whipped overhead with an angry whizzing sound.

"Slate!" Trask called from twenty feet away. The big man was pressed up behind a tree. "Flanking team's bogged down. Trap field."

Slate swore.

"Landis is circling," I said, still not lifting my head. "Once he gets to the top of the hill, he can melt those bunkers right off the rooftop."

"That'll take too long." I felt the futures shift as Slate came to a decision. "Trask, put up a fog cloud, then get Caldera and the front team. We're going in."

I didn't hear Trask's answer, but I felt the signature of water magic. A moment later the air grew cool, strands of mist forming out of the night, spreading and thickening to become a fog. Within seconds everything more than a few feet away had disappeared into the cloud. It was the same spell my condensers used, but much more powerful: the cloud was already more than fifty feet wide and it wasn't slowing down.

I felt a hand on my arm and glanced up to see Slate. His eyes glittered. "Let's move, seer boy," he said. "You're with me."

Briefly it occurred to me that if Slate wanted to take a shot at me, now would be the perfect time to do it. *Oh well, I've already had two Keepers try to backstab me this evening. Lightning doesn't strike three times in the same place, right?* I took a deep breath, then stood up and ran for the building.

It caught Slate off guard—I think he'd been expecting to have to drag me. I left him behind, outdistancing him in the mist, and suddenly I was running alone. The mist cloud blocked sight and muffled sound, and for a brief moment it didn't seem as though I was in a battle at all. The sounds of gunfire were faint and distant, and there was no one close enough to threaten me. It was almost peaceful.

Then somewhere above, the machine gunners shifted fire, and in a scattering of the futures ahead of me I saw myself torn apart. *Okay, not so peaceful.* I slowed to a jog, twisting sideways, sensing the bullets snap past. Behind me I heard someone lose their breath in a gasp, followed by a thud. And then all of a sudden the walls of the White Rose estate were looming up, flower beds under my feet. I'd made it through the gauntlet of fire, and I was too close for the gunners on the roof to reach me. There was a blackened hole in the outer wall where one of Landis's fireballs had struck; I could still feel heat radiating from the stone. I went through . . .

. . . and came out of the mist into a plain wooden corridor, face to face with two men in shirts and jeans. Both were carrying guns but they weren't aiming them at me, and before they could react I pointed at them. "What are you doing? Why aren't you with Vihaela?"

Confusion is the ally of the prepared. The two men paused, looking at each other. I didn't give them time to react. "Order is to pull back to the upper floor. Move!"

"But they told us—" one of the men began.

Slate came out of the mist behind me, black energy hovering at his hands. I dived for cover. The men hesitated—first mistake—and levelled their guns at Slate—second mistake. They didn't get the chance for a third. Black lightning cracked and I heard the *thump* of bodies hitting the floor.

I got to my feet and glanced at what was left of the two men. Slate hadn't used nonlethal spells this time. "Which way?" Slate demanded.

"Working on it." My future selves were moving through the mansion, running and dodging and dying.

Caldera and Trask came through behind us, trailed a moment later by two more Council security men. No more followed; the rest of the team had been lost to fog or gunfire. They spread out, securing the corridor. Caldera covered one side, while Trask set up on the corner to the right.

I kept flicking through the futures ahead. With the interference from Slate and the fighting, it was slow going. Right side was going to run us into trouble. Left seemed clearer. Upstairs was clearer still. Now where was Haken . . . ?

"Well?" Slate said.

"Shh," I said absently. I'd just caught a trace of Cerulean. *So he's still here.* No Vihaela, though. Maybe if I looked for her first . . .

Gunfire sounded to the right, followed by a scream. I heard the rushing sound of a water blast and the firing cut off abruptly. "Get on with it!" Slate snarled.

"You rush a diviner, you get crappy divinations," I said without opening my eyes. Left route wasn't working out. There was a small oasis of calm on the first floor and I split my perceptions, pushing myself to track multiple paths at once. Was that it?

Another burst of gunfire came from the right, and Slate and Trask's response fragmented my path-walk. *There.* I'd only had a glimpse but I was sure it was him. "Found him," I said. "First floor. This way." I walked across the corridor and pulled open a door: it led into a small staircase, winding upwards.

Slate didn't hesitate. "Caldera, Trask!" he shouted. "Moving out!" Then he hurried after me.

The sounds of fighting died away as we jogged up the stairs. The battle was still going on outside, and there were a lot of enemies all around us, but Trask's fog spell had spread enough confusion that most of the White Rose defenders hadn't yet figured out that they had intruders. From above I could still hear the staccato beat of the machine guns, but as we reached the first floor there was a tremor and a thud, and one of the guns stopped firing. Probably Landis's work. I hoped Luna was staying with him and hadn't done anything crazy.

The first floor of the White Rose estate was more comfortably furnished, and I had a brief impression of rugs on the floor and mirrors on the walls. The path I'd planned out splintered into combat around the next corner, and I changed plans on the fly. There was a door two steps away, with a bolt on the outside. "In here," I said quietly over my shoulder to the others, pulled the door open, shut it behind them once they were in, then held a finger to my lips when Caldera tried to talk. She, Slate, and Trask were the only ones still with me; we'd lost the security men somewhere along the way. We stayed quiet, and a moment later, I heard footsteps go running past outside.

The room we'd entered was a bedroom, decorated in pink and white. A muted yellow light cast a soft glow, illuminating a hanging mobile. Stuffed animals were piled on an armchair, and a small table held a reading lamp and a notebook with loopy writing on the cover that read *My Diary*. The bed was frilly and fluffy, with more stuffed animals propped up against the headboard, and a small girl was sitting up in it. She was dressed in a white nightie and couldn't have been more than nine years old. "Are you my daddy?" she asked me.

I stared at her. Her eyes were blue, without any sign of fright, or worry . . . or anything. I looked into the futures and felt a chill. The girl's futures were solid lines, reacting to our input without any initiative or variation. Just like a construct.

"I've been good," the girl said.

I felt my skin crawl. I turned and headed for the other side of the room, where a connecting door was half hidden by a wardrobe.

"Jesus," Slate said. He was staring at the girl.

"Are you my daddy?" the girl asked.

"Guys," I said, not looking at the bed. "Come on."

Slate was staring at the girl, but Trask and Caldera followed me. "Door's locked," I said. A muffled shout sounded from somewhere off to the left, followed by gunfire. "Keep it quiet."

Trask nodded, and I stepped out of the way. The big man put a hand to the door handle: there was a blue glow and the handle, the locking mechanism, and a six-inch circle of door puffed into dust. Trask pushed it open. *"Slate,"* I said over my shoulder. Slate tore his gaze away from the girl and followed. The girl watched us go with dead eyes.

The next room was panelled in stone, with a medieval theme. A fire burned in a fireplace, and oil lanterns were mounted on the walls. At the centre was what looked like an old-fashioned version of a medical examination bench. A side table held a tray of gleaming metal implements that could have been dentists' tools, if you didn't look too closely. I was glad Luna wasn't here to ask questions. None of us spoke; we moved through and out.

Another door, another corridor. Someone almost ran over us as he came around a corner. He wasn't dressed like one of the White Rose soldiers, but in a business suit: one of their clients, maybe. Slate stunned him with an enervation spell and we kept moving . . .

And then all of a sudden we were there. We'd come to what was obviously a cell block, metal doors with sliding windows on the outside. "He's—" I began.

"He's in there!" Slate said. Death mages can sense living creatures: it's not as precise as lifesight, but Slate obviously knew what to look for. "Get the door!"

Trask turned the lock and most of the door to dust. Inside was a plain cell, a toilet, a bunk . . . and Haken, lying unmoving on the bed. Slate took a step forward.

"Wait." Caldera caught him, jerking him to a stop. "Verus, any traps?"

I concentrated. "Can't see."

Slate shoved Caldera off with an effort and strode into the room. Nothing triggered and he bent over Haken for a second, then looked back at us. "He's okay."

"I don't like that look on your face," Caldera said. "What's wrong?"

"This is too easy," I said. "There weren't even any wards . . ."

"Who cares?" Slate said.

Something clicked. "It's a decoy."

"Looks like Haken to me," Caldera said.

"No. I mean, yes, it's him, but that's not what I meant. We weren't—"

"Verus?" Slate said. "Shut up. You've done your job."

"Wait," Caldera said. "We weren't what?"

Slate gave Caldera a look. "Really?"

"I've learnt that if you bring a diviner along, it's a good idea to listen to him," Caldera said. "Especially this one. We weren't what?"

"Vihaela isn't working for White Rose anymore," I said. "She's bailing."

"How?"

I spread out my senses, looking for Vihaela. Too much interference—I needed more to go on. I thought about how all this had started. The data focus and what was on it . . .

Information. The real power behind White Rose. I

snapped my fingers. "She'll be at the archives. Wherever they keep their records. She's going to take them and run."

"Why?" Slate said.

"Because that's what she's after. Look, think about it. What would she want with Haken? She wasn't trying to silence him, she *wants* the Keepers here. Everything she's done has made things worse for White Rose, not better."

"You don't know that," Slate said.

I looked up at the ceiling in frustration. *He's not going to listen, is he?* I turned to Caldera.

Caldera looked back at me for a second, then glanced at Slate. "We *are* still under orders to bring her in."

"You're really buying this?" Slate said.

Caldera shrugged. "I'm just saying."

Slate hesitated, and I felt the futures fork and then shift. "Fine," he said. "Trask, get Haken out. We'll take Vihaela."

"You sure?" Trask said.

"Don't have time to wait." Slate turned to me. "Find Vihaela. And make it fast."

We split, Trask carrying Haken back the way we came while Slate, Caldera, and I headed deeper. With only three of us left, there was less interference to my senses. The machine-gun fire from the roof had stopped, and instead I could hear shots echoing from the ground floor; the fight was still going on, and it sounded as though the Council had brought in reinforcements. Shouts and hollow *thuds* echoed from below, and I could smell smoke. The fighting was getting closer, which seemed like a good indication that White Rose was losing. I didn't know where Vihaela was, but I'd managed to get a good enough sense of the building that I could guess where the more secure facilities were housed, and I picked us a route that would avoid as many people as possible. Running footsteps sounded from all around, but in the chaos we were able to make our way across the building without being spotted.

I reached a corner and stopped, using my divination to peer around the edge. The room beyond had a circular door in the far end that looked like a vault, made of metal and massively thick. The lock had been melted by some kind of intense heat, and the door was swung half open. Bodies lay scattered across the floor. A chair had been knocked over, but apart from that there were no signs of battle, and no bullet holes in the walls. The walls in this section were thicker, blocking out the sounds of the fighting behind, and all of a sudden the corridor was eerily quiet.

Caldera frowned at the bodies. "Any of our guys make it this far?"

"No." Slate came around the corner and saw what Caldera was looking at. "Blue on blue?"

"I don't think this was an accident," I said. I nodded at the vault door. "Get ready. Vihaela's coming out."

"I don't see her."

"Trust me."

Slate and Caldera looked at each other, then walked forward, stepping over the bodies to take up positions flanking the door. The anteroom had two corridors leading off it, one to Caldera's right, the other where we'd come from. I stayed close to the corner.

Footsteps sounded from inside the vault, and Vihaela appeared. She looked much the same as she had when I'd seen her out in the grounds, with one change: she had a light satchel slung over one shoulder. She looked unsurprised to see us. "Oh," she said. "You."

"Mage Vihaela," Slate began. "Under the—"

Vihaela waved a hand. "Can we skip this part?"

"Suits me," Slate said. He was standing in a ready stance, feet spread wide. "You coming quietly?"

Vihaela looked between us for a second before answering. "Three of you." She frowned slightly. "I'm actually a little insulted."

"Yeah, sorry to burst your bubble," Slate said. "We got better things to do than go after freaks like you."

"I mean, three Keepers would be one thing," Vihaela said. "But two Keepers and an auxiliary? You aren't even taking me seriously."

"We're crying," Caldera said.

"Just out of curiosity, what are you charging me with? It's not as though I hurt your boss."

"Bullshit," Slate said.

"Sorry," Vihaela said. "Didn't lay a finger on him. You can check with him when he wakes up."

"If you didn't," Caldera said, "then who are you saying did?"

"Now you want me to solve your case too?" Vihaela shook her head. "Come on. If I really wanted Haken dead, you think I couldn't have done it already? There's no point offing Keepers. Sometimes we have to hurt you a little, just to teach you to stay out of our business, but killing you? Why bother?"

"Keep talking," Slate said. "Your men are losing out there."

I still couldn't hear or sense any people moving in our direction, but the longer this went on, the better the chance that Council reinforcements would arrive. Caldera stayed quiet, and I knew she had to be thinking the same thing. If Vihaela stuck around, sooner or later she'd be overwhelmed.

Vihaela turned towards the right-hand corridor. "Well, fun as this has been, I've got places to be."

"You aren't going anywhere," Slate said.

Vihaela paused, then turned her head to look back at Slate and raised an eyebrow. "Do you really want to do this?"

"You don't want to pick a fight with Keepers, Vihaela," Caldera said.

"Times are changing, Keeper." Vihaela smiled. "The people you work for are going to be changing too. Might want to think about staying on their good side."

I stared at Vihaela. "Now," Vihaela said. "I'm going to walk away. If you're smart, you'll tell your captain that I was gone when you got here. If not . . ." She shrugged. "Your call." She started towards the corridor.

Caldera stepped in her way. Vihaela kept walking, unhurried. She was ten feet away from Caldera, then five. Caldera hesitated and for a second I could tell she was thinking about backing off. I knew I should be doing something, but I found myself staring, fascinated. There was something hypnotic about Vihaela's movements . . .

The moment broke and the futures settled. Caldera reached out to seize Vihaela as the Dark mage came into range.

"Don't!" I shouted.

I was almost too late, but Caldera heard my warning and twisted aside at the very last second, just as Vihaela moved. Green-black light flashed, Caldera went staggering back, and Slate struck instantly, death energy lashing out.

The blast hit Vihaela and . . . something happened, then Vihaela was advancing. Slate hit her again, crackling black lightning flashing from his hands into Vihaela's body, but the dark green light of Vihaela's spells met Slate's attacks and it was Slate who was driven back. Even watching it clearly, I couldn't make out what Vihaela was doing. She was so *fast*, her movements flowing and precise. I've met a lot of battle-mages, but in all my life I'd only seen a handful who moved like that. The closest thing that Vihaela's fighting style reminded me of was a Dark mage named Onyx, but Onyx had relied purely on speed and power. Vihaela was different; every move she made was like a step in a dance, so natural that it seemed effortless. I'd been about to join the fight, but as I looked at the futures, I realised that I was utterly outclassed. All I could do was watch.

Caldera recovered and charged Vihaela from behind. Without turning Vihaela sidestepped the rush, directed a spell into Caldera that sent the heavier woman staggering, and struck again at Slate in the same motion. Caldera sent a ranged spell of some kind: it soaked into Vihaela and slid off, and Vihaela's next strike snapped Slate's head back. I understood now why Vihaela had looked so relaxed. She was fighting Caldera and Slate at the same time, and she didn't even look as though she was going all-out.

Green and black light was thrown back from the walls, mixing with the brown of Caldera's earth magic. The floor shook with heavy blows, and deflected spells punched holes through the plaster; the air was thick with ozone and the scent of blood. Caldera stumbled over one of the bodies and Vihaela hit her in the instant she was off balance. Caldera shook it off with a snarl. Her protective spells had kept her standing through Vihaela's attacks, but she was moving more slowly and I could tell she was being worn down. She moved right to flank Vihaela, her back to the other corridor.

The futures shifted. "Caldera!" I shouted. "Behind!"

Caldera turned—too slow. Air imploded, striking with enough force to pulp flesh, and Caldera went down. Slate moved to cover her, dropping his own attacks as he did so.

Vihaela paused. Green-black energy glowed around her; her hair was mussed, but as far as I could tell she hadn't been scratched. She turned her head to look down the corridor. "I didn't need the help."

A man stepped out into view, dressed in grey. A beard covered the lower half of his face, and he wore dark glasses. It was the assassin from two nights ago, Chamois. He inclined his head back very slightly.

"Protecting his investment?" Vihaela said. She shrugged. "Fine." She turned to leave.

"Hold it!" Slate called.

"Or you'll do what?" Vihaela said without looking back. She walked away.

Slate half-moved after her. Chamois met his eyes and shook his head very slightly. Slate stopped.

Then Chamois looked at me. He stood studying me for a second, then reached into his pocket, took something out, and tossed it at me. I felt the surge of a minor spell, giving extra force to the throw. As it spun in midair the futures flashed before me—no danger. I caught the thing one-handed, then looked down at what I'd been thrown.

It was a brown cloth pouch. Looking into the futures where I opened it, I saw a condenser. The same one I'd decoyed Chamois away with on the train.

I looked back up to see Chamois watching me. He turned and was gone.

Slate made a move after him. "Don't," I said tightly. I

hurried to Caldera's side. She was down on one knee, bleeding from her ears. "Caldera. You okay?"

Caldera looked up at me with a frown and shook her head wordlessly. She hadn't heard me. "Slate," I called.

Slate touched Caldera's shoulder, frowning. "She's deaf, eardrums busted. Be fine if we can get her to a life mage. We need to go after them—"

"With *what*?"

Slate clenched his fist. For a moment I saw the flicker of arguments, then he abandoned them. "I'm going to get them." Slate's voice was tight and furious. "This isn't over. Understand?"

I didn't answer. In the distance, from where Vihaela and Chamois had disappeared, I felt the signature of a gate spell, and I knew they were gone. Slate punched the floor with a sharp *crack*.

I didn't move. Caldera shrugged us off and got to her feet, still unsteady. From behind, I could hear shouts and footsteps, and looking into the futures, I saw that they were friendly. The three of us stood in the anteroom, alone with the bodies, and waited for our reinforcements to arrive.

chapter 14

The rest of the battle was mop-up.

Slate, Caldera, and I fell back to rejoin Haken and Trask. I kept us away from the remaining White Rose forces, and we linked up with a Keeper strike force. Haken and Caldera were shipped out to the back lines, and I went with them.

Slate and Trask went back into the fight, although by this point they didn't have much to do. In the end, the battle was more one-sided than it had felt. White Rose's power was in political influence, not in military strength, and their wards and defences weren't anything like enough to hold off a full Keeper attack force. After half of the defenders had been killed or incapacitated, the rest started surrendering. By the time the Keepers finished rounding up their prisoners, they found a lot of foot soldiers and workers, a lot of slaves, and a scattering of mages and adepts. Vihaela, Cerulean, and Chamois weren't amongst them.

I went looking for Luna and Variam once the fighting had stopped. They were out on the front lawn, a little way outside the ring of lights. Variam was resting against a tree and wrapping a bandage awkwardly around his arm one-handed. "Look, I can go get them," Luna was saying.

"Nah," Variam said. He glanced up as I approached. "Hey, Alex."

"Hey," I said. "Glad you both made it." I nodded at Variam. "Gunshot?"

"He won't go to the Keeper medics," Luna complained.

"It's not like it's serious," Variam said.

"You got shot! How is that 'not serious'?"

"I'll just go see Anne," Variam said. "She's better than the Keeper life mages anyway."

"I know, but . . ." Luna looked away.

Variam grinned at her. "Upset?"

"Screw you."

I sighed and dropped down onto the grass near to them. "Luna? You hurt?"

Luna shook her head, but didn't turn around. I gave Variam a questioning look.

"We were with the security teams around the hill," Variam said. "One of them caught a bullet from those machine guns right in the head. Splattered like ketchup."

Luna twisted around to glare at him. "Vari!"

"What?"

"Can you not joke about it?"

"Hey, you were the one who wanted to get in on the battle."

"Guys." I raised a hand. "Enough, okay?"

Neither Luna nor Vari argued. We sat quietly for a little while. After you go through a battle the adrenaline rush keeps you going for a while, but once that's gone you crash and all of a sudden it feels as though you can barely move. All I wanted to do was sit there.

As we watched, a group of people started to trickle out from the front of the White Rose estate, escorted by Council security. The oldest were in their early twenties; most were younger. The clothes they wore ranged from simple robes and nightgowns to outfits with implications I consciously didn't think about. They moved in an aimless, straggling way, and kept stopping to stare around them, blinking at the lights as though they hadn't been outside for years. Maybe they hadn't.

"Those are the White Rose slaves, aren't they?" Luna asked. "What's going to happen to them?"

The Council security were trying to chivvy the slaves towards an open meadow to the south. It was slow going. "They'll take them to the facility in Southampton," Variam said. "See what they know."

"What about after that?" Luna asked. "I mean, it's not like the Council runs social services, is it?"

Variam shrugged. "Dunno."

A small figure dressed in white had fallen behind the rest of the slaves. As I looked more closely, I saw it was the little girl from the bedroom. She was moving haltingly and kept turning to stare back at the building behind. A security man was standing over her, trying to get her moving, and from his body language he seemed to be getting frustrated. When she didn't react he grabbed her by the upper arm and started dragging her.

There was a commotion and a short, heavyset figure came stalking out into view. As he came into the light I saw that it was Slate. He snapped something at the security man, who let go of the girl. Slate said something, his voice harsh, then pointed back in the direction of the house. The security man backed off quickly; Slate watched him go, then crouched down next to the girl. His back was to us, but there was something oddly protective about his stance.

"They're just going to put them out on the street, aren't they?" Luna said. She was looking towards the main body of the group.

"I don't know," I said, watching Slate. "Maybe they'll have a little help after all."

Slate stood up, guiding the girl gently with one arm. As he looked up he saw me and the scowl returned to his face. I looked away, careful not to smile.

Movement in the futures caught my attention. A Keeper was headed towards me; it was Slate's partner, Trask. "Verus," Trask said as he walked up:

"Hey."

"Wards are down," Trask said. "Going to need you to come back to HQ."

"Oh, right," I said with a sigh. "That." I was still wanted for questioning. "So am I under arrest?"

"Not technically."

"Seems to be a habit." I climbed wearily to my feet. "Come on then."

"Alex?" Luna asked.

"I'll be okay. Make sure he gets to Anne."

"Hey," Variam said. "I can take care of myself."

"I will," Luna said.

I walked with Trask towards the gate point, leaving Luna and Variam alone on the hill. Getting out of here was probably a good idea anyway. Right now everyone was running around trying to get things back in order; once they managed that, they were going to start looking for people to blame. There was going to be a lot of fallout from what had happened here tonight, and I was pretty sure I'd just made some extra enemies.

Then I glanced over at the teenagers and children in the meadow. Slate was still with them, along with a couple of other Keepers. As I watched, a gate opened, and the White Rose slaves started to file through. One boy who reminded me a little of Leo had stopped and was staring back at the building behind him. As we passed by, he turned and stepped through the gate, disappearing from the meadow and leaving White Rose behind.

I turned back to see that Trask was watching me. "Worth it?" he asked.

I considered it briefly, then nodded. "Yeah."

The two of us walked away.

⸱ ⸱ ⸱ ⸱ ⸱ ⸱ ⸱ ⸱ ⸱ ⸱

The next few days were busy.

I spent the first forty-eight hours in meetings and interviews. All the different Council factions wanted to hear the details of how my trip with Haken had gone, and all of them *also* wanted to make sure I reported said details in such a way that would work to their advantage. Before the first day was out, I'd been threatened with death, imprisonment, exile, and demotion (not necessarily in that order), and had been instructed by five separate people to follow four different and contradictory stories. There was no possible way that I could make everyone happy, and I didn't even try. I just stalled, and waited.

I didn't have to wait long. As the days went by, the mages in the Council had their attention pulled away from me to the political crisis unfolding around them. Now that White Rose's organisation was in ruins, all the dirty laundry was coming out. The really secure files had been kept on keyed data focuses or in the heads of Vihaela and Marannis, but as with any security system, the weakest part is the human element, and with the number of prisoners the Keepers had taken, they had a lot of witnesses to interrogate. Some Council members tried to make covert attempts to shut the interrogations down. It didn't work. Within a week, everyone knew who White Rose had been in bed with, with more juicy details coming out every day.

Oddly enough, being in Keeper custody ended up working out in my favour. No one was really interested in prosecuting me anymore, and being held in Keeper HQ ended up isolating me from the worst of the political storm. The only drawback was that it was hard for me to find out what was going on, but in that regard I got help from an unexpected source. Caldera was still off on medical leave, but Coatl started showing up to bring me meals and escort me around—for some reason he'd taken a liking to me, and through him I learnt what was happening in the Council as the political casualties started to mount up.

Nirvathis was one of the first to go. I never did learn exactly how he'd been associated with White Rose and what his apprentice had been doing meeting with Chamois that night, but it didn't matter; he was never going to have a shot at the Council again. One member of the Junior Council and one member of the Senior Council both resigned four days after the battle, within an hour of each other, for "health reasons." Along with the one Nirvathis had been gunning for, that left a total of three Council seats up for grabs. It was announced that the new Junior Council seats would be assigned first, and a political free-for-all began.

On the Dark side of the fence, Marannis found himself out in the cold. Vihaela had disappeared, the Council factions who'd lost influence were hungry for blood, and Marannis was the obvious scapegoat. He probably could have escaped if he'd been willing to cut his losses, but he hesitated too long. The Order of the Star raided his mansion while he was still trying to piece the White Rose organisation back together. Marannis was killed "resisting arrest." Apparently someone on the Council had decided that they were tired of cleaning up White Rose's mess.

With Marannis and Vihaela gone and their main base destroyed, White Rose disintegrated. The houses operated by White Rose were closed down and the slaves and enforcers taken into custody, and the last remaining mages involved in running the organisation slipped away.

And by the time I was finally released from Keeper HQ, everyone was far too busy with all the political chaos to pay any attention to me.

⁙⁙⁙⁙⁙

"I still don't understand what Vihaela was doing," Luna said.

It was a week after the battle and I was back in the War Rooms, sitting in the same alcove in the Belfry where Haken and I had waited to be summoned. Murmurs of conversation echoed across the polished floor, mages and their assistants speaking quietly as they walked. I'd been ordered to attend another hearing—a less important one this time—and I'd taken advantage of my newly acquired status as a Keeper employee to bring Luna along.

"You remember what we were saying about the three factions?" I said. There was no one very close to us, but I kept my voice down all the same. "White Rose, Levistus's group on the Council, and whoever hired Chamois. Vihaela wasn't on White Rose's side."

"But she was working for White Rose."

"Yeah, well, once the Keepers started digging, they found some new information," I said. "Turns out Vihaela was running the organisation a bit *too* well. Well enough that Marannis wasn't necessary anymore."

"So Marannis thought she was going to betray him?"

"He might have been right at that. I had a look at Vihaela's history. Her bosses tend not to live very long."

Luna thought about it for a second. "So he decided to get rid of her, but she found out and beat him to the punch."

"That's what the Keepers think," I said. "We know that she sent Leo to deliver the focus. Well, my guess is that she also leaked the time and place of the meeting. That was how Chamois knew where to find them."

"Why?"

"She was turning the Council against White Rose," I said. Now that I had a bit of distance, I could recognise the tactic. Take two of your enemies and set them against each other. I'd used the same trick plenty of times myself but this was my first time on the receiving end. It was a new experience for me and I was discovering I didn't like it very much. Maybe this was how it had felt for some of the people I'd gone up against. "Remember the rumour that the data focuses could be cracked? The only thing stopping the Council from moving against White Rose was the information they were holding. Once enough mages on the Council believed that all that blackmail material White Rose was holding on to was going to get out *anyway* . . . well, that was it. Kidnapping Haken just sped things up."

"So Vihaela wouldn't have cared about getting the focus back at all."

I nodded. "She knew it couldn't be cracked. As long as it was out there, lost, it was doing its job. She hardly had to do anything, really. Once things were set in motion, she just had to wait for the Keepers to figure out what was going on and move against White Rose themselves. Levistus was the one trying to put on the brakes."

"So what are you going to do with that focus?"

"Keep it as a souvenir, I guess. Not like anyone can read the thing."

"Levistus could." Luna thought for a second. "He was the one behind that attack on you and Caldera, wasn't he?"

"Either him or someone on his team. I think they were hoping that by disappearing Leo they could dead-end the case. If Leo hadn't talked before they snatched him, it might have worked."

"What do you think happened to him?"

"You mean once they finished ripping everything he knew out of his skull?" I shook my head. I knew there was no way Levistus would have let him live.

Luna was silent, and I found myself thinking about Leo. He'd been abused by White Rose, used as a slave and as a disposable messenger. And then when he'd fallen into the hands of Light mages, the people who were supposed to be his protectors, they'd abducted, interrogated, and finally executed him. It was a miserable end to what had probably been a miserable life, and to a certain extent, it had happened because of me—it had been Caldera and me who'd inadvertently led Levistus's agents to where Leo was hiding.

I hated that things worked like this. I hated that children like Leo and that nameless slave of Vihaela's could be casually murdered, while the rulers slept easy at night, protected and safe. Sometimes a mid-level mage like Marannis would fall, but for the most part the ones who paid the heaviest price always seemed to be the ones who had the least to lose.

"It doesn't feel like we won," Luna said.

Luna and I think alike in some ways. "White Rose is gone," I said. "Maybe Leo didn't get to see the benefit of that, but the other slaves did."

"This . . ." Luna took a breath. "This wasn't all because of me, was it? I mean, I was the one who talked you into joining the Keepers, wasn't I? Everyone who was killed in that battle . . ."

"No," I said. "This fight was going to happen, one way or another. If it hadn't happened this way, it would have happened somewhere else."

Luna nodded. I could tell that it was still bothering her though, and I had the feeling that might be a good thing. In a few more years, if everything went to plan, Luna would pass her journeyman tests and become accepted as a mage. She was going to have to get used to her actions having consequences, even for people she didn't meet.

"So who was Vihaela really working for?" Luna said.

"The Keepers don't know, and neither does the Council," I said. "But we can take a guess. Levistus has been weakened, his puppet candidate for the Council seat is gone, and the status quo's in chaos. Who's the one person who's going to profit the most from all that?"

"Morden."

"He's wanted that Council seat for years. Now there's nothing standing in his way."

"So Levistus loses, and it just means Morden wins instead." Luna grimaced. "Great."

I didn't answer; it was too close to what had been going through my head a minute ago. It's not the first time I've been caught in a power struggle between Levistus and Morden, and once again, the most I'd been able to get was a partial victory. I was still alive, but so were they.

But sitting there in the Belfry, I made a decision. I was tired of Levistus and Morden. I'd seen enough people sacrificed as pawns in their political games. I wanted them to pay for what they'd done. Maybe for someone like me, they really were just untouchable. But if I had the chance . . .

Then I'll bring them down. That's a promise.

Something in the futures caught my attention, and I looked up. There was a mage crossing the floor towards us. Luna followed my gaze, and her eyes narrowed as she saw who it was. We watched in silence as he walked up to us and stopped. I didn't say anything, and Luna didn't either.

"Hey," Haken said. Given what had happened to him, he looked in pretty good shape. It wasn't really a surprise;

Keepers get a good health plan. "Can I have a word?" His eyes flicked to Luna.

I paused just long enough to make it clear I was thinking about it. "I'll be back in a bit," I told Luna, then rose to my feet. Luna didn't answer, and her eyes stayed on Haken as we walked away.

Haken and I crossed the Belfry, footsteps echoing on the stone as we traced the lines of the patterns beneath our feet. Other mages were scattered around, but none came close. I could sense subtle wards meant to detect eavesdropping. We rounded a column and turned left, still in silence.

"Committee are dragging their feet about Cerulean," Haken said at last.

"Yeah, I bet they are." Cerulean hadn't shown up for his inquiry, even though they hadn't officially suspended him yet. That one was going to be a major embarrassment for the Keepers. Informing on the side was one thing, but having one Keeper outright betray another was not going to do their reputation any favours. About the only consolation from their point of view was that with all the other political developments, no one had all that much attention to spare for a Keeper being fired.

"The guys we're holding from White Rose are saying they didn't know anything about it."

I shrugged. "Might be true."

"Yeah."

There was a pause. We rounded another column and passed by the reception desks, heading back across the floor.

"So . . ." Haken said.

"Go ahead and ask it."

"Why'd you do it?"

"Do what?"

Haken gave me a look.

"I don't know *everything*," I said. "You'll have to narrow down the question."

"I talked to Slate," Haken said. "He said that it was because of you that they found me."

I grinned. "Slate must have loved having to admit that."

"So . . . ?"

"So?"

"You could have led them somewhere else."

"I could."

"So why'd you do it?"

I walked for a little way before answering. "Maybe it helped me prove my innocence to the Keepers," I said at last. "Maybe I didn't see any profit in holding a grudge. Maybe it was some other reason." I shrugged. "From your perspective, does it matter?"

"Maybe not," Haken said. "All the same . . . I'm curious."

"When Cerulean tried to shoot me, you had a split second to decide whether to try to kill me, or whether to try to stop me," I said. "You tried to stop me. If you want a reason, you can go with that."

"And I assume you're not going to tell me how you went through that wall of fire or how you vanished off our senses."

"Yup."

We'd done nearly a full circuit of the Belfry, and as we turned the final column, Haken stopped. "Then just so you know," he said. "Levistus isn't going to forget this. Right now he's going for that Senior Council seat. But sooner or later, once that's done, he's going to come after you. There won't be any more threats or warnings. If I were you? I'd start working on an escape plan."

I looked back at Haken for a second. "Thanks for letting me know."

"Yeah," Haken said. "Good luck. You'll need it."

| | | | | | | | | |

It was the next day when I stuck my head inside Caldera's office. "You rang?"

"Yeah," Caldera said. She was frowning at her computer. "Be with you in a sec."

I crossed the room and sat in front of her desk, stretching out. To the right was the small workstation I'd been using. To the left was Haken's half of the office. The desk looked a lot clearer than the last time I'd seen it. "Haken moved out?"

"Yes," Caldera said without looking up. Her tone made it clear that she didn't want to talk about it. I took the hint and stayed quiet.

The only noise in the office was Caldera's fingers on the keys. She wasn't a fast typist, and watching her, it struck me how awkward she looked sitting at a computer. Every time I've seen Caldera out in the field she's looked confident and capable, but in front of a keyboard, she just looked out of place. At last Caldera took her hands off the keys and reached down to pull open a drawer. She took something out and set it down on the desk with a click. "Here."

The object on the desk was a small silver signet, with a stylised flame and coat of arms. With my magesight, I could sense a faint magical trace. It was a focus, and as I looked at it, I realised I knew what it did. Keepers carried focuses like these as identification symbols. This one was smaller, with a different pattern, but it was recognisable as the same basic design. It was an official Council signet.

"Congrats," Caldera said. "Welcome to the auxiliary corps of the Order of the Star."

I blinked at her.

"No smart-arse comments?" Caldera asked.

"I'm, uh . . . just surprised."

"About what?"

"Honestly?" I said. "I had the feeling you were going to blame me for what happened with Haken."

"You followed the orders you were given," Caldera said. "You did your job."

I looked at Caldera for a second. "Don't take this the wrong way," I said, "but you don't exactly seem happy."

"About what? That Haken was the one who set us up in Uxbridge?"

I didn't answer.

"I'm not a fucking idiot, okay?" Caldera said. "I put it together. And yes, we've noticed how you kept quiet about it instead of laying another charge against the order. Sure Rain'll appreciate it." She gave me a look. "Picking up our politics fast, aren't you?"

I raised my eyebrows.

Caldera stared at me for a second, then passed a hand across her eyes. "Fuck." She paused. "Forget it."

"The thing with Haken's getting to you, isn't it?"

"He was my partner for a year," Caldera said. "I knew him when we were apprentices. Yeah, it's getting to me."

"If it's any consolation, he did try to help," I said, then shrugged. "A little. I don't know. Maybe give it some time, talk to him. You might be able to work something out."

"Yeah." Caldera pushed a set of stapled sheets of paper across to me. "All right. Take a look at these."

I flipped the report around, started reading it, blinked, skipped to the end. "Smuggling?"

"Yeah, looks like there's a new source of meld. We had a handle on it for a while, but seems like a new supplier's got into the market. Best guess is it's coming from Thailand."

"This doesn't have anything to do with White Rose?"

"Not really."

"So . . . we just go on to the next job?"

"What were you expecting?" Caldera said. "Victory parade?"

"Would have been nice."

Caldera snorted. "How'd you think this was going to go? It was just a case. They come and they go. Some are easy, some are hard. But you know what they've all got in common?"

I looked at Caldera, interested. "What?"

"They end," Caldera said. "And you go back to your desk and start the next one." She shook her head. "You still think like an independent, Verus. There's trouble, you fix it, and everything goes back to normal. But that's not how it works now you're in the Keepers. For us, this *is* normal."

"Mm. By the way?"

"What?"

"You can call me Alex."

Caldera gave me a curious look. After a moment, she nodded.

We sat in silence for a little while, broken only by the

rustle of paper as I turned the pages. "Do you think what we did to White Rose will change anything?" I asked.

"Short term?" Caldera said. "Sure. Longer term?" She shrugged. "Demand's still there. People are still the same. You can make things a little better if you work at it. But in the end, nothing really changes."

I thought about that for a moment. I remembered the Keepers, and the feeling of sitting in the Belfry, watching the mages of the Light Council go about their business. Even in the middle of everything that had happened, there had been a sense of inertia there, a stability. It was easy to believe it would always be the same. Caldera was paging through the report, distracted, and all around us, the bureaucracy of the Keepers hummed quietly. It didn't feel any different.

At least, not yet.

         ı ı ı ı ı ı ı ı ı ı

I t was a month later.

The Conclave is a semicircular amphitheatre, the largest of the three chambers at the heart of the War Rooms. Gold leaf covered the domed roof above, and gilt-framed paintings and works of art looked down from between velvet curtains. I'd never been inside the Conclave before. Usually the room is forbidden to all but an inner circle of Light mages, but there are a very few events where the gates are (reluctantly) opened to outsiders. This was one of them.

The room was crowded. Mages sat in rows at the curving benches, while those who hadn't been able to get a seat stood in the stairs or at the back. Security was everywhere, Council operatives and Keepers standing at vantage points at the lower levels and scanning the crowd from the balconies above. I could feel the presence of literally hundreds of defensive wards and spells, but few of the mages seemed to be paying attention to them. Everyone was focused on the stage below.

Thirteen chairs stood at the centre of the stage, one row of seven, slightly raised, and a second row of six in front and below. Ten of the chairs were occupied. One of the ten

people was Levistus, sitting still and silent. The other nine
I'd never seen before. All wore elaborate mage robes; none
were young. The one thing all shared was that each of them
wore a simple gold chain over their shoulders. These were
the Junior and Senior Councils, the leaders of the Light
mages of Britain, and collectively they wielded more power
than any other group in the country.

I wondered what they thought of what was happening in
front of them.

"Who comes before the Council?" the master of ceremonies asked.

The man he was addressing looked about thirty, though
I knew he was far older. He had dark hair, the polished good
looks of someone who spends time cultivating them, and a
half smile that rarely left his face. His robes were black,
which I was sure had been a deliberate choice. This was
Morden, one of the most powerful Dark mages I'd ever met.
If the mages sitting in those chairs were the strongest
amongst the Light faction, Morden was their counterpart.
"One who is summoned," Morden replied. He didn't raise
his voice, but it carried to the edges of the room.

"How do you come before the Council?" the master asked.

"In humility and in obedience," Morden said.

"Why do you come before the Council?"

"I wish only to serve the Council, in heart and mind and
soul."

"Where would you serve?"

Morden's voice stayed quite steady. "On the Council,
should it please the Councillors."

I heard a slight murmur go through the crowd. It was as
if they hadn't quite believed that this was really going to
happen until they heard the words. I'd read the histories: in
all the thousands of years that the Council of Britain had
existed, a Dark mage had never sat upon it. Until now.

The ritual continued, question and answer, each exchange
scripted. I took the opportunity to look around, scanning the
faces of the mages I could see. A few looked thoughtful.
More looked angry. I didn't get the sense that the Light mages

here were happy about what was happening today, and as I looked into the futures in which I approached people, I saw that anger turned towards me. Of the ones who recognised me, all too many saw another Dark mage like Morden. They were looking for someone to blame, and I didn't think that was going to go away. If anything, as the reality of Morden's presence on the Council sank in, it would get worse—

A voice whispered into my ear. *You know where you belong.*

I jumped, twisted. There was no one behind me. Mages around me turned to look at me, frowning. I looked from side to side, heart hammering. There was no one there, and the futures were clear.

But I'd known that voice. It had been Richard's.

On the stage below, the master of ceremonies turned from Morden to the sitting Councillors. "Who will accept this mage to the Council?"

Everyone fell silent, watching. All eyes were on the nine men and the one woman sitting on those chairs. One of the men was the first to move, straightening his dark red robes before unhurriedly rising to his feet. A moment later, a second stood, followed by a third. One at a time, slowly and deliberately, each of them rose . . . except for Levistus.

The chamber was dead quiet, and I held my breath. Everyone's eyes were on Levistus. An election to the Council had to be unanimous. The appointment would have been decided over behind closed doors, but any member, at least technically, had veto power. If Levistus stayed seated, Morden would be refused his seat. Levistus would almost certainly be removed from the Council himself in the aftermath, but he could do it . . .

Levistus stayed where he was, and I sensed the futures fork, just briefly. Then he rose to his feet. His pale eyes regarded Morden without expression.

"It is agreed," the master of ceremonies said. "Mage Morden, step forward."

Morden stepped forward and bowed his head. The master of ceremonies picked up a gold chain, twin to the ones worn by the ten mages standing behind him. The chain was plain and heavy, almost simple compared to the artworks around the chamber, but it symbolised far more. He placed the chain around Morden's neck. "You are raised to the Junior Council, that it may further endure," the master of ceremonies recited. "May the Light guide you."

Morden straightened. His right hand came up to touch the chain, holding one of the links between thumb and forefinger for a second, then he nodded to the master of ceremonies and walked to one of the empty chairs. He sat, and the other ten sat as well. Now there were eleven.

A faint murmur went through the room, then died away into silence. I don't know what I'd been expecting—an outcry, maybe. Instead everyone just watched. You read a lot about history being made; you don't often see it happen. Sitting on his Council seat, Morden surveyed the crowd. I was hidden away at the back, yet his eyes found me. Maybe it was my imagination, but he seemed to give me a tiny smile and a nod of the head.

I looked away sharply. The master of ceremonies was announcing something else, but I didn't listen. Instead I found myself scanning the faces around me, looking from one mage to another. None were familiar, and it took a moment before I realised who I was looking for. Richard. I couldn't see him, or sense his presence, yet somehow I knew he was there.

Caldera's wrong, I thought. *Things are changing.* I turned and walked out of the Conclave, leaving the Council behind. The Keepers on the door watched me go.

From national bestselling author

BENEDICT JACKA

ı ı ı ı ı ı ı ı ı

hidden

An Alex Verus Novel

ı ı ı ı ı ı ı ı ı

With his talent for divining the future, Alex Verus should have foreseen his friends' reactions to the revelations about his previous life. Anne Walker no longer trusts him. She's also cut ties with the mage community, and the last time Alex tried to check on her, he was told to leave her alone.

Then Anne gets kidnapped. Working with the Keepers, Alex discovers that Anne has been taken into the shadow realm of Sagash, her former Dark mage mentor, and he must find a way to rescue her. But another shadow from the past has resurfaced—Alex's former master may be back in London, and Alex has no idea what his agenda is...

"Harry Dresden would like Alex Verus tremendously— and be a little nervous around him. I just added Benedict Jacka to my must-read list."

—Jim Butcher, #1 *New York Times* bestselling author

benedictjacka.co.uk
facebook.com/AceRocBooks
penguin.com